D1012716

"The authors have already made a name for themselves as writers of intelligent space opera, and *Echoes of Earth* is sure to further bolster that reputation. The book is chock full of marvelous events, cosmic significance, mysterious alien motivations, and the wonder of outer space."

—*Science Fiction Chronicle*

"The science in Dix and Williams's work shines, entrancing with its glitter and innovation . . . and you won't find any of their novels without fully fleshed-out characters, complex plots, vivid settings, and thoughtful exploration of issues."

—*SF Site*

PRAISE FOR
The Evergence Trilogy

"A close-knit personal story told on a galaxy-sized canvas. Filled with action as well as intriguing ideas."

—Kevin J. Anderson,
New York Times bestselling author

"An appropriately wild mix of pulp, Saturday matinee serial, TV sci-fi, and computer games in its DNA, and more than a touch of postmodernist melancholy in its spirit."

—*Locus*

"Space opera of the ambitious, galaxy-spanning sort. A good read." —*The New York Review of Science Fiction*

"Full of adventure of Asimovian imperial vistas. Delivers tons of action . . . Offers wide-screen baroque plotting never out-of-control. With echoes of vintage Jack Williamson and Poul Anderson, as well as Niven, Asimov, and Vinge, Williams and Dix proudly continue a vital tradition in SF."

—*Analog*

"The excitement never lets up."   —*Orb Speculative Fiction*

GEODESICA
ASCENT

Sean Williams
with Shane Dix

ACE BOOKS, NEW YORK

THE BERKLEY PUBLISHING GROUP
Published by the Penguin Group
Penguin Group (USA) Inc.
375 Hudson Street, New York, New York 10014, USA
Penguin Group (Canada), 10 Alcorn Avenue, Toronto, Ontario M4V 3B2, Canada
(a division of Pearson Penguin Canada Inc.)
Penguin Books Ltd., 80 Strand, London WC2R 0RL, England
Penguin Group Ireland, 25 St. Stephen's Green, Dublin 2, Ireland (a division of Penguin Books Ltd.)
Penguin Group (Australia), 250 Camberwell Road, Camberwell, Victoria 3124, Australia
(a division of Pearson Australia Group Pty. Ltd.)
Penguin Books India Pvt. Ltd., 11 Community Centre, Panchsheel Park, New Delhi—110 017, India
Penguin Group (NZ), Cnr. Airborne and Rosedale Roads, Albany, Auckland 1310, New Zealand
(a division of Pearson New Zealand Ltd.)
Penguin Books (South Africa) (Pty.) Ltd., 24 Sturdee Avenue, Rosebank, Johannesburg 2196, South Africa

Penguin Books Ltd., Registered Offices: 80 Strand, London WC2R 0RL, England

This is a work of fiction. Names, characters, places, and incidents either are the product of the author's imagination or are used fictitiously, and any resemblance to actual persons, living or dead, business establishments, events, or locales is entirely coincidental.

GEODESICA: ASCENT

An Ace Book / published by arrangement with the author

PRINTING HISTORY
Ace mass market edition / February 2005

Copyright © 2005 by Sean Williams.
Cover art by Chris Moore.
Cover design by Judith Murello.
Interior text design by Stacy Irwin.

ISBN: 0-441-01269-8

ACE
Ace Books are published by The Berkley Publishing Group,
a division of Penguin Group (USA) Inc.,
375 Hudson Street, New York, New York 10014.
ACE and the "A" design
are trademarks belonging to Penguin Group (USA) Inc.

PRINTED IN THE UNITED STATES OF AMERICA

10 9 8 7 6 5 4 3 2 1

For K.

*With thanks to Simon Brown, Ginjer Buchanan,
Marcus Chown, Richard Curtis, Nydia Dix,
Mikolaj Habryn, Jeff Harris, Jeremy Nelson,
Garth Nix, Robin Potanin, Kim Selling,
Lilla Smee, and Stephanie Smith.*

CONTENTS

+PRELUDE

The Palmer Cell *Jaintiapur* was a long way off its usual course. A regular on the Eliza and Whitewater Detours, it had struck out even farther from the Arc Circuit in response to a plea for help from one of humanity's most distant colonies. Eliza, that colony's nearest neighbor, was over ten light-years away, but weather had been favorable in the Local Bubble and the journey took less than a year.

Palmer Horsfall, chief officer of the *Jaintiapur,* didn't begrudge the long journey. It could have been worse. Humanity's exploration of the galaxy had advanced rapidly through regions with the least amount of matter between the stars. The frontier world of Scarecrow—recently annexed as Mei-Shun-Wah by the Exarchate, around a star identified as 59431 in the Hipparcos catalogue—was the present holder of the record for most distant. Not far behind were Hipparcos 59432 and the *Jaintiapur*'s destination, Hipparcos 66704. The former had been known as Severance before the Exarchate christened it Newbery-Vaas. The latter's new name, White-Elderton, would never stick. Ten years after the *Jaintiapur* docked, eighty-two long light-years from Sol, people would still call it Sublime.

The *Jaintiapur* came at speed in response to a request for scientific assistance from the colony's Exarch. Since that request had been lodged, the news had spread along the Arc Circuit: of a hitherto unknown type of ROTH artifact that had drifted from deep space into the colony's gravity well. People as far away as Little Red began to whisper about what that might mean. A working alien machine offered more than just interesting xenarcheological relics. All of the seven alien races known to have passed through the Local Bubble at various points in the previous million years had been more advanced than humanity.

Palmer Horsfall, chief officer of the *Jaintiapur,* didn't have orders to move the artifact or to take samples elsewhere. She simply brought instruments and personnel from the better-equipped Eliza colony to its frontier neighbor. Among those personnel was her sister, a vacuum physicist normally stationed in Alcor. Deva Horsfall wasn't a xenarcheologist, a fact not lost on the people aboard the Cell.

"Maybe it's a diversion," one of the crew suggested.

"For what?" Deva Horsfall was determinedly pragmatic. Probing the empty places of the universe soon leached the romance out of life.

"Something they've made, rather than something they've found."

"Invent a better VOID drive," quipped the ship's wit, "and they'll beat a path to your door."

"It's more likely to be the other way around," Deva said. "Would they wait for us this long if they didn't have to?"

"You get your kicks where you can, I guess, on a frontier world."

Palmer Horsfall didn't like to encourage speculation until she had the facts in front of her. In that respect, she was much like her sister. She thought it perfectly conceivable that a find could relate to her sister's field of expertise. The details could wait until they reached their destination.

Within twenty-eight hours of the arrival of the *Jaintiapur,* Deva Horsfall and the rest of the payload were delivered safely to the colony. The alien artifact, if such it was, had been carefully sequestered within a containment facility of Exarchate design. The Cell's sensors couldn't penetrate its outer shell. What lay within was a mystery to those outside. The discovery was being treated with great secrecy.

"I hope this doesn't turn out to be a waste of your time," Deva had said when leaving the *Jaintiapur*.

"We've been well paid," said the Palmer, meaning the words in more ways than one. The trip had been an opportunity for them to reacquaint themselves with each other. Long absences and light-speed delays had stretched a formerly close sibling relationship almost to irrelevance. "I have no regrets."

"I'm just trying not to get too excited." The feverishness in Deva's eyes belied her words. "This wouldn't be the first time people have gotten worked up over nothing.

"What's the worst that can happen? If you *do* find nothing—well, that's your specialty. It's a win-win situation."

"Either way, I'm about to find out."

They had embraced and said farewell.

Sublime's Exarch took the scientific payload and put it to immediate effect. The crew of the *Jaintiapur* watched from a distance as arcane sensors stirred and strange energies brewed. Deva Horsfall disappeared into the artifact's containment facility to conduct her investigation under the tightest of security, so what she and the Exarch did was never known precisely.

That they did *something,* however, was of little doubt. The footage of the colony's final moments soon became familiar to every citizen of the Exarchate. It was broadcast across the whole of colonized space, leaving a horrified, stunned silence in its wake.

As though a detonator had been tripped, the artifact suddenly and without warning disgorged devastation on a scale never before witnessed by humanity. A raging, luminous ball of plasma spread rapidly across the *Jaintiapur*'s forward sensors in a blaze of golden light, devouring everything in its path. The containment facility went first, then the colony's main base. Nothing stopped it. The more it consumed, the more it propagated, exploiting a terrible arithmetic progression to gain total dominance of the system. Within hours it had destroyed not just the colony, including Exarch Elderton and everyone under her care, but four of the system's inner worlds as well.

The *Jaintiapur* barely outran the fatal front, capturing images of the destruction as it fled. The expanding bubble of hostile alien replicators left a fine mist of vicious nanotech in its wake. As soon as it was safe to do so, Palmer Horsfall turned her Cell about to consider her options. Endlessly breeding and vigilant, the alien replicators devoured anything that strayed too close, and buried everything within its borders in a howl of electromagnetic noise. Palmer Horsfall sacrificed numerous Cell components in a vain attempt to penetrate the borders of the affected area. She pursued every possible means of communication. A dozen members of her crew lost their lives when the unpredictable ROTH tech took offense at the Cell's continued presence and swatted at it as a human might an irritating fly.

Eventually the chief officer of the *Jaintiapur* decided that nothing could be done for the people of Sublime, if any remained in the infected mess of the system at all—her sister included.

Despairing, the *Jaintiapur* turned tail and fled.

In the following years, other Cells attempted to breach the boiling borders of the alien-infested system. None were remotely successful. Overtures of communication continued to be rebuffed. The theory prevailed that the Exarch of the colony had inadvertently triggered a sophisticated defense mechanism that blindly destroyed everything within a certain radius of the artifact. The artifact made no other response to the civilization that had poked its doorbell and run away—and neither did the defense mechanism, except to strike out every now and again at the automated monitors stationed around the system, ready to sound the alarm should the contagion show signs of spreading.

The Palmer who had obediently delivered her sister to the maelstrom resigned from the *Jaintiapur* and took charge of Horsfall Station, in a deep elliptical orbit around Sublime's primary star. There she waited, maintaining a grim vigil for the many who had died in the budding colony, victims of unknown killers. She would find those responsible, she swore to herself. And she would make them pay.

No matter how long it took . . .

1

According to the map the pipe was rated for humans, but Melilah Awad, one-eighty centimeters long, only just fit into it. Curved, cream-colored walls veined in yellow rushed by as she hurried to the next hub, pushing herself along with hands and feet in the negligible gee. Lights in visible spectra were few and far between, and she navigated by infrared when the darkness was complete.

An air current blew from along the pipe at roughly her velocity. She imagined a bubble of her exhalations accompanying her like an unseen shroud and quickly quashed the thought. It made her throat tighten as though she were actually suffocating.

She pushed on, conscious of time ticking away fast. Her watchmeter told her she still had work to do. Fourteen people were observing her from afar, locked on to her trace as she plumbed the innermost regions of the giant habitat. Seven of them she knew well: fellow gleaners, keeping tabs just in case she'd caught a whiff of some new, rich vein of overlooked information. Four were friends she'd asked to tag along for the ride, until the time was right. Two of the remaining three were unknown to her, possibly pseudonyms for the Exarch and, therefore, of some concern. And the last . . .

She checked the time. Thirty-two twenty. Another three hundred seconds.

"I told you, Gil: leave me alone." She spoke aloud. The echo from the pipe's smooth walls gave her words extra substance, if only to her ears.

"Now, don't be like that, 'Lilah."

She cringed at the use of the nickname. "Why do you go

to so much trouble to track me when you're not even prepared to listen to what I've got to say?"

"And why do *you* resent my surveillance of you? Seems strange for one who expends so much energy on defending the openness of our society."

"It's not the surveillance I mind, Gil. It's *you*."

The distant man chuckled. "Could be worse," he said. "You could be so dull that nobody would *want* to watch you."

"Sounds like heaven."

"I know you're lying."

Gil Hurdowar was right, but that didn't make him any easier to tolerate. Melilah could picture him, a scrawny figure jacked directly into the Scale-Free Bedlam feed. His face was lined, and his hair possessed a disconcertingly piebald quality that spoke of badly maintained antisenescence treatments. She had learned from her one and only in-person confrontation that his cubicle smelled of burnt sugar, as though a saucepan of ruined toffee had been hidden in a cupboard and forgotten months ago.

She—elegantly youthful, in appearance at least, and meticulously clean—took offense at his interest in her, and she made no bones about showing it. That was how the system worked. He could watch her if he wanted to, but she didn't have to like it. Especially at moments such as these, when being observed was exactly what she didn't want.

One hundred fifty seconds. Her watchmeter was down to twelve. At the hub, she kicked right, then almost immediately right again. The new pipe was slightly wider along one axis, giving it a squashed feel. Although there was no real indication that this area of the habitat was experiencing undue structural load, Melilah was distinctly aware of how near the center she was getting. With thousands of kilometers of pipes all around her and unknown cubic hectares of chambers piled high above, it was no wonder that the heart of Bedlam had long ago collapsed into a solid core. What had once been perfectly habitable spaces were now flattened foundations for new architecture. That new architecture would, in turn, one day collapse on top of the layers beneath, if Bedlam kept growing at its current rate.

Melilah sincerely hoped she would be well away from these pipes when that day came.

"Looking for something in particular?" Hurdowar pressed, voicing the question that was undoubtedly on the minds of many of the others watching her movements. "Data cache? Hard-copy store?"

"Who says I'm looking for anything?"

"You only come down here when you are."

"That's not exactly true." Bedlam's basement was vast and, for the most part, empty. The habitat's many citizens naturally tended to gravitate upward, resettling as fast as each new layer could come online. This constant migration left a labyrinthine vacancy in its wake. She wasn't the only person looking for things left behind, and she knew for certain that she wasn't the only one who used it as a repository for her own private data. The core of Bedlam was a graveyard for many things best left forgotten.

Melilah didn't have to justify herself, but she wanted her cover on public record. "Since when has amateur archeology been a crime?"

Hurdowar snorted. "If that's what you're doing, then I'm your guardian angel."

"The information laws are there to protect us all. I'm doing the community—and the Exarch—a service by upholding them."

"And making a tidy profit while you're at it. Hell, you don't need to explain it to me. I'm just jealous. Why else would I be snooping at you every waking moment?"

"I thought that was because you're an insensitive asshole."

"Some would say that. Consider the rest a bonus, then."

Twenty-five seconds. The pipe ended at a chamber large enough to have earned a warehouse rating, way back when. She took a moment to get her bearings. Five exits led from it, two deeper still. She took one of the latter, following her internal map.

"I'll ask you again, Gil: will you *please* leave me alone for a while?" The irritation in her voice was real.

"When the show's just getting interesting? I don't think so, 'Lilah."

Her internal timer hit zero. Far above the lowly tunnel, the system's primary flared. Magnetic fields flexed and snapped like whips. Huge gouts of supercharged particles poured through interplanetary space, frying every unshielded object in their path. The poles of magnetically active worlds and moons flickered blue. With the uncanny promptness of a vast machine, the symptoms of Hipparcos 62512's grumpy restlessness overtook the lumpy, half-made skin of Bedlam's outermost layers—and would have rendered them and what lay beneath utterly sterile, but for the sudden opacity of PARASOL in orbit between the station and the sun.

Melilah's watchmeter noted the departure of her four friends, as planned. Five of the gleaners went with them, and both of the unnamed traces. That left just two gleaners and Hurdowar.

"Is it a big one?" she asked them, knowing what the answer would be. She'd checked the solar weather reports in advance.

"Huge," said Hurdowar. "Pretty, too."

One of the two remaining gleaners took the bait. Melilah slipped into a pipe too narrow for her to stand in and shot along it like a bullet down a barrel. *Close, now.* She stretched in her crawl-suit, enjoying the physicality of her quest.

"Not as pretty as what I see right now," Hurdowar added.

She swallowed revulsion. "Give me a break, will you?"

"No can do, 'Lilah. But please, feel free to watch me back if it makes you feel any better."

"Thanks, but I think I'd rather gouge my eyes out with a blunt spoon." The pipe constricted to the point where she had to put her arms at her sides and let her feet kick her along. "Listen, Gil: you may have your rights, but so do I.

I'm not some animal in a zoo; I'm not your *property.* Try to corral me, and I'll take whatever means necessary to stop you."

"But I keep an eye out for you. I give you leads!"

"My gratitude has its limits. I can cope just fine without you."

"Really?" A sly tone entered the man's voice. "Did you realize that the *Nhulunbuy* requested permission to dock fifty minutes ago?"

At Bedlam? The words were almost past her lips before she could stop them. She hadn't known, and the news took her by surprise. "What business is that of mine?"

Hurdowar chuckled again. "You don't fool me, 'Lilah. You know as well as I do who's running the *Nhulunbuy* these days. And you know he wouldn't come here unless he had absolutely no choice."

"Damn you, Gil," she cursed. The last gleaner winked out, perhaps from embarrassment. "My relationship with Palmer Eogan is none of your business."

"Can't blame a guy for being curious—especially when you still call it a *relationship.*"

She brought herself to a sudden halt. *Here.*

Calling up a series of virtual displays, she scrolled rapidly through them and launched a package of countermeasures, prepared in advance against just such a contingency. If Gil Hurdowar wouldn't go away voluntarily, she would just have to make him. There wasn't a hell deep or hot enough for someone like him—and to hell with penalties, too. The Exarch could cut her off completely for all she cared. At least she'd be alone.

"I'd love to continue this engaging conversation, Gil, but—"

Hurdowar's channel died with a squawk. Her watchmeter clicked to zero at last.

Zero. She focused her thoughts on the task at hand. No one was watching her. This was her chance—and it wouldn't last long. The Exarch would be onto her in moments for shutting Hurdowar up like that. In Bedlam, there were many crimes, but few were as fundamental as restricting a citizen's right to information. Loathe him though she might, Hurdowar was a citizen, and the Exarch imposed the laws protecting him with the same rigor he imposed those of the Gentry.

Damn them, too, she added to herself, but didn't dwell on it. The seconds were flying by. She had brought herself to a halt by a narrow niche that only appeared on the most detailed of maps. Most importantly, it was out of sight of the nearest CCTV feed. She'd checked it some years earlier and found it to be empty. A scan of the area since then showed no signs of anyone moving in. But just because no one had, didn't mean that she *shouldn't*.

Reaching into a pocket of her crawl-suit, she produced a flat packet as round as her palm. Colored to match the pipe's milky wall, it was designed to stick unobtrusively and remain out of sight forever. Should anyone trace her path to the niche, they would assume that she had already cleaned it out and might not bother taking a second look. Even if they did look, the camouflage would probably still fool them.

Melilah reached inside the niche to stick the disk in place, and was startled to find something already there.

What the hell? She pulled her hand away. The niche should have been empty; she was certain of it. Putting her disk back into its pocket, she leaned into the hole and examined what she'd found more closely. It was standard model data fiche, solid-state, unsecured. She pulled it loose and held it up warily in front of her. Some data caches— like hers—were booby-trapped, rigged with viruses or EMPs designed to take out both the idly curious and the deliberately invasive alike. She swept it while she had the chance, while Hurdowar was off-line and the others were busy with the flare.

The fiche was clean of traps. Accessing it, she brought up the contents in an internal window and scanned through them.

Old letters. Some pictures. Two faces recurred: a pair of

women, one with brown hair and a square jaw, the other skinnier, shorter, a redhead. They had been lovers, had gone surveying together; there were maps of a tangled, convoluted space Melilah assumed was Bedlam. Most of the photos portrayed happy times, snapshots of contentment; they had holidayed at Sublime on at least one occasion, before the Catastrophe. But Melilah sensed sadness lurking behind the smiles. People didn't bury good memories without a good reason.

In this instance, it looked like someone had beaten her to it.

She tossed the fiche in her hand, momentarily indecisive. The data she had found was valueless on the open market. It was no business of hers, of anyone at all except the person who had put it there. She would be doing them a service by replacing it and moving on.

But that would leave her business unfinished. The simplest thing, she told herself, was to replace the fiche and do as she'd originally intended. She doubted the person who had placed it would ever come back—and if they did, they probably wouldn't notice hers, tucked away behind it. Most likely both of them would remain there, untouched, as this layer of Bedlam compacted around them. Both repositories would be buried physically as well as mentally.

So that was what she did. She replaced the fiche and stuck her disk nearby. Then she kicked herself away, pretending to be heading elsewhere just in case someone happened to glance at her at that moment and wonder what she was doing.

The flare had been roiling around Bedlam for two full minutes. Her surprise package had kept Hurdowar busy all that time, forcing him to untangle knotted data lines and unclog stodgy feeds before he could get out. She didn't care what he thought of her, what weird sort of kick he was getting, following her around as he did. But pretending it didn't affect her was the surest way of letting him know that it *did*.

The Nhulunbuy *requested permission to dock fifty minutes ago . . .*

She opened a link to Gil Hurdowar. It would look good for her if she made the first overture, made it appear as though the breakdown in comm was a genuine accident. Worth a try, anyway.

"You there, Gil?"

Silence. The link registered as being open, but nothing came along it.

"Gil?"

She tried another line, and another. More nothing. She dialed an acquaintance at random with the same result. Frustrated, she punched in the code for the Exarch himself, and only echoes of her frustration returned to her down the pipe.

"Is *anyone* out there?"

The feeling of claustrophobia returned as one by one all the lines she had opened shut down. For the first time in years, Melilah Awad was truly cut off.

2

The alarm, once triggered, spread rapidly through the colony's infostructure. Exarch Isaac Deangelis normally skimmed the surface of temporal flow like a stone over water, experiencing individual days as though they were minutes, riding the ebb and flow of the economy, watching Palmer Cells come and go like darting pond creatures, embracing the sure vantage point of long time as was his birthright.

When the alarm reached the outer layers of his distributed consciousness, however, his entire self jerked abruptly to a temporal halt. It felt like a transport collision in slow motion. A single moment crystallized around him, spreading out in branched waves of supersaturated connectedness; what had once been liquid and smoothly flowing suddenly coalesced into an incredibly complicated snapshot of the colony as a whole, caught in the seed crystal moment of the alarm. As he changed gears from very long-term overview to minutely microfocused, he sought the source of the disturbance and critiqued his agents' autonomic reactions to it.

The first name he saw prompted a sigh of resignation. *Her again.* He didn't need to see the footage in detail to recognize Melilah Awad's elegantly angular features or her naturally grown hair, dyed brown and white in geometric streaks parallel to her fringe. Her tight-fitting semi–pressure suit accentuated her natural physicality with a brazenness that unnerved him only slightly more than her resentment of him. She seemed to be at the heart of every disturbance in his domain. When the Exarchate had annexed the colony, forty-odd years earlier, Awad had been Deputy Counselor, second only to the system's nominal head. Although the annexation had been conducted with the same swift efficiency as those in other habited systems, with very little loss of life or material assets, the aftereffects were pervasive and tenacious. Awad, left with no functional role to play in the system's new government, made a point of encouraging anti-Exarchate demonstrations whenever she could, and would, he was sure, foment active dissent were it not for the system's antiprivacy laws that would immediately finger her as the ringleader. Deangelis couldn't stop her from talking, not if he wanted to maintain the system's unique character, since imposing absolute rule would prompt even greater resentment than he already experienced. He tolerated the rumblings and was proud that, so far, the situation had never flared into open revolt as it had once or twice elsewhere.

Even if it had, the outcome would have been the same. The Exarchate was unassailable. That was the one, pure fact that Awad had never been able to digest.

She appeared to be on another prospecting mission, insinuating herself deep in the belly of the habitat. That, he assumed, was what had triggered the alarm. Foraging under cover of an attention-grabbing flare was a common tactic, as a great number of observers directed their attention toward the celestial event. Despite it being two hundred years since a similar flare had expunged all life from the system, this was still a significant event and worthy of close study. Deangelis scrolled back through Awad's movements to confirm that her behavior matched that of someone engaged in a secret-retrieving pursuit. There was no discrepancy. She had even launched a software guillotine to cut off the one remaining viewer watching her when the time came, so what she found would remain unseen by anyone but herself.

Ultimately her destination revealed her intent, and he would have been alarmed for that reason alone had he seen her coming in advance. Luckily for him the deeper layers of deception seemed to be holding. The fiche was back in its place, read but not recorded. At least one of the habitat's few secrets was still concealed from prying eyes.

He was about to reinforce the good judgment of his agents—rewarding them so their complex decision-making nets would respond similarly next time such a circumstance arose—when he realized that it wasn't Awad who had triggered the alarm at all. It was in fact a more complex juxtaposition of names and words. The object of Awad's software guillotine had dropped the names into their conversation with the clear intent of provoking her, and those names—innocently in one sense—combined with a comment from Awad had been enough to set alarm bells ringing.

A chill went down his many spines when he examined the data. The agents had made a spot decision based on weightings he had given them, and based on the conclusion they had come to, their response was—again—absolutely correct. If his secret had been sprung, if word of what was slouching to Lut-Deangelis got out, it would undo everything he had worked for. *Everything.*

He immediately set in motion an emergency shutdown of all of the habitat's communications networks. He couldn't let word spread any further than it already had. This was too inflammatory to hesitate over. Even with his relative time slowed to a near standstill, he worried at his tardiness. Awad was busy replacing his cache back in the niche; Hurdowar was still trying to untangle the software bomb. But who else knew? How many other lips were spreading the terrible truth? How fast had incriminating light sped along which optical fibers?

Silence spread like ice through the habitat. Conversations were cut off in midsentence. Data flows ceased without warning. A normally thriving semantic space devolved into a multitude of truncated termini, spasming futilely to reconnect.

Exarch Deangelis reassured himself that he was doing everything he could, that no one could blame him if it wasn't enough. Word was bound to get out eventually, and contingencies were in place to deal with it when it happened. He had his orders, just as his agents had their key words, *Nhulunbuy* and Palmer Eogan among them.

He examined the exact instances in which each trigger word had been used, dreading to see precisely how much damage had been done but knowing he had to in order to begin repairing the damage. Part of him was already drafting an explanation to send to Sol, detailing the instance in which the leak had occurred, the precise mechanisms— once he isolated them—by which the leak had been allowed to happen, and the many ways in which he was already beginning to heal the breach. If the ftl network was decoherence-free, he could have a response within minutes. The swiftness with which judgment could fall both appalled and relieved him. Abrogation of responsibility always came at a price. Sometimes the price was worse than the circumstance from which one was trying to escape.

Even as data flows staggered to a halt all through his domain, a second realization—that he had been wrong twice in as many microseconds—struck him a near-physical blow.

Try to corral me, Awad had said, replayed for his benefit by the software agents, *and I'll take whatever means necessary to stop you.*

He thought of the fabled king who, for the want of a pin, lost his kingdom. Would Isaac Forge Deangelis lose *his* kingdom, now, over an accidental *pun*?

No, he told himself, torn between relieved laughter and despair at the stupidity of the situation. The agents had misread a critical word on which he had placed, perhaps, too much weight. Erring on the side of caution was, he supposed, sensible, but on the basis of that error he had just shut down a habitat containing over forty thousand people, of whom many already resented his interference and all valued their connectivity. His crystalline moment had gone from bad to worse—then back to bad, with a side order of chaos.

He forced himself to view the situation philosophically.

Mistakes happened, and in this instance this one could be corrected swiftly and simply. Problematic though it was, it was definitely better than if the truth had gotten out. In the case of such a leak, shutting down the habitat would have been only the beginning. The truth, as ever, was as volatile as a genie, and once released would not be easily recaptured.

Exarch Deangelis reprogrammed his agents to avoid a similar mistake in the future, and put into motion the lengthy process of reconnecting the many millions of severed lines. Even though the grunt work was usually performed by more specialized agents, this he oversaw personally, thereby ensuring that no further mistakes would be made. Indeed, if the reconnection went smoothly, many people might not even notice the sudden glitch. The task also gave him something to keep his mind off the disaster he had avoided through no quick thinking of his own.

He had been complacent, content to rule from the privileged position of Exarch, even though he knew the coming days to be critical. He understood now that he could no longer afford that luxury, that agents were insufficient to handle the minutiae of day-to-day governance in such critical times, that from now on he was going to be furiously, relentlessly busy—at least until the initial crisis was past. The truth remained buried under layers of deception, behind multiple falsehoods all resembling the truth. Balancing so many lies was a task worthy of a master juggler.

He was confident that, despite this bad start, he was more than up to the task. It was what he had been born to do. From his first conscious thought, the Archon had refined and fine-tuned his every capacity and instinct in order to create the perfect head of governance. He and the other Exarchs were the pinnacle of human evolution, the potent products of evolution both random and self-directed. No matter what the universe threw at him, he was certain he could handle it. In the long term, if not the short, the future was assured.

Still, part of his mind, no matter how furiously he

occupied the rest, stayed firmly focused on the imminent arrival of the *Nhulunbuy*. The Palmer Cell and its contents descended upon him with all the deadliness of an axe. The next slipup might result in much worse than a slight inconvenience to the casual telecommuters of his domain.

3

The *Nhulunbuy* hove to around Bedlam in a graceful arc, strung out like pearls in a necklace. Each of its seventy-eight components was spherical and perfectly reflective. Each reflected the solar storm's radiation—that which wasn't absorbed and put to nondestructive use—back into space, lending them a flickering, brilliant shine. Ranging in size from drones barely the size of a fist to bulky freight containers large enough to contain a small house, each of the Palmer Cell's components had the capacity to function as a completely independent starfaring vessel. Linked by protocols capable of withstanding the stresses of high-velocity space deformation, together they formed a single VOIDship under the command of one man.

Palmer Eogan crouched in the womb of the *Nhulunbuy*'s second largest component, N-2, and watched gloomily as Bedlam loomed large and silent in his instruments. It had been a long and stressful journey; normally he would have been glad to be coming out of the Dark and into port. This time, though, he felt far from glad. He would find no rest as long as he remained around Bedlam; of that he was completely certain.

While his thoughts should have been on the thing in N-1 and the wreckage they'd found around it, compacted and sealed in every available compartment throughout the Cell, instead his mind was on Melilah Awad.

I'm so sorry, he thought. *I didn't ask to come here like this. I didn't ask for any of it. If I could make it any other way, I would.*

He knew better than to call her. Forgiveness was not—and

had never been—an option. But he wanted to anyway. Even after so long, he still missed her.

Fortunately, the communications blackout currently gripping the colony put paid to any suggestion of breaking his vow. The silence from the colony was as ominous as it was unexpected. Could something have gone wrong with PARASOL? Or was the cause more sinister? Reflexively, he tightened the distance between the Cell's components, drawing the *Nhulunbuy* close around him in case it needed to move suddenly.

The thing in N-1 resisted the change in momentum as it had throughout the entire trip. He felt as though he had a tiger by the tail—a very heavy tiger that might wake at any moment and bite the hand pulling so insistently at it.

With a snap of static, the lines were suddenly open again.

"This is Lut-Deangelis Traffic Control," said the smooth androgynous voice of a routing AI. "*Nhulunbuy,* your approach is noted and your vector has been approved. Stand by for further instructions."

Eogan confirmed receipt of the transmission by opening data channels. "What happened back there, LDTC? You went awfully quiet."

"Interference from the flare," supplied the AI. "An EMP took out a major communications hub. The problem has been rectified." Without changing tone, Traffic Control continued: "In accordance with Lut-Deangelis Information laws, you are required to open all memory and channels to public scrutiny. Please immediately supply access codes and encryption keys. Upon verification, you will be allotted temporary citizenship and allowed full access to local systems."

Palmer Eogan hesitated only momentarily before sending the requested codes. Once they were verified, anyone in Bedlam would have access to every piece of knowledge he and his crew had gathered on their journey from Mizar. Theoretically, he would be unable to keep secrets from anyone.

He had no choice but to accept the condition of entry into the system. Without doing so, he would be forced to go elsewhere, and that was simply not an option. Carefully, with no evidence of obvious deception, he had configured the data in the Cell's stores so it wouldn't point directly at the truth. Convenient and very plausible deceits stood in the way of anyone curious about what lay at the heart of N-1. Even the persistent would be hard-pressed to penetrate to its core.

"Codes and keys verified," said the AI. "Welcome to Lut-Deangelis System, Palmer Eogan."

He didn't respond. It would have been a lie to say that he was glad to be there. He felt exposed and vulnerable, and conscious of a large number of games tangled around him. The AI's explanation for the blackout was a little too pat. To take out the communication web enclosing not just Bedlam but the entire system would require more than just the destruction of a major hub. That would require hitting at least a quarter of the hubs at once, or shutting down the Exarch himself.

A flood of information swept over the Cell. His crew broke radio silence to inquire about friends and colleagues last visited many years before. It had been a long time since the *Nhulunbuy* had been this way.

"You have an unusual manifest," said a new voice over the comms. "How intriguing."

Eogan checked the ID before replying, even though he thought he recognized the warm, contralto tones. The ID confirmed his suspicion.

"That was quick, Luisa. Good to see you're still on the ball."

"Quick nothing. Every snoop in the system will have checked you out already. I'm just the only one who can get past your firewall and speak to you directly." He could hear the welcome in her voice, and couldn't help a slow smile in return. Luisa Pirelli had flown several legs around the Arc Circuit with him before settling down on Whitewater, years ago. It was good to hear her voice again, even if she was asking all the questions he wanted to avoid.

The features of her diamond face and the cast of her round eyes were deliberately neutral. He knew that look. "Want to tell me about 2358M1S willingly, or will I have to come up there and find out for myself?"

"There's nothing to find out," he said. "You have all the data we have."

"Yeah, right. It's big, whatever it is. Much bigger than anything else found on a sweeper run. Could it be a ROTH artifact?"

"Your guess is as good as mine, Lu. I'll leave the answers to the experts."

"No experts here, Eogan. We're just a bunch of amateurs—and starved of excitement, to boot. Expect to be thoroughly *probed* in the coming minutes." A thick edge lent her choice of words a prurient double meaning. "You should be used to that, working for the Gentry."

"How's James?" he asked, ignoring the jab. The Palmers were theoretically independent of the Exarchate empire, although in practice it was the only organization with the resources to pay for interstellar travel, and, therefore, wielded a great deal of influence over the guild of starfarers.

"The same," she said. "Still as crazy as coat hangers in free fall. But you know: he occasionally makes sense. The latest glitch will have him jumping."

"The blackout?"

"No. You." She was still smiling, but the comment wasn't entirely playful. "Will you be staying long?"

He hoped not. "I don't think so."

"Drop in, if you deign to come down to our level."

"I will, if you're offering dinner."

"You'd better believe it. I'll keep the vodka on ice. By the sound of your voice, you need it more than ever."

He didn't know how to respond to that. After so long plying the trade lanes, his social skills were rusty. He'd thought he was being perfectly affable to Luisa, and he *was* genuinely glad to hear from her.

"Just call her, Dominic," Luisa said into the conversational void.

"Call who?"

"You're not fooling anyone, you know."

The line shut with a click.

Eogan sighed and forced himself to concentrate on the Cell as it locked into orbit and assumed new symmetries reminiscent of an ancient model of a molecule. Independent fragments drew together; some of them touched, merged into one. He tapped into an external feed to admire the ballet, and was startled at how obvious it looked that the Cell was hiding something. He tweaked the distributed intelligence guiding the maneuver, moving N-1 out of the heart of the formation and putting it on the edge, as though it was nothing important. He downgraded the shields, now that the Cell was under the shelter of PARASOL, and they dimmed to a reflective brown-black. Instead of a collection of highly polished ball bearings, the Cell now resembled a clump of Christmas ornaments made of smoked glass. Angular, indistinct shapes lurked within.

"Palmer Eogan," said a third voice. Brisk and authoritative, this one radiated no welcome. There was no visual.

"Exarch Deangelis," he sent back, wondering if the chill was an act put on for those observing. He had expected the Exarch to call earlier. Now that the moment had come, he was more aware of being watched than ever before.

"You've posted some irregularities in your mission log," said the Exarch. "These will require explanation."

"I am aware of that." He fought the urge to add *sir.* "I'd like to discuss the details with you at your earliest convenience."

"That might be sooner than you were expecting. An envoy is on its way to you as we speak."

Eogan checked telemetry and noted a small vessel powering toward the *Nhulunbuy* from behind the giant habitat.

Bedlam occupied the heart of the Trojan point trailing the system's largest gas giant, Ah Kong. PARASOL, the flare-shield, hung like an improbably large contact lens between Bedlam and the sun, assuming full opacity only when solar radiation was at a maximum. Numerous vessels and other structures huddled beneath its black shadow, jostling each other under the influence of Bedlam's weak gravitational pull. The flare painted the edges of PARASOL bright orange, casting a peculiar light over the assembly. Magnetic field lines, PARASOL's second line of defense, rippled and swayed like the tentacles of a luminous jellyfish, hundreds of kilometers long.

"I'll have my data ready for your inspection," Eogan said. Telemetry put the envoy's ETA at five minutes.

"Do. There are a number of issues that need to be clarified immediately. I trust the *occlusion* is adequately contained."

Eogan caught the slight emphasis. "Inasmuch as I can tell."

"Good. Let's keep it that way."

"I have no intentions of doing otherwise," he said, realizing only at the end of the sentence that he was talking to himself.

Damn him, Eogan thought, allowing himself no external display of anger. *Damn them* all *to hell.*

His gaze drifted to N-1, and he idly toyed with the idea of opening it to the vacuum and dumping its contents unceremoniously onto Bedlam. Or Lut-Deangelis, as the Exarch had insisted it be called since annexation. Let *them* deal with it, whatever came out of its hellish throat. Without that particular albatross around his neck, Eogan would be free to run again.

But even as he thought it, the question "Where to?" surfaced, as it always did. He could no more flee the Exarchate than he could his guilt. Both would always be there, until he confronted them head-on.

The comms bleeped, indicating that he had a personal message waiting for him. He took it with a sinking feeling, knowing who it was from before he opened it.

> *DE*
> *Let's talk.*
> *MA*

A mixture of hot and cold rushed through him. The overture barely comprised a single sentence, but it was the first in one hundred and fifty years, and more than he'd dared hope for. It should have been a good thing.

So why did he feel so terrified? Why did he reach out to his peripherals and give the command to delete it? Why didn't the fact that he knew she was watching him do it give him any kind of satisfaction?

It wasn't about revenge or shame or fear or any such simple emotion. It was none of those and all of them. Until he was certain exactly what he was feeling, his history with Melilah Awad was one Pandora's box he preferred to leave shut.

One out of two, he thought, as the Exarchate's envoy accelerated steadily closer to the thing in N-1. That was the most he could hope for.

4

An alarm rang, signaling that it was time for Melilah's exercises. Grateful for the break, she shut down her interface and her watchmeter. It didn't worry her if people observed her during this particular daily ritual, but it helped if she wasn't distracted by the knowledge that they were there—and so many of them at that moment, too. She dimmed the lights.

Thickening shadows fell across her collection of personal paraphernalia. Her quarters consisted of a double-lobed chamber—a peanut stretched thin in the middle. One lobe, slightly smaller, was her personal area, where she saw to the needs of her body; the other lobe, with its entrance to the outside world, was where she worked, socialized, took messages, and so on. There, she was surrounded by trinkets she had collected or been sent from a dozen worlds. Near free fall enabled her to utilize every surface to its full potential. Viewed from one angle, it revealed a collection of fine, earthy artworks originating on Eliza and New Eire. From another, gleaming novelties fashioned from intricate titanium wire peeked out around delicate Little Red bonsai. The room was a puzzle box with numerous solutions, and each solution was a slice of her life.

She floated in the middle of the room and activated the exercise program.

Immediately, a face appeared in the 3-D screen curving around one segment of the chamber. The man's features were both familiar and friendly. Generous lips curved in a smile; deep green eyes twinkled.

"Hello, Mel." The man's voice was warm and couldn't quite hide the accent of a Friday native. "It's been a while."

"It has indeed," she told the part recording, part simulation. "But I still remember you, Bernard Krassay. You were my doctorate supervisor. As far as I know, you're still alive and living on Altitude."

The image nodded and winked out. A second later, it was replaced by another, this time a woman with a long, narrow nose and a shaved head. Fine, gold lines within her skin traced fractal patterns across her temples and cheeks. A deep tingling in Melilah's occipital implant indicated the receipt of a neural packet.

Melilah hesitated before opening it, not remembering the woman at all. Was she friend or foe? Was the packet safe or loaded with neuron-scrambling signals? A decision either way, in real life, could make the difference between offending someone who had once been a dear friend or risking permanent insanity.

Two things she had learned from her political career were that society depended on interpersonal networks, and that everything could turn on a simple misidentification. In her fifties she had set about ensuring that her memory remained good in order to avoid the latter. Anthropologists had known since the twentieth century that people were born with a ceiling on their social groups. Once Melilah exceeded the Dunbar and Hill number of 150, and rapidly acquiring still more associates, it became progressively harder to keep track of everyone she had to know. As she passed her hundredth birthday, it became only worse. Some of her contemporaries opted for cortical grafts and other memory prosthetics. She, motivated by a gut-level—some would say "irrational"—desire to keep her body as free of technology as possible, opted for other means.

She had found that using a name once every two months was enough to keep the memory fresh. Any longer than that between reminders, and the associations faded, rendering recall unreliable. So she programmed a complete list of her occasional acquaintances and enemies into a database and programmed it to cycle through them every sixty days, shuffling the order each time.

A hundred years on, she was still in the habit of skimming fifty or so names a day, just to keep on the ball. By flicking through images, voice files, place names, and more abstruse clues, she felt confident of recognizing any of the several thousand people more or less likely to interact with her at any point in the near future. The list had grown and shrunk down the years, and many people had dropped off it entirely because of death or distance. Sometimes she had added names to the list only to be surprised that they had been on it once before, decades ago, and she had forgotten them completely. That only reinforced the need for the list and the effort to keep it fresh in her mind.

Some names, however, simply would not fall out of her head, no matter how she tried to ignore them.

"Szilvia Animaz," she said eventually. "I wouldn't open a packet from you if I had a knife at my throat."

The angularly beautiful woman with the gold-inlaid skin vanished. Another face took her place, followed quickly by another. And so it went.

Melilah stuck at it for an hour. It was penance, she told herself, for giving in to antisenescence treatments that reduced the need for physical workouts. Her body would remain fit and healthy for decades regardless of what she did to it; but maintenance, she thought, was an important part of any health regime. She needed to remind herself that existence needed to be worked at, or else it soured. She had seen too many people burn out within decades, despite being wired to the nines with technology intended to squeeze every drop out of life.

She didn't want to be a god, but she *did* want to be around for a very long time. If only to see the end of the Exarchate, as had to come sooner or later. Nothing was permanent; no empire lasted forever.

At the end of the hour, she'd had enough of her own company and headed to ben-Avraham's to get some breakfast.

The restaurant was nearly full. More people arrived in a flood after her, and the maître d' soon began turning them away. As she ordered, a familiar voice rose up above the crowd, calling her name.

"Grandmother Mel! Over here!"

Melilah looked up and saw her four-daughter Yasu struggling to get into the restaurant. She called over the waiter and explained she would need another setting at the table.

Yasu looked flustered when she joined her. "It's crazy out there!" Yasu exclaimed, pushing a long, blue fringe out of her eyes. Natural flesh tones vied with postdermal patches that seemed to float a millimeter above her skin, moving around her body with apparently random but well-coordinated modesty. "You're the hit of the airwaves today. Did you know that?"

Melilah had forgotten to turn her watchmeter back on after her exercises. The reading had been high enough then to dispel any doubts planted by Gil Hurdowar that she was *uninteresting*.

She shrugged. "So?"

Yasu laughed with gusto. "Don't pretend you don't care! I know you better than that."

Indeed she did; of all Melilah's descendants, Yasu was the one she liked most. For a time, while Yasu's father had been stationed on Phad 4, Melilah had been her primary guardian, cementing a bond that had already been strong.

"Is that why you came here?" Melilah asked, throwing the accusation back at her. "To bask in the limelight?"

"That, and to find out what's going on. Who is this Palmer Eogan guy? Why have I never heard of him before?"

"He's old news." She buried a small pang. "You can't expect to know about everyone I've met."

"Only the important ones. And you dropped him a note, so he must mean *something*." Behind the ribbing, Yasu's expression was serious and sympathetic. "Is he my four-father?"

That stopped Melilah short for a moment. Why would Yasu guess that? What the hell were people *saying* about her?

"You have lots of four-fathers, my dear."

"Only one of them that no one talks about."

"When people do that sort of thing, there's usually good reason."

"But if it *is* him, and he's back . . ." Yasu took her great-great-grandmother's right hand in both of hers. "All the reason in the world won't make him go away."

Damn her. Melilah felt a surprising upwash of grief and affection, half-directed at Yasu. She didn't say anything for a long while, just squeezed the young woman's hands and wished she could take herself back almost two centuries and undo her mistakes. It probably wouldn't change a thing, though; she had done what she had done while in a perfectly clear state of mind, and that mind had not changed greatly down the years. But to experience it all afresh, firsthand . . . She was slightly appalled to realize that part of her wanted to go back *because* she would do it all again, not in order to change it.

Her fingers had typed the note to Eogan without apparent connection to her mind. All the justification in the world about pursuing a lead cut no ice when it came to the logic of her gut. She could have called him directly—if she'd been truly serious about it—but she wasn't nearly ready to see his face, to see what he had become.

She had made the first move; the rest was up to him. But she wasn't going to sit around waiting for him. The last thing she wanted was to be back *there* again.

"I'm hungry," she said, safe in the knowledge that only Yasu could read her expression accurately. She genuinely didn't care what the others watching her thought. Life in Bedlam wasn't for the faint of heart.

They ordered breakfast and talked about other things: Yasu's work in transspatial physics; her current partner, a coworker younger than she whose persistent flirting had finally paid off, although she confessed to being more intellectually stimulated by the AI assisting the project; and the flare, which had been officially designated the fifth-largest on record.

"Can you imagine what it must've been like for the First Wavers?" Yasu shook her head, echoing the very same sentiment she had expressed as a stricken four-year-old. "Without PARASOL, they wouldn't have lasted a second."

"They didn't." The current wave of colonists had inherited the habitat from predecessors who had sowed it into the rock of a nickel-iron asteroid over three centuries earlier. The name Bedlam suited the rambling, organic structure it had become in all those years, along with its similarly convoluted custodian AI that had spent much of its long life utterly alone. The First Wave colonists that had brought it into being hadn't stood a chance against the primary's fiery wrath.

"All fried up and turned into walls." The older Yasu looked around her, at the elegant furniture and iridescent drapes. Gone was the horror the thought had once evoked in her, twenty-five years earlier. Eyes as green as emeralds came back to focus pointedly on Melilah. "Like our memories."

Melilah raised a fruit smoothie in salute. "If you want to know what I was doing down below," she said, "just ask."

"Maybe I could come with you on your next expedition and find out for myself."

"I've offered plenty of times."

Yasu acknowledged the deflection with a roll of her eyes. "You know I'm never going to do it."

"Maybe. I still don't entirely understand why you're so certain of it, though."

"Ennui," her four-daughter said. "Information is only interesting if it's, well, *interesting*. What's the point of mucking about in the underbelly if all you find is someone's old tax statement? Without a guarantee of something at the end of it—and I know that's impossible—I'll stay right here, where I know the supply is reliable."

"There's interesting stuff to be found down there, believe me."

"Well, when you've found it, perhaps you can tell me

about it." Yasu tipped a wink to someone behind Melilah. "I'm not a pioneer, like you."

The comment surprised her. "Is that really how you see me?"

"Kinda." Yasu looked embarrassed. "When you're not digging around in garbage, that is."

The young woman got up to lean over the table and kiss her four-mother on the lips. "I love you even if you won't tell me what's going on. Give 'em hell."

With a sweep of energy and life, she was gone.

Melilah finished her smoothie, paid, and left, checking her watchmeter as she did so. The numbers outside the restaurant had dwindled slightly, as had the number of onlookers. Her studied nonchalance had convinced some at least that there wasn't going to be a grand revelation anytime soon. That was good. She had work to do.

When she brought her apartment interface back online, it whistled politely to indicate that she had received a large number of messages. Most were junk, propagating rumors about the blackout. She had instructed her spam filters and data moles to retain anything even tangentially related to her current interests. There was nothing about the couple whose memories she had invaded, not a single recent rumor concerning Lost Levels. Even Gil Hurdowar was quiet, for a change.

She took matters into her own hands and began probing.

First up was to get her civil record cleared after her stunt with Hurdowar, so she *could* dig. Within minutes of her software bomb, she had been issued with a temporary civil rights suspension order. It wasn't the first time a suspension order had been issued against her. The AI responsible for delivering the news did so with a cautionary smugness that made her want to gag. Two more, it warned her, and she would risk permanent downgrade. Two more after that, and she would exceed the maximum allowable for one year. The Exarch could only be *so* lenient. If she persisted beyond that point, she would qualify for expulsion from the habitat.

Fuck that, she thought. *It's going to take more than some freakish hybrid to kick me out. This is my home.*

But right then wasn't the time to fight that battle. She apologized for the incident and went about her pretend business. She didn't ask about the blackout, although she was sorely tempted to. The communications rupture had healed over within moments of forming; to all intents and purposes, nothing had happened. Later, in front of the interface in her quarters, surrounded by the welcoming clutter of two centuries of life, she'd learned that the breakdown had been noted in some quarters but completely ignored in others. As usual, a raft of unlikely and/or paranoid theories abounded to explain the incident: that the colony had experienced a near-catastrophic infostructure failure, and the Exarch was denying the fact in order to hide the precariousness of his rule; that imperialists from Alioth had finally made their move, attacking by viruses, EMP, and other exotic means; that someone had stumbled across something momentous and the Exarch was trying to cover it up. Melilah browsed them all, but was satisfied by none. Except, perhaps, for the last. She couldn't shake the impression that the blackout was somehow related to her. Although the cache she had found contained nothing but personal data, the synchronicity of her finding it and the blackout was too unlikely to be unconnected.

As paranoids and skeptics alike acknowledged, only one person had both the authority and the ability to deliberately bring Bedlam to a halt. That person was the Exarch. But why, she asked herself, would he protect a file of lesbian love letters and some amateur treasure maps? Everyone who came to Bedlam dreamed of finding the Lost Level, a supposed vault of hidden riches long buried on the fringe of the core regions. Melilah had traveled enough kilometers down there to suspect that official maps were mostly accurate and that there were no new large finds to be made. The odds were remote to an extreme that the two women in the file had stumbled across anything new.

Still, when Palmer Eogan failed to respond to her note, she decided to take another look, just in case her cursory steganographic scan had missed information buried deeper than normal in the files. Negotiating with her parole AI for permission to go back down was galling, but she forced herself to be polite and reasonable. Yes, she had done wrong. Yes, she must be punished. No, the data in the disk she had accidentally left behind couldn't be accessed later. No, she couldn't just dredge up a copy. The whole point of burying stuff so deep was that it couldn't be easily accessed.

It let her go on the grounds that she posted the data on a public node so the Exarch could examine it. *Fine,* she thought. If the data belonged to the Exarch in the first place, she wouldn't be showing him anything he didn't already know—assuming, of course, that the data was still where she'd left it. Although she'd checked security scans of the area to make sure no one else had been there, that didn't mean the fiche hadn't been scrambled or destroyed by remote.

The niche, when she returned, was undisturbed. Cool confidence in the face of a near disaster? She couldn't tell. Just in case she had missed something blindingly obvious, she quickly took a copy and replaced the fiche, then proceeded upside to post the data publicly, as instructed.

"Not up to your usual standard, Melilah." The voice of Isaac Forge Deangelis was coolly patronizing. "I expect better of you."

"Count yourself lucky, then," she said. "You'd better hope I don't strike it rich next time."

The Exarch's laugh was mocking, and ended with a click before fully played out.

A deliberate slur, she told herself. The Gentry did nothing involuntarily. Every move was calculated, every word chosen for a particular effect. Even the tone of his voice had been contrived specifically to rile her.

It was working.

+5

Like an ancient mechanical model of the solar system, with planets and moons rotating around a central point in a precisely controlled ballet, Exarch Deangelis's mind was technically in many points at once. Part of him watched Melilah Awad as she followed her instincts back to the fiche. Another part monitored communications traffic along a dozen or so well-patronized networks, tracking public speculation and rumor about the *Nhulunbuy*. Numerous parts dedicated themselves to overseeing the intricate economic and social systems required to keep Lut-Deangelis stable.

Just one satellite mind interrogated Palmer Eogan—but that one was keenly aware that, for the moment, the orbits of all the others were centered on him. What was said and done in the next few hours would determine the course of the future. There was no *could* about it.

"I have examined your mission log, Palmer Eogan," the envoy said, knowing the information was irrelevant but following the protocols of conversation with the same rigor as he would handshake a modem.

"I'd just like to reinforce that we've made no attempt to hide the irregularities," said Eogan. The chief officer of the *Nhulunbuy* hadn't got up on the Exarch's arrival, but that was a result of necessity, not bad manners. The Palmer was still in the process of untangling himself from the Cell he commanded. His body, where it sat hunched in a pod-like chair before the curving interior bulkhead of the container called N-2, seemed at first glance to be sprouting roots like an overripe potato. A more detailed examination revealed that some of the threads originated in the chair, not him. Either way, the roots were retracting, retreating millimeter by millimeter, leaving bare skin in their wake.

The process seemed ludicrously primitive to the Exarch. The Palmers, although significantly more cyborg-savvy than Naturals like Melilah Awad, were generations behind the Exarchate. It felt sometimes like talking to a tree.

"I will grant you that," he said. "But your openness does nothing to explain the irregularities. I and the citizens of Lut-Deangelis deserve a full account."

"You have my full agreement on that point."

Was that sarcasm? The Exarch couldn't tell. The Palmer's face was almost invisible behind a beardlike spray of fibers.

"Good. You can begin by describing the contents of the component you call N-1."

"If I could do that," the Palmer replied, "we wouldn't be having this conversation."

An apt comeback, one perfectly in line with the script they had prepared over ftl before the *Nhulunbuy* had docked. Exarch Deangelis nodded, as though deep in thought, and instructed the Palmer to begin at the beginning and to leave nothing out. The process wasn't for his benefit, but for the audience's. The soap opera was entirely for them.

The *Nhulunbuy* was one of several sweeper Cells plying the trade lanes of the Arc Circuit. Its usual routes were along the twenty-five-light-year sweep taking in Mizar, Alioth, and several other major systems in the area. Its function was simply to keep the lanes clear of the interstellar dust that downgraded average deform ratings, thereby causing voyages to be longer and less efficient. Occasionally, hard debris strayed across the lanes, forming serious occlusions that could cause catastrophic accidents. Such navigational hazards were difficult to clear, and the *Nhulunbuy* had a reputation for reliability and promptness in the face of such crises.

The report of a major occlusion on the lane between Mizar-Cazneaux and Lut-Deangelis had, therefore, led to the *Nhulunbuy*'s immediate dispatch to clear it. Apart from the occlusion, the lane had been relatively clear, so the *Nhulunbuy* had made impressive speed. Averaging a deform rating of just under 5.0 and a subjective velocity of 0.9 c, the *Nhulunbuy* had crossed the six light-years to the occlusion in a little under a year, local time.

Everything seemed normal to that point. It was when they arrived at the occlusion that the data took a turn for the screwy. The occlusion, it turned out, was no cometary fragment expelled from a nearby solar system. Neither was it a brown dwarf, an ejected planet, or a micro black hole.

"Describe what you found."

"You have my scientific data."

"Yes, but I don't have your firsthand experience. Tell me."

The Palmer took a deep breath. "From a distance it looked like a puff of dust, and I thought at first that it might be a holed Cell. But closer you could tell that it was something much stranger. The dust was old and cold, and wasn't rotating. There wasn't one solid core, as there would have been with a First Wave wreck. There were lots of solid bodies in there, and they were cold, too. They'd clumped together in no apparent order, but radar suggested that they were intact, not damaged. We saw smooth hulls, portals that could have been air locks and smaller companion craft that might have been shuttles, all docked."

"You're saying that these objects were space vessels."

"Yes." The Palmer didn't hesitate. "They were ships, all right. ROTH ships. I've never seen anything like them before."

Races Other Than Human. There had been several xenarcheological discoveries made in the last century, scattered across human space. All had been of ancient, dead cultures that had traveled and left detritus behind, much as humanity did. Nowhere had a home or colony world been found; if such existed—as surely it must—it was presently beyond the expanding bubble of the Exarchate's influence.

Exarch Deangelis was human enough to feel a tingle of excitement at the thought of what it must have been like to study those ghostly radar images and to realize that what one was seeing were the works of other hands, other minds, other lives . . .

How terrible, then, that the wonder had been so swiftly turned on its head.

"Is that what you have in N-1?" he asked the Palmer. "ROTH artifacts recovered from the occlusion?"

Palmer Eogan shifted slightly in the embrace of the Cell. "In a manner of speaking, yes."

"In *what* manner of speaking, exactly?"

"I'm sorry, Exarch Deangelis, but I hesitate to discuss this publicly."

"You are aware that the laws of Lut-Deangelis forbid you to hide information, especially when it is in the public's interest."

"Information, yes—but not speculation." The Palmer's eyes stared up at him unblinkingly from his mess of tree roots. "Forgive me if I seem intransigent. The *Nhulunbuy* isn't equipped to carry out the investigation required to do this thing justice. Until we have more data, I'd prefer not to make any judgment calls."

The Exarch imagined a ripple of excited whispers spreading out across the system at the revelation.

"I understand. But why bring it here? The ROTH Institute on Jamgotchian-McGraw is the best equipped on the Arc Circuit to examine such a find."

"I chose to bring it to Bedlam because you're closest," the Palmer explained, "and because your neutral political stance and open information policy would ensure that the information wasn't kept secret. This is an important discovery. People should know about it."

"We're honored you chose us." Exarch Deangelis wondered if the conversation sounded as prepared as it seemed to him. No matter. Most people would lap it up. "We'll take it off your hands and make sure it's studied properly. We have the rough specifications you've given us; I'm building a containment facility as we speak." This was true. A nanofacturing seed was already blossoming alongside the habitat, fueled in part by the energies of the recent solar flare gathered by PARASOL. Within hours it would be the size of a small asteroid and secure enough to handle such a discovery. "Your swift and prudent actions are greatly appreciated."

The Exarch intended the words as a dismissal. Once he handed over the occlusion, Eogan's work was done. There was no real role for the Palmer organization once the thing was out of their hands.

"My science officer has requested that she be part of the investigation," Eogan said. "I trust you won't have a problem with that."

Exarch Deangelis allowed no outward sign of annoyance at the departure from the script. "The examination of the object will take time. I wouldn't like to delay your departure any longer than be necessary, as committing an important member of your staff to such a procedure undoubtedly will."

"Thanks for your concern, but I believe the investigation to be more important than maintaining my schedule. My SO has firsthand experience with the object. That sort of information could be priceless."

The Exarch seethed. Was he being threatened with disclosure of the truth if he didn't submit to Eogan's request?

"Of course," he said aloud. "Palmer Vermeulen will be welcome to sit in on the analysis. I'll notify you of where she should report when the time comes." *And I'll make you pay for blackmailing the Exarchate over something like this,* he swore to himself. *This isn't the time for petty power games.*

"Thank you, Exarch Deangelis. I'll await your word." Eogan looked up innocently from his entangled seat. "No doubt you'd like to take a look at the object while you're here. I've authorized entry for your envoy into N-1. Is its body shielded?"

The question surprised him, as did the sudden depersonalization. "Yes, of course."

"Good. At a standard rating, it should last about five minutes. That'll give you time to become acquainted."

The Exarch just stared at the Palmer for a moment, unable to grasp what he was hearing. The envoy's body was rated to withstand the full force of Hipparcos 62512's solar flares indefinitely. A thousand years of exposure to cosmic rays would leave him functionally unharmed. *What the devil had Eogan brought him?*

Know your enemy, he told himself as he took his leave of the Palmer and entered the shuttle again. The loss of one body was a small price to pay for a closer look.

Half an hour later, standing on the lip of the monster and staring at the throat that lay open before him, he felt an exhilarating sense of despair. Space whipped and spun in Planck-sized whirlpools around him. He could feel their miniscule tides tearing at his hardened flesh, ripping it to pieces molecule by molecule. Cerenkov radiation flashed in the fluid of his eyes. Strange neuronal storms preceded massive cerebral shutdowns. He had almost immediately lost all feeling in his legs and torso, and that numbness crept steadily up his fingers to his elbows. As the nerve and chromosome damage mounted and his ability to communicate with the rest of his mind decreased, he wondered at the wisdom of belling this particular cat.

I'm dying, the envoy thought, alone at the end. *And what for?*

White-stained violet streaks flashed down the sides of the rotating cylinder in which he stood. It wasn't a solid object. The boundary ahead of him was utterly black. Wormhole black.

To be the first to die.

That was the doom-laden thought that accompanied him into the abyss.

The first of many.

+6

When the Exarch left him, Palmer Eogan was immediately bombarded with communications from Bedlam—mainly text, voice, and image but with the occasional more exotic protocol thrown in for good measure. Expecting such a reaction, he ignored them all. The notion of ROTH artifacts at such close proximity spread through the general populace like wildfire, exciting imaginations and encouraging all manner of speculation. Only later, as the ramifications sank in, would more sober concerns float to the surface.

None of the communications were from names he recognized.

"That's a dangerous game you're playing, Palmer Eogan."

He looked up. The voice came over the intra-Cell channels from one of the other components. With it came an image of a round-faced woman with gold eyes and silver hair.

"I'm aware of that, Palmer Vermeulen. We're a little short on options."

"You and me both." She didn't say as much in words, but he could see the reproach in her expression clearly enough. His science officer had requested no such attachment to the ROTH investigation. Vermeulen would probably be happier on the other side of the galaxy, given a choice.

But he needed someone at ground zero. And he owed Palmers Cobiac and Bray the attempt, at least, wherever they were. Without the Exarch's guarantees of assurance

on that score, the Palmer guild could soon find itself cut
out of the equation, as they had been on Sublime, and as he
was sure the Exarch wanted them to be everywhere.

Until the Exarchate Expansion of forty years earlier, the
Palmers—so named after ancient pilgrims who returned
from the Holy Land laden with gifts—had had a stranglehold on interstellar commerce. The only reliable means of
getting from A to B anywhere in human space had been on
the back of a Palmer Cell, following trade routes eked
out—and vacuumed clean—by many years of constant
travel. The VOID drive systems, with their algorithmically
evolved nanotech, possessed advantages no existing competitor could match; within a century of leaving Sol, therefore, almost all human transport beyond the system had
depended on the goodwill of the guild.

That situation was unsustainable, of course, and pres-
sures within Sol had grown to remedy it. After the True
Singularity, technological advancement hit a new upward
slope, and whole new sciences evolved. Unbeknownst to
the First Wave colonies and the Palmer Cells that helped
found them, the Exarchate had devised its own, carefully
guarded means of propagating through the Dark. The system, even forty years later, appeared to be too inefficient to
permit true trade—from what little the Palmers had been
able to deduce about it—but it had been sufficient to seed
invasion fleets in every human-occupied system, and to allow the takeover of human territory within two years. The
posthuman aftermath had seen incremental erosions of
Palmer control, until the possibility that Cells might be
supplanted altogether began to look frighteningly real, perhaps even imminent.

If the Exarchate was throwing him a bone to keep the
Palmers happy, Eogan would take it with both hands. It indicated, if nothing else, that Exarchs were still willing to
make deals. And it proved that Isaac Deangelis was still
human enough to succumb to a little extortion.

His command couch vibrated beneath him, indicating

that his separation from the Cell was now complete. Gingerly, relishing the newfound freedom, yet sad at the same time that the intimate, familiar connection had been severed, he stood up for the first time in almost a year.

"There are those famous legs," commented Vermeulen dryly. "Got yourself some shore leave, handsome?"

"Something like that." He stretched more out of habit than any real need. His body had left behind such inconveniences as stiffness, cramps, and pins and needles long ago. "I'll bring you back a souvenir."

"Some real food would be good."

"You can join me when you've finished with your new toy."

A slight tightness around her eyes betrayed a thought similar to: *If there's anything left of me.* But she was good; it stayed just a thought. He had briefed his Cellmates carefully on the long flight into Bedlam space.

"Trust me," she said instead. "This is one port where you really *should* find yourself a girl."

He smiled, simultaneously amused and unnerved by the bandwidth presently devoted to his history with Melilah Awad.

"I think the Exarch needs it more than me," he shot back.

The memory of Vermeulen's quick laugh accompanied him through N-2's air lock and out into the vacuum of space.

For a wonderful moment, he was an ant exploring a sack of marbles. Sunlight caught the Cell over the limb of Bedlam, daubing its manifold components with warm yellow light. Refracted and reflected a million incalculable ways, that light shivered around Eogan with an intensity he could almost feel. It was like floating through the heart of a quartz crystal. Nature, as his father had once said, was at its most beautiful when least expected.

Then a large, white shape hove into view, emitting bright

flashes of blue light from reactionless thrusters as it adjusted its relative velocity. A giant triangle, not dissimilar to a folded paper plane, its lines were stark and lifeless, designed to intimidate.

The Exarch had come for his prize.

Eogan gave himself a nudge toward N-14, a midsized bauble dwarfed by the new arrival. Intelligent systems in the Cell negotiated docking maneuvers without the help of any of its crew; it didn't need to request authorization, either, as he had already told it to expect something like this. The *Nhulunbuy* knew what it was doing.

But part of him itched to take over anyway—to issue the commands, to chart the trajectories, to activate the thrusters—because what was the point of being chief officer of an interstellar vessel if you didn't actually get to *fly?* It had been a long time since he had piloted anything more complex than a hopper. He missed it.

That feeling, he knew full well, came from the loss of control he was experiencing in the current situation. He felt trapped and impotent under the Exarch's thumb, and to dream of flight was to yearn for escape. Again came the urge to dump N-1 and run, even stronger than before. No doubt Vermeulen would support such a decision, along with the rest of his hostage crew.

The glaring white triangle powered closer. N-2 swung up to meet it. There was no attempt to hide anything. It all happened out in the open, as it was supposed to.

The triangle folded gracefully, and with no small sense of menace, like an origami praying mantis. Triangle-tipped edges converged on the glassy sphere beneath it. Four slender tines impaled it, stretched it into a tetrahedron. More white walls folded down to enclose it. Eogan thought he detected a gamma-ray flash as the Cell containment failed, but he couldn't be sure.

"We'll be compensated for that, I hope," he broadcast into the white shape's flank as it closed shut over the *Nhulunbuy*'s sacrificed component.

"Your trading account has already been credited," the Exarch confirmed.

Eogan checked. It had been, at exactly the right amount.

"Well and good," he said. "I look forward to seeing what you make of it."

"In good time."

Eogan couldn't be sure, but the Exarch sounded distracted. Physically, Isaac Deangelis manifested in the form of a young, blond man with delicate, almost translucent features. Eogan didn't know if it was the Exarch's genuine appearance or designed for a particular effect. Either way, it unnerved him that someone so inexperienced-looking could have access to something of such destructive potential.

"You will be careful opening it, won't you?"

"Be sure of it." The origami-ship banked sharply and angled away from the *Nhulunbuy* like a robot swan.

Eogan thrust to a gentle halt next to N-14 and rapped on the hull. It peeled back, exposing a dozen hopper bays arranged inward in a circle. He picked one at random and folded himself into it. He could have flown on his own down to the surface of Bedlam, its gravity being barely that of a small moon. But Traffic Control imposed strict limits on nonvehicular traffic near the giant habitat, and he'd never got around to renewing his license.

He'd never thought the opportunity to use it would arise again.

The hopper slid out of its niche with a smooth hiss. Facedown on his belly, Eogan piloted the craft with his fingertips instead of direct linkage to the controls. *Surrogate wings,* he thought as he powered away from the collection of spheres that had for so long been his home.

"I still have the helm," he told his second officer, Palmer Flast. "If I plan on going out of range, I'll let you know."

"Right you are, Palmer Eogan," came the calm, masculine tones in reply. "Properly speaking, of course, 'out of range' is not an option here."

"You never know," he replied, as Bedlam's pockmarked face ballooned in front of him. "I hesitate to take anything for granted at the moment."

"Good weather," Vermeulen wished him.

He didn't reply.

By midnight, the object officially known as 2358M1S had been dubbed "the Mizar Occlusion." Network commentators speculated freely about its origins and nature, training instruments on the Exarch's new containment-and-observation facility. Much larger than the Palmer vessel that had ferried the Occlusion from deep space, the Occlusion observatory had grown in a series of concentric polygons around the white tug that had claimed it from the *Nhulunbuy*. Each layer, according to amateur reverse engineers devoted to probing the technological secrets of the Exarchate, offered different means of both inspection and protection for the thing at their heart. Melilah Awad wondered if whatever lay hidden inside it minded the game of pass-the-parcel being fought over it in the skies of Bedlam.

ROTH artifacts were the prize sought by every interstellar citizen. Very little of what the ancient aliens had left behind was on actual worlds. Most of it was space junk following ancient orbits around moons, worlds, and primaries. Some of it drifted through interstellar space. There were hulls of space vessels drilled through by high-velocity impacts, shells of habitats destroyed in accidents so severe that the wreckage was radioactive enough to kill an un-Natural, mysterious machine fragments suggesting technologies that ranged from the mundane to the bizarre—and much more. There were even bodies, every now and again. A jettisoned corpse had been found two decades earlier just off the main trade lane between Phad and Severance. Initial T-scans revealed a creature with two stalklike eyes protruding from a thick, curled shell at the center of ten jointed legs. Each leg was tipped with three opposable digits. Its thick exoskeleton suggested an insectile ancestry, but deeper analysis refuted that theory, revealing that the creature's outer layers were artificial, not natural. The alien, dubbed the Snailer, might have been a Natural of its own species, modified barely enough to survive in the hostile environment of space, or it could equally have been an extreme variant with only passing resemblance to its relatives' usual morphology. There was no way of knowing until they found another corpse or decipherable records.

The knowledge that a ROTH artifact had arrived at Bedlam was genuinely exciting. Melilah could understand the interest of her fellow citizens and the Exarch's desire to handle the investigation carefully. She could also understand why the *Nhulunbuy* had come to Bedlam rather than any of the other, more central colonies. The rivalry between Friday and Alioth would only spark friction, no matter who got their hands on it; New Eire was still rumbling after the attempted uprising ten years earlier; Altitude could have been a good choice, but it, too, fancied itself a player on the Arc Circuit, and couldn't be relied upon to do the research required with complete objectivity.

What Melilah didn't understand entirely was why Palmer Eogan had traveled physically to Bedlam and *still* not replied to her message.

"Feeling snubbed?" asked Gil Hurdowar, after her third check of the Palmer's movements. "It doesn't look like he's going to come your way anytime soon."

"You've got a fucking nerve," she said, shutting down the query window and hating the flush that wanted to rise to her cheeks.

"What I've got is *rights,* Melilah," he shot back.

"That's poor grammar, Gil," she offered lamely.

His tone was smug. "Why fight it? You know you need someone to keep an eye on you, to keep you out of trouble."

"If I did—which I don't—then it sure as hell wouldn't be you."

"But we have such a beautiful rapport."

" 'Rapport' isn't the word I'd use."

He chuckled lightly. "You'll come around."

His conceit was really starting to irritate her. "Don't you have anything better to do, Gil?"

"It may surprise you to learn that I don't."

She took a quick peek at his log. "It's been a while since you cleaned out your junk file. And some of your auxiliary routines are looking a little frayed."

"Minor stuff compared to—"

She turned the volume down without waiting for him to finish. He could talk as much as he wanted, but she didn't have to listen.

Besides, it was time for her weekly Defiance meeting.

Once every eight days, in a small chamber off Bornholdt Chasm, an obscure suburb well away from the main pipe routes, a group of people dissatisfied with the Exarch's rule met to discuss what could be done about it. The meetings were conducted openly and with no attempt to hide their times or the identities of those attending. The inconvenient location had been chosen simply to weed out those who might attend to heckle or waste time. Melilah had no patience with either type. If they didn't mean business and couldn't be bothered going out of their way to be there, they weren't welcome.

The trouble was, she was beginning to lose patience with the people who *did* show up, and there was no easy way to say that without admitting that the cause itself was at fault.

"The Mizar Occlusion is just another example of what I'm talking about," one of the more strident voices was saying. Angela Chen-Pushkaric was a stocky food tech from Havlin, one of Bedlam's three industrial sectors. "We've lost our name, our independence, our governance—and now we're losing our science, too. The Gentry are bleeding us dry. How long until we're nothing but a nuisance, a pest to be eliminated entirely? What are we doing to stop that from happening?"

"The Exarch needs us," argued Werner Gard, a programmer whose skull had been elongated lengthwise to accommodate the Third Hemisphere interfaces required to keep up with specialist AIs. His face was pushed forward and seemed stuck in a permanent grimace. "There are things he can't do."

"Not yet."

"Not ever. He's just one point of view. The Exarchate knows it needs variance and dissent in order to survive."

"The Gentry *say* that, yes, but—"

"I'm not arguing with you over whether they're lying or not, Angela." Gard's long fingers splayed out in front of him like a net to catch her words. "I'm just saying that the Exarchate could have wiped us out or made overtures toward doing so long ago. It didn't, hasn't, and doesn't seem likely to in the near future. Spreading panic isn't going to do the cause any good at all."

"But what *is* the cause," asked white-haired Prof Virgo in her calm, reasoned voice, "if it's not to remove the Exarch from his position of absolute power? He might indeed need us, as you say, but the fact remains that what freedoms we still have exist solely at his whim."

"I don't see an easy way around that," said Kara Skirianos, another person, like Melilah, displaced by the Exarch when the local government had been decapitated. The blow might not have been literal, but it had definitely spelled the end of Bedlam's self-rule. What was the point of maintaining a bureaucracy when one person thought he could do so much better?

That that person was some sort of superhuman and could be in numerous places at once certainly added to the argument that he might be right.

"We can't openly attack the Exarch," Skirianos went on, the attention of the room on her, "because we're technologically outmatched. We can't actively subvert him, because our own laws—the laws he let us retain as a conciliatory gesture—will expose our intentions before we even get started. All we can do is appeal to his sense of reason. If we can convince him that we deserve the right to govern ourselves, and that we're capable of doing it, he may let the reins go."

Chen-Pushkaric snorted. "With all due respect, Speaker, the Exarch didn't invest so much energy into taking over this system just to hand it back to us when we *ask nicely*."

"We don't know that for certain." Skirianos's voice was thin and sad. Before the takeover, she had been Speaker for the habitat, the highest political officer in the system. It was she who had signed the peace accord with the Exarchate that many in the extreme wings of Defiance described as a betrayal of humanity. "Isaac Deangelis has consistently stated that the Exarchate has no intentions of ruling in the fashion of past empires. In other words, no mailed fist. He lets us speak against him when many despots wouldn't. We're free to do as we will."

"But we're still trapped," said Prof Virgo.

"Trapped by who we *are*. Perhaps the point of all this is not to subjugate us but to spur us on to bigger things. We know the Exarch doesn't like Naturals, for instance."

"So he wants to turn Bedlam into a happy little posthuman paradise, like Sol. Great." Chen-Pushkaric swung her wide face slowly from side to side, as though triangulating. "Giving him what he wants doesn't sound like victory to me. It sounds like defeat."

"It sounds like survival," said Gard, his long skull catching the light. "I can think of worse things."

Melilah could see where both points of view were coming from. Her position was simple. She resented the arrogance with which the Exarch's superiors had Gentrified Bedlam without once asking its inhabitants if they wanted it or not. She loathed the automatic assumption that Sol knew best, and that everyone else's opinion counted for shit. The technological superiority of Bedlam's new governor worried her, for she suspected that Chen-Pushkaric was right on one point: that the Exarchate would soon possess the ability to wipe out the rest of humanity. She didn't like the idea of living with a gun to her head, especially when the gun was wielded by someone whose mind she couldn't even begin to imagine.

She didn't hate Exarch Deangelis, nor did she want him dead. She just wanted her world back, one way or another, and her old life with it. The universe was big enough for free humans and the Exarchate to coexist peacefully. At some point, the Exarchate was sure to realize that, no matter how unreasonable a dream that sometimes seemed. She needed to feel as though she was working toward making that dream a reality, at least incrementally.

The Defiance group, on the other hand, seemed more and more to be a bunch of malcontents arguing among themselves, divided by details of their disgruntlement.

"What about you, Melilah?" asked Chen-Pushkaric. "You're being quiet today."

She glanced up from her introspection. "We're tying ourselves in knots," she said. "There are no conclusions we can come to about the Mizar Occlusion until we know what it is. Finding that out should be our first priority."

"If the Exarch doesn't tell us, we'll never know." Chen-Pushkaric glowered theatrically. "No data has been posted on the network."

"The new installation has only been there a few hours. Give him time." Melilah turned to Gard. "Is it even operational yet?"

"Hard to tell. Something's going on in there, but what exactly . . ." He shrugged. "Your guess is as good as mine."

"Wait another day, then start making assumptions," she suggested. "We can at least give him a chance to do the right thing."

I hope you're listening to this, she thought to the absent Exarch, who had the capacity to eavesdrop if he wanted to. *Hard though it is to believe, I'm actually sticking up for you.*

"A day could be too long," said Chen-Pushkaric. "Doesn't anyone remember Sublime?"

"Of course," said Melilah. "It's not the sort of thing we're likely to forget."

"Well, what if we're sitting on top of another one of those? What if it goes off because the Exarch mishandles it?"

The thought, Melilah was sure, had already occurred to everyone in the room. Perhaps everyone in the habitat.

"The odds are against it," said Gard. "There have been other ROTH objects recovered in the last ten years, and many more before that. None has been as dangerous as the one that destroyed Sublime. That was probably just bad luck: a piece of munitions left over after a war, or a cache booby-trapped against tampering. Mostly all we find is just junk."

"It doesn't look like the Exarch is taking any chances," said Skirianos. "The installation is very secure."

"They thought so in Sublime, too, remember?"

Melilah did remember. Everyone on the Arc Circuit did. Shock waves had rippled along the local trade routes, and beyond. All investigations into ROTH artifacts were put on indefinite hold, pending a closer examination of the Sublime Catastrophe, as it quickly became known. Humanity's grip on the stars had suddenly seemed decidedly precarious.

There had been political aftershocks, too. Palmer Horsfall had spared no effort in alerting the systems around her to the disaster that had befallen Sublime and her sister, thereby revealing the existence of an ftl communications link between all Palmer Cells and the Exarchate. How that link manifested was not known—the prevailing theory, that it relied on entanglement between elementary particles, fell apart in the face of the fact that signals decohered too fast to reach more than a light-year or two—but the sure knowledge of its existence rocked the relationship between subjugated colonies and the supposedly neutral traders that plied the lanes between them. The ability to communicate instantly with neighbors would have greatly assisted any effort to unite against the Exarchate. By not offering that ability to all, even for trade, the Palmers had passively assisted the Exarchate in their Expansion.

Tempers had been strained. Cells received unfriendly welcomes in some ports, accused of collaboration with the enemy. Palmers had denied the charge—and denied it still—but suspicion remained. Melilah herself had organized a habitatwide protest against the technological embargo enforced by Sol on other human-controlled worlds. What right did the distant home system have to keep potentially lifesaving technologies from those who needed it?

The fuss had died down eventually. More distant colonies had no choice but to embrace what means of connection with the rest of the Arc Circuit they could maintain, and the harsh reality was that the Palmers had such a stranglehold on interstellar colonies that to spurn them was to choose complete isolation. No matter what one thought of the Palmers *or* the Exarchate, in the minds of most people having them around was better than the alternative.

Despite the political wrangling, the thirteen thousand people who died in the Sublime Catastrophe were never forgotten. They had relatives and friends in many different colonies, on and off the Arc Circuit. Monuments and memorials were dedicated to them, the first known human victims of the ROTH. The lesson had been learned.

And she remembered the buried snapshots of her holidaying couple in the same system. She'd performed a search on the names recorded on the fiche and learned that both women had left Bedlam separately, more than a year ago. Their trail went cold from there.

"Again," she said, "we come up against the fact that the Exarch is in the best position to analyze this thing. Sure, if we had access to his knowledge and technology, we might be able to do better—but we don't, so we just can't. Instead of bitching about what we can't fix, why don't we try turning it to our advantage?"

"How do we do that, exactly?" asked Chen-Pushkaric, skepticism writ large across her broad features.

"Well, we're not worthless chattel. We do have some skills. Lets apply them to what we can lay our hands on and prove that we're worth collaborating with. Going off half-cocked will only ensure that we remain out of the loop forever."

"Collaborate, in other words."

" 'Thinking long term' is how I'd rather put it," she said, cursing the food tech's blunt lack of sophistication. *Read between the lines, you idiot. I didn't say that the Exarch would give us the information* willingly . . .

Melilah gave them another half an hour before giving up. She had better things to do. Their hearts were in the right places, but their methodology was all screwed up. They were a fire burning without fuel, consuming itself and liable to do little more than that, no matter how hot its flames burned. She came away from the meeting feeling frustrated and angry, with no clear vent, apart from the Exarch. She felt like doing something bold and stupid— and that was dangerous for someone already on probation.

Instead she sealed herself in her quarters and set about digging. She didn't tackle the Exarch's defenses head-on. She took her time, nibbling around the edges of the problem like the experienced data-gleaner she was. In the day since the Mizar Occlusion had arrived at Bedlam, many people had crudely probed the core secret and gotten nowhere. She doubted that she could do any better. But there would be peripheral secrets hidden less successfully, and other gleaners whose data she could lift without having to duplicate their efforts. If there was one thing she knew about the Exarchate, it was that there were no easy solutions. Going at it like a battering ram wasn't going to get anyone anywhere.

Time passed. Leads came and went. A picture slowly began to take shape. Two people were missing from the *Nhulunbuy*'s crew register, without explanation. And something about the Occlusion observatory didn't look right to her. The two thoughts, seemingly unconnected, nagged at her as though potentially significant.

So immersed was she that she barely heard her door buzz. When she glanced at who it was, the floor seemed to lurch out from under her, a feeling utterly at odds with her low-gee conditioning. Her first instinct was to bury herself back in the problem—the lesser, it seemed, of two—and hide.

But she didn't.

"Hello, Melilah," said Palmer Eogan, when she opened the door. "I owe you an apology."

She just stared at him, and wondered where the last one hundred and fifty years had gone.

+8

Caught in the moment like a microbe in an ice crystal, the Exarch didn't even notice the reunion that had the habitat abuzz. His thoughts were dominated by much more important issues. Even at the slowest possible speed he could maintain, events were unfolding with disconcerting rapidity.

The Occlusion was safe for the moment, wrapped in a cocoon of instruments and shielding. Preliminary data were suggestive but inconclusive on a number of points. There could be no doubt, though, about what he had in his possession.

And the Occlusion wasn't all he had to worry about. Long-range tracking had picked up two unidentified blips on the borders of the system. They were without doubt vessels running silent, decelerating with drives filtered to resemble astronomical objects, like early airplanes swooping out of the sun. One of them was impersonating the spiral galaxy M97, the other the bright globular cluster 47 Tucanae, just a few degrees removed from the Small Magellanic Cloud. Close inspection revealed emission lines consistent with tanglers from out-system. Where precisely they were from, he couldn't tell—but he suspected that the first was from Kullervo-Hails system. The Exarch of that colony, Lazarus Hails, had a weakness for word games. M97 was also known as Bode's Nebula.

Bodes ill, either way, Exarch Deangelis thought to himself. He wouldn't have spotted the newcomers had he not been looking specifically for them. He wasn't sure if he should feel relieved that his paranoid notions had been confirmed—or worried that he wasn't being paranoid *enough.*

The tanglers must have left their systems barely moments after he had posted his report about the Mizar Occlusion to Sol, months ago. Even as the full explanation of what had happened in Sublime was arriving in his system, others were preparing their own response. He had no way to predict exactly what form that response would take. On the surface, communication with his neighboring Exarchs was as polite as always.

That wasn't all. Palmer traffic was up across the board. Four more Cells had hailed the habitat since the *Nhulunbuy*'s arrival: *Studenica* and *Umm-as-Shadid* from Alioth-Cochrane, *Inselmeer* and *Patrixbourne* from farther afield. He expected more in the coming week. Some were haring in with VOID drives blazing in furious deceleration, indicating the tremendous hurry with which they had left their home systems. He had no way of knowing who was spreading the word. All he could do was batten down the hatches and prepare for the worst.

There were consolations. With attention shifting to focus on Lut-Deangelis, the political landscape of the Arc Systems was drifting away from Friday in 78 Ursa Major and Alioth-Cochrane. That could only be a good thing, from Exarch Deangelis's perspective. Too long had those two neighboring systems dominated the region. The time was overdue for his independent, open alternative to rise to the fore.

Excited and terrified in equal measures, he composed a brief report for Sol—confirming the identity of the Mizar Occlusion and outlining the surreptitious incursions into the system—and sent it on its way.

The reply came almost immediately.

"Stand firm, Isaac. We're on our way."

He didn't know quite what to make of the last sentence until his own tangler reported a rapid influx of data. Ftl transmissions were a severe bottleneck when it came to information flows between inhabited systems. Bit rates rose only as a cube root of transmission power, so it took eight times as much energy to send twice as much data. The most he could manage without crippling the habitat was a few tens of kilobytes a second; Giorsal McGrath in 78 Ursa Major, the most industrialized system in the Arc Circuit, could do a megabyte a second at a stretch. During the Exarchate Expansion, Sol had converted whole asteroids to energy in order to power the transmissions that had beamed Deangelis and his peers to their respective systems, one bit at a time. It had taken weeks for him to upload into the tangler parked out of detection range of the Bedlam government, there to begin preparing in earnest for takeover. Now, the tangler was reporting a transmission rate in the order of terabytes per second. The burst was expected to last three days.

He didn't know who exactly was coming down the pipe at him—but they were big, whoever they were.

Rather than worry about that—too much—he threw himself into research. The Occlusion was an odd beast, hard to pin down. From a distance, it was much as Palmer Eogan had described it: a dimple in space that accumulated interstellar dust much as a navel attracted lint. But it didn't end there. Palmers like Eogan made their living scraping trade lanes clear of dust that might downgrade their VOID drive deform ratings, but that process didn't create a vacuum as pure as the one at the heart of the Occlusion. There was still the quantum foam, seething away at Planck levels: all manner of exotic particles popping into existence, then disappearing again before they could make a difference.

The Mizar Occlusion somehow punched a hole through that foam, leaving true emptiness in its wake. What that emptiness consisted of wasn't space-time as Exarch Deangelis knew it. It was another creature entirely.

After the destruction of his envoy and Eogan's own experiences in transit, the Exarch was reluctant to get too close to it in any of his personae just yet. Instead, the installation designed and made instruments to send into the Occlusion, while clearing it of dust and other debris. The alien vessels Eogan had retrieved went into a smaller in-spection chamber for cursory analysis. They were twisted, spindly things, with oval compartments strung out like seed-pods at odd attitudes. He had seen their type before in archival records. Similar to other wrecks left behind by a civilization dubbed Merchant B, they had already been scoured of all worthwhile data during the trip from their resting place. He arranged for them to be transferred to the habitat for scientists there to pore over at their leisure. A pacifier to appease a grizzling child.

One by one, as that was done, exploratory instruments disappeared into the Occlusion. Data trickled back in mea-ger streams, confirming his expectations. The relative tran-quillity of the hole punched in the quantum foam didn't last long. Nature abhorred a true vacuum: what it lost in one place was more than made up for in another. In the heart of the Occlusion, the underlying substrate of the uni-verse twisted and flexed. Constants vanished in a hail of imaginary and impossible numbers. Equations adopted dozens of new dimensions, or collapsed down to just one or two. Strange new particles popped into existence, then disintegrated in showers of exotic energies.

But that region of discontinuity didn't last long, either. And what lay on the far side was even more remarkable.

Coral, he thought. It was an appropriate descriptor for something upon which his career—perhaps even his life—might founder, like a wooden-hulled boat on a submerged reef.

He opened a Most Secure ftl channel and, bucking the data flow coming in-system through his tangler, hailed a woman everyone assumed was dead.

"Isaac?" Jane Elderton's voice was distant and low-res. "I was wondering when you'd call me."

"You know, then."

"Of course."

"I wanted to ask you . . ." He hesitated, suddenly doubt-ing the wisdom of the conversation.

"Did I go into it?" she finished for him.

"Yes."

"I understand what you're feeling, Isaac. The first glimpse is terrifying. We could never have built anything like that. It's as alien to us as we are to the Naturals—perhaps even more so. And the other side . . ." Elderton sighed. "Yes, I went into it. Who could resist? We're still human."

Exarch Deangelis had never felt more human in his life—in all the negative senses of the word.

"Were you punished?"

It was Elderton's turn to hesitate. "What do you think?" she eventually said. Her voice was sad and impossibly distant. "It's lonely here, Isaac. But I'm too scared to do anything about that. So much has already been lost."

He ignored a shiver of apprehension in his core body. "Someone came to you," he said. "From Sol."

"Yes."

"Who?"

"The Archon."

"Itself?"

"In full."

No wonder the data transmission was so enormous. "What for?"

"To oversee the operation," she said. "To make sure nothing went wrong."

"What *did* go wrong?"

She was silent for a long time, so long he wondered if they had been cut off.

"Jane?"

"They'll be listening now, Isaac. You must know that. We have no secrets from them."

"That thought doesn't frighten me."

"It frightens me," she said. "This whole situation frightens me. I shouldn't be talking to you. You have my data. That should be enough. I don't want to contaminate you any more than you already have been."

"I have your data, yes, but I need so much more than that. You've been through this and I haven't. I need to know what to expect. I need your advice. I need to know—"

What I might lose.

"—what the Archon will expect of me."

"I'm sorry, Isaac. I can't give you anything. It's all changed now. Nothing will ever be the same. I opened the door, and now no one can ever close it."

"But—"

"I have to go." Her transmission was graying. "Be careful, my friend. Don't lose yourself like I did."

The Exarch of White-Elderton colony—formerly known as Sublime—disappeared in a wash of white noise.

On arrival in Bedlam, Eogan had immediately downloaded an up-to-date map in order to avoid getting lost. The surface of Bedlam was a morass of constant nanofacturing, as the indigenous replicators, much evolved from the original seed planted by colonists three centuries earlier, doggedly continued their work. The pitted, seething surface where the expanding boundary of replicators met the vacuum boasted numerous tapered spines that speared up through the steel gray morass. These doubled as instrument berths and docking towers, and looked like thorns on a cactus with acne.

An elevator took him from his arrival point along a wide pipe that spiraled as it descended into the habitat. The gravity was negligible, but more than he had experienced for over a year. It took him a moment to adjust. Few landmarks on the map struck Eogan as familiar. Numerous sections had succumbed to the relentless pressure as the habitat grew, with favorite haunts that had once been on the surface now squashed flat far below. The programming of the replicators was simple: to construct walls and spaces of varying sizes sufficient to house a growing human population. Like much of nature's produce, the end result was a scale-free network, with relatively few large chambers multiply connected throughout the habitat. This meant that routes through the habitat were rarely straight lines and frequently changed as new chambers were added. A map was essential, even for regular visitors. Some names remained the same, despite being housed in radically different locations.

Automated security systems scanned him inside out for various biological and artificial pathogens. Once cleared, he was allowed deeper into the station. The process was entirely unstaffed. Not until he reached a depth of forty meters or so did he see his first local. The woman, a surveyor of some kind, testing a length of pipe with her gloved fingers, looked up at him with vague interest but said nothing. It was clear that she knew who he was. That was only to be expected, he supposed, given the open information policy of the habitat and the circumstances of his arrival. He had been steeling himself against an agoraphobic reaction for days.

He took another elevator to the nearest hub, an enormous doughnut-shaped chamber named after Réka Albert. Throughout all of Bedlam's creeping layers of habitation, there had always been an Albert Hall. This one was as busy as the one he remembered, with numerous restaurants, shops, and entertainment facilities covering the floor, ceiling, and much of the curved walls. Pipes large and small led into the enormous space; slender, brightly colored transports whizzed by overhead with tiny margins for error; the air was rich with numerous fragrances and the sound of voices. Everywhere he looked he saw unfamiliar faces.

It made the blank walls of N-1 look decidedly drab. No matter that sensory addenda allowed any number of backdrops and interactive scenarios, driven by peripheral AIs with easily sufficient power to imitate any human interaction. He still *knew* he was sewn to a chair in interstellar space. There was no substitute for getting out of it and walking around, every now and again.

Stares met his with disconcerting frequency. Most people were curious; he could understand that. Some were hostile, and that, too, was not unexpected. It was the solicitous ones he was keen to avoid, wherever possible. He didn't want to get stuck in a conversation with someone who thought they knew all about him just because they had access to his public file.

He wandered at random, in no immediate hurry. A line of jewelry makers occupied one inner side of the Hall, and he stopped to admire the handiwork on display. Few people in Bedlam actually worked for a living. Nanotech and fusion power gave the habitat all the physical resources it needed to maintain itself. But there was always room for creativity and ingenuity. Craftspeople, poets, dancers, musicians, public speakers—and thieves, spies, con artists and charlatans—all thrived. Over three hundred years earlier, human society, especially those founded in space, had adapted to selling nothing but nonmaterial wares. Wherever money existed, people found new ways to spend and earn it.

"There's a field effect generator in the clasp. My own design."

He looked up from a silver broach so fine it was barely visible. Glassy, artificial eyes stared back at him from the face of a spry, bald woman with fingers that tapered to wicked-looking points. To manipulate the materials she employed with greatest precision, he presumed.

"Remarkable," he said. "I wondered how it could possibly hold together. How much is it?"

"Four hundred Sols."

Sol Dollars, he thought, marveling at how quickly merchants adopted the victor's currency.

"I'll take it."

She shook her head. "Save your money," she said. "Mem Awad already has one."

"She—what?"

"Your friend, the one you're here to see. She bought one very much like this last year."

"I see." He stared at her, feeling like an idiot. "Thank you."

"You're welcome, Mus Eogan."

He walked away shaking his head, dimly acknowledging the artisan's thick Prime accent. She was a long way from home, having probably come to Bedlam by hitching rides on Cells bound along the Arc from end to end. The Arc Circuit had been a busy trade route for over a century, ever since the Sol-ward legs of the Great Bear Run had been severed in the double interests of profitability and self-determination.

Your friend, the artisan had said, *the one you're here to see.*

There was no privacy on Bedlam. People naturally gravitated to the source of greatest interest. At the moment, after the Mizar Occlusion, that was him and his connection with Melilah Awad.

Eogan had forgotten what it was truly like to be in the public eye, caught in a spotlight so bright it made him feel completely transparent. No amount of preparation could steel him against it.

Still, he told himself, the artisan had saved him from wasting money on something Melilah already owned.

"Five Sols say you wouldn't have bought it anyway," said Vermeulen from the *Nhulunbuy.*

He ignored the gibe and spoke to Palmer Flast instead. "How's the transfer coming along?"

"The new installation is sealed and operational," came back the voice of his second officer. "No word from Exarch Deangelis."

"The skulls?" *Skull* was Palmer shorthand for alien remains, wrecked ships in particular.

"On their way to the big house."

"Get me the name of the person assigned to them," Eogan said. "I'd like to assist in their examination."

"Roger. One moment."

Wheels turned fast in Bedlam. Routine decision-making was handled mainly by AIs, and the few humans involved actually *wanted* to be. Operational inefficiencies were therefore minimal. Eogan didn't think it would be long before the wrecks he had scavenged from the dust-heavy environs of the Mizar Occlusion were tucked safely away inside the habitat.

"Dr. Iona Attard is the person you want," said Flast.

"Set up an appointment for one hour from now. Tell her I might have someone with me, and that we'll need full access. There are some unique features I need to point out to her that aren't obvious from our report."

"I'll tell her that. Can she contact you directly if she has any questions?"

"I'd rather not be disturbed."

"Yes, sir."

Eogan closed the line, wondering what the hell he was going to do for an hour, but almost immediately coming up with several possibilities. Hailing a transport and jumping inside, he took a swooping, complicated journey to ben-Avraham's to see if the coffee was as good as he remembered.

It was—but the empty setting opposite him, placed in defiance of his request for a table for one, wouldn't let him relax. He drank the coffee before it had properly cooled, paid, and left.

The address was the same, 14A Jeong Crescent, although the actual suburb had changed. The air of Bonabeau Fold was fresh and smelled faintly of green things growing nearby. Subtle strip lights painted fuzzy geometric patterns on the curved pipe walls, shifting like underwater sunlight in slow motion. Angular, rhythmic music came from one apartment he passed; his heartbeat tried to match its brisk pace, and he felt light-headed as a result. Or was that nervousness?

He kicked himself along the pipe to a door not dissimilar to the one he remembered and soundly pressed the entry buzzer.

The habitat seemed to fall deathly silent. His breath curdled in his throat.

The door clicked and hissed open.

"Hello, Melilah," he said. "I owe you an apology."

She didn't move. Her face was unnaturally still, and her eyes didn't saccade. Her left hand anchored her body to the frame, and Eogan didn't doubt that it was within easy reach of the switch that would close the door in his face. He could feel her warring within herself over the impulse to do just that.

And *him* . . . He felt as though every muscle in his body had turned to inertia gel: perfectly fluid until shocked, then suddenly rigid. At any moment, he could freeze and shatter into a million pieces.

It was *her*.

"You took your time," she said eventually. Her voice was exactly as he remembered it, warm and rounded, with cultured vowels and an unhurried pace. She was as tall as he was, but slighter, more elegant. Her hair hung in alternating stripes of black and gold. Her skin was flawless. Her green eyes were fixed on him, waiting for him to respond.

"I'm sorry," he said. His body wanted to break out into a sweat, but he kept a tight lid on his autonomic reactions. It felt good to say it, at last. He'd been carrying it for so long. "I'm truly sorry, Melilah."

Her head moved slightly: the beginning of a shake, carefully contained. "It's old news, Palmer Eogan. We've both moved on."

"Yes."

"You're lucky I even remember you."

"I've never forgotten—not us, or what happened to us."

"I had to forget, or it was going to drive me insane." Her stare was accusatory. "If you'd apologized back then, it might have meant something."

"It wouldn't have made a difference, though."

"To you, maybe."

"There seemed no other way out." He looked at his feet brushing uselessly against the wall of the pipe. They longed to kick away, to run. Again. "I didn't think I had a choice."

"Is that all you came here for?" She retreated slightly, as though preparing to shut the door. "I'm not interested in hearing an explanation. Not after so long."

Eogan shook his head, reminding himself that there was a reason for coming to her. He wasn't just exorcising—or indulging—an old regret.

"I want to show you something," he said, meeting her challenge. "The skulls we found. The ROTH ships. I'd like you to see them."

She eyed him suspiciously. "Why?"

"I think you'll be interested in them."

"The data will be available soon enough."

"Data is data. It's not standing in the same room with them. It's not touching something made by another race of intelligent beings. It's not standing where aliens once stood, and wondering what they looked like, what they breathed, what they *felt*." He chose his words with care, hoping to appeal to the deep streak of curiosity that was an integral part of her personality. The enthusiasm he felt was real. "You don't have to take it as a peace offering," he said. "Just look at it as an opportunity to do something you've never done before."

"How do you know I've never done it?"

"I checked the public record when I arrived."

She did a double take. "Of course." He could see her thinking to herself, wondering what else he had checked for. Employment history? Public code violations? Lovers since him?

The truth was that he had looked for nothing more than her address and her experience with ROTH artifacts. Nothing else had concerned him.

She looked behind her, then back at him. "Okay. You've got my interest—but don't expect anything more than that."

"I don't."

"And you'd better deliver. Give me a second."

The door hissed shut.

He endured a small eternity, feeling like a teenager waiting for his first date to turn up. She had changed. Physically she still looked young, but there was a palpable weight to her presence that spoke of fifteen decades of extra experience. It manifested in her stare and in her bearing.

Many years of VOID travel had slowed his ageing relative to hers, so he was in effect fifty years younger than she now—and he felt it. Maybe she *had* gotten over him. Maybe his apology was completely irrelevant to her.

She emerged from the room dressed in a businesslike

black one-piece covered with pockets and straps—a work uniform and symbolic gesture both—and locked the door behind her.

"Lead the way, Palmer."

He did so in silence, unwilling to force her into a conversation she probably didn't want. He had what *he* wanted, for the moment. All he had to do was keep her with him until the time was right, and then they could deal with what was truly important.

+10

Melilah kicked alongside Eogan through the pipes of Bedlam with one thought stuck in her mind. *He looks the same.* Despite one hundred and fifty years of separation, of trying so hard to get over him and to put the hurt behind her, he turned up on her doorstep wanting to apologize, and he looked the fucking same! She couldn't let go of it. Had he done it deliberately, to wound her or—God help her—to woo her? Was he wearing that face to hide the ghastly reality beneath, so she wouldn't flinch at what he had become? Was he manipulating her or genuinely trying to be considerate?

He looks the same. Dark hair and friendly, square features. A stocky, strong body with broad chest and reliable hands. His teeth were white and straight, apart from one that had rotated slightly on his lower left jaw. There was a suspiciously smooth patch on his upper lip, as though he'd had corrective nanosurgery as a child.

All fake, she reminded himself. That body was him no more than her work garb was her—or his simple brown shipsuit was his actual skin. He was a ship-symbiont now, physically grafted to the Cell he commanded.

And, dammit, part of her was still jealous.

"Tell me something I don't know about the Mizar Occlusion," she said, trying to turn the situation to her advantage instead of letting it drag her down. "Unless that's what you're taking me to see."

He shook his head. "Everything I know is on public record."

"That's a cop-out," she said. "No one has the time to scour the entire public record. It's hard enough finding specific things, let alone every possible thing."

He kept his eyes forward. "I guess that was always going to be the problem with the Bedlam model."

Melilah responded automatically to the implied criticism. "We don't keep *everything*. Zero access records are deleted after a year, unless considered of particular value. More popular or relevant information lasts longer. AIs maintain the archives, making sure the information is accessible. But still, there are forty thousand people in Bedlam, and every one of them is laying down a minute's worth of data every minute—and that's too much data for even the most determined of peepers."

"But there are filters and search algorithms. It's not as if you can't follow a thread to its conclusion."

She glanced at him; he still wasn't looking at her. "I don't think you realize just how much of a fuss you've created, bringing that thing here. I'm good at finding details; people pay me to do that for them, when other methods fail. But you've got me stumped on this one. The truth is locked up supertight."

"Either that," he said, "or it's exactly what I've said it is."

"Whatever." She kicked ahead of him and into a medium-sized hub. A crowd of people looked up from a game to watch them fly by. Elbows nudged; hands went up to cover lips. Frowning, she hailed a chevron-shaped purple two-seater transport and climbed inside. The gesture was purely symbolic, but it helped.

"Why is someone called Gil Hurdowar hailing me?" Eogan asked as he climbed in after her.

"Ignore him," she said, "and give this thing a destination."

"Dr. Iona Attard," he said. A second later, as though he had just had a silent exchange with someone else, he added, "Four-oh-nine Barabási Straight, Pastor-Satorras."

The transport accelerated smoothly beneath them and left the gawpers behind. Eogan steadied himself with one hand as inertia pressed him into the seat next to her. Their thighs touched.

Dear Jesus, she thought in response to long-forgotten feeling. *He even* smells *the same.*

"Why are you really here?" she asked him, edging away and turning so she could face him. "You're obviously not going to spill any great secrets, your apology is a hundred and fifty years late, and we have nothing in common anymore. Is there a point to this, apart from some old ships I could probably see more clearly in VR?"

Finally, he looked at her. "I wanted to see you. Does it have to be more than that?"

She searched his eyes. Had he been an ordinary human, she would have thought he was telling the truth.

"It's been so long," she said. "You can't just stroll back into town and offer me a trinket, like I'm some Wild West hooker who'll pretend she's glad to see you."

He smiled at the analogy, but it had the look of a grimace. "That's a little harsh."

"Well, I don't owe you anything, Palmer Eogan. And to be perfectly frank, you don't owe me anything in return. There's a statute of limitations on crap like this." *Or if there isn't,* she added to herself, *there damn well ought to be.*

"I know what you're saying," he said softly. His gaze drifted away from her and settled on his hands. "But you can't erase the silence. That's not something you can get rid of, once it's there. You lay it down, and you're stuck with it forever."

"If you try to blame me for that—"

"I'm not. I know where it started. But I got tired of it, Melilah." He spoke her name carefully, as though afraid his tongue might trip over it. "It's quiet enough in space. The journeys are long, and there aren't many other people to talk to. Palmers are an insular bunch; we don't make close bonds easily, so the thought of leaving people behind for years at a time doesn't bother us, on the whole. Most passengers sleep out the long legs, but we don't have that option. We have to be on our toes, constantly. That gives us plenty of time to think. Plenty of silence in which to play back remembered conversations, and to wonder at conversations that never happened." He took a breath as though to gather himself. "Well, the silence is over now. No matter if you and I never say another word to each other after today, at least that stretch is finally behind us."

She stared at his broad, all-too-familiar face, surprised by the side of him he was showing her, and feeling herself relent a little. *This* was new. And she was an idiot for being thrown by that. She had changed in numerous and very significant ways since she had last seen him. She had to let herself believe that—maybe—he had changed, too.

He seemed to have run out of words for the moment, and so had she. The irony wasn't lost on her. Color and motion swept by as the transport carried them headlong toward their appointment with alien wreckage he had brought to Bedlam.

The skulls were much larger than Melilah expected, dwarfing the scientist and her team assigned to study them. Spindly, asymmetrical, and self-contained, they couldn't have been more different from Palmer Cells. Technicians swarmed over them like ants, scanning them with delicate instruments.

"I'm not sure what you expect to show us that we won't see on our own, Palmer Eogan." Dr. Attard was a slight, narrow-faced Natural wearing an all-encompassing white cleansuit. Melilah and Eogan had been sprayed on entry to the examination facility with a quick-setting nanofilm designed to keep contamination from the alien wrecks. The films didn't interfere with their respiration or senses, and would decay automatically as soon as they left the facility.

Eogan strode confidently around the base of the largest of the seven vessels, trailing Melilah and Dr. Attard in his wake. The alien hull of the vessel was pitted and scored like ancient basalt; Melilah couldn't tell if it was supposed to look like that or if its appearance resulted from long exposure to the interstellar medium.

"There are some things best observed *in situ,*" said Eogan. "You see the hatches? They're all open."

He pointed at various oval holes in the wreck's hull.

To Melilah's eyes they looked more like structural flaws than doorways.

"We had noticed that," commented Attard dryly.

"They were like that when we recovered the ships. There were no bodies."

"We have never recovered the occupants of Merchant Bees, whole or in residue. They either decay without trace or are removed from the wrecks."

"Maybe they never had bodies as we know them," commented Melilah.

Eogan glanced at her and smiled. "It's possible. The ships are very old. Any information they contained has long since decayed into noise."

He stopped near a junction between two wide, knobbed "arms." Like a giant, ancient tree, the bulk of the ship stretched up and around them, bulging in odd places and narrowing in others. Even in the low gee, invisible fields were needed to stop the structure from slumping down on them.

"Here." Eogan indicated the oval entrance before them. "Take a closer look at what we've got here."

Attard *tsked* in annoyance. "We will be doing exactly that when you let us. What exactly is it you're trying to show me?"

"We know the Merchant B civilization used matter where we'd use fields. We know they grew doors open and closed where they needed them. We know what their air locks look like." He pointed at the inner lip of the entrance. The material came in layers, alternating porous and solid; it looked fearsomely resilient. "Does this look like an air lock to you?"

Attard leaned closer. "No. There's only one seal." She looked up at Eogan. Her eyebrows met. "What are you trying to tell me? That this is an atmospheric vehicle?"

"I'm not trying to tell you anything. I'm just pointing out an anomaly."

"But that doesn't make sense." Attard leaned back and

put her hands on her hips. "What would an aircraft be doing in deep space?"

"It's your job to find that out, I guess."

She nodded, distracted by the problem. "If you don't
mind, I think I'd like someone else to look at this."

She hurried off.

Eogan took Melilah's arm. "Come on," he whispered.
"In here."

She resisted automatically as he tried to pull her through
the oval entranceway. "Wait a second." She yanked herself
free. "I don't think this is a good idea."

"It's okay. We won't damage anything."

There was an urgency to his gaze that was totally at
odds with his light, almost playful manner. "What are you
up to?"

"Nothing. Trust me, Melilah. This is your big chance."

To do what? she almost responded. She thought of her
probation and wondered what a scientific violation might
cost her. Was it worth it just to step inside a ship of unknown age built by unknown hands?

But a small part of her whispered that maybe this wasn't
what Eogan meant.

She nodded, and he waved her ahead of him. Apprehen-
sive, she kicked herself up a tube wide enough for two people that kinked and contorted like an ossified intestine.
Unlike Bedlam's pipes, the walls were rough under her
hands; if she misjudged a push, she'd suffer a nasty scrape.
The ambience darkened around her as the entrance fell behind them.

He pulled her to a halt in the crook of a right-angle turn.
There was another entrance ahead, but it hadn't quite come
into view. "Here will do."

"I don't see anything special about it," she started to
say, but he put a hand on her shoulder and leaned in close
to her ear. His voice was hurried and emphatic, all sense of
play utterly gone.

"Listen carefully: there's something about the Occlusion

you need to know. I can't tell you in public because the Exarch will hear. I brought you here because the wrecks aren't tapped yet. It's the only place where we can speak in private."

She checked her watchmeter. It said zero.

Her heart beat a little faster. "Okay. Tell me."

His words were hot in her ear. "I will. But you have to be careful. I can understand Deangelis wanting to keep this secret. People might panic if word gets out."

"Is this something to do with your missing crew members?"

"Yes. I have it all on fiche. We—"

He looked up at a slight sound from the entrance above them. She couldn't see anything, but that meant nothing. Airborne drones were tiny. The Exarch could take control of one and fly it into the ship as easily as thinking about it.

She glanced at her watchmeter. It said *one*. If Eogan gave her a fiche now, the Exarch would see him do it. And there would go her only chance to know what was going on.

She grabbed the front of his shipsuit and pulled him hard against her. He resisted for a bare microsecond, then their mouths met. She felt his left hand, shielded by their bodies, slip in and out of his pocket and into one of hers. Then it was pulling her closer to him still, and she knew she should have been pushing him away. Her lips parted automatically, relishing the taste of him . . .

A shrill voice calling their names from below lifted the spell. "What are you doing? Come down from there at once!"

They separated, faces burning. Melilah could feel the heat steaming off him—and her, too. She hadn't been kissed like that for one hundred and fifty years.

Damned pheromones, she swore to herself. *They haven't changed, either.*

"We're on our way!" Eogan called down to Dr. Attard. He glanced back at her, and his flush had become one of embarrassment and apology. "That wasn't what I wanted— or expected—to happen."

She smoothed herself down. For the benefit of the camera watching them, she said, "The cliché upsets me more than anything else, although I hate to admit it."

When they reached the bottom of the shaft, Dr. Attard was waiting for them with a stern expression on her face. Members of her team clustered behind her, clutching scientific instruments as though they were weapons.

"You were gone too long," Eogan explained smoothly, "and we got bored. Melilah has never been inside a Merchant B before. There's no substitute for firsthand experience."

"If you've contaminated the sample—"

"You've still got six more." Eogan didn't feign annoyance at her attitude. "*Contamination's* the least of your worries," he muttered.

"We're sorry if we've caused you any inconvenience," said Melilah, still thinking of her probation. "Thanks for your time. We'll get out of your hair now."

"That's an excellent idea."

Attard escorted them to the door and coldly sealed it behind them. Melilah resisted the urge to make a face at it, like a rebellious teenager.

"Do you have time to grab something to eat?" Eogan asked her, as they kicked themselves along Barabási Straight toward less industrial regions. "It's been a year since I had any real food."

She surreptitiously touched the flexible plastic square that he had put in her pocket.

"I've got a few other things to chew over first."

His nod was steeped in disappointment. "I understand."

"Will you go back to the *Nhulunbuy*?"

"I don't have to. Not yet."

"Perhaps you should stick around for a bit, then." She felt tired, then, afraid that he would take her meaning the wrong way. She just wanted to talk about the contents of the fiche once she had read it.

"I understand," he said again, like a simple voice-response program. That impression—that he was an artificial, false thing, a machine—contrasted with the vividly remembered feel of his tongue touching hers, and she felt suddenly nauseous.

"I'm going this way," she said, kicking into the nearest pipe and propelling herself as fast as she could along it, away from him.

He took the hint and didn't follow. When she dared to look behind her, he was gone.

Tanglers, holes in the quantum foam, a dire warning from someone who had once been a dear friend . . .

The intricate mechanism that was Exarch Deangelis's extended mind had lost some of its clockwork momentum. He felt isolated and beset upon at the same time. All he needed was for word to get out, so he would have a riot to deal with as well.

Only then, as he checked on the whereabouts of Palmer Eogan, did he realize that his greatest domestic security risk had gone missing. He wasn't on the *Nhulunbuy,* having flown to the habitat some hours earlier. Standard surveillance had tracked him on his arrival and followed him through his wanderings. His location should have been instantly accessible.

But it wasn't. A sweep of the entire habitat revealed no trace of his whereabouts. And it wasn't just him. Melilah Awad was missing as well.

Deep in the forgotten folds that had once been known as Milgram's Crossing, Exarch Deangelis broke into a cold sweat. He called up every available record of their movements, and within microseconds had traced Eogan and Awad to the Merchant B artifact examination facility hastily cobbled together off Barabási Straight. There were numerous surveillance cameras and other sensors in the chamber and adjoining areas. None of them contained the missing pair.

Inside the artifacts. He scanned through the recordings to pinpoint their probable location with greater accuracy. Sensitive vibration sensors caught the sound of voices from within one of the alien ships, but the hulls were too dense to

penetrate with the resources available. In the time it took
for Iona Attard to take one step, Exarch Deangelis commandeered a remote probe from its human operator and
sent it arcing at full velocity into the nearest hull opening.

They were exactly where he expected them to be. And
they looked guilty, like illicit lovers caught in the middle of
a hurried embrace. He was about to transmit a warning
when he realized that that was *exactly* what they were.

He wasn't a slave to hormones as less evolved humans
were, but he understood their operation. During his training, he had been deliberately subjected to the emotional
storms such primal chemicals could cause, the better to understand the people who would ultimately be under his
care. Emotions were, like senses and the intellect, a means
of understanding and interacting with the world. And just
like Natural human senses and intellect, they were imper-
fect. Sometimes they overrode the *actual* signals one was
supposed to be paying attention to.

Was this what Palmer Eogan and Melilah Awad were experiencing: an emotional storm ignited from century-cooled
ashes? He knew their history, and what it must mean to both
of them to be reunited after so long. The senses available to
him registered temperature and respiration rises in accord
with that theory. But he couldn't let himself believe that this
was the entire story.

Even when they kissed, and the signs of biological
arousal reached new heights, he refused to accept that he
could relax.

Exarch Deangelis stayed silent, transfixed by their embrace. He who was not a slave to biology could not begin
to imagine what an exchange of complementary chemicals
must feel like. He could only stand outside it and watch
from afar, a stranger staring out of the bushes at the heat of
a campfire and the people warming their hands around it.

He had seen people kiss before. He had watched them
court each other, dance around each other with all the
grace and blind determination of animals convinced that
what they were doing was unique and special. He had seen

them make love, have sex, fuck to utter satiation; he had heard the words they used and comprehended with clinical intimacy the processes involved.

He had never experienced *longing* before.

"Hello, Isaac," said a voice he hadn't heard over light-speed channels since the heady days before the Exarchate Expansion. "I'd like a berth, if you'd be so kind."

He wrenched his attention away from the two lovers, already pulling apart at the outraged cry from the scientist below. Every part of him was focused on that moment, transfixed. Only with difficulty did he realize that he wasn't alone.

"Lazarus?" He hurriedly shook himself together. Lazarus Hails of Kullervo-Hails system, last seen impersonating Bode's Nebula, had arrived. "You've caught me at an awkward time, I'm afraid. My facilities here are—"

"Perfectly sufficient for one small hopper, surely."

Exarch Deangelis scanned the skies for Hails's vessel. Unexpected though it was, Exarch Hails did appear to have arrived in the tiniest of single-passenger craft. His tangler was still stationed far out of the system, carefully camouflaged to all but Deangelis's most perceptive eye.

"You're not an invasion fleet, then," he said.

"Don't sound so relieved, my boy. I'm here purely in an advisory capacity—and already I can tell I'm needed." Hails's hopper curved in toward the habitat with no high-tech displays of deceleration. "Don't give me any special treatment. I'll be just one of the puppets, as far as anyone's concerned."

Exarch Deangelis instructed Traffic Control to allocate the incoming hopper a vacant berth, and took the moment to think the new development through. Lazarus Hails hadn't made the seven-plus-light-year trip from his system just to talk. There had to be more to it than that.

He scanned the hopper as it came in to dock. Lazarus Hails's body contained no obvious threats, overt or covert. It was a standard shell through which Exarch Hails's expanded intelligence could operate. Outwardly it looked perfectly human, taking the appearance of a large man with profuse white hair and strong chin. The only difference to the standard design lay in expanded memory and processing capacities. Hails had packed as much of his extended mind as possible into the shell before committing it to the front line.

Hails's patriarchal physical appearance was designed to trigger subconscious feelings of submission in his charges, thereby decreasing the likelihood of rebellion. Exarch Deangelis had gone down the opposite path, choosing the likeness of a young, slightly sexless male. There was room for such divergent philosophies in the Exarchate, which ruled many hundreds of human colonies, scattered across the bubble of human space, each of which had different needs.

"Everything's under control," he told the new arrival, using secure channels unknown to the people in his charge. "I can manage without your help."

"You think so, now," said Hails as he climbed out of the hopper and flexed his long limbs. "I assure you that will change."

Exarch Deangelis bristled at his words. "Are you threatening me?"

"Hardly, my boy. But there are plenty of others who will. As soon as word got about what you had coming your way, no one's wasted any time."

"How *did* word get out?"

"One can only wonder. Someone's either made an intelligent guess or taken advantage of a leak back home."

"Who did you hear it from?"

"I received word from your friend and mine: Lan Cochrane."

Cochrane was the Exarch of the system formerly called Alioth by ancient Earth astronomers—and the closest to Lut-Deangelis by a hair. She and her compatriot Giorsal McGrath in neighboring 78 Ursa Major had ruled the Arc Circuit ever since the Expansion. Neither of them took kindly to any suggestion that *his* system would be a more sensible choice for regional capital.

Cochrane might well have alerted other systems in order to goad them into action rather than taking direct steps herself. The tricky questions were: who else had taken the bait, and in what fashion?

"You haven't actually told me what you've got," said Hails. "Am I safe in assuming that what I've heard is correct?"

"That depends on what you've heard." Exarch Deangelis repressed a sigh of weariness. "Come on in, and we'll talk properly. I'll give you a false ID to cover you while you're here and show you the data I've recovered so far. If nothing else, I could use a second opinion on that."

"Excellent. A tour of the object in question would be welcome at some point, if I could take one without arousing suspicions."

"Not at the moment, I'm afraid."

Hails cocked an eyebrow. "Natives restless, are they? We'll see what we can do about that, too."

You'll keep your damned hands off my habitat, Exarch Deangelis thought to himself.

But he said nothing.

In response to that silence, Hails laughed and walked grandly among Exarch Deangelis's subjects.

+12

"So what happened in the skull?"

Palmer Eogan looked up from his meal into the know-ing smile of Luisa Pirelli. He couldn't meet her stare.

"You didn't see?"

"Oh, no. It was a complete blackout while you were in there." She put her chin in one hand and narrowed her blue eyes. "You're not going to tell me that was an accident, are you?"

He shook his head. Luisa's partner, James, returned from the kitchen with another bottle of wine and he thought he might be spared the interrogation. The hope was short-lived.

"We may like living in the dark ages, Lu and I," James said, tugging at an imitation cork with a manual opener, "but we're not idiots. And we know *you*, friend. You can't pull anything remotely fleecy over our eyes."

As fragrant Shiraz gushed into his glass, Eogan leaned back in his chair and told himself that they meant well. De-spite his late notice, the evening had been perfect. The two of them had prepared a roast that had all the texture and nu-tritional properties of the real thing—along with the taste, which was exquisite. The act of savoring every mouthful left little opportunity for talk, but he managed in about half an hour to bring them up to date on the years since they'd last dined together.

They waited for him to answer with the patience of ages. Compact, dark-haired Luisa was an archeologist specia-lizing in First Wave colonization. James was taller and long-faced, and a pre–Space Age historian. Both were deter-minedly anachronistic. Not only did they refer to themselves as husband and wife, but they both also wore corrective glasses and sported various degrees of biological imperfections. Their apartment was a fair imitation of a twenty-first-century Western abode, complete with up-down orientation and latched doorways. There were some things they couldn't replicate: the wine for one had to be squeezed out of a plastic bottle and would have floated away had not field effects kept it in the glass. James's tie kept rising up to his chin. But the pretense was an admirable one, and Eogan was grateful for the effort they had made.

He owed them, he supposed. Within reason.

"I just wanted to talk to Melilah," he said, "without a thousand eyes watching."

"Only a thousand?" Luisa looked at James and raised her eyebrows. "Is that all it rated?"

"I think he's being metaphorical." James used a fork to scoop a gravy-soaked segment of roasted carrot into his mouth. Slightly muffled, he continued, "And his point is not invalid."

"Most people would be proud of such a moment," she said to her husband. "When I think of all those soap operas and reality TV shows we had to sit through for your thesis . . ." She grimaced. "If they'd dared cut a climax like that, the viewers would've sued!"

"My life isn't a television show," Eogan protested.

"It is if you come to Bedlam," Luisa corrected him.

He couldn't argue with her on that point. He had known the laws before setting course. There were no exceptions—except, maybe, for the Exarch, and no one had yet found certain signs of that. Any odd blank spots inevitably attracted attention.

He wondered if that was why Melilah had seemed angry when they'd parted. It couldn't have been the kiss, since it was she who made the first move. Nor could it have been the offer of information. Was it that he had robbed her public record of a dramatic moment many people would have longed for?

The theory wasn't unlikely to be true, but it didn't accord

with what he knew of her. He would have to wait to see what she did next, after she had read the fiche.

"Okay," he said, resigned to telling at least part of the truth. "I was afraid of looking like a fool. You know how long it's been since we last saw each other. I had no idea how either of us was going to react. I didn't want to screw things up with the entire colony watching."

"And *did* you screw it up?" James asked, eyes alight.

"You both looked a bit flustered when you came back into view," said Luisa.

"I don't know," he confessed. "It's too early to tell."

"Yes, probably." Luisa diverted her gaze from him at last. She looked satisfied by his answer, as though she had expected nothing more. He was briefly tempted to shock her by revealing that he had in fact kissed Melilah, but the impulse quickly passed. He still didn't quite believe that it had happened himself.

"Don't eat too much," she said, helping herself to another spoonful of peas. "There's dessert to come."

Eogan went for seconds, safe in the knowledge that he could eat as much—or as little—as he wanted.

"We'll ease off on the Melilah front," James said, washing down his food with more wine, "if you tell us what you found between here and Mizar."

Eogan feigned exasperation. "Don't you people *ever* let up?"

"Not when one of our best friends lies to us," said Luisa, poking him in the side with one purple-polished nail. "You said you didn't know if it was a ROTH artifact—then there were skulls practically dropping from the skies."

"It seemed prudent to keep the truth under wraps," he said, knowing the excuse wouldn't cut plasma. "Think of it as a reflex action. I'm sorry."

"Forgiven—if you tell us what *else* you brought." She raised her chin in challenge. "What's in that observatory up there, Palmer Eogan?"

He shook his head. "I really don't know for sure, Luisa. Honestly this time."

"But you have an opinion," she said. "Why not share it with us?"

And the rest of the colony? He wondered what would happen if he tried. The Exarch could kill him before he finished the sentence, if he so desired.

"I'll pass for the moment."

"There are a number of theories in circulation," said James, wiping his lips on a cloth napkin. "One is that you found a whole new class of vessel—maybe even a working Merchant Beehive. With crew still in hibernation, waiting to be woken up."

"Now that would be a find," Eogan said.

"There are numerous variations ranging from operable superweapon platforms to research stations containing the original exogenesis germ line."

"James accepts that all of them *might* be true," said Luisa, fondly patting her husband's knee.

"There's always a chance, no matter how remote."

"Your mind's as open as ever, then," said Eogan. "That's good to hear."

"Well, there's the lunatic fringe," James went on. "Those who think you've found the Grail, the Ark, a generation ship stocked with Yeti, whatever fantasy's triggered them off this month."

Eogan laughed easily. "I can solemnly swear that there are no Grays within a light-year of this habitat."

"Most people just assume it's got something to do with the Sublime Catastrophe," James concluded. "And I can understand that. It's the one big setback we've had with the ROTH, and it happened only ten years ago. Putting it together with this thing—which seems to have both you and the Exarch completely on edge—is an obvious if not entirely logical operation."

Eogan did his best to maintain the smile. It had died inside the moment James mentioned Sublime. "I guess we'll see. The Exarch has to tell us what he's found eventually."

"Deangelis doesn't have to tell us a damned thing if he doesn't want to. And neither do any of the Gentry. They're as bad as you are." James took the sting off the comment by raising his glass. "And here you are, my friend. Whatever brought you here, wherever it takes us, it's nice to see you again. Here's to happier times."

Eogan toasted with his friends, although the taste of the wine had turned bitter on his tongue, and all appetite for the feast had vanished.

What are you doing right now, Melilah? he wondered. *We gorge ourselves on the brink of destruction. We take our fill while, unknown to us, death may already be spreading its dark wings over this fine, strange world you have made. Is there anything I would say to you now, if this was the only moment I had left?*

Eogan's depressive mood swing did not go unnoticed. His friends let him go when he protested weariness, even though they knew as well as he did that physical tiredness was another complaint from which he need never willingly suffer. Taking a transport, he instructed it to fly at random through Bedlam's many tangled ways, wherever its miniscule AI whim took it. He turned down numerous offers of accommodation from the generous and the mercantile both. A room didn't interest him. The last thing he wanted was to be shut up alone again.

Read the fiche, Melilah, he wanted to tell her. *Read it, and find us a way out of this god-awful mess.*

13

Melilah floated in the center of her pitch-black apartment. To the casual observer, she would have appeared asleep, but she was very much awake. She had gone back to her apartment as soon as she'd left Eogan, but hadn't immediately accessed the fiche. That would have drawn too much attention. Instead she memory-exercised for an hour, then joined Yasu for a quick meal. Her four-daughter had been full of questions and speculations about Eogan again, and to avoid them would also have looked suspicious. She had to go about her life as though nothing more urgent than usual was pressing.

She said nothing about what had actually happened in the alien wreck, but Yasu knew her well enough to guess that a secret was being withheld from her. Her sly almond eyes gleamed.

The fiche Eogan had given her weighed in her pocket like an anvil.

There's something about the Occlusion you need to know.

She shrugged off Yasu as soon as politely possible and headed back to her quarters.

But you have to be careful.

She went through her usual preparations for sleep, getting into silken purple pajamas that tied at wrists and ankles, setting an alarm for three hours hence, and turning down the lights.

I can understand Deangelis wanting to keep this secret.

The fiche was in her left hand, palmed as she had undressed. She sank into low gee and brought it up to her face, half-opening her fingers as she did.

People might panic if word gets out.

And well they might, thought Melilah, if there was any connection between what had happened in Sublime and what had come to Bedlam—as Angela Chen-Pushkaric of her Defiance meetings suspected. The Exarch might fear political and economic instability more than the sheer loss of life should the Catastrophe be repeated, but she knew squarely where her priorities lay. If either Eogan or the Exarch had willingly put her home and her friends at risk, she wouldn't rest until she saw them both take a long walk out an air lock.

For a moment, though, she hesitated. What if it wasn't an ordinary data fiche at all? What if it contained dreadful Palmer programs that would get into her system and corrupt her, change her, *dehumanize* her? She didn't want to be like Eogan. She didn't want to be Alice foolishly swigging at the bottle just because it said, "Drink me."

Trust me, Melilah. This is your big chance.

Her lips tingled as she raised the fiche and pressed it close to her chest, where her skin could read it. She opened the fiche and browsed its contents, keeping her hand carefully over it so no one would suspect its existence. It contained an extremely large amount of data, many, many terabytes mostly in the form of detailed reports and analyses, much of it in exotic formats she couldn't read. It had the air of something dumped unceremoniously and at great haste, when an opportunity presented itself. She would probably need Eogan himself to decipher half of it, or else would need access to more sophisticated decrypting tools to nut out the rest. For a good minute she cursed him for forgetting how much she disliked Palmer protocols.

But he *did* know that, she reminded herself. That had been the whole point of their breakup. And he had as good as told her that he had been obsessing over their final moments for one hundred and fifty years, so that wasn't the sort of thing he was likely to forget.

He wasn't stupid. If he wanted her to read it, he must have provided a way.

Melilah looked deeper, beyond the information itself to the way it was arranged on the fiche. Directory structures, file labels, sector assignment, fragmentation . . .

She found it. Buried in a cluster of recovery files was a string of labels that, when taken as a series in order of size, spelled out a message in old ASCII code. She unreeled the string one way, and read nothing but gibberish. Parsing a simple pattern recognition net over it took less than a second, and generated instant results.

The string had been garbled using an eight-digit modifier based on the date 04-03-2287: the day they had last seen one another.

You sentimental fool, she thought, touched despite the cynic inside of her who insisted he was trying just a little too hard to demonstrate just how much emotional baggage he had, where she was concerned.

Putting that aside, she turned over in the darkness and read his message.

```
    Melilah, forgive me. By telling you
this, I might well be putting your life
at risk. But you need to understand that
your life is *already* at risk,
irrespective of what I might involve you
in. You have a right to know the truth.
    What we found between Mizar and Bedlam
wasn't an artifact, at least not in the
sense that you and I would probably use
the word. It wasn't a ship like the
Merchant Bees we brought back, although
we did find them alongside it. I'm not
entirely sure *what* it is—but I know
what it looks like to me, and I think
it's dangerous to suppress that
possibility, for any reason.
```

A lot of the report is true. The
Occlusion was drifting across the lane in
the location specified. It looked from a
distance like a haze of dust. The dust
became a real navigational threat as
we approached, even with our magnetic
cowcatchers. We had to shut down the VOID
drive half an AU out and use thrusters
the rest of the way; otherwise, we
would've been holed for sure. None of us
had ever seen anything like it. No wonder
it was screwing up deform ratings so
badly.

But it was manageable. Dust is just
dust, after all, and there wasn't *that*
much of it, not compared to a brown dwarf
or microsingularity. All we had to do was
take some broad sweeps to mop up the bulk
of it, then let robot cleaners do the
rest. It'd be gone in a week. Even when
we found the Bees clustered around the
heart of it, we didn't think we'd have a
problem. The skulls made the job
interesting. They didn't make it
difficult.

Only when we took a closer look did we
realize we had something weird on our
hands. The dust cloud and the wrecks were
just symptoms. The real occlusion was in
the center, where our probes couldn't get
any sensible data. We noticed it first
because it was interfering with the
signals between the *Nhulunbuy*'s
components. We got lags where there
should have been none, and odd
reflections off things that couldn't
possibly exist. When we'd isolated our
hardware and determined that they weren't

causing the problem, we took a closer
look at the environment in front of us.
There was a patch of space that didn't
measure up—and I mean that quite
literally. When we tried to pin it down,
we got readings ranging from millimeters
to light-seconds across. The best we
could do was measure the edges, where it
didn't screw up our signals. We placed
it at around five meters across. A
perfect sphere, right at the center of
the dust cloud. A sphere of something
very odd indeed.

We cleared it off as best we could.
I don't understand the science too well;
it's not my field. Palmer Vermeulen, my
SO, described it to me as a "tightly
bound region of distressed space-time."
We found nothing visibly maintaining
it; it didn't seem to be spreading or
shrinking, for all the weird measurements
we took of it; it was just there. When
we sent a probe into it—that was when
things got really strange. The probe
disappeared from all our sensors, except
for those trained into the sphere.

It's a hole, Melilah. A wormhole.
Not a singularity; there's no warping
outside the boundary; there's no event
horizon as we understand them. But it's
definitely a hole of some kind. The
sphere at the center of the dust cloud is
the outside of a kind of multidimensional
throat. I don't know what kind of throat
it is. Vermeulen couldn't get her head
around that part. But it's hellish in
there, to say the least. Our first probe
was instantly fried, and so was the next

one we sent in. The third managed to get
back a few microseconds of data before it
melted, too. The fourth hinted that there
might be something on the other side of
the throat, then it, too, burned out.

I don't mind telling you, Melilah,
that this thing scares me. I've been
traveling the lanes for a century and a
half, and I've never seen anything like
it: a hole in space you can float right
through, if you come at it just the right
way, but fry before you reach the far
side. What sort of thing is that? Why
would someone build it, then set it
adrift? I dread to think what would've
happened if a Cell had hit it at speed.

That's when I called the nearest
colony. I was completely out of my
depth, and I needed advice. I had a
choice. I could've called Mizar, where
we'd come from, but I chose Bedlam
because it was closer. I described the
thing we'd found, and sent what data we
could. The bandwidth is terrible out
deep, so I could only give Deangelis a
vague description. I thought he'd just
laugh at us, call us crazy, and tell us
to stop wasting his time. But he didn't.
He told us to bring it in immediately.
He didn't seem thrown at all by what
we'd found.

We were thrown instead. I replied
saying that I didn't have the first idea
how to shift the thing out of the lane,
let alone haul it all the way to Bedlam.
He came back straightaway, cool as
anything, with detailed instructions
of how to convert one of our cargo

components into a magnetic cage. The cage would enable us to move the thing we'd found, just like any other piece of space junk. Vermeulen said it was never going to work. But at Deangelis's insistence we tried it, and it *did* work. He may have neglected to tell us how *heavy* it was going to be, drag-wise, but he was right about everything else. The cage took hold, and the thing was caught.

What the hell, I thought. The Exarchs are way ahead of us; they know all sorts of crazy shit. They probably concoct dozens of things twice as weird as this in Sol every day.

We delayed barely long enough to wipe the lane clean and pick up the skulls. The Occlusion itself was tucked up nice and tight, and Vermeulen was happy that we'd have some months yet to poke at it before we handed it over. At the time that didn't seem like such a bad thing. This was obviously the product of advanced ROTH tech, and the more we got from it, the better for us. We burned up several tons of mass on probes, algorithmically designing them so they'd withstand the strictures of the throat. What it's made of, we never found out, but Vermeulen kept talking about exotic matter and negative energies with the Cell AI. None of us could follow them when they started—and probes kept coming back with even stranger data.

After the throat, things level. It begins to look like almost plain sailing. Almost.

Vermeulen was becoming pretty good at keeping the probes alive, and the data they were sending back from the far side was amazing. Zero radiation; zero gravity; zero hazard. If this thing was a hole, we asked ourselves, then where does it lead? The pictures from the probes couldn't have been less interesting, only adding to our curiosity. A wormhole could take us anywhere in space *or* time. Even if this one opened in the heat-death of the universe, that would be something!

Vermeulen wanted to go through, but I wouldn't let her. Two volunteers went instead: Palmers Cobiac and Bray, two people I'd served with for thirty years. Vermeulen kitted them up like high-tech torpedoes, morphing their bodies back to the bare essentials and giving them everything they'd need to survive the passage through the throat. At that point in the journey, we were one month from Bedlam. Deangelis didn't know what we were doing. The ftl link doesn't work when the VOID drive is on, so there was no way to tell him, even if we'd wanted to. All of us were aware that we had a shrinking window in which to find out what was on the other side before the Gentry took over.

But even then I was having second thoughts. Deangelis's reply had been too quick, too assured. He *knew* something about this thing: what it was, or how it worked, at least. How had he pinned it down from our quick description? He or another member of the Exarchate must have

seen something like it before. But where?
There was nothing in the records that I
had found. If the Sol labs have been
building holes in space behind our backs,
we've yet to see any sign of them. And
the only other truly anomalous ROTH
artifact we've ever come across, and
about which we know next to nothing,
caused the Sublime Catastrophe.

By the time the connection truly began
to worry me, it was too late to cancel
the expedition. Cobiac and Bray were
ready to go. Vermeulen was acting like
she expected me to pull the plug at any
moment; maybe she was hoping I would,
since she didn't have the guts herself.
But with nothing but my own misgivings
to go on, I didn't feel I could do
anything, and let the mission go ahead
as planned.

Cobiac and Bray went into the
Occlusion, and they survived the throat
intact. What they saw on the other side
wasn't unexpected; we'd had pictures back
from the probes, after all, and it wasn't
interesting viewing. But the subjective
experience, the knowledge that *one of
us* had gone through something so strange
and emerged unscathed, *was* amazing. It
gave us a sense of subjectivity—of
reality—that had previously been
lacking.

Space is curved on the far side,
wrapped around itself to form a tunnel
that stretches into the distance in a
perfectly straight line. The throat is at
one end. We still don't know what's at

the other. Cobiac and Bray took passive
readings, but picked up nary a photon
from more than twenty meters into the
tunnel. They tried radar and got nothing
back from that, either. The vacuum is as
pure as our detectors had ever registered
before—which is saying something;
remember that the *Nhulunbuy* is a sweeper
Cell—so that ruled out any sort of sonar.
Seismic readings were nonexistent.
Cobiac tried going a little farther up
the tunnel and reported some odd spatial
distortions. At five meters from the
throat, he stopped, then came back to
check the link. He measured his return
journey at over seven meters.

I should've called them back then. My
gut was screaming that something was
severely fucked up, that if we pushed
our luck any further, it was all going
to go wrong. But Vermeulen kept at me,
and I knew we might not get a second
chance. We *had* to know what was at
the other end of the tunnel—and both
Cobiac and Bray wanted to find out. If
I'd been in their shoes, I would've
wanted to go, too.

So I let them. I authorized an advance
to fifty meters. They sent back a
transmission from forty saying that
everything was fine, that the way ahead
was clear. And that was the last we heard
of them. One minute they were there; the
next they were gone. Telemetry completely
lost them. We waited—hours at first, then
days—but they never came back.

Vermeulen sent a probe after them. It

disappeared, too. A closer examination of
its final transmissions picked up further
weird special effects. There were signal
lags over the final few microseconds
suggesting that its actual distance was
far greater than forty meters from the
throat. The last ping taken off the probe
put its location at just under three
hundred kilometers away—as though
something had reached out of the depths
of the tunnel and snatched it from us.

That was it. I wanted nothing more
to do with it. I ordered N-1 sealed until
we were in Bedlam. I locked what data
I felt safe to give the Gentry into a
deep-crypted file and briefed the crew
on what they were and weren't to say
when we arrived. I wanted Deangelis to
think that we'd left the Occlusion
alone—because that was the only way we
were ever going to get a chance to warn
someone about what might actually be
going on.

The data is inconclusive, Melilah,
but it *is* suggestive. If this thing
really is a wormhole, then there has
to be another end to it. So where does
it go? What's waiting for us at the
other end?

There's no way of knowing the answer to
those questions at the moment, not now the
thing's in Deangelis's hands. All I know
is that I've already lost two crew
members, and I want to leave it at that.
Bringing it to Bedlam was the worst thing
I could have done. Either way, I lose. The
best-case scenario is that everything I've

guessed about this thing is wrong: I've
lied to the Exarch, risked an interstellar
incident, and forced my fears onto you
with no sound provocation at all.

Or I'm right . . .

In my worst nightmares, the other end
of the tunnel is in the heart of Sublime,
and even as you read this file another
Catastrophe is boiling our way.

14

On the lip of hell, an arcane fire burned. In a distant, distracted way, it hurt. Deangelis tried not to notice it, because if he did, it might snare him as it had snared the others who had preceded him and burn him back to nothing. The effort wasn't entirely successful. Deep inside, unacknowledged, part of him was screaming.

"There's a storm coming."

The Exarch pulled himself out of the viewpoint of the fragment of him standing on the brink of the Occlusion. He had too many events happening at once to reply immediately to Lazarus Hails's comment. While the Exarch of Kullervo-Hails system strolled by the mundane temptations of Albert Hall, nodding pleasantly at people he passed and indulging in the occasional real-time conversation, Deangelis was monitoring no less than five significant situations unfolding in widely separated parts of the habitat and beyond. Some of his eyes were on the tangler still masquerading as the globular cluster 47 Tucanae. Hails's tangler in Bode's Nebula—if that was indeed who it belonged to—was quiet, but there were faint signs of activity on the other side of the system. Deangelis could do little more than guess at its nature, while at the same time battening down the hatches for whatever it augured. Habitat security, internal and external, had been surreptitiously increased on several fronts. It didn't appear that anyone had noticed yet, but he kept a close watch on that, too.

The influx of data from Sol continued to mount. His hourly reports were met with the most cursory of replies from home, assuring him that help was on its way. Although tempted to connect such blandishments with the mysterious tangler, he was wary of accepting such a comfortable assumption without further evidence. And without knowing what sort of help Sol was sending, exactly, it wasn't much of a comfort.

Defiance, the local and largely ineffectual resistance group, had met again, this time without Awad and some of the more reasonable voices to keep them in check. Their stridency warranted close observation, lest they provoke unrest at a critical juncture. The local crime rate was up, as were information infractions. With several Cells now on station around the habitat and more on the way, numerous destabilizing influences were entering the picture, one by one. The *Inselmeer* had come, its chief officer declared, to renegotiate the terms of its trading agreement with the colony, seeking to renege on a science and technology clause the Palmers had signed decades ago. The Arc Circuit's Negotiator Select, Palmer Christolphe, had made the long journey from Ansell-Aad to stick his nose into the situation, and had already hinted that he knew more than he had previously let on. A bluff, Deangelis assumed, but one he couldn't afford to ignore. A clane of identical bodyguards accompanied Christolphe everywhere he went. They were in the process of unloading the Negotiator's administrative paraphernalia and relocating it all in the habitat's business district.

At any other time, this development would have pleased him. To have Palmer Christolphe in-system was a boost to Lut-Deangelis's significance in the region. But with so much else going on—and the Occlusion that provoked it all still requiring constant study—he barely had a moment to consider the ramifications. He could only take it at face value and assume that Christolphe hadn't come for a social visit.

A storm was coming. Hails was absolutely right, in his bluntly provocative way. Deangelis could feel it in every part of his extended being—like a spider sensing vibrations in the web from which it hung. Crisis was inevitable, sooner rather than later. He just couldn't tell which direction it was coming *from*.

"Try the Pinot Noir at Ormerod's," he advised Hails, feigning disaffectedness. "You'll find it surprisingly pleasant."

Hails did, smiling charmingly at the maître d' and paying with a debit line put in place by Deangelis. He settled into the zero-gee bar like a debonair autocrat from the late twentieth century, ruby red wine in one hand and eyes that took in everything around him. Outwardly relaxed, he, too, was surfing the channels, dipping into the habitat and tasting its many flavors. Deangelis monitored his mental movements closely, wondering what conclusions the visiting Exarch was drawing.

"You're not fooling anyone, you know," Hails said. "This is too big for you."

"The situation is under control."

"There's no shame in admitting otherwise, Isaac. I'd have been outclassed, too, if the Mizar Occlusion had come to my system. You need help, and I'm here to offer it to you."

"Sol will provide."

"We're a long way from Sol, my friend. Their objectives are not necessarily ours."

Deangelis couldn't argue with that. The Exarchate had its rifts and tensions just like any human society. The Arc Circuit, although part of the Exarchate, regarded itself as semiautonomous, when it suited it, and the individual systems within the Arc Circuit did the same. Deangelis wasn't immune to the impulse, either, but he remained acutely aware that he was in power by the grace of the home system.

"That doesn't mean," he said coolly, "that Sol's objectives are wrong."

"They sit in their ivory towers and dictate to us, unaware of the harsh realities of colonial life."

"If they're not aware, it's because we have failed to *make* them aware. That's one of our primary functions."

"They're as removed from us as we are from the puppets. They've forgotten what it's like down in the trenches. No—they've never known. Sol might as well be in a different galaxy, sometimes. What holds there doesn't apply here."

Deangelis wondered what the Archon would think of such talk. "That's why they're sending someone here," he said, hearing the naïveté in his words even as he uttered them.

Hails laughed derisively. "They're coming to take over. At the first whiff of trouble, they dispel the illusion that we're even remotely autonomous and apply the iron heel. We would do that to *our* subjects; why wouldn't they do it to us?"

Deangelis's first instinct was to deny that he *would* do that to his subjects. Even with activists like Awad and Defiance wandering freely through the habitat, he had never had to apply force to maintain control. Authority was an emergent property; it couldn't be forced on a system. Not for long, anyway. After the initial Expansion, he had tried to insinuate himself into the life of the habitat so the thought of doing without him was inconceivable. In return for granting him that authority, he allowed the system its odd perks—open information laws and the like.

He felt that, for the most part, his method was working. Awad and Defiance were exceptions, not the rule. Most people in the habitat had become accustomed to his presence and, through him, that of the Exarchate. Undisturbed, he was certain he could guide his wards to the best possible future available to them.

Undisturbed . . . That, he supposed, was the problem.

Palmer Christolphe hailed him to schedule a meeting. The Defiance group decided that they should take action immediately, somehow. A fight broke out in a public reading room that left one woman with a broken nose and another hollering for security. Lazarus Hails sipped his Pinot Noir and cast a knowing, aloof eye across the people around him.

Deep in the heart of an impossible space, another fragment of Exarch Deangelis vanished from sight, perhaps never to be seen again.

He remembered:

On the morning of his birth, the sun was shining. He opened his eyes on a world of color. Wind blew across a field of green grass, making it ripple. Leaves rustled. Clouds scudded through the sky in slow motion, casting liquid shadows upon the world.

He knew where he was and *who* he was. Spring had come to the Clare Valley early, in a profusion of colors. He was leaning with his back against a rough-barked eucalyptus near the summit of a low hill, high enough to see that there had once been a settlement near a small creek below. Stubs of walls protruded from thick tufts of grass; straggly rose-bushes clutched with skeletal hands at long-decayed water tanks; tilted, crumbling slabs of tarmac revealed where roads had once led.

Part of the one who had made him had lived there, once. A long time ago, when humans had walked the Earth.

The name *Isaac Forge Deangelis* had been chosen for him by his maker. The Archon wasn't his parent, and he wasn't the Archon's son, but intrinsic to their relationship—even at such an early stage—was the awareness that one had generated the other. The process was complicated, intuitive, and unpredictable. As with biological breeding, input was taken from many sources, and much was left to chance. Not even the Archon, with its godlike intelligence, could know what Isaac Forge Deangelis would be like when allowed to live in his own right.

And Isaac Deangelis *was* alive. There was no doubting the fact. He might not have been conceived of human parents or grown in a flesh-and-blood womb, but he felt life coursing through him just as vigorously. He wasn't a robot, or a homunculus, or a golem. Nor was he a puppet dancing at the Archon's will, with an illusion of self pasted over it to make it think it was alive.

The wind stroked his bare arms, and the sun bathed his face. The scent of a clean, free world made his nostrils tingle.

Then something very strange happened.

On the moon, another version of him was born. He, too, opened his eyes and embraced the world before him: the rolling gray regolith and the vault of stars above. An orbital tower cast one single stark, brilliant line across the sky, where it caught the Earthlight and reflected it down upon him. He, too, wondered at the complicated process of his creation and his relationship to the Archon.

The awareness that there was another person exactly like him cut across Deangelis's existence as a siren would through a symphony. They were identical in every initial condition, but they weren't the same person. Their experiences diverged with every passing moment. The version of him on the moon was delayed by some seconds, giving their overlapping thoughts a jarring, disconcerting beat, like two tones almost alike played at the same time.

Six seconds was the time it took light to travel from the Earth to the moon, and vice versa. It was likely, then, that the two of him had awoken at exactly the same moment, and only once the light-speed lag had been surmounted had their thoughts begun to overlap.

Another six seconds passed, and he began to receive his twin's response to feeling *him* awaken on Earth. The discord was alarming. He, Earth-Deangelis, had automatically assumed that Moon-Deangelis was a secondary creation, but Moon-Deangelis thought exactly the same thing about *him*.

They tried communicating. The lag was difficult to overcome. Next they tried cutting the link between them. It was fixed, part of them. Lastly they tried calling the Archon, but received no reply. They were on their own, momentarily.

Mars-Deangelis woke to a gloomy dawn high on the red world. Dust storms raged around the base of Mons Olympus, obscuring the details from his elevated position. Earth was a brilliant star, far, far away.

Venus-Deangelis chimed in not long after, followed by versions of him on Mercury and several of the larger asteroids. Jupiter-Deangelis joined with a selection of others who had woken on the gas giant's major moons, already knitted into a confused collective by the time light had crossed the distance to Earth. So it went through the solar system: Saturn, Uranus, and Neptune, plus *their* moons, were followed by Pluto and other Kuiper Belt Objects. There were even minds identical to his riding three long-period comets out to the Oort cloud. How far did he extend? he wondered. If he waited four years, would he receive the waking moments of his selves in Alpha Centauri?

The noise was incredible. He could barely hear himself think through the ceaseless babble of his selves. He was drowning, smothering, fragmenting.

But moments came and went when it seemed that, just for an instant, everything gelled. Despite the confusion and the time lags, all his disparate selves fell into synch and reinforced each other, creating a powerful, surging sense of connection. He could tell, instinctively, what Triton-Deangelis was thinking and how Venus-Deangelis felt about their predicament. He was part of a whole, not a piece of a disintegrating mosaic.

He felt grass against his cheek (which Mars-Deangelis distantly acknowledged) at the same time he experienced the taste of sulfur on Io's turbulent winds. He wondered what was happening to him when he reached out one hand to try to sit up and felt methane snow crunch under his fingers. He was dissolving into the relentless rush of self, drowning in the sights glimpsed by eyes identical to his, overwhelmed by so much *him* he could never contain it.

As time went on, the moments of synchrony became more common, until he began to long for them. He imagined that something had arisen from the chaos—not another version of him, but a new creature emerging *out of* him, made from him but not the same as its many parts. It was to him what a tank regiment was to a single tank, or a flock of ducks was to a single duck. A single tank couldn't surround another army; a single duck couldn't control the graceful movement of the flock. The new creature was an emergent property of everything he was, everywhere he was.

A new, permanent standing wave formed from all his different voices. Just as his thoughts rose spontaneously from the cells of his brain, the workings of its mind rose spontaneously from the many copies of him scattered across the system, simultaneously smoothing the chaos and thriving on it. In a matter of days, all the copies of him were integrated seamlessly into the workings of a much larger mind that allowed them freedom and independence, yet depended on the reliable quirks and details that made him who he was on an individual level. No one else could join the collective, just as foreign cells couldn't survive for long in his body. The various versions of him had joined like the flat facets of a magnificent gem, creating something much more wonderful than simple two-dimensional shapes. They contained within them the makings of a whole new dimension of thought and existence.

He underwent in a matter of days an evolution of being that had taken humanity as a whole many thousands of years to attain. He went beyond humanity to another state entirely.

He remembered:

On the morning of his birth, the Archon greeted Isaac Forge Deangelis in a way his components could not begin to comprehend. Linking minds across the great volume of the solar system, he felt embraced by the greater collective that humanity had become. Sol system might have looked empty, apart from the components of numerous minds slowly waking and joining together, but it was in fact full of vast and potent intelligences. They had brewed there for decades, centuries, staring up at the stars and making plans to attain them.

Isaac Forge Deangelis was an Exarch.

The time had come to branch out into the universe.

It was strange, then, sixty years later, to be standing on the brink of another continuum entirely, an artificial space that had been made by minds unknown. He sent his many selves out into the habitat to test its mood and monitor its changes, readying himself for anything. He walked among staring Naturals and more adapted Arc Circuit citizens, all of whom knew his face from pictures but few of whom had met him in person. He sent one to monitor the exploration of the skulls, although he had already determined everything he needed to know from the alien wrecks. He sent one to sit with Hails, joining him for a glass of wine and continuing their discussion face-to-face, by means few of the people around him would recognize as communication at all. He took several transports and traveled the pipes of his domain as an ordinary person might. He passed the one containing Palmer Eogan several times, but did not hail him.

The experiences washed through him like a vitamin tonic, centering him. The Mizar Occlusion was a distraction from his primary concern, which was the maintenance of his colony. Being an Exarch wasn't about seeking personal gain—although having a sense of ambition was important. He had been on the fringe for too long to realize just how far from the center he had drifted.

He smiled at Hails over his glass of Pinot Noir and toasted the mouth of hell.

15

Eogan woke from a nightmare with a jerk that sent him bouncing around the cramped, unlit interior of the transport. Gripping an armrest and bringing himself to a halt, he cursed himself for nodding off. Palmers didn't need to sleep, but the instinct wasn't excised entirely from their bodies. Some slept for release from consciousness; others for the dreams. Eogan hadn't slept since finding the Occlusion.

Until now.

He had dreamed that he had been standing in a long, straight corridor. Gravity had held his feet to the floor; his clothes had hung from him like lead weights. Behind him was a door—an antique wooden door with a metal handle. The door was shut. He suspected it might even be locked, but he didn't try to open it.

He turned back to the corridor. It stretched ahead of him to infinity, undeviating, lit in regular patches all along its length. His eye caught on the vanishing point, and would have held there but for the feeling that he was being watched back.

He glanced away. *Where to now?* he thought, even though there was only one way to go.

He took one step along the corridor, then another. The door receded behind him, dropping away like the ground during a vertical ascent. Gravity pulled at him, made his knees want to buckle. The vanishing point seemed to draw closer, although he knew that had to be an illusion.

Two more steps, and he reeled as though the corridor had shrugged beneath him. He hadn't had a panic attack since childhood, but this felt very similar. His skin prickled. His heart rate increased.

Two more steps made six in total. The sense that he was completely alone, utterly vulnerable, struck him an almost physical blow. Although constrained in four of the six directions—left, right, up, and down—he felt as though he was hanging in an empty void. Were there dimensions he wasn't aware of? Could something be slouching toward him through time, or along one of the rolled-up Planck-scale spaces?

He managed just one more step before the corridor defeated him. The vastness of the space before him distorted like some cheap visual effect. Something was rushing toward him out of infinity—and with a gut-wrenching jolt he realized it was infinity itself. The atom-sharp point where the curved walls of the corridor met flexed in upon him, folding space so it could stab at him like a rapier. He recoiled with one arm flung up in front of his face and ran for the door.

One step, two steps. A wind sprang up around him. Three steps, four. He heard a howling noise, growing louder. Five steps, six. Space-time crackled and snapped, tearing itself into splinters. Seven steps—the number he had taken into the corridor.

Then—*eight*.

He panicked. How was this possible? He took nine steps, ten steps—but the door was still out of reach.

Eleven!

The corridor snarled.

He lunged for the handle as infinity's teeth snapped at his heels—

—and woke in Bedlam, flying through an anonymous, random pipe with his heart hammering like an overstimulated Natural.

Eogan sighed and tried to put it from his mind. If the Mizar Occlusion was what he dreaded it might be—a wormhole connecting Bedlam to the force that had destroyed Sublime—then it was only natural to be afraid of it. But letting that fear dominate his thoughts, getting in the way of what he needed to do, was irresponsible and dangerous.

Knowing exactly what he needed to do, of course, was the difficult part.

He checked the *Nhulunbuy*'s telemetry and found that he had missed an interesting development.

"When did you hear from him?" he asked Vermeulen, whose component, N-11, was already preparing for disconnection from the rest of the Cell.

"Ten minutes ago." She affected grumpiness. "Just when I thought I was out of the firing line."

Eogan replayed the conversation between his science officer and Exarch Deangelis. It had been brief and to the point. The Exarch intended to honor his agreement with Eogan, allowing a Palmer presence inside the Occlusion observatory. If Vermeulen was willing to observe, she could join the project immediately. Slightly stunned by the offer, she had accepted.

With Eogan out cold, she and Palmer Flast had begun making the necessary arrangements before the Exarch changed his mind. That could happen at any moment, they knew. The Exarch had no obligation to them.

"You don't have to do this if you really don't want to," Eogan told her.

"Oh, I do," she replied. "I may not like it, but I don't have any choice. I owe it to my profession, curse it, if not to myself."

"You'll keep us up to date, of course."

"As and when I can. That thing is sealed tight. Nothing's gone in or out since it went up."

"If you get into trouble, we'll do everything we can to get you out of it."

"Thanks. It does make me feel better, knowing that you'll be there to rescue me. If you can stay awake long enough."

He laughed to hide an undercurrent of doubt. Was Deangelis giving them access because he thought he had the Occlusion under control—or because he was as stumped as they had been? Or was Eogan missing the point entirely?

He fought the impulse to check in on Melilah, to see if she had read the fiche. Then he gave in to it. She was awake and active, but not on any overtly Occlusion-related business. He could tell from her public record that she was in the middle of some sort of legal wrangle. On probation herself, she was lodging a claim of public harassment against the man called Gil Hurdowar. While she didn't mind Hurdowar watching on principle, she told the appeals AI, Hurdowar had a social obligation to do the right thing by her in return. When she asked him to leave her alone, he should either comply or be discreet. Bombarding her and her associates with constant requests to communicate got in the way of her work. His resistance to her pleas for consideration provoked arguments that affected her public record. She wasn't the only guilty party, therefore; he should be punished, too.

The laws of Bedlam were complex, but no more so than those of any society. Abnegation of the right to privacy was compensated for by the shoring up of other rights: the right to access information at all levels of government at any time; the right to personal physical security; the right to travel unhindered and free of charge within the habitat; etc. Gil Hurdowar could watch anyone he wanted, thirty-six hours a day, and no one could legally stop him; but should he make the slightest move to enter someone's apartment or to damage his or her personal property, he would be hit with severe penalties, including imprisonment or expulsion. "Property" was occasionally defined as goodwill or productivity, so Hurdowar's interference in Melilah's work counted in her case, she argued, as an infringement of the law.

The AI agreed with her argument. Gil Hurdowar lost a slew of privileges he probably wouldn't exercise anytime soon, and then only temporarily. It wasn't much, but it was recorded as a small victory on her part.

Melilah went back to work, searching archival material for information on two women Eogan didn't recognize. If she knew Eogan was watching, she made no sign. Maybe she was ignoring him, or just didn't care.

Eogan allowed instinct to guide him again. He didn't know what made Hurdowar so persistent, and he had no right to act in Melilah's defense. But Hurdowar had tried to contact him as well, and that fact alone made him curious and suspicious.

"The famous Palmer Eogan," said Hurdowar in response to his communications request. The man's face was puffy in low gee. His graying hair stuck out on one side, drifting like lank seaweed. Eyes as brown as a bog regarded him half-lidded, while dry, thin fingers tapped restlessly on naked thighs. "I'm glad you ignored 'Lilah's advice regarding not talking to me."

"I didn't ignore it. I just didn't follow it." He shifted position as the transport took a sharp corner. "What do you want from me?"

"Nothing more than your attention."

"What for?"

"I'm a watcher," the man said. "I see lots of hidden things. Some are down deep, where no one thinks of looking; others are right out in the open, where no one notices. 'Lilah is good at finding the former, but she needs my help with the latter."

"I don't mean to be blunt, but it doesn't look like she wants your help at the moment."

Hurdowar grimaced, sending a landscape of wrinkles spreading across his face. "Ever, to be honest. It's frustrating. There are things she needs to know. I told her that you were coming, for instance. She's very fragile where you're concerned."

Eogan bit down on a sharp response. "Melilah is perfectly capable of looking after herself. She doesn't need you to do it for her."

"She can't watch everything." Hurdowar's lidded eyes were muddy and cool. "She's distracted."

By me, Eogan knew the man meant. And now Melilah had restricted Hurdowar's access to her. "You want me to pass something on to her, I suppose."

A nod sent lank hair waving. "Yes. Obviously you have your own secrets: the missing crew members, for instance. If she doesn't know about them already, then you can tell her in your own time. But there are other details. She needs to know about them, too."

"Like what?"

"The Occlusion observatory. It's very well defended, don't you think?"

"Yes. It would be."

"People remember Sublime and don't wonder that the Exarch is taking precautions."

Eogan frowned, wondering how much the man had guessed. "What's your point?"

"I've studied the design of the station—as much as I can, anyway. 'Lilah's Defiance group has some clever brains among them. They've noted details I couldn't work out on my own. But they haven't worked out what's wrong with them, why they don't make any sense."

"Go on."

"If Sublime is truly the Exarch's concern, why is the Occlusion so well protected from the *outside?*"

Eogan let the thought sink in before responding. "That *would* seem strange, I suppose."

"I've tried asking the Exarch about it, but he hasn't responded."

Of course not. "Perhaps your speculation is wrong. The level of technology is very high. Deangelis doesn't need to explain his actions to anyone."

"He should if the habitat is under threat."

"You really think that's likely?"

"*Likely* I don't know about. *Possible,* yes, I do."

Eogan pictured the colony pinched like a seed between thumb and forefinger, with the threat of the Occlusion itself on one side and something much more nebulous on the other. Who or what would attack the station? And, more importantly, why?

He couldn't think of an answer to the last question—at least not one he wanted to believe, anyway.

"I think you're barking up the wrong tree," he said. "But I hear you, and I'll keep it in mind."

Hurdowar looked resigned to getting no more than that from him. "I'll tell you if I find anything else. There's so much traffic coming in at the moment. There could be anything hidden in it all."

Eogan nodded. He had noticed that, too, before sleeping. One of the manifests had listed the Negotiator Select. If Palmer Christolphe was really in Bedlam, events were taking a truly significant turn.

"Just take it easy," he warned Hurdowar. "Melilah will know we've talked and what we've talked about. If your information is good, she'll listen eventually. Don't let it get personal is my advice to you. She doesn't owe you anything."

Hurdowar's pupils rolled back under his lids. "She's here now. She's listening to us."

"You'd better go, then," Eogan told him. "You're on probation, too, remember?"

The man winked out.

"You don't have to talk to him," Melilah said, her presence sliding into his like cream into coffee, audio only. "I already knew about the station—more or less. Something about it was bugging me. I would've worked it out."

"You're preaching to the choir, Mel."

"About our earlier conversation . . ." She hesitated, and he could tell that she wasn't being literal; she was referring to the fiche. "You mentioned a connection between—you know."

Clever, he thought. Eavesdroppers would think they were talking about each other, not the wormhole.

"I did."

"I don't think you're imagining things. There *is* a connection. But it looks like we disagree on what to do about it. You think it's a bad thing, that it's something we need to sever."

"Of course. Don't you?"

"Not in itself, no. It might even be a good thing. It might be just what I need to get myself out of a sticky situation."

He felt himself grow tight around his midsection. "I'm not sure I follow you." *I hope I don't, anyway.*

"There's a third party—someone whose attentions I'm trying to distance myself from. Do you know who I'm talking about?"

Not Gil Hurdowar, Eogan thought, although many people would assume so. *Exarch Deangelis. The Exarchate.*

"Yes," he said. "I think I do. But the means don't justify the end."

"The means are the whole point. And perhaps that's what you're *really* afraid of, Palmer Eogan. That the means might destroy your precious monopoly."

She was skating perilously close to openly stating the truth. He kept his voice calm and measured. "I'm not interested in monopolizing anything," he said. "I had my hands on it before anyone else here, but that doesn't make me its owner. If I'd wanted it for myself, I could've tried keeping it long before now. Do you think that would've worked? Do you think something like this *can* be owned?"

She was silent for a second. He wished he could see her face. God only knew what those listening in thought of the conversation.

"No," she said in the end. "But it can be *used.* I'd be irresponsible not to try."

"You're making a mistake," he said, feeling it in every artificial cell of his hollowed-out bones. "I came to you for help—not this."

"So we're at cross-purposes again. What's new about that?"

The conversation's sudden shift to old territory left him feeling as though the transport had fallen out from under him. "I'm sorry, Melilah."

"Don't start that again. Either help me get what I want, or stay the hell out of my way."

The line went silent. A transport whizzed by in the

opposite direction. Eogan glimpsed a pale, fair-haired face looking back at him and thought: the Exarch?

He shook his head, and wished again that he had never come to Bedlam. Nothing ever seemed to go right there.

+16

Melilah closed the connection to Eogan with the mental equivalent of a slammed-down headset. All her incoming lines failed with it, so she found herself in an illusory quiet, as though she was suddenly and completely alone.

You fucker! she wanted to yell. First he forced her into a position where she sounded like she wanted him back; then he deigned to judge her when he didn't like the conclusion she came to! She was infuriated. Of all people, he should have been sympathetic. He *owed* her!

She knew she was just being petulant, though. She had known in advance that he wouldn't approve of her opinion. He was a Palmer through and through. Anything that threatened the guild's cozy little hegemony was bound to upset him.

But that didn't stop her being disappointed. Part of her, so deep she hardly dared acknowledge it, had hoped that—

What? she asked herself. That they would overcome their differences and work together to cast the demon out of Bedlam? That they would gain access to the Occlusion and use it to strike back at the Exarchate? That wormhole technology would be the key to set humanity truly free? That they would reconcile their differences and give the relationship another go?

You fucker, she cursed again, but with resignation this time, rather than anger. *You screwed up my life once. You won't have me on your side, this time.*

She opened her inputs one by one, reconnecting herself to the constant ebb and flow of information through the station. She didn't need to be in her apartment to access the data. She simply preferred to do it the old-fashioned way as often as possible, without resorting to virtual overlays and other synesthetic means. It wasn't that she was afraid of forgetting what was fake and what was real; she just didn't like fake very much.

For several years she had studied origami, the ancient Japanese art of folding paper, partly as a mathematical exercise but also to clear her mind. She could have fed the patterns into an assembler and had a machine create the finished product for her, with every fold crisp and clean, every point as sharp as a stiletto, but that wasn't the issue. The process was what was relevant, the *experience* of doing it herself. It was the same with the tunnels of Bedlam: she could have sent a remote into the pipes as easily as gone herself; it would've shown her as much detail as her flesh-and-blood senses could retrieve, maybe even more. But it wouldn't have been *her* doing it, and that meant something—to her, if no one else.

When she thought of the Exarchate ruling her home, her gut recoiled just as it did at the thought of using a machine to make a Hojyu ammonite or a simple *yuan bao*. The means might not justify the end, as Eogan had said, but without the right means the end was simply irrelevant.

The Mizar Occlusion could be the key to Bedlam's cage. A wormhole through space offered a way of not just communicating faster than light, but actually traveling between the colonies with greater swiftness than anything the Exarchate could manage. A resistance movement could sweep around the Arc Circuit—indeed, through the entire human territories—in hours, always one step ahead of their oppressors. Ditching it in deep space—as Eogan seemed to wish he'd done—would be as bad as rolling over and accepting Sol's domination.

Yes, there were complications: the real dangers of the wormhole throat for one, and the more nebulous threat of the Sublime Catastrophe for another. But to give up without even *trying?* She wouldn't have it.

She called up a grid showing the location of the Exarch as a series of points plotted on a three-dimensional map of the habitat. Exarch Deangelis was unusually dispersed; he normally kept to himself in a deep section of the habitat, coming out only as required to deal with people face-to-face. Speculation occasionally flared that he kept some sort of secret hideout there, a high-tech retreat for all the many parts of him, but no one had ever confirmed the hypothesis.

Now, Deangelis was crawling over the habitat like a swarm of ants. His deceptively youthful face was everywhere: cruising the pipes, talking to vendors and scientists, in meetings with specialists. One was sitting in a bar in Albert Hall, drinking wine with an imposing white-haired man listed on the public register as a visitor to the station. *Fiddling while Rome burned,* she thought.

Two in tandem were meeting to discuss trade agreements with Palmer Christophe. The Negotiator Select bristled with high-tech modifications, many of them hidden from the visible spectrum. To a casual glance, he was a solidly built man with no body hair at all and striking orange eyes, dressed in a garment that clenched and unclenched around him like a fist. Microwave links cast a complex web from transmitters on every exposed patch of skin. Delicate-looking fan-shaped field effects fluttered all over his infrared body, their purpose unknown.

"We were unprepared for Sublime," he was saying. A chirruping electronic chorus enhanced his words, making sure his audience captured every possible nuance. Subtitles described his tone as conciliatory but firm. "The ROTH artifact found there took us by surprise. In retrospect, we should have expected such an event before long. There is much in the Dark that has not yet been charted."

The Dark was Palmer slang for the gulf between stars. Melilah could accept the Negotiator Select's point. Inhabited systems and trade lanes comprised a very small percentage of the total volume of space over which humanity claimed dominion.

"I'm sure you do not deliberately discount the loss of life in White-Elderton colony," said one of the two identical Deangelises facing Palmer Christophe. His tone was biting, no doubt also protesting the use of the pre-Exarchate name of the destroyed system. "That, not scientific or technological gain, is our prime consideration."

"Yes, yes." The Negotiator Select waved away the concern with a gesture. His hands, Melilah noted, had no fingernails. "But we must consider all outcomes when anticipating future developments. You have another ROTH artifact in your custody now. Its origins are similarly unknown."

"That is public knowledge."

"Indeed, but precious little else is. The Palmers would like access to your discoveries, when and as you make them. We are prepared to pay well for such access."

"It is not mine to sell. The information belongs to all humanity."

"But while access is limited, as of the moment, it is tradable."

"Access to data is a right in this system, not a privilege."

"Then why have you released none to those in your charge? You cannot expect us to believe that you have had this thing in your possession for two days and uncovered nothing at all!"

"What I have uncovered is mysterious even to me. That's why I've asked the science officer of the *Nhulunbuy* to assist me. What information we find she will be free to share as she sees fit."

Christolphe's smooth brow creased. "This is a circuitous route toward disclosure. I fail to see the necessity of it."

"And I see no reason to explain myself to you. Our existing agreement has sufficed for thirty-eight years. You haven't offered me a reason to change it now."

Melilah watched with detached amusement as the Exarch stonewalled Palmer Christolphe at every turn. The Palmers were going to get nothing out of Deangelis, just as she had got nothing out of him in the past. He was using the same technique on the Negotiator Select as he had on her. Moving his point of view constantly between identical bodies was distracting. Christolphe, who should have been used to occupying a room with cloned individuals, seemed disconcerted by the constantly changing spokesperson.

Two members of the Palmer's bodyguard stood behind him, listening patiently to the exchange. The clane—a neologism combining "clade" and "clan" with "clone" to describe something that hadn't existed until two centuries earlier, and still wasn't a common variant of humanity—consisted of twelve women of average height, each with the same pointed features and muscular forms, each dressed in identical all-encasing light armor that faded to transparent over face and hands. Slight bulges at thigh and waist hinted at concealed weapons. Grown from the same seed body and imprinted with the same reflexes and personality, their minds operated in perfect tandem, thinking the same thoughts and responding to the same stimuli. The clane was in effect a single person with twelve pairs of eyes, twenty-four hands—and eleven extra lives.

Melilah didn't like them. They made her uncomfortable. The particularly sharp purple of their armor made her eyes want to itch. The remaining ten were, like Deangelis, spread out over the habitat, going about their business with serious, impenetrable expressions. They gave away nothing that was going on in their combined heads.

She sent her point of view upward, out of the habitat to where the *Nhulunbuy* was parked nearby. One of the components was missing, supporting Deangelis's claim that Eogan's science officer had joined the investigation of the Occlusion. She was annoyed at herself for missing that. As much as it galled her to admit it, Gil Hurdowar was right: she *was* distracted. At any other time she would have been taking advantage of the numerous newcomers filling the systems—the Cells, the Negotiator Select and his clanes, the Occlusion itself—to go data-hunting. In all the chaos, all sorts of fragments would be cast adrift, deleted improperly, or simply forgotten. This should have been an opportunity, not an impediment.

Her daily alarm rang to remind her of her memory exercises. She ignored it. *Stuck in the past,* she told herself. That was as dangerous as forgetting.

It had been just two days since she'd last gone gleaning through the deeper tunnels. It felt like weeks. She uncased her crawl-suit and enjoyed the tingling, faintly erotic sensation as it swarmed up over her legs and torso, then down her arms. She had no specific target in mind, but that didn't matter. It was the journey that counted, not the destination; the search, not the rescue.

And maybe, she thought, it was time to pay the Exarch a visit on *his* territory, for a change.

Isaac Deangelis had never claimed to read minds, but he had a very real ability to decipher the signals passing between them.

The clane's thoughts were highly encoded, sweeping constantly from brainpan to brainpan. The two with Christolphe exchanged frequent packets of information with the other ten. Managing so much additional sensory input required considerable sophistication. Signal processing between the twelve bodies, in order to present the illusion of a single self, was a deeply demanding task. A clane, unlike him, was therefore inherently fragile. Disrupt the signals between its bodies, and the illusion would collapse; likewise when separated by more than a few kilometers, so signal lags could accumulate.

Encoded and complex though its thoughts might be, Deangelis could tell that it was waiting for something. A signal of some kind. A sign. Its mind stirred restlessly in its many homes. It was nervous.

Perhaps Palmer Christolphe thought the endless rights negotiations sufficient to distract him from his vigilance. If so, he was going to be disappointed. For whatever reason he had brought the clane to the habitat, Deangelis was watching them both very closely indeed. On top of everything else.

There's a storm coming . . .

"Okay, I'm in." The voice came from Palmer Vermeulen, within the Occlusion observatory. Her integration within the station's infrastructure was complete. "Can you hear me, Flast? Eogan?"

Replies came immediately from the *Nhulunbuy* and the

habitat, confirming the connection. Eyes from all over the system were drawn to the exchange.

"Deangelis is as good as his word," she said. "I have access to all the raw data I want."

"That's—pleasing," said Palmer Eogan. Deangelis could tell that he meant *surprising*.

"There's a lot of it," she said, her enthusiasm not matching his. "He's using instruments I'm not sure I even understand. It's going to take me a while to work out what's going on."

A while was an understatement, Exarch Deangelis thought. He doubted a single human, even a Palmer, could penetrate in less than a month the vast amounts of data he had collected so far. And more came in every second.

"Perhaps you can understand, now, why I have been slow releasing it," he said to all of them. "This is no simple skull we're investigating. I am following a carefully coordinated approach, examining every iota of knowledge gained along the way. I do not wish to replicate mistakes that have been made in the past."

That, at least, was the utter truth. He didn't want Lut-Deangelis to vanish in a hellstorm of alien replicators any more than they did. But at the same time he wasn't afraid to tread where Jane Elderton had tripped ten years earlier. He wasn't going to skirt around the edge and let such a pristine opportunity pass him by. Lut-Deangelis was in the thick of things, not out on the Exarchate's frontier.

"I understand." Eogan granted him that much with barely a hint of disapproval. The transport the Palmer occupied was winding its way to the surface of the habitat, heading for the hopper he had arrived in.

Leaving so soon? he thought to himself with a hint of satisfaction. Things obviously hadn't gone so well between the estranged lovers.

Remembering Awad, he checked her location and found her back in the tunnels at the heart of the station. Gleaning again. Running away from reality.

Hails drained his glass and locked it into place on the arm of his low-gee chair.

"Well," he said, clapping his hands down on his thighs, "that's the wine-tasting done with. Unless you've got something else to say, Isaac, there are a number of sights I haven't caught yet. Might as well make the effort while there's time, eh?"

"The art gallery would be my next recommendation," Deangelis said. "You'll find the low-gee environment very congenial to sculpture and dance. In fact, at thirty o'clock there's a performance of—"

He stopped when movement at the periphery of his vision caught his attention.

"Yes?" prompted Hails.

"Wait." Instruments swung around to focus on the globular cluster 47 Tucanae. Emissions on several spectra were flaring. Something was breaking cover.

Hails followed his shift in focus. "Ah. It's begun, then."

The part of him sitting opposite Lazarus Hails looked up sharply. His many hearts beat faster. "What do you know about this?"

"Only what I've told you, my friend." The statesmanlike presence rose to his feet and made to move off. "Don't say I didn't try."

"Where do you think you're going?"

Hails shrugged. "Elsewhere."

A cloud of gleaming, darting shapes boiled out of 47 Tucanae, expanding as it approached the habitat. Instruments scattered across the system rapidly triangulated on the cloud. Its distance was a little under twenty million kilometers, its speed appreciable—nearly twenty percent light. The cloud was not solid right through, consisting of numerous small projectiles that left brilliant drive flames in their wakes.

Missiles—many, many thousands of them aimed squarely at the habitat—and due to arrive in less than a minute!

Deangelis's reaction was automatic. He sounded impact alarms through all quarters. Pressure doors irised shut in slow motion, dividing the habitat into numerous small sections. He set up pressure differentials to encourage people to move into safer locations. All external operations were halted immediately. Cells and other vessels were advised to move clear as a matter of some urgency. Thrusters on the Occlusion observatory nudged it deeper into the shadow of PARASOL. Defenses swung around to bear on the attack.

He broadcast a message to the aggressor requesting an immediate cessation of hostilities. He hid nothing from the occupants of the habitat. They heard his words over all channels, in all quarters. He was speaking on their behalf, not just his own.

Whoever you are, he wanted to shout, *you're not going to get away with this.*

The reply, when it came, was unexpected.

A hand tapped him on his shoulder. He didn't need to turn to see who it belonged to. Cameras throughout Ormerod's wine bar gave him an excellent view of the clane, one part thereof, standing stiffly behind the couch on which he sat.

"Don't mess with what you don't understand."

The words came from every mouth of the clane at once, wherever they happened to be. Somehow, without him noticing, it had positioned itself near eleven of him across the habitat.

"Consider this a warning, Isaac Deangelis."

The explosions—twelve of them in perfect synchrony—tore the clane to atoms, and took a large chunk of the Exarch with them.

18

Eogan felt the transport kick under him. The Scale-Free Bedlam feed dissolved into chaos.

"What the hell's happening?" he asked his Cellmates, feeling abruptly cut off from the world. He'd been just moments from reaching his hopper when pressure doors had closed around him, cutting him off. His complaints had gone without response.

"Something's going down," said Flast, his voice distorted by unusual interference. There seemed to be several of him all talking at once, all slightly off-key. "You heard the Exarch warn off whoever's attacking?"

"Yes."

"We're picking up explosions from inside Bedlam, although the missiles are still a good half minute off. Hang on. I'll see if we can get you some telemetry"

One half minute, Eogan thought to himself. That was barely long enough to quibble over. There were going to be many more explosions if the things hit.

"Okay," said Flast. "Here it comes."

It felt as though a third eye had opened. Where a moment ago there had been nothing but the inside of the transport and chaotic voices, now clarity bloomed. He saw raw data from numerous viewpoints, rotated a logarithmic diagram of the space around the habitat, and charted the precise location of every component of the *Nhulunbuy,* including N-11 inside the Occlusion observatory. The Cell was relatively safe, not the sitting target Bedlam made. The incoming missiles were tipped with blood red, growing rapidly closer.

Eogan snapped through dozens of internal views in less

than a second, seeking the source of the explosions. He saw eleven locations in all, ranging from secure meeting rooms to public places. A bar in Albert Hall was the most chaotic. A black shield had dropped around the locus of the blast, containing it to just a few dozen cubic meters. That was enough, though, to fill the air with smoke and blackened fragments, billowing about in free fall. Several bystanders had sustained minor injuries, one a tall man with hair burned completely away. Their blood added to spilled wine in a terrible floating cocktail. It would take hours to settle.

"Any casualties?" he asked, thinking but not daring to say: *Melilah!*

"Palmer Christolphe was in the thick of it. We're not getting a signal from him anymore." Flast hesitated a beat. "You've got bigger things to worry about, boss. There's something coming in the wake of those missiles. Something big. If the Exarch's defenses are sloppy, you're going to end up looking like a colander."

"Right." Fed up with waiting, Eogan ordered the transport hatch open and kicked himself out of it. He wasn't going to sit still while the world fell apart around him. And he wasn't going to let a nonintervention agreement or two stop him from doing what he needed to do. His left arm was already rearranging itself as he reached the pressure door. It took just three seconds to analyze what the door was made of, determine the best means of cutting through, configure his hand into the appropriate tool, and start drilling. Ten seconds after that, he was on the far side.

Red warning lights flashed in his wake. He ignored them. The view through the telemetry feed was dismaying. The missiles were just moments away, and still nothing had come forward to meet them. He cursed his sluggish body—which wasn't *in toto* anywhere near as fast as its individual components—as he hurried to the hopper bays. He didn't care what he found at the dock; he would appropriate whatever would do the job. He just wanted to get out of what might soon become a floating coffin and get to where he could do some good.

Even as he hurried, his mind reached behind him, into the habitat, looking for Melilah Awad. The feed was still jumbled and chaotic, but not nearly as bad as it had been. Her apartment was empty. She had last been noted traveling the depths of the habitat. Her present location was unknown.

"Keep your head down, Mel," he said, although he knew she couldn't hear him. "I'll be back for you as soon as I can."

19

Melilah had barely reached the lower levels when the alert sounded. The sirens were piercing, unfamiliar. Their whooping shrieks echoed through the pipes of Bedlam like the cries of deep-sea beasts. It took her a second to interpret them. She hadn't heard their particular signature since the Exarchate Expansion, forty years earlier.

Bedlam was under attack!

She kicked herself forward, carried by a wind that seemed to spring up out of nowhere. Although she was deep in the habitat, she wouldn't be completely safe until she left the pipes. Seismic shocks could propagate unpredictably through the complex tangles of the habitat, snapping links where the pressure waves overlapped and reinforced.

Caught up in her own emergency, she barely had a chance to note what was going on outside. Something about missiles. The Exarch was calling for a cessation in hostilities.

Then the feed abruptly died, and it felt for a moment as though Bedlam died with it. The wind carrying her blew itself out. Silence enfolded her. With no voice and no nervous system, the habitat was drifting through space, derelict.

An icy river of fear swept through her. Had a new Catastrophe struck already? Were swarms of alien replicators already burrowing down to her level, devouring everything she loved with deadly voraciousness?

The reason for the wind's sudden cessation became apparent when she reached the end of the pipe. The way was sealed shut, clenched tightly ahead of her like a hose with a knot in it. She turned back the way she had come, hoping the other end was still open. If it wasn't, she would be trapped.

The feed flickered halfheartedly, granting her frustratingly incomplete glimpses of fires and blood. Explosions. She had felt nothing. She was cut off, irrelevant. Melilah cursed the urge to go deep right when she was needed most!

The pipe curved around to her right. The exit, if it was still open, lay some distance away. She kicked herself along it as fast as she could—so fast she swept by a tunnel mouth almost before she had seen it.

She reached out for the pipe wall and spun herself around. Her inner ears protested. The junction hadn't been there moments before; she was sure of it. It wasn't on the map, either. But it was open and offered an alternate escape route.

A youthful, blond face appeared from the opening. "Awad, get in here," said the Exarch. "There's not much time."

Deangelis's expression was grim. Were they tears drying on his cheeks? She swallowed her surprise and did as she was told.

Following him along a short tunnel that was barely wide enough for her to crouch in, she entered a large chamber shaped like an oval sombrero: fat in the middle and thin around the edges. They emerged to one side of the central bulge, where she was confronted by no less than ten identical versions of the Exarch apart from the one who had called her by name.

"Where am I?" she asked, looking around in amazement.

"Somewhere you're not supposed to be," said the nearest Deangelis. He shook his head. "You of all people, now of all times."

A jet of foam struck her from the ceiling, forcing her to the ground. She struggled against the enfolding whiteness but was soon enveloped.

"Wait!" she cried, despairing as the secret chamber disappeared from her sight. "You can't—"

She got no further. The foam tightened around her, and everything went black.

+20

Deangelis knew suffering of a sort he had never experienced before. In all his years of life, spread out over many bodies and experiencing time as a flexible thing, able to creep and race at will, no part of him had ever unwillingly died. From Sol to Hipparcos 62512, the system he now called home, he had only ever grown in complexity and vitality. Apart from those who had sacrificed themselves to explore the Occlusion, he had never been reduced.

Until now.

Don't mess with what you don't understand.

The moment the clane had confronted him, its blank expressions more revealing than its words, he had sensed what was coming. A quick scan revealed how their interiors had reorganized themselves into chemical explosives powerful enough to take a significant chunk out of the station. His mind had raced, seeking an explanation, even as more immediate reflexes kicked into play. What good would it do to destroy part of him? Why have two bodies in one place and singletons elsewhere? Who had sent it?

Consider this a warning—

Unlike the clane, his individual bodies didn't need light armor to protect themselves. There were more subtle methods available to him within the habitat. But protecting *him* wasn't his first concern. There were people all around him: Lazarus Hails and Palmer Christolphe were just two among many innocent bystanders who would be killed if the bombs were allowed to explode unchecked. He couldn't let that happen. The care of his citizens was ingrained into him from birth. His multifaceted, robust existence could tolerate an excision or two, but theirs could not.

—Isaac Deangelis.

Not "Exarch" or "Exarch Deangelis." The message came from someone confident enough to address him by his full name. Even as complex shields expanded to enfold him and the clane in a fatal embrace, his thoughts stuck on the mystery: *Why me? Why now?*

The matter of the missiles went completely forgotten as the clane blew itself up and part of him died with it.

He felt—violated. Someone had reached into his living mind and torn a piece out of it. The physical pain was over in an instant and paled in comparison to what was to follow. The dynamic equilibrium of his thoughts shattered like a chandelier in a hail of bullets. What had been for sixty-four Sol years an effortless, vibrant symphony of existence suddenly became a dissonant nightmare. He shrieked and vanished into the discord.

For the first time since his birth, the greater version of him lost consciousness.

Into that fragmentation stepped Melilah Awad. The individual parts of him remained conscious and active. Earth-Deangelis, deep in the heart of the habitat, felt his higher self slough from him like a dream and found himself suddenly weeping with his siblings. It was hard to remember what had happened. One moment they had been an Exarch, their thoughts combined in a magnificent, vibrant wave form; the next they were detached, unraveled, dislocated.

They were still connected, however. Earth-Deangelis could tell what the others felt and thought. He could reach out and touch the survivors elsewhere in the station. All was not yet lost.

They assembled a clumsy facsimile of what they had once been. Io-Deangelis oversaw the habitat's defense mechanisms, swinging powerful X-ray batteries to bear on the incoming missiles and firing clouds of particulate debris into their path. Triton-Deangelis began reconnecting communication channels severed by the explosions.

Charon-Deangelis checked the status of the Occlusion observatory and found it to be unharmed.

Earth-Deangelis took charge of the habitat's evacuation
and safety procedures. Most people had been swept into
the chambers by the safety winds and their own need to
hurry. All knew that an emergency was in progress and
willingly complied with his instructions. He helped a number of stragglers to the bunkers, following his innate reflex
to protect his charges.

When he found Melilah Awad caught in a pipe just meters from him, he wished he could shut down that reflex for
a moment and let her take her chances.

But that wasn't an option. The missiles were just seconds away. He couldn't risk the possibility that she might
perish when they struck. Opening a concealed entrance
from the pipe to his secret retreat was as easy as shutting
down the security monitors tracking her. If she lived to tell
the tale, there would be no evidence to back her up.

"Awad, get in here. There's not much time."

For a moment he thought she was going to resist, but her
instinct for self-preservation soon kicked in.

What had happened to *his?* he wondered. For all he
knew, she had been involved in the attack. She and Defiance could have conspired with someone out-system to
ferry the clane into position, using the Negotiator Select as
an innocent courier. She could have been coming to him to
deliver the final hammerblow, and he had just led her into
his very heart!

No. A quick check of her body revealed no sign of explosives or replicators. Nothing that could harm him. If she had
treachery in mind, it was of a sort he couldn't recognize.

She protested as antiaccelerant foam pinned her to the
floor, but he didn't have time for niceties. The missiles
were almost upon them, and not even Io-Deangelis's best
efforts could keep all of them at bay.

There was something riding the wake of the missiles,
obscured by their energetic afterwash. This, he assumed,
was the main thrust of the attack. No matter what happened

in the next few seconds, the worst of it was still to come.

Lasers flashed. The habitat shook like a living thing. Earth-Deangelis tucked himself into a ball and rolled with the quake. The loss of his higher self was a pain greater than any the attack offered. Alone, just one among many, he rode out the attack as best he could.

21

Eogan burst out of the dock in a stolen hopper. In one sense, he couldn't have chosen a worse possible time to launch. Missiles burst like fireworks in the skies of Bedlam, sending streaks of particulate debris in all directions. High-energy collisions created secondary explosions everywhere he looked. It was impossible to avoid them all. He felt sharp stings in shoulder and knee as shrapnel left fiery tracks through him, barely deflected by his flesh and the substance of the hopper. He flinched but didn't worry overmuch; his most delicate areas were resistant to particle strikes at high velocity, designed to tolerate the dangers of near-light travel in deep space; he doubted that anything here could come close to such energies.

Still, there was the hopper to think about. Its workings suffered from the battering. Fighting unreliable controls, Eogan guided it up into the burning heavens, to where the *Nhulunbuy* awaited him.

"Can you hear me, Palmer Flast?"

Data struggled to rise above the fierce crackling noise of combat. "—clear, boss."

"Send N-6 down to pick me up." Sparks sprayed from the hopper's port flank as another missile fragmented nearby. "I don't think I'm going to get much farther than this."

"Confirmed. Hold tight. We're on our—"

Flast's voice dissolved into a squeal of static. The sky lit up in an insane mural of overlapping razor-thin rays and spirals. Eogan felt as though he was trapped in a cloud chamber, the target of a cyclotron's devastating energies.

It was hard to see or sense anything—and it occurred to him then that this was exactly how it was supposed to be. The missiles disintegrated in just the right way to inhibit most forms of near-habitat transport and telemetry. As long as the pounding continued, Bedlam was effectively blind and impotent.

While that realization offered him some hope for the habitat's immediate survival, it also opened another avenue of worry. The thing coming in the wake of the missiles was effectively hidden from sight. It could be anything. Any sense of relief was premature.

The hopper lurched. He literally reached into its stricken circuitry, dissolving his right arm and seeping through cracks in the internal shell, in order to give it a few more moments of functionality. Electronic storms swept along their melded structures; he tasted ozone and melting plastic. He pictured the hopper as a burning terrestrial biplane tracing out a graceful arc through the air, doomed to intersect with the Earth below. Again, he could survive such a collision with Bedlam, but it certainly wasn't optimal. He would be stuck there, a harder target for the *Nhulunbuy* to collect and wedded to a much easier target for whatever was coming.

The particulate storm eased up long enough for him to see a mirror-finished sphere swoop alongside him. He fought the bucking of the hopper, trying to match trajectories, then gave up and simply rammed the Cell component broadside. The mirror finish parted smoothly. Complex engines absorbed his momentum and brought him to a gentle halt. Darkness and silence enfolded him.

He retracted his right arm and forced back the blackened, crackling shell of the hopper. The electroactive womb of the Cell fell over him as the component accelerated away from the surface of Bedlam. The tangle of missile fragments and debris resolved into something much more comprehensible.

The first wave of missiles had entirely disintegrated two kilometers from the surface of the habitat. A second wave, tucked in behind the first, had had more luck reaching its target. Two shallow but large craters gaped in the habitat's midsections, jetting white smoke into the void. Furious nanofacturing showed in infrared around the crater rims as the habitat's living skin tried to seal the breaches. Other, smaller hot spots pockmarked the surface from pole to pole. Seething chain reactions swept like lateral lightning bolts where aggressive replicators fought the local defenses, leaving blackened, dead habitat skin in its wake.

A third wave of missiles sliced in from the sky. Needle-tipped at both ends and as reflective as the *Nhulunbuy*, these weren't designed to fragment.

"Penetrators," said Flast, confirming his diagnosis.

"How many?"

"Five hundred-plus."

"Risk to us?"

"Minimal. Bedlam's a different story. Deangelis's reactions are—surprisingly—no better than ours, and we're not guarding a thing the size of the habitat. Some are bound to get through. Hopefully he's more capable on the ground."

Eogan hoped so, too. "We'll have to help, just in case he isn't."

"I knew you were going to say that."

"You disagree?" He could tell from the telemetry that the other Cells parked around the habitat had made for safer locations rather than get involved.

"Not emphatically." Flast hesitated, as though debating how honestly he could speak. "I question what difference we can make on such a scale. It's not as if we have much training in this sort of thing."

"Good point. For a second I thought you might be questioning my motives."

"I've served with you long enough to know that you wouldn't put the *Nhulunbuy*'s safety ahead of any one person's," he returned soberly. "Not unnecessarily, anyway."

Eogan smiled. "That's good. Because I *am* concerned about Melilah, and I need you to tell me if my judgment is compromised."

"Trust me. The first opportunity I get to take charge, you'll know about it."

Eogan settled back into a hastily morphed flight chair as N-6 powered away from Bedlam to where the rest of the Cell awaited it above. The shell of the hopper crumpled and vanished into the interior bulkhead, its molecules destined for recycling in the component's complex guts.

22

Melilah woke to the hissing of rain. The sound brought back memories of her earliest years of life, on the colony world called Little Red. She had lived there with her mother until ten years of age; and she retained little more of that time than the sound of water falling freely from the sky. There was no precipitation on Bedlam, and low-gee fountains were a poor substitute. Sometimes, late at night, she would float in the darkness and imagine what it had been like to hear rain hitting a metal roof. A gentle wistfulness would envelop her, for both the lost sound and the mother she'd lost in a spacing accident when she was ten years old. She'd never even had the chance to see their new home in Bedlam.

Bedlam . . .

Melilah twitched against the restraining foam holding her still, memories of where she was—and why—overriding any regrets from the past.

"Let me out of here!" Her voice was muffled but loud enough. "Deangelis, you son of a bitch! What the hell is going on?"

The white foam parted. The Exarch's fresh-faced visage leaned into the gap. His blond hair hung in disarray; a bruise was forming on one cheek.

"I am genuinely sorry to inconvenience you," he said. "I did so only for your well-being."

She didn't believe him at first, but as tattered threads of the Scale-Free Bedlam feed wound themselves around her, the truth began to grow clear. Bedlam had been attacked—and was, in fact, still under fire. Penetrator missiles, a meter long and barely a millimeter wide, were slicing like deadly rain from the hostile sky.

Not aliens, then.

The relief was fleeting. She had seen such things before.

"You've got to let me go."

"You're safer here, Melilah."

"I don't care. This is my home, for Christ's sake! I have to help defend it!"

Deangelis pulled back. His expression lacked its usual smug self-assurance. She remembered seeing tear tracks on his cheeks, and wondered if that could possibly have been real.

"Please," she entreated him.

He nodded. "Very well, Melilah. Our objectives are, for the moment, the same."

His sudden backing down surprised her. She began to shake as the foam retreated completely. The floor trembled beneath her, and the air had an acrid smell to it.

Deangelis helped her to her feet once her legs were free. There were at least a dozen Deangelises standing in the curving, hidden space, milling protectively around a glowing object in the center of the room. It looked like a crystal sarcophagus.

"You'll need this," said the first Deangelis, pressing a small, sharp-pointed object into her hand. She went to look at it, but it had already dissolved into her skin. Uncertainty, a sudden feeling that she had done the wrong thing, made her pull away from him.

"What is it?" she asked, as a strange high swept through her, much faster than any chemical drug. "What the hell have you done to me?"

"Made you sufficient." He turned her and propelled her toward the door. "Do not return here."

"But—" The force of his push was sufficient to carry her clear through the portal. By the time she'd tugged herself to a halt, the entrance was gone.

"Damn you," she hissed under her breath. The tingling had spread to the back of her eyes. Images appeared in her forward vision, overlaid across a map of the habitat. Bright sparks flared into life in the upper levels, and she instinctively—the instinct granted via the nanoware graft Deangelis had given her—knew that these were places the penetrators had broken through.

She kicked herself along the pipe, trying to ignore the way it vibrated under her palms and soles. Fragmentation bombs were designed to cut communications and keep mundane vessels grounded; penetrators were commonly used to breach interplanetary cargo vessels. Everything, therefore, pointed to a takeover, not a wipeout. The origin of the takeover was unknown but not presently relevant. Repelling the invasion was the main thing. They could assign blame later.

A high-speed transport awaited her at its far end. She slid smoothly into it and let its electric engine hurry her away.

"Yasu?" Communications within the habitat were severely curtailed, but it seemed the Exarch had granted her priority. Melilah's four-daughter responded almost immediately.

"Oh, Grandmother Mel, you're back! We were so worried."

"I'm *back*? What are you talking about? I never went away."

"You dropped completely off the system. We didn't know where you were. We thought—well, it didn't look good, given what was going on. Palmer Eogan was nowhere around this time."

Off the system . . . Melilah momentarily regretted leaving the Exarch's secret space so soon. Where exactly had she been?

"Never mind about me," she said. "I'm okay. But what about you? Where are you? Are you safe?"

"I'm in a shelter on Granovetter. There are lots of people here. It's kind of exciting—like a drill, but we know it's for real. Things got bumpy for a while there; we've all got bruises. What's happening out there? It's hard to tell with the network so patchy."

Melilah did her best to bring her four-daughter up to

speed, knowing that anyone who could would be listening in. It was important to her that the citizens of Bedlam were kept in the loop—even if, in the end, she could share only her own fragmentary knowledge with them. The Exarch was either unwilling or unable to do it for them.

"An invasion?" Yasu sounded almost scandalized, rather than concerned. *Kind of exciting,* she had said. She was too young to remember the Exarchate Expansion and the last time the shelters had been used. "Who would invade us? We're not a threat to anyone."

"Not normally, no." Melilah thought of the Mizar Occlusion and wondered at how quickly things could change. The transport passed through a rapid series of junctions, choosing routes with unaffected ease despite the occasional lack of lighting and clouds of acrid smoke.

"Stay exactly where you are," she told Yasu. "Wait for the all clear before coming out. Let as many people as you can know what's going on. I can't come join you right now, but I will as soon as I can."

"What will you do, Grandmother Mel?"

She had been pondering this question while they talked. The answer was obvious, and deceptively simple. "I'm going to help."

Melilah disconnected from Yasu and called the members of Defiance.

23

I'm still here.

Flickers of consciousness returned to the higher Deangelis as his many parts strove individually to repel the invasion. Sense of selfhood came and went in an overwhelming torrent of information. He clutched each brief awakening as a person struggling to swim through rapids gulped for air when he or she surfaced.

What the hell happened?

He knew the answer to that question: brain damage. The clane had destroyed one fifth of his individual selves. Repair took time, required rapid reorganization of his remaining resources. His return was fragile, patchwork, impromptu—and delayed.

Someone had knocked him out of the picture long enough for penetrators to reach the habitat. Dozens of the invasive needles had struck external levels and flattened like old-fashioned bullets as momentum carried them deep inside. Nanotech swarms attacked the outer layers of the projectiles, but were unable to reach the crucial cores in time. Such defenses were deactivated automatically when the penetrators reached inhabited areas lest they cause injury to bystanders. Lumps of red-hot quicksilver dropped from ceilings in widely scattered pipes and chambers. Barely had they hit the ground when the cores unraveled, revealing their deadly payloads.

Deangelis snarled to see them. Tiny in size but rich with malevolence, the invaders were programmed solely to destroy. Ranging in size from the nanoscale to a grain of sand, they swarmed over and through anything that got in their way. Breeder factories produced new breeders every ten reproductions, ensuring the plague spread rapidly. If the incursion sites weren't sealed soon, the habitat would soon be overcome.

Not incursion, he corrected himself. *Infection.* The habitat quivered around him like a feverish child. Its ancient mind was too primitive to interact meaningfully with his, but he could feel it reacting to what was going on. It was *hurting.*

The worst thing about it was that he could do little to help it. The habitat's own defenses, and those of its inhabitants, were better equipped to handle localized attacks within the habitat's many spaces. He could only direct them from above, and assist where he could. Earth-Deangelis's instinct to help Melilah Awad had been a good one. Already she and the Defiance movement were mobilizing to locate and isolate infection sites in their area. Evacuating people was a priority, followed by severing each location from the rest of the habitat, so the infection couldn't spread. If the infection couldn't be destroyed *in situ,* it would be kept isolated for later expulsion.

What was happening in the skies concerned Exarch Deangelis more. The deadly rain had allowed something much more sinister to approach the habitat. With data limited from sources outside the habitat by continuing fragmentation interference, he couldn't get a clear look at the thing. It blocked the stars behind it with silent, ominous menace, an inky black shape growing larger with every second.

Only as a sheer mass of fragmentary data accumulated, and as his many fragments coalesced once again into a whole, did he realize that this new arrival wasn't aimed at the habitat at all.

It was heading for the Mizar Occlusion.

Ice spread through him. Every one of his minds turned their attention to this new development. He reached out for the fragments of him working in the observatory. It was still tucked safely under the protective umbrella of PARA-SOL, forgotten in the opening salvos. There were five of him there, intermittently connected to the greater him. They realized as soon as the rest of him did that they were the true focus of the attack, not the habitat at all. Everything—the fragmentation, the penetrators—was designed simply to grant the invader access to the observatory.

I won't allow it, he thought with furious resolve. This was his system, his prize, and he wasn't about to let anybody take either of them away from him . . .

As the battle for the habitat waged on, he sent a priority signal to the observatory, activating its defenses.

24

"It's a Reaper," said Flast. "A big one."

Eogan closed his eyes and let the grim data flow through him.

The black shape riding the tail of the penetrators flickered in and out of view, its signature masked by interference from the stricken habitat. When visible, its silhouette was jaggedly geometric, like a spider or a multiarmed robot; the *Nhulunbuy*'s instruments put its size at somewhere between five hundred meters and one kilometer across; the forces propelling it were carefully shielded, making them especially difficult to pin down.

"I thought they were all decommissioned after the Expansion," Eogan said.

"Apparently not. Or someone built a new one."

Eogan expelled a breath in frustration. "Either way, it's not good news."

"It gets worse." Flast's voice threaded the data like a black ribbon, tying it into a new shape. "My best guess is that it's heading for the Occlusion observatory, not Bedlam."

Eogan studied the telemetry from this perspective. The evidence was inconclusive but compelling. It also necessitated a change of plans. He didn't know what use the *Nhulunbuy* was going to be against a Reaper, but he couldn't in good conscience leave Vermeulen in its path without trying to help.

"We have to split the Cell," he said.

"That makes sense: half for the habitat, half for the station. I suppose you'll take the half to Bedlam."

Eogan took a split second to examine both his instincts

and what was best for the situation. They conflicted, which was a sure sign that he should tread carefully. His concern for not just Melilah but for Luisa and James Pirelli as well was particularly keen.

"Actually, I think I should take the Occlusion run," he said. "It's my fault Vermeulen got mixed up in this, and it's therefore my job to make sure she's okay."

"You want me to take the Bedlam run?" If Flast was surprised, it didn't show.

Eogan grunted acknowledgment. "Do what you can to help. I don't know how messy things will be. Find Melilah and do as she says. If you can't find her . . ." He hesitated, remembering how she had dropped off the scopes last time he'd looked for her. "Just use your judgment. And keep in contact as best you can."

They split the remaining crew down the middle. Although not strictly designed for combat, the Cell wouldn't look out of place on a battlefield. What it lacked in dedicated armaments it more than made up for in other ways. There was no need to divide the components up according to mass or resources, since they were naturally flexible. Flast could convert his allotment into dozens of pip-sized baubles, if he wanted to, while Eogan configured the remainder into any shape he desired. The basic design principle of the Cells made them infinitely variable.

He took a moment out of the preparations to ask himself a simple question:

Why am I fighting? He didn't owe anyone here anything, except himself and his crew. So what exactly was he trying to prove?

He was sure the Negotiator Select wouldn't like his answer—if he was still alive—but at least he could honestly say it wasn't all about Melilah.

If someone was coming to steal the Occlusion, then they—along with the rest of humanity—didn't know what they were in for.

The Cell divided.

Nhulunbuy was a region of Australia's midnorth that had had a special significance for the Cell's previous chief officer's grandparents. Although Eogan knew nothing about Yolngu traditions and felt no ties to Palmer Weightman's old homeland, he had kept the name upon assuming command five years earlier. It was a way of honoring Weightman, who had groomed him for the job before choosing to settle on a remote outstation on Altitude. Eogan would have been well within his rights to change its name, but something had stopped him. A fear of stamping his mark too deeply on the Cell, perhaps, as though fearing that it might return the favor.

Flast celebrated his sudden rise in responsibility by coining his half of the Cell the *Kwal Bahal.* Now a functional vessel in its own right, it had to be differentiated from the remainder of the *Nhulunbuy* somehow, so Eogan allowed him the indulgence. There was a small chance that the two Cells would remain permanently separated after the fight. Palmers recognized no minimum or maximum size for a Cell, and new ones were simply budded off as need arose.

"Congratulations, Palmer Aesche," he told his new second officer, an efficiently humorless woman who had been plying the trade lanes longer than he had. She presented no face at all over intra-Cell communications, just voice and a series of complex emoticons. "You've drawn the short straw."

"Better out here than in there," she replied, indicating the habitat. Purple blotches were spreading across the variegated surface, indicating where aggressive replicators had taken root. "Ground battles always struck me as somewhat pointless."

Distractedly, he nodded his assent. Palmers considered anything with more than 0.05 of a gee pull as "ground." What was the point of fighting over a lump of dead mass when the infinite sky was your playground?

The truncated *Nhulunbuy* swept out of the habitat's meager gravitational well with thrusters on full, sweeping over the worst of the fragmentation mines remaining from the initial barrage. Flickering, ghastly light still sprayed in the habitat's immediate vicinity. Signal-to-noise ratios improved dramatically as their distance increased, but there was precious little to listen to beyond the habitat. The system possessed several moon and asteroid stations, mostly unstaffed. A handful of hardy explorers braved the long cold into the near-Dark halos, looking for evidence of exospermia. They were keeping quiet for fear of the invader targeting them next. They hadn't yet realized that they were irrelevant.

Eogan hadn't been caught in a combat situation since the complicated Expansion years, but the lessons learned then were ingrained. Arc Circuit systems had heard rumors of hyperadvanced vessels appearing in other systems that had managed to mount a stiffer-than-expected resistance to the Exarchate incursions. Quickly dubbed "Reapers" for their stealth-black appearance and lethal capabilities, the vessels functioned as destroyer-sized smart bullets, committed to rooting out every possible threat to Sol's imperial aspirations as quickly as possible. Finely targeted strikes took out hardware first—weapons and intelligence outposts; mine clouds; communications arrays. If resistance persisted, the application of force quickly turned deadly. The blackest whispers spoke of satellites ditched on populated areas, bubble cities opened to the vacuum, moons razed, and whole ecologies disrupted. Once they had beaten the locals into submission, the stories went, the Reapers moved on to the next target, ready to dispense Sol's version of tough justice.

Two systems in the Arc Circuit—Schiller's End and Phad 4—had received visits from Reapers during the Expansion. No shots had been fired in either case; the simple presence of such dark emissaries had been enough to stifle resistance. Sometimes Eogan had wondered what had been the most effective weapon in the takeover—the Reapers themselves or the rumors that had preceded them.

Either way, the one looming fast on the Occlusion observatory was certain to be armed with more than just gossip.

He dipped into the Cell's extensive shape-library and chose from several possible attack formations. Twenty-five of the thirty-seven remaining components merged into a configuration that was simultaneously reminiscent of a raptor and a flower, with five tapering "wings" angling forward and out from a central thorn fifty meters long. The remaining twelve components followed randomly determined paths around the raptor, affecting highly reflective profiles.

Although he suspected it wouldn't do any good, he broadcast Cell registration codes and a request to negotiate over all frequencies. He even tried the secret ftl link. Exarch Deangelis didn't intervene. The vacuum between the major players was light on communication, heavy on threat.

"This is an unnecessary violation of interstellar and inter-human treaties," he tried, resorting to voice where other protocols had failed. "What are we: savages throwing sticks at each other?"

Much to his surprise, he received a reply.

"That's exactly what we are, Palmer Eogan," said a woman's voice over the ftl link. "Comparatively speaking."

It took Eogan much less than a second to produce a voice match. The Reaper belonged to Frederica Cazneaux, Exarch of Mizar system. He had last spoken to her a year ago, while leaving to clear what he had thought was a simple occlusion from the Mizar-Bedlam trade lane.

"You're making a big mistake," he said.

Her response was incredulous. "Are you threatening me?"

"Merely stating a fact."

"The facts are simple, Palmer Eogan. *You* are the one who made a mistake: you brought this thing to Bedlam. I'm here to put that right. I advise you to get out of my way before you get hurt."

The *Nhulunbuy* was caught between two opposing Exarchs. Eogan seriously considered the virtues of fleeing right then, before he buried himself any deeper than he already was.

"I can't do that," he said. "One of my crew is—"

Cazneaux didn't wait for him to finish. The Reaper transformed from deep black to glaring white in an instant as energy surged for the Occlusion observatory. Eogan's senses were instantly overwhelmed. The *Nhulunbuy* spun like a dust mote in a laser beam. He heard shouting, felt the sudden thrill of mortal fear in the fabric of the Cell as it strained to get out of the firing line. He urged it on with every iota of willpower he possessed.

He hadn't even begun to hope that they might make it when, from behind them, the observatory unfolded like a predatory flower, and the universe hit him with the weight of worlds.

With a deafening, white-noise hiss and a rush of blast-furnace air, the nanotech infection rushed up the pipe toward Melilah. For a moment, she froze, staring at it as it burst out of the potential breach she'd gone in to investigate. The insatiable replicator was simple and deadly. Designed to disrupt complex molecules wherever it found them, it effectively tore matter apart. If it touched her, the replicators would spread through her flesh like black rot. She wasn't, therefore, embarrassed in the slightest at turning tail and running.

"Infection confirmed!" she yelled at the top of her voice. Kicking like a springbok off the walls of the pipe, she hurried as fast as she could to the truncation point. "Seal it off! Seal it off!"

"When you're through!" shouted Vernon Gard through the opening. "Not before!"

Don't be an idiot! she wanted to yell back at him. *If just one breeder gets on me, I'll contaminate the rest of the habitat!*

But when she shot through the portal and slammed to a halt on the far side, she was glad that he'd waited. She looked back just in time before the pipe was sealed off forever, imagining the contagion boiling just millimeters behind her shoulder blades. It was in fact still some meters away, encroaching like mold in fast motion toward the one remaining link to the outside. She didn't think it was intelligent, in any communal, guided sense of the word, but its black tendrils seemed to wave at her with increased agitation as the portal slammed shut on them.

Until next time, the forces of dissolution seemed to be saying. *It's only a matter of time before you make a mistake.*

Subtle forces flexed. The pipe pinched and folded back on itself, forming a tight U-shaped loop. Its previous destination—and a bubble roughly ten meters across around it—was isolated from the rest of the habitat behind alternating layers of matter resistant to the replicators and complex field effects that would persist for hours even if the local power supply was severed. Within those layers, the replicators could breed to their heart's content, until there was nothing left but itself to devour.

Melilah was still breathing heavily when Angela Chen-Pushkaric gave the all clear. The woman's gruff tones were briskly matter-of-fact, as though listing a supply order.

"That was too close," said Prof Virgo, over the dedicated feed the Exarch had given them. "We should have sent a remote."

"Not when transmissions are so unreliable," she said. "Someone had to go in there, and it had to be me. Are you suggesting that any of you were more qualified?"

There was no response. Gard, with his third-hemisphere capabilities, was far more valuable linked directly to the habitat, overseeing the sudden changes required to seal off the pockets of infection. Angela Chen-Pushkaric and Prof Virgo were helping direct people to safe areas. They needed accurate, up-to-date intelligence on each of the outbreaks, and she couldn't trust the machines to give that to her.

"We have another breach," said Gard, closing his eyes and sniffing as though tasting the air. His elongated skull swung from side to side. "In Faloutsos Junction. A big one."

She smoothed down her crawl-suit. Her breathing and heart rate had begun to return to normal. "Okay. Let's go."

Other emergency vehicles made way for them as they rushed through the pipes. Hatches opened and closed automatically. Melilah oversaw the efforts of the others to clear

the infected area. Five people had been caught in the
breeding mass of replicators when the ceiling came down
on them. Overrun in less than a second, there had been no
chance of rescue. Their matter was now part of the invasion, co-opted into a battle they had wanted no part of.

A seething, background rage filled Melilah at the
thought of what the attack would cost Bedlam. To her
knowledge, her home had done nothing to provoke such
action; the explanation had to lie in the Occlusion and what
it promised. Someone else must have guessed its secret and
come to steal it. That was the only reason she could come
up with for the chaos into which the system had been
thrust. The mission's objective was theft; everything else
was just collateral damage.

Only Exarchs thought that way, she told herself. And no
one else in the Arc Circuit had access to this kind of firepower. When it was over, either way, she swore to identify
the extropian freak responsible and see that their plug was
pulled.

"Something new," said Gard. "I'm picking up a physical
incursion. Hardware, not nanotech."

"Where?" she asked quickly, thinking: *What now?*

"Bacon Cathedral. We can be there in two minutes."

She briefly considered her options. The incursion in
Faloutsos Junction could be handled by local emergency
services without her; her value was reduced now that she
had shown them what to do. On the other hand, if the attacker had sent some novel means of attacking the habitat,
it might be best to face it head-on.

"Take us there." The transport banked sharply and
swooped into the next left turn. "Give me visual."

A virtual window opened, courtesy of the Exarch's
nanoware. She swallowed her distaste and looked into it.
Bacon Cathedral, like Albert Hall, was a permanent land-
mark of Bedlam. A teardrop-shaped chimney crisscrossed
with platforms and walkways, it stretched all the way from
the deepest levels almost to the surface, its ceiling rising

automatically as new levels grew around and over it. The new invasion had come through that ceiling, the thinnest point for kilometers around. The thought made Melilah feel physically ill. Not a place of religious worship, the Cathedral was decorated with commissioned art from many of the habitat's inhabitants. Public rallies had been held there during the Expansion; Melilah had led one for eight days straight, lifted up by the united voices of her supporters as they called for freedom. That the Cathedral might require sealing off and excision was intolerable. She imagined replicators spilling down murals and devouring sculptures as they went.

There has to be a way to save it!

No visible nanotech but an awful lot of smoke filled the view Gard gave her. Her gaze swept up and down through numerous frequencies, seeking one that could penetrate the murk.

When it finally cleared, she saw a string of pearl-shaped craft descending gracefully down the Cathedral's chimney.

"I'm not getting a match from the weaponry database," said Gard.

Her breath caught in her throat. "That's because it's not a replicator incursion," she said. "It's a Cell!"

He nodded, then shook his great head. "Neither its signature nor mass is in the register."

Excitement ebbed. "You think it could be a Trojan?"

"Anything is possible."

"Just get us there ASAP," she said, "and tell everyone else to stay away."

Seconds later, the first attempts at communication came from the Cell.

"—the *Kwal Bahal,* seeking Melilah Awad. I repeat: this is Palmer Flast, chief officer of the *Kwal Bahal,* seeking Melilah Awad. I've come to offer you assistance. Please respond."

She replied immediately. Talking wasn't going to hurt anyone, even if the transmission was bogus. "I hear you,

Palmer Flast. Where are you from? We don't know your Cell."

"It used to be the *Nhulunbuy*—half of it, anyway." The possible Palmer's voice was brisk as the mirror-finish orbs sank deeper into the Cathedral and assumed a swirling, faintly hypnotic configuration.

"What happened to the other half?" she asked, steeling herself for the answer.

"Eogan has work elsewhere; otherwise, I know he would've liked to be here instead of me."

Any relief she felt was almost certainly premature. "How can you help us, Palmer Flast?" The transport she rode was only moments away from reaching the Cathedral. She had to make a decision soon.

"The infection is spreading," he said. "You can see it from outside the colony. As hard as you're trying, you don't have the resources to quash this kind of invasion. We can make the difference. We're more mobile than you are, and we're expert at dealing with nanotech. We have to be, in the environments we're used to."

That made sense. Although extensively shielded, Palmer Cells required vast amounts of exotic technology to keep their once-human crews alive. A large part of that technology consisted of nanoware designed to maintain, repair, and destroy living cells. So inimical was life in the trade lanes, even those most frequently swept by the Palmers, that the repairers themselves sometimes suffered radiation damage. Whole Cells had been wiped out when a single corrupted molecule had turned a beneficent collaborator into a rampaging killer. Extensive feedback systems ensured that such disasters were rare in recent times, monitoring the ebb and flow of passenger replicators to ensure that nothing got out of hand. Such corrective systems would be extremely helpful in combating the incursion afflicting Bedlam.

Cancer ships, she remembered, distracted from Flast for a moment. There had been a pirate once, an interstellar bandit associated with such vessels. A long time ago, when

the Arc Circuit had been barely a sketch across the
starscape, he had made a habit of cruising silently along
the trade lanes, then suddenly crashing his intended victim's VOID drive by ramming in too close. Pellets of corrupted nanotech seeded mutations in the target's immune
system analogue, encouraging the growth of destructive
replicators. While the crew struggled to deal with that
problem, the pirates moved in and took what they wanted.
Whole manifests were emptied in the twenty years the pirate had reigned; thousands of people had lost their lives.
Only when the pirate's vessel had been found drifting in
empty space, gutted by one of its own mutations but still
flying under the sign of the Crab, did the trouble cease.

That had been before the Palmers, she knew. Such
events had encouraged the formation of a self-regulating
organization in a frontier that simply could not be policed.
She remembered word spreading that trade lanes were safe
again—but she couldn't remember the name of the pirate
who had caused so much dread.

"Okay, Palmer Flast," she said. "We accept your help."

"Good. Show me to the nearest site, and I'll take some
samples. When we've got something concrete to look at,
we'll start talking countermeasures."

Vernon Gard lifted deep-set eyes to focus on her as the
transport pulled up at the main entrance of the Cathedral.
The entrance irised open at his command, and a shining,
giant pearl necklace unreeled from within. Each of the Cell
components was two meters across, small enough to fit
through a minor freight pipe but seemingly too slight to
hold a living human.

Melilah attempted to patch into the Cell's manifest to
examine it in more detail, but received only the most cursory sketch in return. She learned little more than that it
had a crew of two dozen people and was barely hours old.
She made a mental note to report the information infringement when things settled down, if Flast didn't fix it
first.

"More outsiders," said Gard with a grimace, watching

the Cell as it stretched almost boastfully before them, like a snake warming itself in the sun.

She couldn't think of a reply that didn't expose her own prejudices—since when did someone with a head like a giant banana have the right to criticize people just because they came from a different *place?*—so she ignored him and told the newcomers what to do.

+26

Space boiled, and so did the Exarch.

Frederica Cazneaux, you will pay for this!

Magnificent destruction cast a deathly light over the side of the habitat facing the observatory, projected by weapons so advanced that unevolved humans couldn't begin to understand them—could only gawp in wonder at them as the sky turned bright above them, like Neanderthals struck dumb by lightning. Gone were the days of wars depending on heavy projectiles, rapid chemical reactions, and runaway heat. Even nuclear energy was tired. The two antagonists who traded blows over the Occlusion did so using forces that under ordinary conditions barely existed in the universe. Such energies were found only on the surface of neutron stars, in the accretion disks whipping around stellar-sized black holes, in the hearts of suns. When desperate needs met extreme ends, space-time was an innocent and unlucky bystander.

Deangelis was all too aware of the proximity of the habitat to the conflict. He didn't mind the thought of losing more of himself to the equivalent of a stray shot or a ricochet. His mental integrity would hold up. But such were the forces involved that the slightest echo could tear the habitat to atoms, or erase it entirely from the universe, as though it had never existed. He wouldn't allow that to happen—and that meant that he was fighting two battles at once: one to protect the habitat, and the other to repel the invader.

Frederica Cazneaux!

The name was a battle cry urging him to greater efforts.

Never before, to his knowledge, had one Exarch attacked another. There might be rivalries, disagreements, bitter exchanges, trade wars, even threats of conflict, but no open hostilities such as these. The Exarchate was bound by loyalty to Sol and a unifying common purpose—to nurture humanity in its new home among the stars, whatever forms it took. Fighting ran nakedly counter to that purpose. And for what?

Deangelis had no doubt regarding the motives of his attacker. Cazneaux wanted to get her hands on the Mizar Occlusion, believing—as did he—that whoever first grasped its purpose would win an unassailable advantage over everyone else. Wormhole technology could open doorways all across human space, not just the Arc Circuit. Once the dangers were overcome, his system would become the gateway to the rest of the universe.

Cazneaux would take that from him. She would argue, no doubt, that because the Occlusion had been found on the trade lane between their systems, she had a partial—if not total—claim to ownership over it. She deserved a proportion of the riches that would inevitably result.

And perhaps she did. He might have been prepared to negotiate something to that effect, had she but talked to him before opening fire. That was the thing that irked him most: Cazneaux *knew* him. All the Exarchs knew each other. She must have realized that he would talk, that he would rather not fight over something that could be settled diplomatically. The Mizar Occlusion could be shared, if it had to be. He would allow that—and she should have known it.

Instead, this wild, furious attempt to overwhelm his observatory's defenses and steal what he had claimed. But he'd be damned if he was going to let her get away with it. War overrode diplomacy. He would defend himself to the ends of his abilities. She would not win!

He might be distracted by the safety of the habitat, but *she* was a long way from home and using a weapon that had last been in service forty years ago. Its systems were vulnerable to perturbation from afar, if nudged the right way.

He watched closely as the Reaper swept through a rapid series of configurations, each one displaying a different lethality. At one moment, it was a swanlike shape with vast bat wings extended to enfold the observatory; the next it had morphed into a four-dimensional trident attempting to penetrate his defenses by sliding around their gross physical surface. He was prepared for both, and ready with a response. The observatory shrugged ghost-shells from its rippling exterior, sheets of brilliant silver energy that broke over the Reaper like waves on an island, wrapping around its every facet and burning deep. Mass flashed to energy and back again; the vacuum seethed with short-lived particle explosions, blossoming into vast, branching shapes that just as suddenly collapsed down to nothing; the light from the system's primary red-shifted to infra, then flashed a startling clear blue.

There. A hesitation as the Reaper absorbed the damage and prepared to strike again. The conflicting demands of offense and defense were taking their toll on a machine that had been self-repairing for too long. Such a stutter could be exploited, like a weakness in a suit of armor. Through soft joints a dagger could slip, crippling an opponent. All he had to do was fashion the blade . . .

In the midst of that thought, he became aware of a third player on the battlefield. A speck he had initially dismissed as a by-product of the firefight turned out to be a small craft bravely but ineffectually weathering the storm around it, a Palmer Cell displaying the signature of the *Nhulunbuy* despite a much-reduced mass.

Deangelis withdrew some of his firepower from its location and considered his options. There was a narrow window of opportunity for him to hail the Cell, should he decide to take advantage of its presence. Caught between two Exarchs, even with him trying to spare it, the Cell simply wouldn't last long. It would be destroyed as casually as an ant on a football field.

Ants can bite, he thought. One solid nip might be all he needed.

+27

Eogan gritted his teeth to blot out a bone-rattling howl that began deep in the bowels of infrasound and ended well beyond the range of any terrestrial creature. It rose and fell in waves too powerful for N-6 to drown out completely. The voices of his crew were barely audible over it; he could barely think through it. Buffeted by forces the Cell had not been designed to weather, he had the strength to wish that he'd never got involved, but little else.

Then, suddenly, the turbulence eased. As though it had burst into the heart of a cyclonic storm, the *Nhulunbuy* found itself in an eerily calm space, one that he didn't dare hope was permanent. With all his senses ringing, jangled, Eogan did his best to get his thoughts in order while he had the chance.

"Is everyone still here?"

Affirmatives from his crew staggered in, accounting for all of them. His relief was profound. The Cell he wasn't so worried about; it could be blown into a million pieces and still function perfectly well. People, however, weren't so resilient.

"Palmer Vermeulen? Can you hear me?"

There was no answer from his science officer. The firestorm curtailed all communication with the observatory—indeed, outside the Cell itself.

"What now, Palmer Eogan?" asked Palmer Aesche.

Outside the bubble of relative stillness, blue-purple light whipped and snapped like auroras with bite. Staccato points of light stabbed in long, curving streamers, resembling rail-gun fire but clearly not made of matter. Pulsing explosions blossomed and died in a constant stream.

Behind the conflagration, the dark shape of the Reaper flexed and writhed into half-glimpsed, nightmarish shapes.

If Aesche was being sardonic, he couldn't read it in her voice.

"I have an idea," he said, "but I fear it might be throwing good money after bad. I need to know if you think I made a wrong call."

Aesche's response was immediate. "No, sir, and I believe I speak for all of us on this issue. We've come this far; we might as well keep going."

He nodded, and the motion was transmitted via the couch he had blended with into a general indicator of approval. Body language was just as important to Palmers as any other human variant, even between bodies separated by many hundreds of meters.

"Very well," he said. "Then I want to retune the VOID systems. I believe that to be our best shot. The vanes are worthless out here, as are the thrusters; with that sort of technology we're like bees trying to attack a whale. If we can bootstrap ourselves up to their level, we might be able to do some damage."

"Retune how?"

He outlined his idea as quickly as possible, fearing the collapse of the bubble around them with every passing second. Palmer Cells were utterly different from the early space vessels humanity had built. Unlike craft with single engines, single life-support systems, and control systems bearing only the most basic redundancy designs, Palmer Cells owed their considerable flexibility to a single, simple design concept. The work of all their systems was spread across the entire Cell, performed by millions of machines on the micro- or nanoscale. Every cubic centimeter of the Cell contained hundreds of components dedicated to air purification, water reclamation, field effect generation, VOID maintenance, and more. Every cubic centimeter was, in a sense, a reflection of the Cell as a whole—in the same way a fragment of a hologram contained an image of the entire hologram in miniature. A Cell could take any shape, any size, and still contain all the elements it needed to be a functioning, human-bearing space vessel.

"I want to strip out the VOID drive microunits," Eogan said, "and turn them into bullets."

"There's a lot of junk around," protested Aesche. "The drives won't be effective."

"Then we'll just have to give them some of our thrusters. All we need to do is get them up to speed. When the VOID drives are activated, they'll generate a warp on a small scale. This, combined with the drive units' masses, is bound to have an effect."

"What sort of effect?"

He shrugged. "I guess we'll find out soon enough."

"You do realize that this will leave us pretty much dead in the water."

There was a note of skepticism—perhaps even criticism—to her voice. "I know," he said. "We'll tailor our trajectory to take us out of range on momentum alone. That'll have to be enough, until we can replace what we give the bullets."

Aesche considered the plan for a moment. He steeled himself for more questions, but none were forthcoming. The truth was, he didn't know exactly what the drive units might accomplish, but it was the best he could think of under the circumstances.

"I approve," said a totally unexpected voice over the open channel. "But I would suggest some fine-tuning."

"Deangelis? Is that you?"

The Exarch didn't reply to his question, either assuming it was rhetorical or the answer self-evident. "Your plan will be ineffective unless it is implemented correctly. I will provide you with a target and a time. Stick to both, and you have a chance of succeeding."

Data trickled in over a highly secure link from the habitat behind them, not the observatory. Eogan didn't examine it in any detail, but it did look at first glance to be strategic information.

"Let me talk to Palmer Vermeulen," he said.

"That's impossible at the moment. I can assure you, however, that she is safe. She will be able to communicate with you once you have completed your mission."

Are you blackmailing me*?* Eogan wanted to ask. There was little he could do about it if Deangelis was.

"Very well," he said. "We'll look at your data and decide what to do."

"I wouldn't think too long if I were you. I won't be able to maintain this bubble indefinitely."

Another thinly veiled threat. "You must be worried," said Eogan, "to be throwing your weight around so much."

The Exarch didn't reply.

28

"A Reaper?" Melilah stared at Gard in astonishment. "You've got be kidding."

"That's the conclusion I keep coming to, based on the limited telemetry available," Gard said. "The Exarch is fighting it off."

"Fighting one of his own?"

The programmer tilted his overlong head in something like agreement. "We live in interesting times."

Her attention was suddenly drawn forward as their transport was blocked by a component of the *Kwal Bahal*. It filled the pipe like a swollen crystal billiard ball, gray at the edges and fading to black in its heart.

"I'm sorry," said the Palmer within. "It is dangerous for you to proceed any farther."

Melilah checked an internal map. They were close to Faloutsos Junction and the site of the latest replicator outbreak. She couldn't tell just how far the infection had spread; feeds in and out of the area around the junction had been purposefully severed to prevent the spread of software viruses.

"I'm not staying back here," she said. "I want to see what happens."

"You don't trust us?" asked the Palmer.

"At this stage, caution seems the best option."

"Understandable." The Palmer was silent for a moment, then said, "I have obtained permission to offer you a berth."

She must have misheard. "A—what?"

"Come aboard. I'll take you the rest of the way in perfect safety."

"But—" Her automatic protest died before becoming a proper sentence. *But I don't want to go in there!* "A certain amount of trust is still required."

"Indeed."

Nothing else was forthcoming; that was clearly as far as the Palmers were prepared to go. She cursed under her breath. It had been almost two centuries since she had last been inside a starship, when she had traveled to Bedlam, and they had been primitive things back then. Who knew what this one might do to her, or how it might *change* her?

That was irrational fear talking, she knew. She swallowed it and willed her voice level.

"I'll be over in a second."

Gard watched her open the transport hatch with sharp, flickering eyes. "Ping me when you're inside."

"Don't worry; I will. If we lose contact . . ." She hesitated as a dimple appeared in the side of the billiard ball, quickly widening and deepening, forming a hole big enough for a person to slip through. "Sound the alarm; tell Deangelis. Give 'em hell."

He nodded like a bishop in danger of losing his mitre.

She kicked herself across the gap between the transport and the Cell component, which become ovoid in shape to accommodate its extra passenger. Its glassy surface loomed ahead of her, reflecting the brown-and-white streaks of her and a distorted image of her face. She forced herself to reach out with hands to arrest her forward movement and was surprised to find plastic warmth against her palms, not cool smoothness. The component hummed to itself, just above the threshold of her hearing.

A light sprang to life inside the Cell, and Melilah fought the urge to run as fast as she could.

The Palmer was barely recognizable; she was, in fact, hardly visible at all. The interior of the component was a cramped, fleshy space with bulging walls and—its only redeeming feature—a smooth, dry surface that looked a little like suede. Its inhabitant sat crouched forward as though playing dice on the ground; her knees were high on her chest, her arms tucked close to her sides like chicken wings. Her eyes were open, but it was clear she didn't see directly through them. They didn't track to look at her. The orbs were held in place by dozens of tiny black fibers that issued from the white of her eyeballs and traced delicate patterns across her cheek and forehead before disappearing into the bulkhead behind her. Thick ropy strands, like dreadlocks, terminated in her black-finished scalp, carrying information to and from the Cell. Her hands and feet were invisible, completely subsumed into the component. Her knees made two angular bumps beneath her chin, which was mercifully clear of modification.

"Don't be afraid," said the Palmer, audible through her ears alone. "You won't hurt anything."

Melilah took a deep breath and slid her long frame feet-first into the component. There were no instruments before its pilot, no controls. Just a blank, translucent bulkhead that curved around her on all sides.

As the opening passed over Melilah's head and began to close, she felt a powerful wave of claustrophobic fear break through her.

"My God! What was I thinking?" She tried to kick through the hole before it shrank too small, but her balance had gone along with her self-control. All she did was flail about like a child and crack her head on a wall. "Help me!"

A hand gripped her ankle, steadied her. "Easy, Melilah. I assure you, you're in no danger."

"But—" She pulled herself out of the Palmer's grasp and kicked to the far side of the cramped space. "You're—"

"My name is Sarian." The woman had eased partially out of the Cell's embrace. Her hands were free, as were her breasts. The sight was shockingly asexual. A flicker of annoyance crossed her face. "We're on the same side, for the Dark's sake."

"Melilah, are you okay?" Gard's voice came startlingly loud and clear from outside the component.

"Yes," she forced herself to say, willing her muscles to desist from their frantic attempts to escape. She *knew* she had nothing to fear, even if everything she felt contradicted that knowledge.

She slumped down in the space and looked Palmer Sarian in the blank eyes.

"I'm sorry," she said. "I have a—a phobia, I guess, of extreme modification. It's not usually a problem. I can control it, unless I'm taken by surprise."

Sarian eased back into her notch, mollified by the explanation. "I apologize also," she said. "I was not aware—"

"You couldn't have been." She gestured vaguely in a direction she hoped was forward. "Shall we get moving?"

"Yes, of course."

Melilah assured Gard that all was in order as the Cell component accelerated to join its siblings farther along the pipe. He sounded appeased but not entirely convinced. She imagined the transport he occupied receding into the distance, and tried not to think of it as a safety line just slipping out of her grasp.

29

Helene-Deangelis watched the battle from the interior of the Occlusion observatory. Connected in fits and starts to the bulk of his higher self in the habitat, he had an ever-changing and sometimes frustrating view. In concert with four other versions of himself in the station—all named after satellites of Saturn—they were responsible for the upkeep of the defenses when the rest of him wasn't able to oversee it for them. The five of them comprised an island of selfhood that wasn't fully independent, yet could function for a while without direct connection to the rest. It felt like slipping in and out of sleep, mixing reality and dream.

His higher self was pushing Cazneaux hard, taking the Reaper to its limits. When the momentary hesitation recurred, the arrow of the *Nhulunbuy* would be ready to fly.

"You guys really know how to put on a show."

Helene-Deangelis broke his concentration to focus on the science officer of the *Nhulunbuy*.

"It's not your concern, Palmer Vermeulen."

"It will be if whoever's piloting that Reaper gets through your defenses."

"Don't worry. She won't get that far."

" 'She'? So you know who it is, then."

"I told you—"

"It's not my concern. Right, I heard you the fifth time. Call me old-fashioned, but I like to know the name of the person who's trying to fry me to a crisp."

Irritated at Vermeulen for distracting him, Helene-Deangelis almost forced her to do as she was told. There was a preservation capsule waiting for her and her Cell component. If she would only get into it, he could stop worrying about her well-being and get on with his work.

But he could see her point. Were their positions reversed, he would also want to know at whom to point the finger afterward.

"Exarch Cazneaux has come to Lut-Deangelis to lay claim to the Occlusion," he said. "She thinks she can waltz in here and take it from us. I assure you it won't be so easy. Getting into the system is one thing, getting out again another entirely."

"I can imagine—and she would know that, too. Is negotiation an option?"

"She has spoken briefly to Palmer Eogan. Apart from that, she's not broken silence."

"So she wanted you to know who she was, but she didn't want to talk to you direct. I see." Vermeulen, so extensively woven into the fabric of her Cell that she no longer possessed a recognizable head, managed to convey a suggestive smile purely through the tone of her voice. "I think that makes you more than a little miffed."

"Of course I am! She attacks my system, injures my people, tries to steal what's rightly—" Helene-Deangelis bit down on the word "mine." "She risks another Catastrophe purely in order to further her own ends."

"Isn't that what *you're* doing?"

"At least I'm not doing it on someone else's turf, in a manner that puts innocent people in danger."

"Has anyone been killed yet?"

"There have been thirty-nine fatalities, including Palmer Christolphe." He didn't mention the eleven versions of himself who had been destroyed when the clane self-destructed, or the version of Lazarus Hails that had been grievously damaged in Albert Hall. Whether the latter would be salvageable or not remained to be seen. "Eighty-eight casualties are undergoing treatment."

"That's not so bad," Vermeulen said, "considering the ordinance she's packing."

"*One* involuntary death is one too many," he retorted, defaulting automatically to Exarchate policy.

She had no reply to that.

Outside, the conflict had heated up again, severing communication with the habitat. Helene-Deangelis swaddled himself in the thoughts of his siblings—Pan-Deangelis, Dione-Deangelis, Telesto-Deangelis, and Enceladus-Deangelis—and focused on the task ahead of him. His strategic map of the volume around the observatory was fiendishly complex, full of transitory reefs and sharks, and other, stranger, secondary phenomena resulting from the interaction between them. The Reaper slid from shape to shape as it pressed the observatory's defenses. Its mighty engines were unfettered now, able to fire without need of cloaking. Between it and the observatory, the *Nhulunbuy* followed a relatively safe route to one side, avoiding the hottest loci while staying within range if needed.

As Deangelis pressed, so did Cazneaux resist. His entire attention focused tightly on their jostling for ascendancy. They were evenly matched, but that didn't mean they were deadlocked. The nature of the battlefield changed from instant to instant. They fought on many fronts at once, in many different ways.

But in the midst of the fighting, Vermeulen's words nagged at him. She was right: Cazneaux wasn't inflicting the civilian damage she could have been. Had she attacked the habitat directly with the Reaper, instead of bombarding it with relatively simple munitions, the death toll could have been in the thousands. That was something to be grateful for, if nothing else. She could easily have used such a tactic to distract him while she took the Occlusion away.

Perhaps, he thought for a wild moment, he should just give the accursed thing to her and be done with it. That would solve the problem quite neatly and stop anyone else from getting killed . . .

As though she could sense his momentary lack of resolve, the Reaper unleashed a new offensive in his direction, a blistering wave of high-energy vortices that would have torn the observatory apart but for his quick reactions. He slammed up fields and launched a counterattack. Strange

ripples spread across the battlefield as space-time warped
into threadlike defects, arrayed in contour lines between the
two combatants. The Reaper morphed into an oblate sphe-
roid, a last-ditch defensive maneuver.

Helene-Deangelis grinned in triumph. He had Cazneaux
on the back foot at last! Diverting power from his shields to
the defect generators, he maintained the attack, not letting
up for a nanosecond, and warned Palmer Eogan to get
ready.

The Reaper sprouted points at two ends, giant spikes
easily one hundred meters long. The one facing away from
the observatory flashed a brilliant white, drowning out the
sun. The forward spike was a deep, light-eating black. The
Reaper as a whole surged forward, following that leading
point.

The move took Helene-Deangelis by surprise. He had
anticipated a retaliatory wave, not for the entire vessel to
move. He sent countermeasures to meet it. The Reaper's
drive-spike flashed deep blue in response, but its shields
held and it kept coming. Helene-Deangelis fired narrow
beams of warped vacuum that pierced the invader's shields
and carved red lines on the Reaper's black surface. In the
wake of the beams, he poured thousands of micro-
singularities into the wounds. Large, semispherical chunks
appeared instantly in the Reaper's hull, as thirty percent of
its mass collapsed into black holes.

Still it came.

Helene-Deangelis, his mind moving so quickly that the
dance of electrons through a wire seemed sluggish, could
only stare at the battlefield in puzzlement. What was
Cazneaux doing? He was going to cripple her if she kept
attacking like that. She had to know it. What was the point
of coming all this way only to sacrifice her greatest asset in
such a futile gesture?

Vermeulen said something then that he should have realized much earlier—four words that changed everything.

"She's going to ram!"

Before she had finished the final syllable, he was moving.

He belatedly powered the shields back up and angled them to deflect the Reaper away. They swung like wings through molasses from his point of view, far too slowly to come into full effect in time. The Reaper speared for the heart of the observatory at full power, its rearward spike blazing with a sun's intensity, its pockmarked forequarters gaping like an open mouth. He launched a halfhearted counterattack—and noticed only then what the singularities had done. In converting such a large chunk of the Reaper into black holes, they had turned the Reaper into an even more dangerous battering ram than it had been before.

More mistakes. He had miscalculated on so many points that, for a timeless moment, he simply watched the Reaper looming ever closer, convinced that death was the reward he deserved for his stupidity.

Cazneaux's objective wasn't to steal the Occlusion. She wanted to *destroy* it!

But it wasn't just about him. There was the habitat to consider, and the rest of him. Helene-Deangelis and his Saturnian siblings hadn't made their decisions in isolation. They had all been fooled.

He had time left to do two things. He gathered up Palmer Vermeulen, her Cell component, and the preservation capsule in one move. Ignoring her half-formed protest, he thrust her into the one place he knew she would be safe, relatively speaking.

At the same time, Telesto-Deangelis hailed the *Nhulunbuy*.

He would not go quietly into the Dark.

+30

"Now, Eogan, now!"

The cry burst out of the ftl channels with none of Dean-gelis's usual cool reserve. He sounded almost hysterical.

"You heard the man, Palmer Aesche. Let's get moving!"

"Sir, I think you should—"

A shock wave hit them before she could finish the sentence. The Cell shook like a leaf on a rubber tree. Complex vibrations thrummed through the components, increasing in complexity and amplitude until it seemed to Eogan as though the universe was unraveling. He could barely make out what was happening outside—and what he *could* see, he didn't quite believe.

"Cazneaux's ramming the observatory!"

All thoughts of attacking were temporarily suspended. Events unfolded too quickly. Energy scattered in all directions as the Reaper burst through the observatory's defenses like a bullet shooting an apple in slow motion. The geometric shape the Reaper had adopted began to come apart, sending exotic shrapnel flying. Eogan ducked instinctively as fragments passed near the Cell.

The observatory unfolded like an onion, flinging layer after layer of glowing shells at the attacking vessel. They all hit their mark—but still Cazneaux came on. The Reaper's rear spike burned a sickly purple. Eogan could actually *hear* the vessel's distress as topological waves propagated through the vacuum to the Cell. It sounded like a whale crying. The deathly moan rose in volume and intensity as the Reaper plowed on.

The tip of its leading spike hit the observatory's heart with a resounding flash; and then everything stopped.

In the timeless instant that followed, Eogan understood: *Cazneaux and I agree on one thing, even if we disagree about the best method of dealing with it. The Occlusion is dangerous. If whatever destroyed Sublime comes out of it here, we can kiss Bedlam good-bye. And if it spreads far-ther this time . . .*

The implications were troubling to say the least. Alioth, New Eire, Mizar, Megrez—anyone in the Arc Circuit could be the next to fall.

He appreciated Cazneaux's concern, but he could not countenance her methods.

Said the tic to the hippopotamus, he thought, as both Reaper and observatory vanished into a spray of light.

"Get ready," he warned his crew. The tight-beam feeds connecting the components were still working, for the mo-ment. "*Something*'s going to come out of this alive. If it's not Exarch Deangelis and Palmer Vermeulen, we have to strike hard and fast."

"We're set to go," said Aesche. "Just give us the word."

Eogan performed the mental equivalent of a squint, peer-ing into the raw data for any sign of what might emerge from the titanic collision. Space flexed and buckled around them, tossing them on a restless sea of potential energies. Light-ning flashed from the exterior surfaces of the Cell compo-nents, earthing into nothing at all.

"There's something . . ."

A shadow flailed through the bright fog, threatening to take shape, then sinking back into the glare. He couldn't make out exactly what it belonged to. It had been curved, perhaps part of the observatory's spherical shell, but it had also seemed to taper back to a point, like the Reaper's nose and tail. He held off a moment longer to be certain.

No word had come from Deangelis or Palmer Ver-meulen since that one, urgent cry.

VOID bullets be damned, he thought. If Cazneaux had killed his science officer, he'd take her apart with his bare hands.

"There!" A slender black spike stabbed out of the

nova-bright flare. With it came a slight ebbing of the sustained explosion issuing from the collision point. "That's good enough for me. Take us in, Aesche. Let's see what damage we can do!"

The Cell surged beneath him, its streamlined shapes blurring with acceleration. Shock tubes hung posed to fire modified VOID drive pellets by the thousand into the target he had provided. The point he had seen kept rising, dragging a jagged, skeletal shape after it, looking like a corpse half-dissolved in acid. It shuddered and lurched, clearly dying but not yet spent. Beams of sickly yellow light strafed the brightness below it where, presumably, Deangelis or automated systems still fought back. The Reaper's form flowed like electroset metal from shape to shape, never fully attaining one of them.

It stuttered, just as Deangelis had said it would.

"That's what we want to see." Eogan locked the *Nhulunbuy*'s targeting systems on the stricken Reaper and released the VOID bullets. Streams of silver flecks arced away from the Cell, leaving visually odd trails behind them as they warped space. He was reminded of footage he'd once seen of a school of knife fish in an Elizan ocean. The flecks flew in an asymmetric curve to where the Reaper crouched in the throes of dissolution over its prey.

White points of light stitched lines across its coal black skin.

"Got it!" cried one of Eogan's Cellmates. He said nothing in response. Hitting the remains of the Reaper wasn't the important thing. *Killing* it was.

"Now what?" asked Aesche.

"We keep firing," said Eogan, as the Cell drifted across the battlefield with little more than attitude thrusters to nudge it along. "And we hope."

"I hope you know what you're doing, Palmer Flast."

"Don't worry, Melilah," said the chief officer of the *Kwal Bahal,* as replicators spilled in a thick, shining wave over the surface of his component. "It's all under control. I'm just taking a sample—"

At that moment, a quake rolled through the station that made everything else Melilah had experienced seem like a mere ripple. The walls of Faloutsos Junction concertinaed, then stretched like a rubber band. Pressure waves sent replicators flying in a silver spray. The gleaming marbles of the Cell bounced and rolled in flickering, failing light. Total darkness came down with a soundless slam.

The Scale-Free Bedlam feed died without a crackle.

Melilah, arms and legs anchoring her grimly in place so she wouldn't have to come any closer to Palmer Sarian than she had to, emitted an involuntary cry of alarm.

"What happened?" she asked.

"Something big," said the Palmer, blind eyes flickering with wild REM motions. "Give us a second."

"Regroup, regroup!" came Flast's voice. Sarian had extruded screens and instruments for Melilah's benefit, since most of the channels normally available to her were dead. The chief officer's voice came over one of those. "We're unharmed and don't seem to be in any immediate danger."

The Cell's components bunched together like grapes on a windswept vine.

"What about the habitat?" Melilah heard a note of panic in her voice but couldn't swallow it. What had the Reaper *done*?

"It's—" Flast hesitated. "I can't tell. Our instruments picked up an event outside, right off the scales. There was a gravitational surge; that's what we felt a moment ago. But that wasn't enough to shut everything down like this. I'm not getting anything at all from the habitat."

"That's impossible."

"I'm telling you, I'm not getting anything at all."

Melilah refused to believe it. "Vernon, can you hear me?" she shouted into the dead feed. "Angela, Kara— Yasu! Exarch Deangelis! Answer me!"

Silence.

It's dead. Bedlam is dead!

No, she told herself. *It's not possible. It takes more than that to kill a habitat of this size. You'd have to blow it apart from the core out—and if* that *had happened, then even I wouldn't be here right now. None of us would be.*

A premonition hit her, as hard as the pressure wave.

Bedlam died the moment the Occlusion came here . . .

"Wait," said Flast from a component nearby. "I'm picking up an energy reading."

"What sort of reading?"

"I don't know. It's weird-looking: not an instrument artifact or an echo of what's going on outside."

"What *is* going on outside?" asked Sarian. "Is the *Nhulunbuy* okay?"

"No signal."

"Fuck the *Nhulunbuy,*" said Melilah. "Find out what's happening to my home!"

A glimmer appeared in the distance, a gleam of deep-sea phosphorescence. She thought she was imagining it at first, then a wave of light swept over them as the Junction returned to life. Momentarily blinded, Melilah blinked in puzzlement at the screens in front of her.

Alive or dead? she thought. *Make up your mind, for God's sake.*

"Citizens of Lut-Deangelis," boomed a voice from every channel at once, unhurried, authoritative, and sexless. "Please remain calm. Order will shortly be restored."

"Who is this?" asked Flast. "I don't have your voice on file."

"I am a guest to your system. I am here to assist you."

"Where are you from?" asked Melilah, thinking of the Reaper. If the person—or persons—behind *that* had taken control, she wasn't going to be so easily reassured. "Give us your name, not empty words."

"Your Exarch knows me as the Archon," said the voice patiently, "and that is how you will address me, too."

" 'The Archon'?" she repeated. "I've never heard of you."

"That is as it should be, under ordinary circumstances." The voice paused for emphasis. "These circumstances are far from ordinary, as you well know. I have come from Sol to set them to rights. Will you assist me in this, Melilah Awad, or hinder me?"

She opened her mouth, then dumbly closed it. Her mind was stuck on the phrase: *from Sol.*

The last time something had come from Sol, it had taken her freedom away.

"I suspect," she managed, "that you and I have very different ideas of what is right."

"And I suspect that I can prove you wrong on that point."

A groan rolled through the habitat. Only then did she notice how quiet it had become.

"My systems are dead," said Sarian, her voice little more than an alarmed whisper. "I can't move."

"Enough talking," declared the Archon. "All unnecessary vehicular activity is now curtailed. Emergency services will act only with my direct authority—but that authority will be instantly given in the case of any genuine emergency. Until your Exarch has recovered sufficiently to resume control, I will be running this habitat. There is a terrible mess for us all to clean up."

Melilah felt overwhelmed. A Palmer Cell inside the habitat and a Reaper outside, the Exarch out of action and something—God only knew what—from distant Sol stepping in to take its place. She felt as if she had somehow drifted into a surreal dream state.

"I want to help," she said. That was the one thing she remained certain of.

"So do I," added Flast. "That's what we're here for, after all."

"Good," said the Archon. "Then let's get started. Continue as you were, Palmer Flast. Your assistance in reducing the nanotech threat will be greatly appreciated."

"Right you are. We'll keep you informed."

As the Cell returned to its original task—capturing active samples of the invading replicators in order to dissect them and design effective countermeasures—Melilah returned to something the Archon had said about the Exarch's needing to recover before assuming control. She remembered the battered look she had seen on one of Deangelis's faces deep in his hideout. She wondered what had happened to him and whether he was going to be okay.

Part of her, unable to forget the way he had saved her during the initial attack, was unsure which way to hope.

32

Deangelis woke from a dream of being chopped into numerous tiny pieces.

"Citizens of Lut-Deangelis, please remain calm. Order will shortly be restored."

The voice echoed through all the corridors of the habitat and propagated across the system at the speed of light.

Deangelis recognized it instantly.

The Archon!

At long last, the tangler had finished receiving and assembling the ftl data sent from Sol. Deangelis struggled to gather his thoughts, to put on a good face. He had lost so much of himself. The five Saturnians must have died in the collision between the Reaper and the observatory. Eleven of him had been killed by the clane. And he had been too casual with the Occlusion when it had arrived, thinking that he had plenty to spare on such games. The risks were high, but the benefits . . .

He had seen no benefits so far, and now he struggled to gather enough sense of himself to address the one who had made him in the fashion it deserved.

"No, Isaac, don't overexert yourself." The calm, mannered voice was full of compassion. "Let it come in its own time, as you know it will. I am here now. The urgency is past."

"But I have to—"

"Rest easy, my friend. Recover. We have great works to perform, you and I. When you are ready."

An icy current rushed through him. *Was that what you told Jane Elderton?* he wanted to ask. *Are these the same assurances you offered before the Catastrophe that almost killed her?*

The Archon's voice came to him from all places, speaking to many different people at once. The same even tone, the same message—a myriad of different words. Exarchs were able to function in parallel to a certain extent, but with none of the capacity or ease of the Archon, their creator and superior in every respect. What the Archon's origins were he didn't know; it could have been human once, or many humans combined; it could have been a seamless blend of biological and made, or even purely artificial. Whatever it was, it was immensely powerful.

"All unnecessary vehicular activity is now curtailed," the Archon announced over the open lines, uniting all its many voices into one again. "Until your Exarch has recovered sufficiently to resume control, I will be running this habitat. There is a terrible mess for us all to clean up."

A terrible, burning shame rose up in him at that. He had failed in his duty. The Archon had been forced to step in and fix what he could not. He'd let his citizens down.

"This is only temporary," the Archon reassured him in private. "I mean that, Isaac. Once this flash point is dealt with, as it will be soon enough, all will return to normal."

He tried to take comfort from the words. After all, the Archon had never lied to him before. Why should it now?

But he knew that what it said was wrong. No matter what its intentions were, it was impossible for things to go back to the way they had been.

He had failed.

In the secret spaces of the habitat, his remaining selves sagged a little at the thought.

33

"All unnecessary vehicular activity is now curtailed."

The unfamiliar voice broke through the interference but went unnoticed at first by the crew of the *Nhulunbuy*. Facing the skeletal remains of the Reaper rising like a hideous ghost from the burning wreckage of the Occlusion observatory, Eogan's attention was more on the likelihood of his impending death than what was happening in the habitat. Although grievously damaged and not long for the universe, the Reaper was far from toothless—like a wounded dragon rising up over the knight who had speared it, preparing to take one last victim into the grave.

The *Nhulunbuy* could do nothing to fight it off, or to run. Its weapons were ineffectual, and its drives were expended in the attack run. Eogan had nothing left up his sleeve.

"I'm sorry, people," he said. "It wasn't supposed to end like this."

"We had to try," said Aesche. If she regretted following Vermeulen to an early death, it didn't show in her voice.

Almost beautiful in its grimness, the burning Reaper loomed over them.

Good-bye, Melilah, he projected into the vacuum. *At least I saw you again, one last time.*

He tensed for the killing blow.

It didn't fall.

"Stand down, Palmer Eogan," said the unknown voice. "You have done enough."

"Who is this?" Eogan broadcast. "What's going on?"

"I am the Archon. There will be no more fighting."

The Reaper crumpled in on itself like a burning log, its

shape dissolving into fragments with a shower of high-energy sparks.

"We've lost what thrusters we had left," said Aesche. "We really are drifting, now."

Eogan thought fast.

All unnecessary vehicular activity is now curtailed.

"Where's Deangelis?" he asked it.

"Until your Exarch has recovered sufficiently to resume control," it said, "I will be running this habitat. There is a terrible mess for us all to clean up."

"He's not *my* Exarch," Eogan retorted, although he agreed about the mess. "What about Cazneaux? Who's to say she won't try again?"

"I assure you, Palmer Eogan," it said evenly, "she will not."

The words were calmly delivered, with no sense of braggadocio, and Eogan believed them utterly. The Archon had somehow reached out and killed his motive power without firing a shot, and stopped the Reaper when it was on the verge of destroying him. Whatever resources the Archon had at its disposal, he didn't doubt that they were sufficient to the task of keeping a rogue Exarch under control.

And who else, he asked himself, had that capacity but someone from Sol?

"You're a long way from home," he said.

"I am indeed."

"Will you be staying long?"

"Only so long as I am needed."

"You're here because of the Occlusion, I'm guessing."

"That is correct."

The tangled wreckages of the observatory and the Reaper burned on, blurring into each other like a small lava moon. "It's not destroyed, then?"

"To accomplish that would require more energy than contained in this entire system."

Eogan's unvoiced hopes died then, that Cazneaux might have succeeded—in her terrible, destructive way—at achieving what he could not.

Vermeulen, Cobiac, and Bray. The roll call of victims was growing steadily longer. How many more of his crew would the Occlusion kill, directly or indirectly, before it was finished with him?

"If you give me back my thrusters," he said, "I'll stabilize my orbit."

"Do so," said the Archon. "I have no wish to inconvenience you further."

"What *are* your intentions?"

"That entirely depends," said the Archon, "on what happens next."

+INTERLUDE

One hundred eighty years before

Things had seemed so simple. Bedlam was the newest Arc Circuit colony: a foundling system built from the legacy of a failed expedition, its marvelous, ever-growing habitat a marvel of human ingenuity, its citizens embracing a novel form of society that promised to avoid the pitfalls of usual top-down government. On the frontier of many territories, Bedlam became known as an exciting place to live. It accepted nationals of all systems, provided only that they adhered to the information laws. The lives of everyday people took on new significance when what was normally hidden from view became accessible to all. Traditional notions of scandal and gossip were transformed. The whole system was a giant soap opera, with cast and audience indistinguishable. Some people came simply to observe; others hoped for a starring role. Many found it not to their tastes; many relished the challenges and the opportunities alike, and stayed for good.

Interstellar traders came and went, perhaps not as frequently as they did to other systems but often enough to ensure that Bedlam wasn't completely isolated. People came and went, too, as populations shifted sluggishly from home to home. It would have seemed strange to pre–Space Age humans, but one could grow tired of an entire planet, and surprisingly quickly, too. Melilah Awad had settled on Bedlam almost by accident, carried there by the momentum of her lost mother's conviction. Enamored of its political and ever-changing architecture, she threw herself wholeheartedly into the life of the colony. She made friends, took lovers, held parties, embraced life.

Dominic Eogan was a spacer she met at an ancient music recital, not long after her eighteenth year on Bedlam. He was solid and square, and his dark hair drifted lazily in the low gee. She hadn't met many spacers who could match her height, and she was instantly attracted to his easygoing manner. His eyes were a refreshingly muddy green, unmodified from the shade his genes had given him. In a crowd of startling blues—the current trend—his natural tones stood out.

She was immediately taken by him and took the first opportunity she could find to get him one-on-one. She made certain the group he was with merged with hers and that they sat next to each other over dinner. That night they just talked—about art, their backgrounds and family, opportunities for study in-system, recent scientific advances, and more—with ever-growing familiarity. He described his love of the stars, and she tried to convey what she saw in Bedlam, which he was visiting for the first time and hadn't quite grasped yet.

Later, she was able to scan back through the archives and relive that first meeting. The entire conversation was recorded as a matter of course by the habitat's monitors. She noted the way his eyes followed her, the fleeting touch of his hand to her shoulder, the fullness of his lips when he drank from a bulb of vodka. She saw herself unconsciously lean in close until they were almost touching, the attention she paid to his hands and arms, and a brief moment at the end of the evening when she had wondered if he was about to kiss her.

That instant was especially vivid in her mind. Her heart had pounded. She didn't understand why he had hesitated and pulled away, and why she hadn't grabbed him to urge him back. Why hadn't they taken it further? And why was she scouring the records afterward like some teenager frantic for a clue?

Either way, they had parted on an agreement to meet for lunch two days later. The attraction was still there, but she was cautious now, wondering if he had a relationship elsewhere that he was honoring, although he hadn't mentioned as much before. Did he think *she* was attached? All he had to do was check the social register to see that she wasn't.

Lunch blended into drinks, then dinner, and finally she could stand it no longer.

"I feel like I know you very well, Dominic," she'd told him, as they stood on the cusp of the night, reviewing the day and wondering what would happen next, "but I know that I don't. I'd like to correct that."

He took her hand. "You and me both."

She kissed him. He didn't pull away. The scent of his skin was rich and heady in her nostrils.

"Don't go back to your ship tonight," she whispered, through the heat of their commingled breath. "Stay with me."

All hesitation was gone, now. Their embrace became more intimate. She broke away long enough to hail a transport.

He didn't go back to his ship for two days.

That was how Melilah remembered the beginning. It matched the facts pretty well. If ever she wondered whether she had imagined the intensity of their early days, all she had to do was glance back at the records. They supported every pheromone-steeped recollection. She had it in hard storage, excised from her personal archives and partitioned so she could view her relationship with Dominic Eogan as a single, continuous arc—or not view it at all, as the case might be.

The arc lasted seven months, spread out over thirty years.

"It's not so simple," he said on the third day they had known each other. "We have to be clear-eyed and unromantic about this. I'm a trader, and you're a colonist. We both love what we do, and it would be unfair for either of us to ask the other to give that up."

"Wow. You're really looking ahead." They were floating together in the close confines of her apartment. A single-lobed chamber then, lacking the amenities she would enjoy many decades later, it was a little too cramped for two. She didn't care about that. In free fall with the lights out, it felt as though they were floating in space, surrounded by infinity.

"Is that wrong? I know what I want and how I feel, but I'm not a slave to either. I have a choice: to find out what you want now, before things get complicated, or just dive in and hope we can fix the mistakes later. Me, I don't want to make any mistakes."

"Nor do I, Dominic. But unfortunately they're inevitable. Murphy's Law still works in Bedlam."

"It works everywhere, Mel. But you must understand what I'm saying. I'm here for a week, then I'll be gone for at least two years. We can be long-distance lovers, we can even remain faithful to each other, but we can't be together as often as we might like. As I would like us to be."

She received the impression that this was a speech he had made several times in the past, and that it was as much for his benefit as for hers. "This isn't a fling for you, then?"

"Is it for you? Tell me if it is; that'll make things much simpler."

"Do you *want* simpler?"

She felt his cheek flex against hers: a smile, she thought. "I don't have a lay in every port, if that's what you're thinking."

"And I don't make a habit of picking up traders."

"Well, then. We're both crazy to be getting involved like this."

"I know."

"It's hard enough maintaining a friendship between systems. A romance—"

"Do you want to stop now?"

He was silent for a long time. The darkness pressed in on them like a coffin. What had earlier seemed so vast and limitless became claustrophobic, moribund, the longer it lasted.

"Enough," she said, kissing him. "You don't have to answer that. I'm not sure I could, if you asked me."

His smile returned. "What if I said that we *should* end this now? Would it make you want me more?"

"That which cannot be possessed," she said, "that which common sense rails against, that which I know will probably be bad for me in the long run . . . ?"

She didn't need to answer with words. Despite life-extending upgrades and a substantial knowledge of human biology, they were still creatures of flesh and blood. Matters of the heart never responded well to logic.

"I can handle whatever life throws at me," she said, a seventy-four-year-old woman feeling like a teenager again.

"Are you sure?"

"As sure as I'm ever likely to be."

She went into it with her eyes open, telling herself that was a good thing. Like someone facing a firing squad without a blindfold, it didn't help at all.

Time was short. She gave him a tour of the habitat, forgoing transports for a more intimate look at her home. He reciprocated with a flyby of the ship on which he served, a clunky mess of magnetic vanes, cargo containers, and VOID drive needles all wrapped up in angular scaffolding. Its lack of symmetry dismayed her; she sensed that something wasn't quite right about it, that there must be a better way of crossing the gulf between stars. But she wasn't a space engineer, and she didn't criticize his way of life just as he hadn't criticized hers.

On the fourth day, they flew unassisted over Bedlam,
naked to the sun. If the primary chose that moment to flare,
they would both be boiled in their suits. Even though
PARASOL's sensors had given them the all clear, the hint
of danger made it all the more exciting. They held hands
and spun gently through the vacuum.

Three days later, he was gone.

They steeled themselves for his departure. Continuity,
not fidelity, was the issue. Whatever happened while they
were apart, they would be there for each other when he returned. They would at least try to make it work.

Melilah managed to watch the clunky ship accelerate
into the starfield without shedding a tear, but it was hard.
When it had disappeared, she swore that she would return
to the life she had known and been perfectly happy with.
She soon found, though, that nothing was the same as it had
been. Dominic Eogan was a dye that had seeped into her,
coloring everything. She saw the same friends, did the same
work, and went to the same places. But now they all lacked
him, as though she was seeing the world through a filter that
made it a darker, unnatural place.

Eogan maintained irregular contact over the time he
was away, constrained by VOID drive relativity effects and
low-bit light-speed communications. Time passed more
quickly for him than for her, but she never once resented
him for that. He hopped ships at Altitude and took another
straight back to Bedlam.

His return was triumphant and wonderful. Melilah's
friends—who had had two years to become acquainted
with him, in absentia—embraced him as if he was one of
their own. He made friends of his own and explored the
habitat itself, making it as close to a home as anything else
he had. For two weeks they were together, and happy.

Then he was gone again, this time for three and a half
years. They took a month to reacquaint after that, to catch
and cling to each other like trapeze artists, getting back
into the swing of things. It was exhilarating, better than

anything Melilah had experienced before. There were ups
and downs, naturally, but there was a sense of certainty
underlying the bad times that made them easier to endure.
All she had to be was patient, she felt, and all would be
well.

Still, patience was expensive. The years between each
life-giving oasis were hard to endure. She devoted herself to
work and to hobbies, finding solace in activities both soli-
tary and social. On occasion, she allowed a certain intimacy
to develop with others, but never anything of the intensity
she experienced with Eogan. She knew where to draw the
line, as she was sure he did, too. There were boundaries she
would not cross for fear of shattering something that was, at
its heart, delightfully fragile. Sex was sex, but love—
commitment, common goals, *continuity*—was something
else entirely.

That he never once checked the public records to see if
she had remained faithful to him—a fact she knew for certain, for that, too, was on public record—spoke volumes.
They trusted each other to *come back,* no matter where
they went.

And for a while, it had been good.

Some journeys, however, were too perilous. Interstellar
space and patterns of intimacy were well-charted territories,
crossed many times in human history. Newer frontiers were
gradually unspooling, along with new ways of exploring. On
Eogan's tenth return to Bedlam, for their twenty-fifth an-
niversary of meeting and her ninety-ninth birthday, he told
her that he was thinking of joining the Palmers.

"The Palmers?" She remembered her lack of compre-
hension with dismaying clarity. A few early Cells had
drifted through Bedlam during his most recent absence.
She found their design more pleasing than that of their
awkward predecessors. Their safety record was impressive,
too. If Eogan wanted to join the trading movement, then
that was fine by her.

So why his worried look, as though he was about to confess something further beyond the pale than a new assignment?

"There are"—he hesitated—"*conditions* of membership. You should know what they are before I accept."

"You've already decided." Melilah didn't inflect it as a question. She knew him well enough, now, to read that much.

"I know what I'd like to do, but I don't know how you'll feel about it. I can't decide until we talk about it."

"So talk." She felt nervous without knowing why. Although they were floating naked once again in her apartment, touching all along their lengths, he suddenly seemed as distant and frigid as a deep-space satellite. His hair, still impractically long, brushed gently against her forehead. She pulled away.

"Tell me, Dominic."

He did, and her sixth sense was justified. She was a Natural, disliking obvious or unnecessary biomodifications on ideological grounds. He was suggesting a total submission to nanoware support systems that shocked her deeply. Every Palmer was expected to form a symbiotic relationship with the Cell he or she rode between the stars. Eogan's body would melt into the walls of the Cell components when they were in transit, leaving only the patterns of him intact, the flows of information that defined his thoughts, his memories, his decisions. He would retain the illusion of selfhood, required to keep him sane and at least nominally human, but human he would no longer be. He would be a posthuman hybrid—a monster.

"Not a monster, Mel." He tried to make her understand. "I know it's hard to accept. A lot of people don't see the need for radical biomods here. But out in the Dark it's different. If we want to survive, we have to go to extreme lengths. I'm already modified, but not enough to endure more than another decade out there. In a Cell I'll be safer. I'll be able to travel faster. We can see more of each other."

"But you won't be *you*."

"What am I now? You can't see beneath my skin. I could be the same as you, or I could be completely different."

"I'd know if you were." *If you came back more Cell than man . . .*

"Would you?"

Something about his tone made her pull farther away. The thought that he might already have made the change, might be adopting a semblance of his old self to preempt her, trick her, made her feel physically nauseous.

Her first instinct was to lash out, to hurt him back. She forced herself to examine that urge before acting on it. Was she truly worried about his possible inhumanity, or was she simply disappointed that he obviously planned to keep traveling longer than *another decade or so?*

It was both, she decided. The two emotions were too intimately entangled to separate. She just wanted him: *more* of him, the *real* him, not less of some thin-skinned imitation.

"What would you do if I said I didn't like the idea?"

He shrugged. "I'd think about my decision very carefully."

"That much at least, I hope."

"You know I love you."

All reservations vanished at his simple words. She wrapped herself around him and tucked her head into the crook of his neck. She hated the welling of tears that made her eyes feel fat and heavy in the low gee. "Yes," she said. "I'll always know that."

And I love you, she thought. Just *you . . .*

He was still there the next morning, and the morning after that. Then he left with the ship he'd arrived on, giving her his assurance that he would return the same way in two and a half years' time.

His words were as good as granite. He came back to her in one piece, altered neither in his affection nor in himself.

The matter of the Palmers didn't come up again, and she assumed it over and done with. They continued their relationship unchecked, reacquainting and relishing the chance to do so.

Later—older and, as she would like to believe herself, wiser—she could see the cracks. She could see the thing in him that she didn't want to acknowledge. As the Palmers grew in influence and spread to dominate the trade lanes, the number of ordinary starships making long runs decreased. More and more of the old vessels retired to individual colonial systems and stuck to interplanetary routes, ferrying colonists and resources back and forth on journeys measured in days not years. Dominic Eogan would never be satisfied with that. For all that he feared the Dark, he loved it, too. The Dark was his true companion, and always had been; Melilah Awad was a mistress who kept to the hot spaces, where her cold competitor could not venture. She had thought her and her relationship safe in Bedlam, and perhaps hoped for more still: that Eogan might one day turn his back on the void, choose her. If so, she had been dreaming, just as he would have been dreaming to think that *she* might follow *him*. To lose her home, her body, her *self*—that would have left her with nothing at all.

She had in effect asked him to do what she could not. And instead of telling her that the request was unreasonable and trying to find a way around it, he kept the desire close to his chest, where it ate at him. Or so she imagined it. She could only wonder in retrospect what had led him to such extremes on their last sojourn together—when everything had seemed the same as always, when their relationship had felt as solid as ever, when she had finally convinced herself to get rid of the last of the lingering doubts. She'd had no idea of the pressure building up inside him.

On the second day of March 2287, the brand-new Palmer Cell *Cirencester* hove to beside Bedlam. Unknown to her, although available on the public record afterward, the *Cirencester*'s chief officer contacted Eogan to repeat the offer made to him five years earlier: to join the Palmers. The timing was impeccable, and suspiciously so. The captain of Eogan's existing trader had only recently announced that he and his vessel would be traveling next to Schiller's End and there ceasing interstellar trade for good.

The net had finally closed in around Dominic Eogan. He spent the third of March 2287 with Melilah, giving no sign of his internal conflict. In retrospect she wondered if he had been a little *too* attentive, devoting himself to her more than he normally would have—but not so much that she had noticed and become suspicious. It had been a day together like many others they had shared on Bedlam. She didn't know, as the habitat's calendar clicked over to the fourth of March, that it would be their last.

She woke alone. He had left in the night without waking her, without apology or explanation, without even saying good-bye. While she had slept, he had signed his life over to the *Cirencester*. The Cell broke dock at about the same time she stirred, and was out of the system before she realized what he had done. By then, the replicators had taken her lover apart and made him something irrefutably *other,* bonded with him more intimately than she could ever have dreamed or wanted to—and they had done so long before she truly understood that he wasn't coming back to her.

The pain was awful.

At first she despaired that Dominic Eogan had ceased to exist. The thing now called Palmer Eogan might imagine that it was still him, that it had a connection to the people and things it had known in its past, but she swore that it would receive a terrible surprise if it tried to come back to her. She couldn't forget what it was, and she couldn't forgive how the idea of it had seduced the Dominic she had loved away from her, hurting her more deeply in the process than if she had lost her own body.

Then she wondered if she had ever known him at all . . .

Wrenching emotional dislocation, betrayal of the worst kind—one that might have been avoidable had he only *talked* to her about it, or made a clean break—and a sense of utter powerlessness conspired to erode her self-esteem, which she resisted as powerfully as she would have fought him, had he been an available target. She went from being a popular, confident person to one who shunned the limelight and hated the open policy of Bedlam. She tried to cleanse herself of the stain of him, to reset her life to the way it had been before he had become part of it, but that was as difficult as it had been between visits. Most of all, she tried to forget how good it had been before everything had turned bad—but how could she do that without turning her back on the thirty years of her life in which he had been so pivotal? It would be like killing part of her.

Sometimes she wished that he had died, not just disappeared. That would have been easier than coping with his utter rejection of her—and the thought that he was still out there somewhere, imagining himself free.

Only as time passed was she able to parcel up the pain and put it behind her. By moving on—to new relationships, new professional challenges, new phases in her life—she was able to lay down progressively more buffers between her and the mess of emotions that would always be there, whenever she remembered or was reminded of him. The situation wasn't ideal, but she could see no other way to persist.

All it hinged on was never seeing him again.

Life was simpler when she had loved Dominic Eogan, and it was simpler when she had hated him, too. Both were undeniable, and equally false comforts. One hundred and fifty years later, she knew that life resisted such simplifications. Life—like her feelings for Eogan—was a snake in a bottle. Given enough time, it would either find a way out, or die. And when it got out, its bite was full of poison.

+34

"Okay, Sarian," said Melilah. "You can drop me off here."

The Cell component came to a gentle halt. "I don't think I could've gone much farther anyway. The way is tight ahead."

The Palmer wasn't mistaken. Recent shocks to the habitat had prompted a premature collapse in some of its deeper levels. A pipe Melilah had followed with ease just days before was now flattened like a kinked hose. There was a chance that the route she sought was gone forever, subsumed by the core.

"Are you sure you don't want me to wait?" asked the Palmer.

"Positive." The ride in the component had been claustrophobic and uncomfortable. "Thanks for going out of your way, though. I appreciate it."

"Stick to the route we mapped, won't you?" Sarian's blank eyes expressed no emotion, but her face was a mask of concern. "I'd feel better knowing you're not going to stumble across a patch of infection on the way back."

"Of course. And good luck clearing up the rest."

A hole opened in the side of the component, finally giving her a way out. Melilah slid headfirst through it. The warped confines of the pipe seemed luxurious in comparison.

She patted the humming flank of the component, genuinely grateful for the help the Palmers had offered. "Godspeed," she said, not knowing the right words.

With the faintest of sighs, the component healed itself and rushed back up the pipe, leaving her alone at last.

She took her bearings and headed deeper. Five hours

had passed since the arrival of the Archon and the suspension of hostilities. In the wake of the attack by the Reaper, the first priority of the habitat had been to regroup and take stock. The gradual recovery of the Scale-Free Bedlam feed enabled most sectors involved to report casualties, injuries, replicator infections, and penetrator impact sites. The list was long, but less than she had feared. Yasu's response had been typical: to get into a shelter and ride it out. Only one shelter had been holed during the attack, and even there fewer than a dozen people had died.

Still, her blood boiled as the tally of dead and dying rose. None of it had been necessary. She didn't believe all the rumors she was hearing, but whoever had been behind the Reaper would pay dearly for the hurt inflicted on her home. She would make sure of that. If the destruction of the Occlusion had been the objective of the attack, that only made it worse. Bedlam wasn't a *distraction;* those who had fallen during the fight weren't *disposable.*

It came as only a small consolation that someone had had the same thought she had. The Occlusion was important. Getting her hands on it was rapidly becoming her next priority, once everything returned to normal.

Normal.

She'd almost forgotten the meaning of the word.

The tunnel kinked and twisted, taking her farther away from the nearest network node, deeper into silence. She slithered and wriggled where she should have soared. Once, facing a hairpin bend that threatened to be too much for her spine, she considered giving up and turning back. But she needed to keep going. She needed to rid herself of the itch that nagged at her, of the hook in her lip that simply wouldn't let her swim free . . .

The narrow niche had very nearly squeezed shut since her last visit. There was just enough room for her to slide her arm in and pat around inside. The disk she had placed there was still securely attached to the wall; it popped free with a gentle twist, giving way in response both to the torsion and the presence of her fingerprints. She held it in her hand for a moment, weighing it, then slid it out into view.

Black, flat, and unadorned. There was nothing on the outside to indicate the bombshell within. Someone stumbling across it by accident might think it contained just banking records or an embarrassing attempt at an erotic novel. There were many people who went to such lengths to bury one aspect of themselves they didn't want in the public domain. In Bedlam, it took a concerted effort to forget.

And even then . . . Melilah felt tears spring to her eyes as she contemplated the contents of the disk. *Dammit!* She knew the contents of the disk by heart. She had taken the records of the time she and Eogan had spent together and buried them deep, metaphorically and physically. Many, many times she had consigned them to a memory disk and hidden them in the habitat's core, fully intending to let them be subsumed by Bedlam's ever-growing, dead heart. Inevitably, though, she reclaimed them—usually under the pretext of moving them to a safer location, where their lonely destruction was more perfectly assured. But she knew the game she was playing with herself, the cycle she had wittingly followed for a century and a half.

Eogan was a glitch that had haunted her for too long. Until she could polish him up and place him beside her other trinkets, that was what he would always be. Keeping him dusty and hidden in the attic of her mind was a sure way to keep stumbling across him forever.

She wanted to let go, but part of her couldn't. She wasn't done with those memories yet. And the harder she tried to destroy their electronic vestiges, the stronger they seemed to burn into her mind.

She was scarred, tortured, and haunted by the past.

And now he was back.

Before she could talk herself out of it—letting emotion carry her like a soliton wave in the wake of the attack on her home, the kiss in the alien wreckage, and the injection of Gentry nanoware into her system—she gripped the disk tightly in both hands and snapped it in two. The sound of it broke the silence of Bedlam's heart: a simple *crack* that echoed for a microsecond from the twisted pipe walls, then disappeared.

It was done, she thought. Done at last. She held the fragments of her life with Eogan, one-half of the shattered disk in each hand, and felt no different.

"Melilah?"

The voice came electronically, not through her ears. She stirred herself and replied in kind. "Is that you, Prof?"

"I'm glad I found you." A tiny drone buzzed up the twisted pipe toward her, broadcasting Virgo's voice where the network couldn't reach. "Palmer Sarian said she dropped you off somewhere down here. The Exarch is looking for you."

"I don't suppose he told you what for?" she asked.

"There's a debriefing meeting in one hour. The Archon has asked for someone to represent Deangelis's nonspecialized subjects. We thought it should be you."

Melilah grunted. She hated that word: "subjects." It made her feel like the chattel of some inbred king.

"I'll be there," she said.

The tiny drone buzzed as a pressure wave rolled through the habitat's depths. "I don't think it's very safe down here, Melilah."

She agreed. "Hang on," she said. "There's just something . . ." She stuck her hand back into the flattened niche and searched for the data fiche that had been there the last time she had visited. She hadn't found it while looking for her disk, and that puzzled her. The two had been next to each other; she should have noticed it.

She slid her hand across the buckled surface of the niche's interior, feeling for any sign that it had come dislodged. Nothing. It was gone.

The walls groaned around her like peristalsis in a giant's belly. Prof Virgo nervously cleared her throat. Time to go. She slid her hand free and turned about in the flattened pipe. The air thrummed in time with the vibration under her palms and toes; her ears popped.

She kicked forward just as the pipe began to shake.

Buzzing furiously, the drone led her back the way she had come, along pipes that flexed and writhed like snakes. The hairpin turn that had earlier almost forced her back loosened just enough to let her by a second time. Then it slammed shut, guaranteeing that she would never come that way again.

The fragments of her memory disk lay in the collapsed bowels of the habitat. There would be no recovering them now, should she change her mind.

Not so, she thought, for the owner of the other memory cache. Whoever the fiche belonged to, they had obviously retrieved it before the collapse. That implied that the memories contained on the fiche were more important than simple throwaways. It also implied that the person they were important *to* was still somewhere on the station.

Lesbian lovers gallivanting around the Arc Circuit my ass, she thought, taking up the mystery again as she and the drone headed for the lower inhabited levels. She would find out what lay at the heart of it, she promised herself. And more besides.

The mind of the habitat flexed like a squid in lightless ocean depths, casting tentacles about to touch loci of pain, chaos, and disease.

Exarch Deangelis, no stranger to pain himself, watched its throes with a feeling of compassion. *Poor, ancient thing,* he thought, *twisted and time-encrusted.* After the death of the First Wavers centuries ago, it had grown alone in the Dark, deprived of intelligent companionship and guidance for decades, until humanity had rediscovered the home it had made and inhabited its living halls once again. For almost two centuries it had known people and vitality; not even the Exarchate Expansion had tried to take that away from them. And now monsters had come out of the void to threaten it, sting it, poison it.

The habitat physically shrugged, as though hunkering down against a chill wind. Seismic detectors registered vibrations in all quarters. Subsidence monitors flashed. Sensors accurate to micrometers recorded the slight shrinking of the habitat's outer layers as the core carefully added another layer of abandoned levels to its growing mass. Wrapped tight within its ever-thickening layer of compressed material, the AI, perhaps, felt a little easier for it.

The process took just seconds. Aftershocks rumbled for several minutes, then they, too, faded away.

"This is a most remarkable ecology," said the Archon.

Exarch Deangelis looked up from the point of view of his self from Earth. The Archon had no outward physical presence; the computations that comprised the visitor from Sol were performed by processors scattered throughout the habitat, plus an increasing number manufactured to precise specifications in the hours since the end of the crisis. Still, the body of Earth-Deangelis straightened to attention, feeling that at least one of him should make an outward show of reverence, like a child before its stern parent.

"I agree," he said. "But then, you already know that."

"I do, Isaac. That's why I chose you for this colony. It's unique, just as you are. None of your siblings would tolerate what goes on here. None of them would indulge such peccadilloes as you do. And I am proud of you for doing so."

Deangelis felt himself flush, although he wasn't sure why. A mixture of shame and satisfaction rushed through him, momentarily snagging his thoughts in its wake.

"You know," the Archon went on, "that the principles on which this colony was founded stand in direct opposition to those of the Exarchate. It is not possible for openness to exist between all levels of society. It simply cannot last."

"Once I would have agreed with you," Deangelis said, his words cautious at first, but becoming less faltering as his confidence grew. "I would have said that authority couldn't exist without effective barriers to communication. I would have argued that the truth must be hidden, sometimes, to protect those who would be harmed by it. I would have pressed for secrecy, as I did when I first came here, to keep to myself that which I did not want to reveal."

"And now . . . ?"

"Now I'm not so sure." There was no point lying to the Archon. "Where secrecy exists, conspiracies thrive. When the citizens of this habitat have free access to all commercial and personal information, it's simply not possible for unnatural power imbalances to emerge among them— either spontaneously or by design. Who would be threatened by someone whose most intimate details are public knowledge—and when the threat itself is visible from all corners of the habitat?

"That's not to say that exploitation doesn't still exist. There are always the negligent, the willingly dominated, the stupid, and the imperceptive—who consent to relationships that most others will not. But they do so at least *theoretically* informed. It's entirely their responsibility what they do with their lives. If they let it happen, that's their decision."

The Archon chuckled. "But where do *you* fit into all of this, Isaac? Are you part of this pretty picture you paint? Or are you the artist, manipulating the canvas until it meets your satisfaction, but never placing yourself upon it? Do you allow one rule for them and another for you?"

Deangelis sighed. "I tried. I honestly did. You can see from the records the efforts I went to; I've erased nothing from them."

"I know," said the Archon.

"Then you already know the answer to your question."

"I know what the facts say. I can see that you let your citizens observe you as freely as you observe them. You let natural differences in technology create the barrier you would not deliberately enforce. No matter how they watch you, no matter how they study your inner workings, they have as little chance of deciphering you as an Elizabethan accountant would a quantum computer. Yet some persist, attempting to pattern-match the signals between your various selves in the vain hope that they will one day come to know your secrets. The fools."

The Archon paused, as though giving him a chance to deny the accusation that he deliberately allowed censorship by default.

"I know that you have secrets, Isaac; the facts tell me that much, very clearly. But I want to hear what your heart says about them. That's what concerns me more."

Deangelis fought a strange urge to weep. The longing between Melilah Awad and Palmer Eogan surfaced unwittingly, from a place unknown.

"Must it be this way forever?" he asked. "Must we always lie to and conceal from those we love?"

"Sometimes, yes. And sometimes we must betray them, too."

"Like you betrayed Jane Elderton?"

"What makes you ask that, Isaac?"

He bit his lip. The question had burst out of him in a rush, out of the body he inhabited, not the greater mind from whose horrified viewpoint he watched. For one terrible moment he saw the exact same scene through two very different sets of eyes.

"I'm sorry," he said, blinking to bring himself back into focus. "I'm afraid, too. The Sublime Catastrophe was—awful. I have no wish to see a repeat of it here."

"None of us do," said the Archon. "I don't want anyone else to die. That is why we need to prosecute this matter as quickly as possible, with the maximum possible decorum. The front we present to the community here must be absolutely united. Are you with me on this, Isaac?"

Earth-Deangelis took a deep breath. "I will continue to keep my secrets. *Our* secrets."

"That's not what I meant."

"I would never defy the Exarchate, or you."

"Would you follow us willingly?"

"Yes."

He felt the Archon's attention sweep across and through him like the fiery stare of a god. He trembled in the face of it.

"Yes," he repeated with more conviction. How could he not willingly obey Sol? The Archon and the Exarchate were more than just colleagues. They were made of the same stuff; they were *family.*

Like all families, there were squabbles. And worse.

"I want to see Frederica Cazneaux punished for what she did to me," Deangelis said, his voice low and determined. "Her, at the very least."

"I've already said that I'll look into it," the Archon said. "Let's get the pieces back on the board first, Isaac, then decide where to concentrate our efforts. It may turn out that the most worrying threat has yet to reveal itself."

The Occlusion. It had floated passively throughout the conflict while vast forces tugged back and forth over it. What would happen if it awoke?

Deangelis had no answer to that question, just as he had

yet to exact a guarantee from the Archon that he would be avenged upon the Exarch who had attacked his colony. He wondered fleetingly if the Occlusion was being used to distract him, if the Archon had some reason for protecting Exarch Cazneaux from his wrath.

He dismissed the thought as utter fantasy. His mind was still addled from attrition and disorientation. He couldn't entertain such paranoid fantasies if he was ever to regain his balance, his *self*.

An autonomous agent nudged him, reminding him of his meeting to discuss the habitat's woes.

"There's work to be done," he said, shrugging aside his fears and his anger. His first responsibility was to the people under his care. If he failed at that, nothing else mattered. "I need to inform everyone of your decisions."

The Archon smiled upon him, filling him with warmth.

"Of course, Isaac. You're a good Exarch. One, as I have said, that I'm very proud of."

Good dog, Deangelis thought guiltily as he cast his mind across the station. *Roll over. Fetch.*

The habitat shuddered again, reminding him of the ancient AI lurking in its depths. If only, he thought, he could feel secure by burying himself in another layer of dead skin.

Play dead.

+36

In the relative peace and quiet of space, Palmer Eogan stood guard over the remains of the Reaper and the observatory it had attacked. The vast, flickering wreckage stood out against the stars, a self-contained, angular aurora with darkness at its heart. The *Nhulunbuy*, in its normal extended configuration, had taken extensive scans of the complex knot that was all that remained of both. Strange spines speared at odd angles, trailing sparks. Warped rings and hoops spilled from jagged, cavernous rents. It was difficult to tell what had belonged to what.

Part of him admired Exarch Cazneaux for her bold effort, even if, in the end, it amounted to nothing but a monumental folly.

"We're not picking up anything," said Palmer Aesche from N-4 on the far side of the wreck, currently identified by the newly reinstated Lut-Deangelis Traffic Control as "Hazard One." The Cell had returned to its usual, strung-out configuration and recovered enough motive power to move three of its components at will. The rest had little more than attitudes to keep them from drifting. Several drones had arrived recently from Bedlam and, like the *Nhulunbuy*, studied the wreck with close attention. Thus far they had done nothing to interfere, so Eogan warily let them be.

"Keep trying," he told her.

"Do you really think there's anything alive in there?"

He didn't, but he wasn't going to be the one to admit it. "Until I have Palmer Vermeulen's remains in front of me, I'm going to keep an open mind."

Aesche's skepticism was as radiant as Hazard One itself,

but she didn't press him any further. Both of them knew that his intentions weren't entirely honorable: the opportunity to probe Exarchate technology in such a broken state was rare and had to be pursued. Vermeulen would have insisted. So would have Palmer Christolphe.

They had just heard rumors of the Negotiator Select's death. It had come as a shock—not because Christophe was particularly well liked, even among his own, but because Palmers weren't used to death coming in the relatively safe confines of a habitat. In the Dark, yes, where a single particle could slam through a weak shield with the force of an atomic warhead. But not while docked, surrounded by many layers of dead matter traveling at barely a few kilometers a second.

Exarch Cazneaux and her booby-trapped clane had sent a message to the Palmers at the same time as she hurt the Exarch. *Be careful with whom you ally yourselves. There are more dangerous things in the universe than mysterious alien artifacts.*

Perhaps, thought Eogan, but now Cazneaux's best shot at destroying the Occlusion was a glowing menace to navigation, destined to be dumped into the sun once the Exarch got his act together.

His mind wandered as he waited for word of any kind. He doubted the Occlusion would suffer such an ignominious fate—although the experiment would be interesting to conduct. What would happen at the Sublime end of the wormhole if this one was exposed to the stellar atmosphere? Would the extreme temperature and pressure flush the passage clean of any remaining aggressive tech, so humans could use it in safety? Or would the walls burst under the insult, ruining the wormhole forever and thereby robbing humanity of a valuable xenarcheological artifact?

Again, Palmer Vermeulen would have had an opinion. She would have voiced it, asked or not, either in her capacity as science officer or as a friend. The more certain Eogan was that she was dead, the more he found himself missing her presence in the Cell. Her absence unbalanced it more than the half Flast had excised to form the *Kwal Bahal*. Even if that half returned, the *Nhulunbuy* would still feel out of kilter.

"The Dark take you and keep you," he whispered, mouthing the words of an old Palmer verse often quoted at assemblies for those lost in transit. "The light of ancient stars guide you to rest . . ."

Icons rippled across his field of view. Someone from the habitat was trying to hail him. He glanced at the origin of the signal, but didn't quite believe what it was telling him.

"Melilah?"

She didn't waste time with pleasantries. "Where are you?"

"I'm still alongside the observatory, waiting for the Cell to recover."

"How soon will you be back at Bedlam? There's a reconstruction meeting in one hour."

"I know. I've been invited, but it's going to be too difficult to get there in time." He tried to read her tone, but wasn't able to. "Why? Are you okay down there? Does Palmer Flast need backup from us?"

"No." The response came almost too quickly, but wasn't ungracious. "I was just wondering if you wanted to meet. We have a lot to talk about."

"I daresay."

In his mind, he heard her telling him, the last time they had spoken: *Either help me get what I want, or stay the hell out of my way.* He wondered what had changed.

"Call me when you have an ETA," she said.

"I will."

The signal closed.

He sat for a moment in the embrace of N-6, turning memories over in his mind. They were like sticky sand, presenting the illusion of slipping through his fingers but always leaving his hands gritty and soiled afterward. There were moments he would have been happier to excise entirely from his recollection, but even with advanced Palmer technology such precision amnesia was not possible. He could have crudely removed the chunk of his life that had contained Melilah Awad, but he had known people who had undergone such procedures. No matter how careful the excision, no matter how sure they were that they'd done the right thing, they always tripped over the days, months, or years forcibly wrenched from their life. They seemed permanently puzzled, as though not quite believing that they could have done such a dramatic thing to themselves, and constantly wondering *why*.

He didn't want to end up like that, a stranger in his own head. But he didn't want to turn the same hourglass over and over, either. The sand had worn his fingers to the bone. He still felt every grain.

While reception was good from the habitat, he hailed the Pirellis, who, he learned, had waited out the attack in a bunker not far from the alien skulls.

"It was no great hardship," said James, somewhat more jovially than the circumstances warranted, Eogan thought. "We even managed to grab a bottle or two before evacuating."

"Actually, the blackout was scarier than the attack." Like her husband, Luisa sounded more amused than worried, as though the crisis had been an adventure put on just for them. "You may think of us as Luddites, but we're as dependent on the feeds as anyone else. We felt completely cut off—even crammed in a room with fifty other people."

"And don't think we haven't been watching *you,* dear friend, since the lines went up again. You have been busy, haven't you? Practically holding off invaders with your bare hands!"

"I lost a friend out here," he said, not in the mood to make light of the situation.

"We understand." Luisa instantly sobered. "So did we all. That's one thing about living in Bedlam. Everyone knows everyone else. Our casualties may have been low, but the cost was high."

"Too high," added James.

"I'm sorry," Eogan said. "I didn't mean to snap."

"That's okay. We're all a little off-color, behind the brave faces."

"All the wine in the system can't make up for the fact that we've been attacked," said Luisa, "for something over which we had no control and didn't much want in the first place."

"At least we've learned something from it," said James. "If the rumors are true, that is."

"What's that?"

"That the Gentry aren't as homogenous as we'd assumed: there's dissent in the ranks. And there's someone or something higher up that ultimately calls the shots."

"I don't know about you," said Luisa, "but knowing that he has enemies—and a boss—makes Deangelis seem almost—well, human."

James snorted. "I wouldn't go that far, my love."

"I did say *almost*."

Eogan smiled, comforted at last by the familiar interactions of his friends. The issue of the Exarch's humanity was a well-worn one. In the early days of the Expansion, speculation had been rife that the new rulers were AIs posing as humans in order to erode resistance. The issue wasn't entirely resolved, certainly not to the satisfaction of skeptics like James Pirelli, but it had become irrelevant to most people. When what constituted "human" took many diverse and superficially alien forms, quibbling about the Exarchs seemed a little petty. At the end of the day, the Exarchs had to be judged on their actions, not their origins.

"I'm glad you're okay," he told them, cutting into their good-natured debate. "Stay that way. I'll be back in Bedlam soon."

"So we hear," said Luisa with a sly tone to her voice. "Tread carefully, my friend. Now's no time for a covert kiss-a-thon."

"I have no intention—"

He broke off at the sound of her laughter. The Pirellis were gone before he could properly respond.

He waited a beat for a caustic comment from Vermeulen. It didn't come, reminding him sharply of her loss. Irritated, he opened another line to keep himself distracted.

"You made it through okay," he told Gil Hurdowar.

"So it would seem." The man looked no different for the experience. Dark bags hung from his half-lidded eyes.

"I just wanted to thank you for the tip you gave me, about the observatory. You were obviously right. Deangelis was gearing up for an external attack. If we'd known that more in advance—"

"It wouldn't have made any difference against a Reaper. Don't doubt that for a second. Frederica Cazneaux was determined. The only person who could have made a difference was Deangelis, and he barely scraped through."

"The Archon—"

"Didn't appear until the fight was practically over. Cazneaux—or whatever part of her was involved—was probably dead by then. The Reaper would have been running on AI. All the Archon did was switch it off and let it melt with the observatory."

"Is this an educated guess, or do you have information we don't?"

"It's all guesswork, Palmer Eogan. But I defy you to prove me wrong."

Eogan had no inclination to try. Even if Hurdowar was right, and all the Archon had done was hit some sort of kill switch in the Reaper, that was still a powerful demonstration. The kill switch had affected the *Nhulunbuy,* too, and the *Kwal Bahal,* and every other vessel in the system. What else could the Archon do if pushed?

"If you get the urge to share any other guesses," he told Hurdowar, "feel free to let me know."

The man grunted, practiced surliness mostly hiding the fact that he was glad to have earned Eogan's ear. "Don't expect anything soon. I'm still sifting through the mess, trying to work out the details."

"There's no hurry. We're all doing the same."

"I doubt it. *The details,* Palmer Eogan. That's where you'll find the devil. The big picture is just a camouflage."

Rather than get caught up in Hurdowar's cryptoparanoia, Eogan made his apologies and killed the line.

He took a moment to glance at the reconstruction meeting Melilah had mentioned, but found it to be much as expected: focusing on a myriad of minor details, not the core problem.

"Anything?" he asked Aesche, fighting a wave of bone weariness.

The negative was instant and disheartening. "We're wasting time and energy," she said, bluntness finally replacing bland disapproval. "We should give up."

Eogan turned his attention back to Hazard One. The wreckage was utterly lifeless to the *Nhulunbuy*'s sensors. The only movement came from stray energies leaking gradually into the vacuum. Light still played across its angular visage, but with less viciousness than before. The drones from Bedlam had become more numerous while he was distracted.

"What about the Occlusion?"

"We can't detect it directly, but we can measure the pinch of space it closes off, deep down in the tangle. It's the same as always: completely inert."

That was a relief. No alien replicators had come boiling out of it yet. Eogan wondered what it would take to prompt such a response, given that the collision of the observatory and the Reaper around it had failed to elicit anything at all.

Now that the wreck was cooling, it was becoming increasingly difficult to justify hanging around.

"All right," he said, thinking: *It's not much of a memorial, Palmer Vermeulen, but it'll have to do.* "Call off the search. There's nothing left to learn here. Get what flight-worthy components we have and find a configuration that will get us back to Bedlam as a whole. We might as well help Deangelis put things back together."

"You don't want one of us to remain behind, just in case?"

He seriously considered it. "No. We might as well accept the fact that—"

"Eogan, wait." Aesche's voice coincided with a sudden rise in activity from Hazard One. "We're getting something."

Eogan returned his attention to the raw data flooding in from the wreckage. Sudden spikes of energy were registering across all frequencies. "What is it?"

"I don't know. I've never seen anything like this before. It's—" Uncharacteristic concern filled her voice. "It's coming from the Occlusion!"

Cold rushed through him. "Pull us out. Get us the hell away from it." He noted the Bedlam drones doing the same. "I want us well back if that thing's about to go off."

"Consider it d—"

Light flashed against the starscape. Something bright and fast-moving shot out of the wreckage, trailing a misty white comet tail behind it. Eogan's fingers, intimately merged with N-6, reflexed to send the component out of its path, forgetting that only attitude thrusters were available to him. The component moved sluggishly as the object curled around in a tight spiral and came right at him.

"Aesche—"

"There's nothing I can do!"

He clutched the component to him and called up emergency collision systems. The object came at him as fast as a meteor, blossoming in his forward feeds, flaring like a supernova—

The impact pushed him face forward into the fabric of the component. Inertia gel flooded the space around him, gripping him like a fist. There was a tearing, screeching noise that was so loud it actually hurt.

Then N-6 was tumbling, and he was tumbling with it, rocking and spinning giddily against the stars. The object was an ungainly lump sticking out of the component like a half-melted, glowing club.

"Palmer Eogan!" came Aesche's voice over the component's battered comm. "Palmer Eogan, are you all right?"

"Don't say anything," said a voice in his ear. "Don't say anything until you hear what I've got to tell you."

He fought the inertia gel, struggling to free himself and see who had spoken. The signal came mechanically through the impact-welded planes of the component and the thing that had collided with it. It sounded as a faint buzz to his ears. The voice emerged out of heavily encrypted Palmer protocols carried by the buzz and was instantly recognizable.

"Vermeulen?" he gasped, incredulous.

"That's right," she said. "And you're not going to believe where I've just come from."

"But you're—"

"Dead? I'm disappointed you gave up on me so quickly—but not really surprised. That was some blast, wasn't it? I've been waiting for the wreck to cool to the point where it was safe to come back out again. Took much longer than I thought. I can't tell you how glad I was to see you on the other side."

Surprise was slowly turning to relief, and puzzlement. "Are you hurt? How in the Dark did you survive?"

"Ah, well, I can thank the Exarch for my present rude health. As soon as things turned nasty, he bundled me and N-11 in this fancy capsule and shoved it in the safest place available: *inside* the Occlusion."

"I thought of that, but the boundary effect—"

"Deangelis solved that in a hundredth of the time it took us. He's been steadily sending probes into it, ever since we gave it to him. All I had to do was sit tight and ride out the collision, then come back out again when things calmed down."

Something in her voice told him that this wasn't the whole story. Ignoring Aesche's continued demands for a

response, he took everything he knew about Vermeulen—
and her precipitous return to the universe—and bundled it
together in one leap of reason.

"But you didn't," he said. "You didn't sit tight at all."

"Absolutely not. I'm back from my little holiday—and
wait until you see the postcards."

Detailed displays cataloged the outrages enacted on Bedlam and its immediate environs down four walls of the conference space. Frozen air glittered over exterior surfaces; debris radiated in an expanding cloud; occasional flashes of light marked regions where fires still burned.

Melilah sat in the midst of the visual record with her stomach roiling, reliving the terrible moments when her home had come under attack. She hadn't known Eogan was in the thick of it until afterward, when images he had recorded of the collision between the Reaper and the observatory circulated freely around the network. Her instinct to call him had been strong but ambiguous, as was the urge to see him again. Part of her, having cut free of the deadweight of the past, wanted to establish a new pattern of coping—one that didn't involve total avoidance and denial. *That* method had clearly performed badly over the last century and a half. If she could see him again, talk to him, she could kick-start the rest of her life. A life free of doubt and anger. Free of him.

"Do we know who did this?"

The voice knocked Melilah sharply out of her reverie. Deangelis, at the head of the table, his youthful appearance composed and his expression neutral, faced the woman who had voiced the question.

"There are several suspects," he said. "An investigation is under way as we speak."

"I'm still not sure what actually happened," said another. "We're hearing nothing but rumors out there."

"Are we at war?" pressed a third voice. "Did the Occlusion attack us?"

"Have we been invaded again?"

"Is it over?"

Deangelis flexed his will, and the walls became windows on the outside universe. The sun was a brilliant point behind his head, casting his face into shadow and making Melilah squint. To her right was the scarred visage of the habitat; to her left, the dark umbra of PARASOL. Between the two, directly opposite the sun, was the tangled wreckage of the Occlusion observatory. The skeletal remains of the Reaper clutched the destroyed station like the fingers of a corpse. A hideous glow wreathed the wreck.

"Earlier today," Deangelis said, "we were attacked by forces external to the system. The attack began with a surgical strike designed to excise a significant percentage of my operational capacity."

"Blew up some of your bodies, in other words," Melilah said.

A wince flickered across his smooth visage. "A crude but effective tactic," he admitted. "While I was distracted, several waves attacked the habitat. The first was designed to interfere with telemetry and communications. The second restricted EVA. The third directly targeted the habitat and its occupants. You are all familiar with the effects of that wave."

Nods around the table.

"It was a smoke screen," he went on. "While we were all distracted, a fourth force moved on the Occlusion, intending to destroy it."

"Why?" someone asked.

"That seems pretty obvious to me," Melilah said. "What I'm more interested in is who was behind the attack."

"As I said—" Deangelis started.

She interrupted him. "We know there are suspects. But who *are* they, exactly? Is it true that another Exarch did this? How do we know it wasn't actually the Archon—using it as an excuse to move in and take over?"

"The Archon played no role in the attack," Deangelis said.

"How do you know that?"

He hesitated slightly. "I know that because it is simply not possible."

"*Who,* then?" asked Palmer Flast of the *Kwal Bahal,* a thin-faced, bald man with surprisingly full lips. "You must have some idea, or else you'd be a lot more worried about another attack."

"I can only assure you that the threat has been minimized. The weapon used in the fourth attack was not a commonplace one. It has been destroyed, so the odds are extremely small that another will follow."

"You didn't answer my question about another Exarch," said Melilah.

"No," he said quickly. "I did not."

She bit down on a sharp comment. That he hadn't denied it was enough. The others stared at the Exarch with undisguised horror at the idea the colony could have been attacked by another like him. They must have felt the same shock she had upon coming to that conclusion.

But she was discomforted to note that her skepticism was not representative of the gathering's mood. They were looking to Deangelis for guidance and encouragement. She and Flast were the ones truly daring to challenge him.

"You put something in me," she said. "I want it out."

"It has already decomposed."

She didn't feel even slightly ameliorated. "What was it?"

"A simple tracking and telemetry interface. You accessed the navigational data it gave you. I was able to access your movements in return."

"That's all?"

"Please; have yourself scanned, if it makes you feel easier. I have no reason to deceive you."

She sighed. "Do you have *any* good news to offer us?"

"We're making steady progress against the infection," Flast offered. "We've developed a countermeasure now. It's simply a matter of helping it propagate."

"Your efforts are greatly appreciated." Deangelis inclined his head at the Cell's chief officer, and Melilah echoed the sentiment: the *Kwal Bahal* put to shame other Cells that had fled the moment events took a turn for the worst. "Curfews will remain in effect until the very last of it is neutralized. I estimate that this will take another fifteen to twenty hours."

"This is unreasonably draconian," she protested. "Not to mention impractical. Emergency services must have free access to all areas. People are injured; their homes are burning—"

He raised a hand, nodding. "Perhaps I am being over-cautious. Category C personnel can have permission to cross checkpoints as circumstances dictate, but they must undergo rigorous scans to ensure they don't track replicators with them. A single dormant breeder could undo all our good work."

Melilah was satisfied by the compromise. "Thank you."

"It should be me thanking you, Melilah. *All* of you." He swept his gaze around the table, at her and Flast as well as the dozen sector heads and municipal representatives he had gathered. "While I was unable to defend either myself or the habitat, you worked together to minimize the damage caused by the attack. I am grateful and relieved that we can cooperate when we need to, regardless of our differences in other areas. Some things are simply more important than ideology."

He received a murmur of agreement in response. Melilah was mollified, even if she doubted the fragile peace would last for long.

"What's the status of Palmer Christolphe?" asked Flast.

Deangelis's lips turned down at their corners. "It is my sad duty to confirm reports that the Negotiator Select was killed during the attack. I will inform his colleagues in Ansell-Aad as soon as communication lines are open again."

That prompted another murmur. "They've been cut?" someone asked.

"Only temporarily," he assured them. "The state of emergency in which we find ourselves will persist a little longer, as together we make every effort to restore the status quo."

"How long will that take?" asked Melilah, unnerved by the knowledge that Bedlam was for the time effectively isolated from the rest of the Arc Circuit.

"That's one of the reasons I've gathered you all here." Deangelis's cool gaze studied them all. "Are there any specific requests? There is much to consider and coordinate before I can release a workable timetable."

A torrent of demands issued from the various sectors, simple, practical needs that the Exarch promised to take care of. Melilah estimated that the majority of the work could be done within two days. Population flows would return to normal before then. Rationing of resources would not be necessary.

Not an unsatisfactory outcome, she thought, given the circumstances. Something to be proud of.

But it completely failed to address the root of the problem. The Occlusion was still in place, an easy target now that the observatory containing it was destroyed. What if the attack they had just endured was the first of many? Could the Archon wave its magic wand again and keep them all at bay?

The new arrival was conspicuous by its absence. Problem *and* solution were absent from the discussion, and that unnerved her. She doubted the others would want to hear it, though. They had come for reassurance, not more nagging from her. There was a time and a place to get what she wanted.

It came as the meeting devolved into a mess of conflicting requests, with everyone trying to push his or her particular concern forward. Melilah was watching Deangelis, trying to work out his exact motivation for the meeting, since it was clear he didn't really need anyone else's input to put things back together. It was probably just a publicity stunt or a means of making people feel involved, even if they really weren't.

His attention darted away. She could see it in his eyes. Suddenly the Exarch wasn't really there.

Curious, she cast her own attention out of the room. Something was happening near the ruins of the observatory, where the *Nhulunbuy* was stationed. That was enough to make her wonder if the meeting was in fact a distraction, hiding something much more important . . .

"Come back," she said, getting out of her chair and whispering in Deangelis's ear. The argument continued unabated behind her. "Listen to me. You talked about cooperation before. I'm not entirely against that idea. We do, after all, want the same thing: revenge against the person who did this to us."

His eyes swiveled to look at her. The greater Deangelis was back.

"Don't say anything." She kept her voice low, barely more than a subvocalization, knowing he could discern her words clearly enough. "Just because we want the same thing doesn't mean we're on the same side. I know you're hiding something—you and the Archon together, from us. The Occlusion is a doorway, one you can't hope to keep closed forever. If I find out that anything you've done has led to people here getting hurt—"

At the mention of a doorway, he pulled back as though physically struck. His calm reserve cracked, just for an instant, and she saw plain on his face the uncertainty and fear he had successfully contained through the meeting.

"How—?" His Adam's apple bobbed, and the mask came back down. He spoke using the network, rather than speaking aloud. "I don't know what you're talking about."

"You know damned well."

"I swear—"

"Spare me your meaningless promises."

His lips tightened. "I don't like your tone, Melilah."

"And I don't like *anything* about this situation, so let's just see what you can do to fix it."

"I'm doing everything I can."

For a moment, she believed him. The glimpse of panic she had seen suggested that he was as perturbed as she was, that maybe he had as little control over events as she did. But that wasn't her problem. If the Archon was his problem, just like *he* was *hers,* then he would have to take steps, too. She couldn't nursemaid him through the process. She could only nudge him onward.

Suddenly exhausted, and unable to avoid being worried about Eogan, she'd had enough of the meeting. "I guess we'll see about that," she told Deangelis, then turned and stalked from the room.

+38

Exarch Deangelis stared at Melilah's retreating back, still stunned by the revelation. *She knew! Impossible!* How *could* she know? She had been watched every second of every day, observed more closely than any individual in the habitat. She had the data he had hidden in the bowels of the station, but it was undoubtedly too complex for her to decipher on her own. Unless she and Palmer Eogan had exchanged more than just a forbidden kiss in the wreckage of the alien vessel, three days earlier, when she had been momentarily out of sight . . .

And if the Archon found out . . .

Dread filled him. He told himself that Eogan and Awad were just guessing, extrapolating from scanty details and using their hunches to apply leverage to him, but he wasn't convinced.

The voice of Jane Elderton came to him unbidden. *I opened the door,* she had said, *and now no one can ever close it. Nothing will ever be the same.*

The alarm that had distracted him from the meeting sounded again, raised by all his autonomous agents at once. He turned his attention back to the source of their clamor: the wreckage of the Occlusion observatory and Cazneaux's Reaper.

The Occlusion was active. Bright light pulsed in a pattern indicating that something was emerging from its hellish throat. Space-time flexed as the Occlusion spat an object no larger than a hopper back into the universe.

He identified it immediately. The object was one of the observatory's escape capsules, modified to withstand the physical trials of the throat. Clearly someone had fled through the Occlusion in order to escape the destruction of the observatory.

His heart beat again. Part of him had survived!

Then he noted the way the capsule was changing course and realized that it wasn't likely he at all behind the controls.

The survivor could only be Palmer Vermeulen, and she was heading for the *Nhulunbuy*.

"Intercept that capsule!" His command whipped out to the observation drones orbiting the wreckage, overriding telemetry feeds and all other communications. "Bring its occupant to me!"

The drones accelerated to match velocities with the capsule, swarming from all sides of Hazard One to catch it in their net. Uncrewed and relatively slight in mass, they were capable of much greater acceleration than Vermeulen's battered vessel. They were also equipped with sampling field effects that could be wielded as weapons. Dozens of them converged on the capsule's path as it arced away from the wreckage.

But they were too slow. Deangelis knew that the moment the capsule suddenly changed course, angling for one of the larger components of the *Nhulunbuy*—the one containing Palmer Eogan—on what looked like a collision course. No gentle docking for this survivor. Not if she wanted to escape the Exarch's clutches.

He snarled in frustration. Why was everyone so resentful of him? Why did they go to such extreme lengths to thwart him? Didn't they see that he was on their side?

The capsule slammed headlong into the *Nhulunbuy* component, and merged with it, sending them off on a new course that was the sum of both their previous ones, in perfect accordance with Newton's laws of motion. All acceleration died. All electromagnetic emissions ceased. Spinning like a top, the crashed vessels—echoing in miniature the wreck behind them—receded from the habitat.

The drones changed course to follow, as did three other components of the *Nhulunbuy*. He fought a sudden urge to fight them off, to claim Vermeulen for his own, to contain what she might have learned on the far side of the throat before it spread any further. But that, he knew, would only draw more attention than the incident was already getting.

"Back away," he told the drones. "Palmer Aesche can handle it from here." He did his best to project the appearance of someone perfectly satisfied that the situation was now under control—the exact opposite of what he was actually feeling.

"Thank you, Exarch Deangelis." Aesche took a moment from her attempts to hail the occupants of the two craft to acknowledge his involvement, then returned to her efforts. Either deaf to her calls or ignoring her, Eogan and Vermeulen tumbled silently on.

"You could plug this leak right now," said the Archon, "if you would only let yourself."

The voice and words of his creator sent a ripple of alarm through all of him. This was potentially a much greater security breach than Melilah Awad's half-mumbled threat. "I am not in the habit of killing those in my care."

"Just two in exchange for the greater good. That's a simple enough equation, wouldn't you say?"

He thought furiously. "Forgive me, Archon, but this isn't mathematics. We're talking about people, not numbers."

"Let's not quibble over the metaphor, Isaac. You know what I'm saying."

"Yes, I do. But I'm not coming to the same conclusion. There are too many variables in play. We don't know what Vermeulen has seen. To kill her now would only draw attention to the fact there is indeed something to hide. If she has seen nothing, or nothing she can understand, then sparing her poses no security risk at all."

"True—but we must balance this eventuality against the possibility that she *does* know what the Occlusion hides. That outcome must be weighted in excess of the other, so even if its likelihood is the same, we must act to avert it."

There was a small silence as the entangled capsule and Cell component continued to race ahead of the *Nhulunbuy*'s pursuit team.

"You could make it look like an accident," whispered the Archon.

"Are you ordering me to do so?" Deangelis asked, despairing. If the Archon *did* order him, he could not possibly disobey. He would have to accept that his judgment was wrong and do what he was told to do—even though the very thought of it burned like acid.

"I would never order you to do something like that," said the Archon. "I am simply exploring your motivations, Isaac. You are not being judged. Understanding is all I seek."

The relief Deangelis felt was profound. "I'm glad," he said, with total honesty. "I have no wish to become a murderous dictator. Humanity evolved beyond that point long ago."

"Indeed it did," said the Archon. "But superior evolution does not free us from situations that challenge us or occasions on which we must act in ways we find abhorrent. All it gives us is the capacity to see with greater clarity why we do what we must do—to see beyond the present, to where our actions might lead. The evolution we have wrought for ourselves gives us perspective, nothing more, and the new altitude from which we observe the world requires a keen sense of balance. We remain part of the universe, no matter how high we climb; gravity is ever waiting to drag us back down."

The Archon's words didn't reassure him. He felt as though he might fragment again, lose himself in a tangle of secrets and crises. He needed to talk to someone who would understand, someone at his level . . .

The rest of the *Nhulunbuy* caught up with the still-inert capsule and the component it had struck. Like a small flock tending one of its wounded, the Cell gathered around the two, expanding protective fields to shield it from the vacuum.

Maybe she's already dead, Deangelis thought, not believing it but unable to completely quash the hope.

Eogan sat in the darkness for what felt like a small eternity. In the scant minutes since the impact, the capsule had peeled back to reveal N-11, Vermeulen's component. His and hers had merged, allowing them to come face-to-face in the tumbling debris. He could hear her breathing, close to his ear. He felt her silver hair brush his face. Her scent was one of fear and excitement.

"I don't need to ask you if you're absolutely certain," he said. "You wouldn't be telling me if you weren't."

"You'd better believe it. I've *been there*, boss. There's no mistaking what I saw."

"Why didn't we realize before?"

"Because we weren't looking before. Or at least we weren't looking with our eyes open, anyway. A wormhole's a wormhole, right? We thought we knew what we were seeing."

"Cobiac and Bray? What about them?"

"No sign of them, but then I didn't go far. Even though Deangelis had taken the first steps—"

She stopped as something banged from the outside. Their angular momentum changed abruptly, rattling them about like two cats in a barrel.

"Shit." Eogan pulled himself out of the component until he was free from the waist up. He needed his head absolutely clear in order to think what to do next. It all depended on who had got to them first.

His dream—of taking seven steps into a corridor and eleven to get back again—recurred with unwanted intensity.

Another bang. Their headlong rotation slowed. He felt N-6 passively succumb to the grip of another vessel.

Vermeulen tried the same trick she had with him, communicating via sound through the hull of the capsule.

"If that's you, Aesche," she said, "don't broadcast anything just yet."

"No." Eogan suddenly saw the way things had to unfold in his head, as though they were already happening. "We don't need to run silent any longer."

"I can hear you," said Aesche, following Vermeulen's lead anyway.

That it *was* she and not Deangelis gave him a moment of relief—but it was short-lived. Her component was open to public scrutiny. Anything they said would be overheard by Bedlam.

"We've been running silent because our systems were unstable," he said via more conventional means, confident Aesche would recognize the cover story for what it was. "Now that we're piggybacking off yours, it should be okay."

"You're not hurt?" she asked.

"We're fine. Palmer Vermeulen lost control of the escape capsule and only just managed to catch mine before it spun right out of range. We're lucky we didn't have to chase her halfway across the system."

He felt Vermeulen watching him closely, trying to work out what his intentions were.

"Well, we're glad to have you both back with us," said Aesche. "It looked a little hairy, there."

"Too hairy by half," Eogan agreed. "I'm starting to think we made a mistake, sticking around so long."

A second's silence greeted his announcement. Then: "You know you're not alone in that," said Aesche cautiously.

He nodded, pleased that she had caught on so quickly. "I didn't think so. You've all been very patient with me, but it's time I did the right thing by the Cell. We've got to look after ourselves, first and foremost. Nearly losing Vermeulen has brought that home hard."

"What would you like me to do?" Aesche asked.

"Notify Lut-Deangelis Traffic Control of our intention to leave."

"When?"

"Immediately, of course," he said. "And tell Palmer Flast, as well. I'd like him to join us, either as my second officer or as chief of the *Kwal Bahal*. Whatever suits him."

"I'll give him the option."

Eogan had no doubt which option Flast would choose. "Thank you, Palmer Aesche."

The only reply was a soft groan as the three components began to merge into one, absorbing the foreign material of the escape capsule in the process.

Vermeulen's hand found his and squeezed softly. "Don't go all soft on me now, Eogan."

He nodded, wishing he could genuinely put the safety of his crew ahead of the situation in Bedlam. The lie was easy to say because it wasn't entirely untruthful.

"We've been out of the Dark long enough," he said, thinking of everything Vermeulen had told him and feeling very, very tired. "It's time to go home."

+40

Yasu had been waiting for Melilah when she left the reconstruction meeting. Effectively ambushed, Melilah had had no choice but to be swept along with her four-daughter's enthusiasm at their reunion. Ordinarily she would have been more interested in what had happened in the shelters during the attack, and she felt bad for being distracted. But she had been intending to sit down with the file she had uncovered in the depths of Bedlam in the hope of gaining some sort of advantage over Deangelis. Even as she talked to Yasu, she scanned the surface layers of the data, looking for a way in. Images of holidays and half-baked treasure maps mingled in an untidy mess, getting her nowhere.

The events occurring around the Occlusion gradually overtook them as they traveled by transport in the rough direction of Melilah's apartment. She felt a stab of concern at the thought that Eogan and the crippled *Nhulunbuy* might be destroyed if the Occlusion chose that moment to blossom. The strength of the feeling confirmed that, although she might be as angry with him as ever, she'd long gotten over her wish that he was dead.

And then came the bombshell.

"Leaving?" Yasu sounded as though she couldn't believe what she was hearing. "He can't be!"

"Looks very much like it to me." A numbness spread through Melilah, as though she had been dipped in liquid nitrogen.

"But you spoke to him barely an hour ago. He said he'd call you, that he'd be coming back!"

Melilah shrugged. "I guess he changed his mind."

"So what are you going to do about it?" Yasu took her hands. "You can't let him get away from you again!"

Melilah felt a rush of affection for her descendant. Yasu was young and entirely too enthused by what she saw on the Scale-Free Bedlam feeds. The world wasn't a soap opera; it didn't have story arcs, coherent themes, or happy endings.

"Calm down," Melilah told her. "You're blowing all of this right out of proportion."

"But after all you and he went through—you can't just stand back and watch him leave!"

"Yasu, listen to me. Palmer Eogan is not your four-father."

The words emerged without premeditation. If she'd stopped to think, she might have talked herself out of revealing the truth. That had always been something for her to know, no one else. But the revelation had the desired effect. Yasu's mouth shut with a snap; her eyebrows converged; her gaze swept Melilah's face as though searching for a lie.

"I'm sorry," Melilah went on. "Your great-great-grandfather was an anonymous sample recovered from a First Waver cache I stumbled across, two years after Palmer Eogan left. There was no actual person involved; there was just a dead donor, and me. I was adrift, struggling to get back to who I was before Eogan; I needed something to keep me focused. That something ended up being a baby— Athalia, your three-mother, and I'm sure she's the one who put all these ridiculous notions in your head. She could never accept the truth. But if you dig deep enough through the records, you'll find it there, Yasu. Not that it matters now, of course. It shouldn't. Does it?"

Yasu surprised her by bursting into tears. "Oh, Grandmother Mel."

Not sure what had brought that on, Melilah took her four-daughter into her arms.

"I'm sorry," she said again, patting Yasu on the back as she would a child—as she had when Yasu *was* a child, two decades earlier. "I didn't mean to upset you."

"No." Yasu's voice was muffled by her shoulder. "I'm the one who should be sorry. I've been going on and on about Eogan, and he's probably the last person you want to talk about."

"It's okay," Melilah soothed her. "I'm all grown-up, remember? I can handle it."

"But you must have been so *lonely*." Yasu pulled back enough to look at her with swollen, red-rimmed eyes.

"Yes, I was." She faced the truth of the statement without flinching. "But I'm not now, and that's the main thing. I have plenty of friends."

"And family." Yasu wiped her nostrils with the back of her hand.

"I have family I'm proud to call friends, and family I don't care if I never see again. You—" She took Yasu's face in one hand and squeezed it. "Yasu, you are most definitely in the first category."

"I'm glad." They hugged again, and Melilah felt the strange rush of emotion ebb, leaving her drained. She wasn't just "all grown-up"; she was entirely too old to be experiencing such violent mood swings. That was the domain of the young.

"I still hope you call him," Yasu confessed, as the transport pulled up outside Melilah's house. "It doesn't matter if he's not my four-father. I'd like to meet him one day, and that's not likely if you never talk to him again."

Melilah felt herself staring at Yasu as though she'd suddenly sprouted antennae and turned into an alien. "Why on Earth would you want to do that?"

The girl shrugged shyly. "One hundred and fifty years later, and not even the Gentry get you so worked up as he does. Eogan must be a rare person to flap the unflappable like that."

"Are you serious?"

Yasu just smiled and indicated the door. "You've got a lot to think about, Grandmother. I'll let you get on with it. I just wanted to make sure you were okay."

They kissed each other and said farewell. Melilah climbed out of the transport and waved as Yasu sped off into the distance.

When she was gone, Melilah turned to go inside, withdrawing into herself as she would to worry over a loose tooth.

41

The body of Lazarus Hails—bound up in layers of recuperative nanoware like a moth in a spiderweb—blinked and opened its eyes.

"Welcome back," said Exarch Deangelis, with genuine feeling. "You should be able to hear me now."

"I do hear you." Hails answered using his vocal cords, then continued via less obvious means: "I wasn't expecting to, though. I wasn't expecting to do much of anything. I remember—"

The gaze of Hails's milky gray eyes locked on Deangelis and studied him closely. Hails had lost all of his white mane and eyebrows. He looked vulnerable, even weak without it, as though genuinely suffering from old age rather than indulging the semblance of it.

"Cazneaux got to you," Hails said. "I thought she might. You're too trusting, Isaac. You'd do well to cultivate some good, healthy paranoia before it's too late."

"She didn't succeed," Deangelis told him, with some satisfaction.

"Oh? I guess not, or we wouldn't be having this conversation."

"And the Archon is here."

Hails was silent for a long minute. His gaze drifted, turned inward. "Well, then."

"You'll be discharged in an hour. This is"—Deangelis indicated the brittle cocoon—"cosmetic. You can leave anytime you want."

"Leave? When things are just getting interesting?"

Deangelis hoped his relief didn't show. He wanted Hails awake and able to talk. They weren't friends, but they were the next best thing for trillions of kilometers. He could use some advice.

He explained the events of the previous day, supplementing his words with images and raw data. He automatically did his best to present the illusion that everything was under control, but suspected Hails could see through it easily enough. He wasn't a fool. He knew what Palmer Eogan's decision to leave might mean.

"So the Occlusion remains intact." Hails's gaze was on him again, probing.

"The throat is still open. I'll give you full access to the data when your peripherals are completely restored. But at this stage the situation is complicated."

"You should have seen this coming, Isaac. The Coral is dangerous. Those it touches, it kills. Its very existence is antithetical to everything the Exarchate—and Sol—stand for. The knowledge that it's surfaced again was bound to provoke an extreme reaction. Those of us who've spoken to Jane Elderton—and there are a few of us, now—have had a taste of what we stand to lose. There was always going to be someone who went too far."

"I need to know . . ." Deangelis stopped to take a deep, calming breath. Talking about the attack never failed to shake his newly restored coherence. "Did you support Frederica Cazneaux?"

Hails shook his head, and grimaced. "I wouldn't be here, done up like a mummy, if I had."

"What about Lan Cochrane?"

A nod. "She supplied the clane, and made sure it was ferried here on Palmer Christophe's Cell."

Deangelis had suspected as much. Hails had mentioned the Exarch of Alioth-Cochrane as the source of his information about the Occlusion. That doubled the number of people against whom he wished revenge.

"Are there more?"

"I honestly don't know. There's a whole lot of talk going on out there. Several factions are swinging into gear."

"Why didn't you tell me about them?" he asked Hails. "Why didn't you warn me?"

"I didn't tell you, my boy, because I wasn't completely certain of my intelligence. All I had, really, were insinuations from Cochrane and Cazneaux that they were taking steps, plus some solid reasoning on my own part. It wasn't much to give you, and there were many other ways it could've gone. It's the same now. The best I can do is to encourage you to make contingency plans, to consider every option. I'm genuinely sorry that wasn't enough, last time." Hails shrugged minutely under the white crust. "You can't blame me for being cautious."

"They used a Reaper." Deangelis fought to keep his voice level. "They sent a Reaper, and they fired on my habitat—on my *people!*" He could feel himself shaking. "There is no greater crime."

"Oh, there are worse crimes than that, Isaac. Believe me. Pray this is as bad as it gets." Hails shifted again, as though uncomfortable in his cocoon. "That's what I'm doing."

"What do you mean by that?"

Hails sighed. "Wrong question, Isaac. You've got eyes. Open them occasionally, and you'll see what I see. Until then, why not ask me if I know whether Cazneaux and Cochrane had any allies? Ask me what happened to Alioth-Cochrane's tangler. Ask me what I've done to protect my own people."

Deangelis was shaking so badly he couldn't speak.

"I'll save you the trouble," said Hails. "I don't know the answer to any of those questions, except the last. And again, the fact that I'm here right now should make it fairly clear what that answer is. I can't tell you what to do, but I can guide you in the right direction. You have to go the rest of the way yourself, as we were designed to do."

Deangelis nodded, understanding at least part of what Hails was trying to say. The Exarchate, thanks to the tyranny of distance, wasn't intended to be a close-knit community. Individual Exarchs had to be fiercely self-reliant. If they'd needed outside help in the early years, all of them would have failed. Critical decisions simply couldn't wait on consensus from the Exarchate or word from Sol. So Deangelis and his peers were independent to the core. They could run an entire colony single-handedly for decades, and would react strongly against any suggestion otherwise. If ever technology did shrink the distance between the stars to the point that Arc Circuit systems became neighbors, separated by hours or even days, the balance of the Exarchate would inevitably shatter.

And no one wanted that.

"Fine," he said, allowing himself to accept that Hails was probably telling the truth. His sense of relief was powerful. "Circumstances are continuing to develop. I may need to call on you for advice. Would that be all right?"

"I'm keen to help, Isaac. I can't lie around here all day. Just don't expect me to make the tough decisions for you."

"I won't." He had expected nothing else. The Archon had made it clear that he was on his own, when it came down to the crunch. As appalling, though, as that felt at times, he knew it was the right thing.

"Don't worry about me." Hails closed his eyes and eased back into the cocoon. "I'm sure you have more important things to think about."

You have no idea, thought Deangelis, as his point of view detached from the body in the infirmary and prepared to cross instantly to the other side of the habitat.

"Send the Archon my regards," said Hails, as Deangelis jumped.

Deangelis froze in midleap like a transport slamming into a solid wall.

There are several factions swinging into gear.

In the complex no-space of his dissociated mind, Deangelis frantically replayed his conversation with the body of Lazarus Hails.

The best I can do is to encourage you to make contingency plans, to consider every option.

The Exarch of Kullervo-Hails system had been circumspect while seeming to be completely direct. He had dropped hints of conspiracies springing into life when word of the Occlusion leaked, but he had only described one of them—the one containing Cazneaux and Cochrane, hellbent on eliminating the threat the Occlusion represented.

But what about the *other* conspiracies? How many were there? Who belonged to them? What were their objectives?

You can't blame me for being cautious . . .

Hails was insinuating something very serious, and the way he was saying it was the most important clue of all. Telling Deangelis to pass on his regards to the Archon was both bizarre and meaningless—on the surface, anyway. Hails could talk to the Archon anytime he wanted; in fact, it was a fair assumption that the Archon had already heard everything that had passed between them. What was the point in giving Deangelis an instruction that made no sense?

Because it made sense in a completely different context. Hails was trying to tell Deangelis something he didn't want the Archon to hear. Something about conspiracies, and about the home system. Something that must have been nagging Deangelis's subconscious or else he might never have noticed it at all.

I can't tell you what to do, but I can guide you in the right direction. You have to go the rest of the way yourself, as we were designed to do.

Deangelis was glad he hadn't returned to his body before rethinking the conversation, for he was sure if he had that he would have physically staggered from the enormity of its conclusion. It struck him as though from nowhere, yet every point was there in Hails's conversation, carefully planted so as to make sense one way at first, then a completely different way in retrospect. The audacity of it astounded him. What if Deangelis hadn't seen through such a clumsy ploy? What if the Archon had?

Even as he contemplated the last, awful possibility, he reassured himself that it was unlikely. As advanced as the

Archon was, there were subtleties of communication that one could only appreciate from within. An ordinary human could marvel at the complexity of birdcalls, and even go so far as to decipher approximate meanings, but the details—the metaphors and similes, the allusions and hints—would go forever undetected.

He wondered for the first time what the humans in his care got away with, even with him constantly watching. Was this how Eogan and Awad had exchanged information about the Occlusion without him knowing? Was this how word would spread if Eogan and Vermeulen decided to reveal what they might have learned from the far side of the Occlusion?

The Coral is dangerous. Those it touches, it kills. Its very existence is antithetical to everything the Exarchate—and Sol—stand for.

So much for coming to his fellow Exarch for reassurance and advice. Lazarus Hails's information might have been out-of-date, but it was clear he already knew too much, and the conclusion he had come to was radically different from his own.

For one wild, exhilarating second, Deangelis thought he might laugh aloud, everywhere at once. The idea of defying the Archon was simply absurd.

But then he shuddered, more appalled now by the possibility Hails had raised than by the fact that he had raised it at all. The idea of rebellion was crazy—but a rebellion with Geodesica behind it might very well succeed . . .

42

"Still nothing from Alioth," said Aesche. "The channels are completely blocked."

Eogan glanced up from the controls of the hopper as it descended over Bedlam.

"It doesn't matter," he said. "I can guess what they'll do."

"Embargo?"

"Undoubtedly." The death of the Negotiator Select would send ripples of anxiety and alarm through his colleagues. Where once they had been keen to negotiate over rights to the knowledge gleaned from the Occlusion, now they would want nothing more than to stay away. Until the fuss died down, the potential costs outweighed the gains.

Eogan didn't, therefore, harbor any hope of calling for help from his colleagues. No other Cells had remained in Bedlam since the attack, and he couldn't help a rush of disappointment at the ease with which the Palmers had been scared off. The Occlusion offered either salvation or destruction—depending entirely on who got their hands on it first. In economic and social terms, this was the most critical juncture in the history of the Palmers—and they had run away at the first challenge.

"Either way," Aesche said, "we're on our own."

Aesche's words fueled his grim determination to act before the chance was taken away from him.

"This is LDTC." A new voice replaced Aesche's. "Palmer Eogan, your approach has been disallowed."

He blinked, surprised, at the image of the habitat floating before him. "Could you repeat that, Traffic Control?"

"Your approach has been disallowed, Palmer Eogan,

pending repairs to docking facilities. Please return to your Cell. We'll notify you when it's safe to return."

For twenty seconds, while he thought the development through, Eogan didn't change course. The cowardice of the Palmers didn't surprise him, but the Exarch's directness did. Clearly Deangelis was afraid of what Eogan had learned from Vermeulen, and with good reason. The Exarch wasn't an idiot. That he was taking such direct action so soon—concocting excuses so transparent anyone with half an eye could see through them—only highlighted his desperation.

Eogan was tempted to ignore the warning and keep on going. Only the fear that Deangelis might use the recent security scare as an excuse to blow him out of the sky turned him against that plan. Best not to give the Exarch more reasons than he had to.

"Understood, LDTC. Changing course now. Good luck with those repairs."

"Thanks, Palmer Eogan. Try us again in a day or two."

"Will do," he said. Thinking: *And fuck you, too.*

Eogan kicked the hopper onto a new trajectory, one that would take it around Bedlam's equator, then back up to the *Nhulunbuy.*

There went his best chance to talk to Melilah face-to-face. But it wasn't his *last* chance.

"Palmer Flast," he broadcast, "did you catch that?"

"I did indeed. These are heady times."

"Tell me about it. How far away are you from departing?"

"An hour. We have some last-minute patches to oversee, then we're gone."

"Good. I assume those damaged docks won't be a problem going in the opposite direction." Eogan didn't hide a slight sharpness in his tone. He waited a second for LDTC to interrupt. This was the Exarch's chance to speak up if he had a problem with the *Kwal Bahal* departing.

When no such protest came, he went on: "Before you leave, there's something I need you to do . . ."

+43

The call came as Melilah settled back into her apartment to continue scouring the data cache.

"Melilah, it's Eogan."

She considered rejecting the overture, just as she had resisted the urge to call him, against Yasu's advice. If he really was leaving again, it was probably best just to let him go. Why risk opening another wound at such a late stage?

But he *had* called her, and she had told herself that she would respond if he did.

"I know you can hear me, Melilah. I'm patched into the feed."

She sighed. "What do you want, Eogan?"

"To talk to you."

"So badly you've already booked your departure. I get it. What do I have that you could possibly still want?"

"Maybe it's the other way around."

She couldn't see him. The lack of image frustrated her. She couldn't tell if he was being serious or trying to make light of the situation.

"Just go," she said softly. "Just leave me alone."

He wouldn't give up. "I'm sorry, Melilah. I can't do that. Some things are too important. I need to see you."

"Come on down, then. No one's stopping you."

"Actually, they are. LDTC has locked the docks."

That surprised her, but the ramifications of the fact didn't sink in immediately. "Then what do you propose? That I should go up there?"

He didn't say anything. He didn't need to. The silence said it for him.

I should go up there?

"No," she said with a sudden lack of breath. "I can't do that."

"It's not difficult. Palmer Flast can be at your door in five minutes. He and his Cell are joining me anyway. They can give you a lift, and drop you back afterward."

"No, Eogan. I'm sorry."

"An hour of your time: that's all I'm asking."

"It's too much."

"Melilah, I wouldn't do this to you if I didn't think it truly important."

His insistence was what caught her. That wasn't like him. Then there was the fact that Traffic Control had locked him out of the habitat. Why would Deangelis do that if all Eogan wanted to do was say good-bye to his ex?

He knows something!

She felt the beginnings of excitement in her gut. The only knowledge with any real currency concerned the Occlusion. If it had been anything else, he could have just told her over the air.

"An hour," she said. "Tops."

"That's all I'll need." He sounded relieved. "Flast is on his way. Be ready to move quickly. You might need to."

She puzzled over his last instruction as she waited for Flast to arrive. Deangelis surely wouldn't stop her from leaving. Would he? She supposed it would depend entirely on what he thought Eogan knew.

Melilah looked around her apartment, at the gathered souvenirs of a long, productive life. She was healthy and in good spirits, and likely to live another two hundred and fifty years if she stayed that way. She would deal with Eogan first, then conduct a fifty percent cull of the names in her memory exercise file. She had to stop living in the past. The future waited.

Her doorway chimed for attention. Assuming it was Flast, she opened it and went to leave.

A stranger stood outside—a large man dressed in white with a pink, blotchy scalp. She recognized his face from the wine bar in Albert Hall. He had been drinking with Exarch Deangelis.

"Please accept my apologies for disturbing you," he said in a voice that boomed improbably. "We have only a moment in which to speak."

"Who are you?" She backed away from him, unnerved by the intensity of his eyes. She considered calling security. "What do you want?"

"To tell you that you are not alone. Your goals are shared by others. We want the same thing."

"Which is?"

"Independence, of course."

He reached out to touch her, but she pulled away.

"Hey!"

"There's no reason to be alarmed." His manner belied his words. Shooting a quick glance either way up the corridor, he tried again. "Melilah, you *must* let me give you—"

"Get the hell away from me!" She braced herself against her doorframe and shoved him back. He tumbled in the low gee just as the first alarm began to buzz. A swarm of flat, disk-shaped security drones rushed up the corridor.

"Be careful of him," said an urgent voice into her ear. "I don't think he's human."

She recognized the oily tones instantly. *Gil Hurdowar.* "What—?"

She stopped, coughing. The stranger had done a strange thing, pursing his lips and emptying his lungs at her as though blowing out the candles on a birthday cake. She recoiled, blinking away sudden grittiness. A taste of peppermint flooded across her tongue.

The security drones rushed into the space between them and forced the stranger back.

My name is Lazarus Hails, said a voice into her mind— the same voice as the stranger. *I know this is surprising, my dear, but you must not react. Your life may depend on it.*

The man backed away and held up his hands as the drones harangued him. She stared at him in alarm. *Nanotech!*

Indeed. Now, pay attention. The Kwal Bahal *is here. You should meet Palmer Eogan as planned. I'll explain on the way.*

Why should I listen to you?

Because it's the only way you're going to hear the truth.

She was about to protest—audibly, so everyone could hear what had happened to her—when the name the stranger had offered finally fell into place.

Lazarus Hails—the Exarch of Altitude!

I don't think he's human, Hurdowar had said—and he was absolutely right. According to Melilah's definition of humanity, Hails was as alien as the entities who had built the Occlusion and destroyed Sublime.

But he, too, was offering her a version of the truth, and he hadn't actually hurt her. *Yet.*

"Melilah?" It was Sarian this time, from the great, gray bauble heaving to up the corridor. "Are you okay?"

"I'm fine," she said. A rush of light-headedness threatened to trigger an attack of vertigo, but she swallowed it down. That could have been a side effect of Hails's nanoware, or because things were happening so fast that she felt as though she were rapidly being left behind.

Hails had his hands raised behind a ring of drones. "Freak," she told him, for the benefit of the people watching, and also for her own satisfaction. She kicked past him, leaving him to sort out the situation.

"I'm coming," she told Sarian.

The Cell component was already open, gaping like a mouth.

"Is everything under control, Isaac?"

The Archon's question cut across Deangelis's view of events as they unfolded in the habitat. From one angle, he saw the components of the *Kwal Bahal* converging across all quarters in preparation to leave. From another he saw Lazarus Hails—fresh from the infirmary and as hairless as a babe—arguing with a human security officer after his confrontation with Melilah Awad. She, unexpectedly, was back in a Cell component and heading to a rendezvous with Palmer Eogan—who was waiting in the *Nhulunbuy* outside the habitat, already configuring his Cell to leave the system with Vermeulen and whatever secrets she had uncovered.

His options were limited. Melilah Awad was at or near the center of so many situations it frightened him. She was a hub, connected to many people at once, like one of the junctions in the habitat's scale-free network of pipes and corridors. He couldn't let Awad talk to the Palmers, given her recent, mysterious exchange with Hails and her continued worrying over the data he had hidden. Hails and Eogan were hubs, too. He would have to eliminate them as well as her in order to bring current events to a complete halt. But there was no way he could do that—even ignoring the local information laws working against him—without raising tension even higher. And he couldn't let Palmer Eogan leave, especially if Vermeulen had learned what he feared she had.

Is everything under control, Isaac?

How to answer the question without exposing the utter depths of his own uncertainty?

"Let me ask *you* a question, Archon," he said.

"Of course."

The question had been nagging at him ever since his conversation with Lazarus Hails. The Archon had intervened in the attack on the observatory, but it couldn't have known about that before it left, so that wasn't the answer. It claimed not to want to make his decisions for him, so that wasn't the answer either. Since its arrival it had done little more than watch, pass the occasional comment, and tinker deep in the bowels of the habitat. Sol had been silent since the Archon's arrival, but the tangler wasn't idle. Moved from its usual location since Melilah Awad had glimpsed it during the attack, it had become the Archon's responsibility. What it was doing was kept secret even from Deangelis.

"Archon, why are you here?"

"I am here because what happens here is ultimately my responsibility. And by 'here' I don't mean this system; I mean the Exarchate. I created it; it's my project. Were Geodesica to have manifested anywhere else, in any other way, it wouldn't be my direct concern. But it *is* here, and now, and I must oversee the way it's handled. Not just for me and the Exarchate, but for all of humanity."

My project. The Archon made the Exarchate sound like an experiment, a hobby. Was that what an empire of over a thousand suns was to its evolved mind: a reaction in a test tube that could be poured down the drain if it went sour?

"I understand," he said. "I think I do, anyway. But how will your being here make a difference? What are you going to *do?*"

"Palmer Eogan asked me much the same question," the Archon replied.

"And what did you tell him?"

"That I don't know what my actions will be. How could I? My plans are contingent on events as they unfold. There are many things I *could* do, of course, but knowing what I *will* do is too difficult even for someone such as me. *More* difficult, perhaps, because I can see so many more possibilities. A shortsighted person can do little more than follow the road she's on; someone blessed with clear sight sees all the turnoffs she could take—and numerous alternate paths besides, running parallel to the one beneath her feet. One is only lost when one has some perception, no matter how dim, that there is somewhere else one should be."

The reply did little to quell Deangelis's unease. "I fear, Archon, that this situation is far from optimal, in your estimation."

"Don't worry about me, Isaac. Simply do what you think is right. I trust you and I expect from you only what I expect from myself—that you will do your best in any circumstance. Remember that this is not an exam; there is no *failure*. There are only consequences, as in all moments of life. Do not imagine that I have come here to judge you."

The Archon hesitated, then continued on a slightly different tack: "Perhaps I am misreading your question. Do you ask because there is something you would *like* me to do? Is there any way in which I can help you feel more in command of this situation? All my resources are at your disposal."

The offer was unexpected, and momentarily threw Deangelis. What wondrous devices had the Archon been building with the tangler and all the know-how of Sol? There might be nothing he could conceive of that lay beyond his creator's capacities.

He thought of all the elements of the situation that seemed to be spiraling out of his control: Hails and his insinuations; Eogan and Vermeulen; Melilah Awad. They were all people, and he wasn't sure he entirely trusted the Archon's instincts when it came to dealing with them. If he was to ask for help, it would have to be in an area that wouldn't cause him greater concern.

"The observatory," he said. "It was destroyed in the attack. Only the ruins protect the Occlusion right now. It worries me that it's been left vulnerable, but I've been so busy focusing on the habitat that there's been little time to rebuild. Would you be willing to assist me in that area while I deal with the others?"

"Your mind can rest easy on that score, Isaac." The Archon's reply was gracefully unctuous. "I will begin work at once, while you deal with the situation at hand."

Deangelis's gratitude was mixed with a dose of discomfort at relinquishing even a small measure of control. He reassured himself that there was little the Archon could do without his knowing. The observatory site was in full view of the habitat. Nothing too dramatic could go on there and remain hidden for long.

That left only the convergence of Palmer Eogan, Lazarus Hails, and Melilah Awad to worry about. They were hubs, and so was the colony Awad insisted on calling Bedlam. He wondered if he was a thorn in the Archon's side, as she was in his.

That thought, more than any other, made him hesitate.

+45

"Your behavior hasn't gotten any less reckless, I see," said Vermeulen. "Deangelis is never going to let them leave."

"There's a big difference between keeping someone out and locking them in." Eogan hoped he knew what he was talking about. He still had the equivalent of a watchmeter running in the *Nhulunbuy*. A large percentage of Bedlam's citizens—reconnected to the network and worried about what was going on—were observing his every word, just as he was watching events in their homes.

The many components of the *Kwal Bahal* met and formed the same great pearl necklace it had been on its arrival in the habitat. Flast announced his intention to exit via one of the main docks.

Traffic Control didn't respond.

"Do we have permission or not?" asked Flast.

"You weren't given permission to enter," said the Exarch himself, "so you don't need permission to leave."

"Fine. I'll remember that next time we help you out."

"This isn't ingratitude. Neither is it an argument about law. We trade insult for insult. Can you tell me now, before all my charges, that your intentions are honorable?"

"I have no quarrel with you," said Flast. "I just want to get out of here."

"Then go." Deangelis's various bodies stood stiff and stony-faced as his words echoed through the habitat, emerging from no single mouth but as though out of thin air. "I will not stop you."

"Great," muttered Vermeulen. "He's making *us* look like the bad guys."

"Maybe we are," said Eogan. "Sometimes the truth can harm."

"Hiding the truth is *always* wrong."

He smiled. "That sounds like something Melilah would say."

"You disagree?"

He thought carefully before replying. "I think life is too complex to make such general statements about it. It'd be the same as my insisting that electrons travel in circular orbits or that space is flat. I could believe it as much as I wanted, but reality would keep on surprising me."

The *Kwal Bahal* emerged from the main dock and swept away from the habitat. Eogan felt numerous instruments tracking it, as though it was at the center of dozens of crosshairs. He didn't know how far Deangelis or the Archon would go to protect their secrets. He only hoped they hadn't already crossed the line.

"I've had enough surprises to last a lifetime," said Vermeulen.

"You and me both," he agreed.

The *Kwal Bahal* pulled up alongside the *Nhulunbuy* and handed over its systems to Eogan's command. He kept the two Cells nominally separate, even if they effectively constituted a single Cell once more. Keeping two chief officers in place had the potential to be unwieldy, but they didn't have to maintain the illusion for long.

Melilah hadn't said a word throughout the short trip. She didn't look comfortable in K-3, braced with every limb against the interior walls as though expecting it to lurch at any moment. Sarian, the pilot, respected her silence and did her best to make the ride comfortable. There wasn't much she could do to improve it, though; with minute reactionless thrusters propelling the component on all sides, there was little chance of her feeling any motion at all.

"Our VOID capacity is still down," said Aesche. "With the *Kwal Bahal* and fair weather, we might just make a de-form rating of two and half. Maybe three. That puts us a long way from anything."

"A long way from *here* is where I want to be," he said, maintaining the half lie. "Just tell me you can get us moving. We'll work the details out as we go."

"Moving, yes. Running, no."

"Good enough."

A mental command saw his component separate from Vermeulen's and thrust toward K-3. The two components exchanged protocols and prepared to merge. With a faint sigh, their protective fields overlapped. A hole opened in the bulkhead in front of Eogan to reveal Sarian's startled-looking passenger.

"Hello, Melilah."

"We've got to stop meeting like this," she said dryly. "People will talk."

He smiled at her attempt at humor. "Come through here." He had detached himself as much as possible from the Cell, but he could tell that she was still unnerved by his appearance. His back and shoulders were fused with the bulkhead behind him, as though he had eased back into a seat made of taffy. When he leaned forward, the connections stretched like chewing gum.

This was the first time that she had seen him in his normal environment, but there was no point hiding it. The nature of his existence had to be confronted at some point, if only out of a need for closure. He wanted her to see the person he had chosen to be—the person she had rejected by asking him not to become a Palmer. He could still see the look of horror in her eyes when he had raised the merest possibility.

Her lips tightened. That was the only outward sign she gave that she even noticed.

"Well," she said, when the hole sealed shut behind her. The components separated inaudibly. "I'm here."

Not just you, he wanted to say. The Cell was picking up a stream of highly unusual signals pouring out of her body. This was more than the usual information flow surrounding everything in and near Bedlam. It was as though something—an intelligence much more advanced than any he was used to interacting with—had taken over her body and was using it as an antenna.

"Thank you," he said, wondering who else he was talking to, exactly. "This is a very difficult situation. It forces us to do things we might not normally like to do."

"Don't flatter yourself," she said. "I got over you years ago."

"I'm not talking about that," he said. "And I'm not talking about being in the Cell, either." He turned his head symbolically aside to address Aesche, and spoke aloud for Melilah's benefit. "Are the systems ready, Palmer Aesche?"

"As ready as they're going to be."

"Good. Then let's get out of here."

He caught a momentary reaction from Melilah. A flash of panic passed across her face, but was quickly suppressed.

"We're leaving Bedlam?" she asked.

"And taking you with us. I'm sorry, Melilah."

He waited for her to protest, to argue, to shout for help—but she said nothing. She looked frightened, but not in the least surprised.

The *Nhulunbuy* and the *Kwal Bahal,* united in all but name, curved away from Bedlam and aimed for the stars.

Melilah went to say something, but Eogan raised his hand for silence.

Ten thousand kilometers away from the giant habitat, one minute into their journey, the Cell passed outside the colony's territorial jurisdiction. With perfect legality, and in complete accord with usual custom, it severed contact with the network and turned control of its navigation to internal systems.

Eogan's watchmeter program clicked instantly to zero.

Information flows returned to normal within the Cell. Eogan severed all contact with anyone outside the component.

At last, they were truly alone.

46

Melilah crouched in the dimly lit component, not daring to move a muscle. The Cell, touching her peripherals as lightly as a feather, offered her a feed not greatly dissimilar to the ones she had accessed in Bedlam, and she took it, nervously at first but with greater confidence once she was certain no tricks were intended. Through it she saw the *Nhulunbuy/Kwal Bahal*'s many components sweeping in a long arc, accelerating steadily as they went. Bedlam receded into the distance behind it. A long time had passed since she had last left the colony she loved. That she didn't know when—or if—she would return made her eyes water.

Melilah blinked back the tears. She didn't want to give anything to Eogan other than what she had come to tell him.

"We must be clear by now," she said.

"Almost. I'm just waiting for the signals from the nanoware you're carrying to give out. We're almost at the limit of their range."

She looked down at herself, still alarmed by the intrusion of Hails into her person. The nanoware had done little more, she'd thought, than convey a message from the Exarch to her. That it was still functioning when that message was complete made her shudder even more than Eogan did.

She kept her eyes down in an attempt not to stare at him. From the waist up and to the front, he might have been perfectly normal. His chest and arms were bare; his skin was hairless and covered in freckles. She didn't recognize the pattern, much to her relief. There were none of the gross physical intrusions to his eyes and face that Sarian tolerated.

But he had no legs, and he appeared to be melting into the unbroken wall. Every time he opened his mouth, she expected the whirring of gears to emerge, not a voice.

This is his home? she wondered. *This is what he wanted badly enough to ditch me for?*

Melilah tried to quash the bitterness, but it wouldn't stay down.

She cleared her throat, and said, "I have a destination for you."

"Good," he responded with disarming frankness, "because otherwise I was just going to pick a direction at random."

The heading Hails had given her wasn't hard to remember. "Aim for Bode's Nebula. Keep going for around two light-hours."

"And what will we find?"

"A tangler," she said. "Do you know what that is?"

"I have a pretty good idea."

"It's an end point of the Exarch's ftl web," she explained. "Our reverse engineers have been trying to work out the Gentry's communication systems for decades. It turns out they *have* been using entanglement, but with relays every two or three light-years to boost the signals. At each end point is a tangler—and it does a whole lot more than just receive data. It uses nanotech to turn the data it receives into physical objects. That's how the Gentry arrived in force from Sol, during the Expansion, without anyone seeing them on the trade lanes. They sent out the tanglers first. While we were whizzing around in our clunky ships, they were leapfrogging between the stars, nothing more than data. The tanglers built them and their Reapers out of space dust and comets."

Eogan was watching her as she spoke, his green eyes impenetrable.

"If it wasn't *them* behind it," she admitted, "I'd think the idea pretty clever."

"Tell me," he said, "how you know all this."

"Lazarus Hails told me."

"He's the one who gave you the nanoware?"

"Along with the destination, yes."

Eogan nodded. "I've instructed the Cell to follow the vector you gave us. We'll see if Hails is as good as his word when we get there."

Melilah hadn't noticed anything to indicate that he had spoken to the *Nhulunbuy/Kwal Bahal* or its crew, or that they had changed course. "How long?"

"Six hours."

"Is that to a dead stop or for a flyby?"

"Dead stop, unless we change our minds on the way."

She was reassured that his intention wasn't really to leave the system—yet. "They'll be tracking us for sure, Deangelis and the Archon. They'll know when we start to decelerate."

"There's not much we can do about that from here."

"True." She tried not to look nervous, but she could feel herself beginning to talk for talk's sake. "Either way, we've got plenty of time to kill."

"It certainly seems that way."

There followed an awkward pause. "Do you want to go first?"

"That depends on what else you've got to tell me."

She nodded. "Okay. Hails wants us to lead a revolution against the Archon."

Eogan's eyebrows went up. "That's unexpected. Did he tell you that we could use the Occlusion to do it?"

"Not in so many words."

"I guess he knew I'd do it for him."

She felt her pulse quicken. "So it *is* a wormhole," she said. "Nothing could make me happier."

He shook his head. "It's not a wormhole as we understand them. I told you before that a wormhole had to have two ends, that it would lead *somewhere* or else what was the point of it?"

She nodded.

"Well, I was partly right and partly wrong. It's not *a* wormhole, Melilah. It's many of them, all tangled up in a knot. A maze."

She frowned, remembering Greek legends and pictures of old Earth hedges.

"A maze?"

"That's right. And there could be more than two exits. *Many* more."

She stared at him, forgetting for a moment to blink. "Fuck," she breathed, the implications hitting her almost immediately.

A maze with more than one exit wasn't a maze; it was a traffic grid.

"You'd better keep going," she said, completely forgetting about her surroundings in order to hear the rest.

Eogan wasn't the one to tell her all of it. He filled her in on the broadest details, then had his science officer join them to do the rest. Another component, dimly visible as a point of light through the translucent shell around her, grew larger against the backdrop of space until it looked like it was going to crash. Melilah felt a thrum of furious activity through her hands and toes as another portal opened before her, revealing Palmer Vermeulen.

Vermeulen sat cross-legged in the center of her component, legs folded beneath her and arms at her sides. Like Eogan, she looked normal at first glance. Only when Melilah noticed that her hands disappeared into the floor beneath her and her legs seemed to overlap peculiarly was she certain that Vermeulen was fully interfacing with the Cell.

So what is this? she wanted to ask them. *Pretense of humanity for the hick visitor?* Part of her would rather they just acted natural. She could deal with it.

But she was glad she didn't have to stare at naked posthumanity as she had with Sarian. No nanowires sticking out of eyes or melting torsos here.

"When the Reaper came to ram the observatory," Vermeulen said, "I thought I was finished. It was Deangelis who got me out in time. He whisked me into that escape capsule and pushed me through the throat so fast I barely had time to realize what was going on. Conditions inside the throat make for a rough ride, especially at speed; but it was short, and Deangelis had done his homework. The capsule made it through just fine. I've been taking it apart since I came back. I think I've found the trick to it."

Good, thought Melilah, although she didn't interrupt. They would need a reliable way to get through the Occlusion if they were ever going to use it to their advantage.

"The far side is much as Cobiac and Bray recorded it," Vermeulen continued. "A straight tunnel; perfect vacuum; nothing much to see apart from that. But it's obvious that Deangelis has been busy. There are instruments everywhere—in webs, growing into the walls, stretching roots farther than I could see up the tunnel. He's been having a ball, and he obviously hadn't expected anyone else anytime soon. The systems were encrypted, but it didn't take long to get in. I got the data he's gathered."

Melilah nodded. Reams of images and multidimensional graphs were streaming around her, projected by the Cell onto the walls of the joined components. None of it made any sense to her—except for one, a stark tangle of lines that reminded her of something she had seen recently.

"What's that?" she asked, as it flashed by again.

"It's a map," said Vermeulen. "Not complete by any means; it may be no more than the tiniest percentage of what's in there; and it's fiendishly difficult to follow. But it's definitely a map of sorts. Without it, I would never have gotten back."

Melilah turned sharply from the image. "Back from where?"

"Nowhere in particular. I just took a couple of corners, to make sure I was reading the map right. I was. The tunnel really does branch. It crosses other tunnels, loops back on itself, and stops dead, too—all in at least five dimensions. It's not the sort of place I'd spend long in without some sort of guide. If there's a pattern to it, I couldn't see one."

Neither could Melilah, at first glance. "Did you find another exit?"

"No. I don't think I went far enough. Conditions are very unnerving in there. Space doesn't work like it does out here. The warp that caught Cobiac and Bray by surprise is typical of the longer corridors, it seems. The greater the distance between two points, the higher the apparent acceleration someone passing between them will experience. It's not *actual* acceleration; it's more a kind of stretching, not so different to the Alcubierre effects that underlie the VOID drive. Space—as defined by the shape of the walls around you—flexes, so one step takes you farther than normal. You just seem to rocket along. And if you're not careful, you can get lost in seconds."

Melilah shivered. "So that's what happened to Cobiac and Bray. They warped up the opening tunnel and got lost."

Vermeulen nodded. "I don't think I can convey to you in words—or even with pictures—just how disorienting it is in there. Nothing works the way it does outside. Taking all left turns won't bring you back to where you started. Same with right turns. You might think you're going in a straight line, but you could actually be twisting in circles. Whoever designed it had a mind very different from ours."

"Or at least a very different way of looking at things."

"Cobiac and Bray could still be alive in there," Eogan said, his tone bitter. "If we'd waited a little longer, maybe they would've made it back."

Vermeulen didn't say anything. Her eyes were hard. Melilah could tell that she didn't want to give Eogan any unfounded hope. If the maze was as complicated as she described, if one short walk up a corridor could cross impossible distances in unfathomable directions, then Melilah could accept, at least notionally, that the two Palmers had become irretrievably lost. And that they had probably continued to wander after getting lost meant the chances of them ever being seen again were very slim indeed.

"So you went exploring," she said, "then you came back. How else did you kill your time in there?"

"That's the other weird thing," Vermeulen said. "According to Eogan, I was gone for fifteen hours. To me it was more like three."

"So time warps as well as space?"

Eogan nodded. "Makes sense," he said. "They're aspects of the same thing, after all."

"I think the warps are side effects," said Vermeulen. "Most of them, anyway."

"Of what?" Melilah asked her.

"Of the architecture itself. It clearly doesn't belong to this universe; it probably lives in its own unique continuum nestled alongside ours, connected in places by means of the wormholes. Its continuum is much smaller than ours. Its only contents are the maze and *its* contents. Or, more properly speaking, the interior of the maze is the true extent of the continuum it defines: there may be nothing at all outside the walls. So anything *inside* those walls will have a profound effect on the topology of the entire continuum."

"This is where I get a bit blurry," said Eogan to Melilah.

"Blurry my ass," Vermeulen said. "You're just not looking at it properly. The idea that any travelers within the maze actually cause the warps that push us along isn't so crazy. Neither is the possibility that neighboring corridors and their contents could affect each other, even if they are separated by light-years in the 'real' world. What happens inside that other continuum is what matters; that's all. At first glance, I felt sure that it was some kind of superscience transport system, a means of connecting stars, maybe even galaxies together. But now I'm not so sure. Why make it so damned complicated? Why not right angles and straight lines? Why not put signposts up everywhere?"

"Maybe because to the builders it isn't complicated," said Melilah. "Or maybe there were guides you just didn't see right."

"It's possible," said Vermeulen. "In fact, this is probably what Deangelis was looking for."

"We have to stop him from finding it," Melilah said. "We have to get there first."

"At the moment," said Eogan, raising a cautionary hand, "we don't have proof of anything much. There's no actual evidence that it's connected to any other point in our universe. We're only *assuming* that there's more than one entrance, that it's related to the thing they found in Sublime. We might have something completely different here. Strange as it sounds, this might not even be artificial. It could be a natural phenomenon."

"A living thing." Vermeulen stared at him with a slightly appalled expression. "A space-time mosquito, sucking the vacuum from one universe to another."

"And you went right up its mouth." Eogan didn't smile. "Sublime might have been its other end."

"Well, shit," Vermeulen said.

"Exactly."

Silence filled the joined components for a moment, as the Cell continued accelerating toward Bode's Nebula.

"Okay. It's my turn." Melilah reached out to the Cell with her peripherals, proffering the data she had been cradling ever since agreeing to meet the Palmers in their home environment. "I found this hidden on a fiche in the heart of Bedlam, a common place to hide data out of sight of the information laws." She didn't look at Eogan. "On the surface, it looks like nothing but letters and amateur maps, but I think there's more to it than that."

"Why?" asked Vermeulen.

"Several reasons." She waved away most of them as irrelevant. "The main one is because the map you displayed before looked familiar. It took me a while to work out where from. Take a look at the sketches in the file I've just given you. Tell me what you think."

Neither moved, but an instant later the data flashed onto the walls of the component around her. The maps were

crude and incomplete. Again, they reminded her of out-
lines of Bedlam's many crisscrossing corridors. She had
checked two days ago to see if it matched any region
within the habitat, without success. It had to be a map of
somewhere else, then.

"I think it's a map of the maze," she said after a moment. "What else could it be?"

"It does look similar," Vermeulen conceded, her pupils
moving, tracking things Melilah couldn't see. "That is, the
individual images do share a certain resemblance with the
ones I brought back."

"Just a resemblance?" asked Eogan.

"Don't forget that any map of the maze in three dimensions is an approximation of the real thing. It'll take me a
while to make sure they're one and the same."

"Take your time. We need to be certain before we make
any decisions about what to do with it."

"I haven't got very far with the rest of the file," Melilah
conceded. "The letters could just be a cover, to distract
from the real data."

"Or they could be the real thing." Eogan nodded. "We'll
work on it as we travel. If the Exarch has been storing any
data at all this way, I suspect it'll be worth getting our
hands on."

"I wouldn't be too sure about that," said Vermeulen.
"After all, he had a perfectly secure setup inside the Occlusion itself."

"Not perfectly secure—nor even safe, as Cazneaux's attack proved. He might have created the cache as a backup."

"And I was lucky enough to stumble across it," said
Melilah, a slight twinge that she hadn't immediately recog-
nized was evened out by the knowledge that she and the
Exarch had similarly demanding tastes in hiding places.

"What?" asked Eogan then, as she frowned.

"Nothing," she said. She had no intention of telling
them what she had been doing when she'd stumbled across
the cache, but the thought had just occurred to her that

Deangelis might have chosen the niche because he subconsciously wanted the data to be found, just as she didn't actually want to forget.

"Let's get on with it," she said. "This trip isn't going to take forever."

47

The sudden peace and quiet had to be an illusion. Or so Deangelis told himself as he wandered the halls of the habitat, tasting its inhabitants' mood. Everywhere he went, he saw relieved faces and determination to put things back the way they had been. Autonomous repair systems operated in tandem with human workers—the latter often more a hindrance than a genuine help, although he kept that carefully to himself. A sense of contributing to the reconstruction was good for morale. Bulkheads and pipes devoured by the infectious replicators grew slowly back into place. Water, air, power, and data lines were reconnected. Waste systems went back online. Only in a handful of areas were some secondary services on hold—such as food production and hard recycling—and he expected that to be a temporary restriction only. Before long, everything would be back as it was supposed to be.

On the surface, at least—and therein lay the problem. He could feel a tension everywhere he went, as though the cooperation and good-natured industry camouflaged a deeply felt but just as deeply buried concern. The habitat had been attacked; the reason for that attack was still nearby. What would happen next?

Deangelis sympathized with that feeling, even though the number of his problems was rapidly diminishing. The observatory was showing signs of activity under the guidance of the Archon. Hails was in protective custody. Melilah Awad was in the *Nhulunbuy/Kwal Bahal*, apparently leaving with Palmers Eogan and Vermeulen. He should have been relieved at having them finally out of his hair.

But it wasn't that simple. Even if there were no further attacks on the Occlusion, there would be recriminations down the line, should word ever get out. He had delayed dealing with the problem, not avoided it. He had gained a reprieve, nothing more.

Although he tried his best to ignore the uncertainty, it ate at him like vitriol. He hadn't handled the situation at all well. The best he could say about it was that the crisis had gone away. What sort of leader could he call himself, with that track record?

Still, his loss to the clane had earned him some sympathy among the general population. He was greeted by nods and waves. The occasional group invited him to join them in toasting a recently completed project, or merely to participate in the relief they felt that all was returning to normal.

He took the first few offers, but then declined them all. He didn't feel like celebrating. Instead of being cheered, his mood worsened. The sense of approaching doom grew stronger. He felt as hollow as a china doll, waiting for a hammer to fall.

The feeling only worsened when the Archon announced that he was taking the colony's tangler and relocating it in the ruin of the observatory.

"A temporary measure, Isaac, to save the resources ferrying materiel back and forth would consume."

Deangelis could see the sense in the plan, but that didn't mean he liked it. The tangler was his link to Sol; without it, he would feel more isolated than ever.

"The move is not permanent," the Archon reassured him. It failed to ease his mind at all. He watched a flotilla of cargo spheres exit the habitat's main docks with trepidation. Without the tangler at hand, his escape was no longer assured, should the worst come to pass.

"Don't worry," said a voice along a little-used communications channel. "She'll be back in no time."

Deangelis followed the communication back to its source. A quick glance took in the man's identity and his recent activities. Gil Hurdowar seemed to have taken up Exarch-watching in the absence of his usual target.

"I presume you are talking about Melilah Awad."

"Who else? Yasu and Defiance might think she's off on some wild, romantic tryst, but she can't fool us. Right?"

"I don't know what you mean." Hurdowar spoke with a camaraderie Deangelis disliked. "Whether she comes back or not is no concern of mine."

That earned him a laugh. "You can't fool me either, Deangelis. I've watched you watching her. I know that look."

"Are you suggesting . . . ?" He stopped, appalled by the man's insinuation. "That's the most ridiculous thing I've ever heard."

"Is it? Maybe you should listen to yourself sometimes."

Hurdowar killed the line, but Deangelis couldn't tear his appalled gaze away from his surveillance of the man. Agonized thoughts slowed his mind like clotted cream. Filthy, antisocial, and invasive Hurdowar might be, but was he as perceptive as he liked to think he was? Could he possibly be *right?*

Yes, Deangelis did spend more time observing and pondering Melilah Awad than he did most other citizens. That was only because she was at the center of so many critical situations. That was *her* issue, not his. If she hadn't been a borderline terrorist, always probing into secret places and trying to turn things against him, dissenting and brewing rebellion among her peers, he would happily ignore her, let her get on with her life like any of the other forty thousand people under his aegis.

The thought that he might be obsessed with her— romantically or otherwise—was patently absurd!

You should listen to yourself sometimes.

The strength of his response undercut his certainty. Was it possible that he was thinking at cross-purposes with himself, that part of him was indeed expending a disproportionate amount of time and energy focusing on Melilah

Awad, that he could have developed some strange, perverse attachment to this blatantly Normal woman? He didn't see how it could be possible. He might have saved her during the attack, but he would have done the same for anyone. He had shied away from blowing her out of the sky when she had run to Palmer Eogan, but both the urge to do so and the decision not to would have been identical if Gil Hurdowar had been in her place. He was sure of it. There was nothing he could see that set her apart, in his mind, from everyone else. There was nothing special about her at all.

A pinhole of doubt remained. He remembered his feeling when he had found her and Palmer Eogan embracing in one of the ruined alien vessels found alongside the Occlusion. The moment had struck him powerfully, and he had never been able to understand why. Could it be as simple as envy for the flesh? Was he desirous of her passion, her intimacy with primal emotions, her blindness to her own faults that propelled her along paths no rational mind could countenance? Did he long, bizarrely, to be as Naturally human as Melilah? To be Naturally human *with* her?

Deangelis honestly didn't know. Gil Hurdowar was probably just projecting his own feelings on another person, giving his obsession validity by mapping them on the system's ultimate authority. But he had raised a concern that couldn't easily be dismissed. Isaac Forge Deangelis, posthuman intelligence capable of experiencing all aspects of the universe from the breaking of a hydrogen bond to the stately rise and fall of economic trends, was aware of himself to a degree never experienced by ordinary humanity. There weren't supposed to be hidden nooks and crannies supplying twisted urges and self-destructive desires. That lack was one of the things that made him such a good colonial administrator.

But his life wasn't supposed to be so complex, either. He wasn't supposed to have been violently diminished in an attack from one of his own kind. He wasn't supposed to be living with the threat of destruction hanging constantly over his head. He wasn't supposed to be working under the watchful eye of the one who had created him.

Would it be any great wonder if he developed a flaw under such circumstances, if a hairline fracture formed and spread across the edifice that was his normal sense of self?

That fracture could take the form of obsessive feelings for one in his care. He supposed it was conceivable. Underneath all his synergistic cognation, he still had emotions and needs. He was still human in his frailty.

Not for much longer, he swore. Reconstruction progressed apace. He would soon be fully accustomed to the new dynamics of his higher mind. The Occlusion couldn't be a problem forever. When things settled down, the fracture would heal, and he would be back to his usual self.

The feeling that thunderheads were gathering just over the horizon was the only thing marring that plan.

+48

The moment the *Nhulunbuy/Kwal Bahal*'s forward sensors found the tangler, Eogan pasted an image of it onto the wall of the component.

"If that's what it really is," Vermeulen said. The faint image was barely discernible against the background sky.

"Hails had no reason to lie," Melilah said, rubbing weariness from her eyes with the tips of her fingers.

"You defending an Exarch?" Eogan made the point softly, not wanting to jab too deep. "That doesn't match your reputation."

She lowered her hands to look at him. "Lazarus Hails had no reason to tell me the truth, either. The whole lot could've been a load of bullshit—and we could be walking into a trap designed to get rid of everyone who knows anything about what the Occlusion really is."

"*Now* she raises the possibility," said Vermeulen, with a grimace.

"But I still trust him," Melilah said, "as far as I *can* trust him. We haven't proven him wrong yet."

"We'll know in an hour, I guess." Eogan didn't bother explaining that there was no way to bring that time forward. The *Nhulunbuy/Kwal Bahal* was still too deeply mired in the dust of Lut-Deangelis to activate its flawed drive efficiently. The point at which it was able to wouldn't come for some hours yet, when it passed the system's heliopause and entered the interstellar medium. There, with nuclei averaging less than one per square centimeter, the vacuum would be pure enough to allow superluminal effects to come into play, and the stars would be within its reach.

If it kept going, of course . . .

Eogan tried to keep his thoughts focused on the information in front of him, not on what might be. The files Melilah had brought from Bedlam were fiendishly complex to unravel. Deangelis's steganographic algorithms had to be at least five generations more sophisticated than any he had ever seen. The data was encoded by layers of transformations he could barely fathom. It was like trying to find his way through the maze on the other side of the Occlusion with his eyes blindfolded and his arms tied behind his back.

But he had to persist. Unraveling the file could be the most important thing he ever did. Palmer Vermeulen's suppositions and guesses weren't enough. He needed hard data. Specifically, he needed to know if the maze had more than one entrance, and if so *how many.* If there were more entrances in human-occupied space, and they could be accessed as easily as the one he had retrieved, then it would change everything.

He felt for Frederica Cazneaux. The Occlusion was even more of a threat than a single wormhole throat or wormhole technology in general. In the wrong hands it would mean the end of the Exarchate and the irrelevance of the Palmers.

But what should he do about it if his suspicions were confirmed? Destroy it, as Cazneaux had failed to? Destroy those who would use it against the Palmers? Take it for himself?

For the moment, it seemed as though Deangelis and the Exarchs were keeping it under wraps. That was a good thing. He had no intention of telling his superiors until he was absolutely certain of what it was, and what needed to be done about it. He recoiled from an image of the scramble that would erupt when word of a new means of getting around the galaxy emerged. Bedlam would become a war zone—and so, potentially, would every occlusion that drifted across every trade lane in the Exarchate.

And that was ignoring what might yet come out of it, if humanity probed too deeply. Even if the Occlusion was completely unrelated to what happened in Sublime, *someone* had to have built it, and they might not take kindly to trespassers . . .

"Why here?" asked Melilah.

He dropped out of the complex decrypting programs he had been employing to crack the file's secrets.

"Why where?"

"Here—near Bedlam. If the maze does have a multitude of entrances, why haven't we seen it elsewhere before now?"

Clearly her mind had been wandering, too. "I put it down to the VOID drive," he said. "It relies on deep vacuum, and we have more of it out here where the Local Bubble stretches farthest. Here, the interstellar medium is much hotter and thinner than elsewhere around Sol. Because of that, the Arc Circuit covers more light-years than any other trade network, and more traffic flows along it than on any other frontier. That increases the chances of an exit stumbling across a Cell, or vice versa."

She nodded, satisfied with that answer. But there were so many other questions. "The entrances mustn't be fixed; otherwise, the Mizar Occlusion would have been spotted on the trade lane immediately, and all this would've happened centuries ago. Same with Sublime. Maybe the whole structure is drifting, moving slowly through space."

"Or the galaxy is rotating through it," he suggested.

"That's assuming," said Vermeulen, "that the structure's motion in its continuum relates at all to the position of the exits in this universe. They may be connected, but they could also be completely separate. All you need is for the mouths to have a bit of give, and the exits could drift about at random while the thing itself stays put."

The effort required to visualize such a situation made Eogan's eyes cross. "So there are three components to this thing: the exits, the mouths, and the maze."

"That's my best guess, at the moment. The exits are holes in this universe; the throats link those holes to the continuum in which the maze sits; the maze gives that continuum shape." She shrugged. "The structure is likely to be much more complicated than that, but it's a start."

It was indeed, Eogan thought. Especially given the scant data they had to play with. Glimpses on the way to Bedlam; files stolen from the Exarch; coded information buried deep in the giant habitat. It might all come together in a way that made sense, but it didn't have to. Eogan was prepared for disappointment.

He wasn't so sure about Melilah.

"I've got into some of the file structure," he said, returning to the virtual displays surrounding him. "A lot of it's still hidden, but there's some basic information that *can't* be hidden, or faked. The dates on a number of the directories are problematic, if the files they contain do indeed relate to the Occlusion. They appear to have been created years ago."

"They must be dummies, then," she said, "planted to put us off the scent."

"I don't think so. They account for most of the data."

"Then you must be looking at it wrong." She frowned and turned away.

"I don't know, Melilah." Vermeulen spoke with uncharacteristic hesitation, as though nervous of Melilah's reaction. "It's not adding up the way you'd like it to. Those maps you gave me: they do assemble into a 5-D maze, but it doesn't match the one I found inside the Occlusion."

"Could it be an earlier version? A rough draft?"

"No. I can't make the hubs fit, no matter how I fiddle it. And besides, the scale isn't right. If this is an early draft, it should be smaller, right? In fact, it's larger. *Much* larger. That's why it's taken me so long to get my head around it. I've had to check every multidimensional branch and twig to make sure part of it doesn't match the one I found."

Melilah looked downcast and very tired. Eogan wondered how long it had been since she had slept—and how long she could function without it. The limits of her Natural body were blurry, depending on her needs. It all depended on what her needs had been just prior to the arrival of the Occlusion as to how far she could push herself.

"Then it's not the maze," she said dully. "We've wasted our time."

"So it would seem." Vermeulen looked sympathetic.

"I just don't understand. Why would someone go to the trouble of burying information like this if it wasn't important?"

"Maybe it was something they were embarrassed about. Love letters, bad art: I'd be ashamed, too."

Melilah looked defensive for a moment. Why, Eogan couldn't imagine.

"Wait a second," he said, a new possibility suddenly occurring to him. "Why couldn't it be a map of the maze— just not a section of the maze we know?"

Vermeulen frowned. "I suppose it's possible, if what we saw through the Occlusion is typical of the rest."

"That would mean there's another occlusion," said Melilah. Her eyes widened. "Sublime!"

"That would be my guess," he said.

"It has to be!" Such was her excitement that she nudged off the bulkhead she was squatting against and tumbled about the interior of the component.

"Easy," he said, grabbing her arm and stabilizing her.

"You know what this means," she said when she had secured herself again, floating just centimeters away from him. Her expression was very serious. "It means the Exarchate is in there, where Sublime used to be. They've got past the—what's it called?"

"Horsfall Station. That wouldn't be hard, seeing they built it."

"The replicators must have burned themselves out, or

been beaten back. The Gentry have been in there without telling anyone. Maybe they've been in there ever since the Catastrophe!"

"That's why Deangelis didn't seem surprised by what we found on the trade lane," said Vermeulen grimly. "And why he knew how to move the damned thing so easily."

Eogan nodded. It all fit. "They might not have known there were more entrances until we found this one. Until then, it was just a weird, dangerous anomaly. Now, everything's changed. And some of them don't like it."

He thought of Cazneaux and could understand her fear more clearly. He pictured the maze as a vast, invisible anemone drifting through the galaxy, the tips of its tentacles occasionally passing through or near colonized worlds. If those tips were deadly, like they had been in Sublime, how many colonies were at risk? Maybe all of them. Learning how to close the throats, perhaps by destroying them, could be the key to humanity's survival.

A chillingly familiar image came to him: of Bedlam's destruction boiling through the maze like steam out of a pipe. The source of that destruction might be very deep within the maze, so deep it was taking days to arrive. Sublime hadn't fallen for months after the discovery of the artifact they found. Bedlam might have just long enough to imagine that it was safe before the end came . . .

"We've obtained a clearer image of the target." Flast's voice intruded on the moment. "Eogan, I think you need to see this."

He pulled himself out of the revelation concerning Sublime and forced himself to concentrate on the images the *Nhulunbuy/Kwal Bahal* had recorded. The tiny dot of the tangler had resolved into several dots clustering around a long spear-shaped structure.

"What the hell is that?" he asked.

"I can't answer that precisely just yet," said Flast, "but we're working on it."

"It's a fleet," Melilah breathed, staring wide-eyed at the image. "Hails left it for us."

"As a gift for us," Vermeulen asked, "or in wait for us?"

"I guess we'll find out," said Eogan, "when we get there."

+49

The *Nhulunbuy* detected an unauthorized transmission one hour from the coordinates Hails had given them. Eogan broke off a detailed examination of the fleet's composition to inform Melilah of the new development. The source of the transmission was the nanoware she had unintentionally brought aboard the Cell.

"Whatever Hails put inside you is wanting to make contact." Eogan indicated the fleet. "With that."

A great weariness swept through her, and no small amount of alarm. She'd assumed that, since her new peripheral had been silent since leaving Bedlam, it had quietly dissolved away. Now she found that it had only been biding its time, waiting for them to reach their destination.

Her home had been invaded, violated, attacked—and now her body had been taken over, too.

"I want it out of me," she said. "You're good with nanotech. Get rid of it."

Eogan looked uncomfortable. "We're good under the right circumstances, Melilah. But flushing a living person clean is very different from scouring an external environment, especially if that person is physically unknown to us. I'd hesitate to do anything right now, just in case we scrub out something we didn't mean to."

"Like your mitochondria," put in Vermeulen. "Besides which, I think we should let it talk."

Both Melilah and Eogan faced the science officer in surprise.

"Why not?" Vermeulen said. "It might say something we need to hear. And even if all it does is sic the fleet on us, we're not so close we can't run away. I can't see what damage it could do."

Eogan turned back to Melilah. "It's up to you."

She stared back at them, then resigned herself to the situation with a shrug. "What the hell. As long as it *only* talks."

"We'll monitor the transmissions," Eogan reassured her. "We won't let it hurt you."

That didn't reassure her much. She bet the Gentry had tricks the Palmers had never dreamed of.

"Okay," said Eogan. "We're giving it free rein." A faint pink-noise burble filled the Cell component: an audible depiction of the transmission, she presumed. "It looks like garbage, so far. Handshaking, presumably."

A stronger tone, deeper and more rapid, drowned out the one she was producing.

"That's a reply," said Vermeulen. "Still no recognizable content."

Melilah waited in nervous anticipation for anything—anything at all—to happen to her. She monitored all of her body's rhythms, ready for the slightest change. Her heart was beating faster in response to adrenaline. The nanoware was probably draining sugars to fuel its activities and bleeding off waste heat into her circulatory system, but neither effect was strong enough to feel.

Maybe, she thought, she wasn't the intended recipient of Lazarus Hails's message at all. Maybe the vague hints he had given her in Bedlam about rebellion were just to get her moving. Maybe she was nothing but a courier, and the real message was only now arriving . . .

Ah, Melilah Awad. The polished tones of Lazarus Hails were suddenly between her ears again. *You were one of several people I thought likely to end up here. It's a pleasure to speak with you.*

She sighed. "Listen," she said aloud. "If you're going to talk to me, then do it openly through the Cell, or I'm not going to pay attention."

I could make you, but— Very well.

"We're being hailed," came Flast's voice. "The target is signaling us."

"It's Hails," Melilah said. "Open a channel."

"Come on down, Exarch Hails." Vermeulen took the development in her stride. "We have you in our sights."

"I'm sure you do. And vice versa, of course." Hails's leonine features stepped into the holographic depths of the component wall. He looked identical to the version Melilah had met several hours earlier, except this one was dressed in what appeared to be a business suit from the days of the Capitalist Spasm. He clearly wasn't the same Hails as the one on Bedlam, since there was no light-speed delay between question and answer, and he had a full head of white hair. He was just another part of a much larger whole.

"What a pretty kettle of fish we have here."

"Meaning?" asked Eogan.

"It means I've never seen an unlikelier set of allies."

"We're not allies yet, Exarch Hails," said Eogan.

"True. This installation is here for your use, however, should we come to an agreement on *how* to use it—or at least to what end. That should be incentive enough to start you talking."

"What do you want us to do with it?" Melilah asked.

"I'm sure you already know the answer to that, my dear." Hails smiled at her as though humoring a schoolgirl. "You are, after all, the one I brought here. The monkey on your back should have brought you up to speed."

She forced herself to ignore his tangled metaphors. "You want us to attack the Archon."

"What I want is to send a clear signal that Sol is no longer welcome in the Arc Circuit. Attacking the Archon and taking the Occlusion for ourselves won't be the end of it, but it will certainly be a definitive beginning."

"Why us?" asked Eogan. "You've got everything you need right here."

"Isn't it obvious? I don't want my name attached to this rebellion. You can consider me magnanimous if you like, preferring to give you the glory while I slink back into the Dark, but I'd rather you understood perfectly where I stand. You'll take the risk instead of me. Fail, and retribution will be upon your head, not mine. Succeed, however, and we all get what we want. I think that's a fair exchange for the only arsenal in eight light-years with any chance of winning."

"What happens when the Archon is gone?" Melilah asked. "Will you be our ruler? If so, I'm not sure what we stand to gain. An Exarch by any other name—"

"Your sentiments are noted," Hails interrupted in a long-suffering tone. "Consider that life with the Archon is likely to be more uncomfortable than it is now. Sol has significantly less tolerance for the peccadilloes of its primitive wards than our mutual friend Isaac Deangelis. Already, I fear, the thumbscrews are on."

Melilah thought of the Archon's reticence since the end of the attack, the blackout of the system, and Deangelis's increasing stress levels. She decided that on this point she completely trusted Lazarus Hails.

"Tell us about the Mizar Occlusion," said Vermeulen. "How much do you know?"

"I know that there is still much to be learned." The illusion of Hails folded its hands behind its back and began to pace around the component, circling them. "But tell me what *you* know, first."

"We know the Exarchate is still in Sublime," Melilah said, going out on a limb to get a reaction. "We know we've been lied to about that."

Hails didn't break step, but he did raise an eyebrow. "Have you been contacted by Jane Elderton?"

She shook her head. "No. Why? Are you telling me she's still alive?"

"Oh, yes. Poor Jane is in an unenviable position. She has suffered much since the Catastrophe. An Exarch without a colony is like Jupiter without its moons. Technically, she is completely isolated, cut off from everyone around her—but unofficially word has been leaking this last year. She still has her tangler, somewhere in that mess. Even with it at hand, the loneliness would be crippling. She may not often initiate conversations, but she will answer when approached."

"What's she doing in there?"

"Isn't that obvious? She's studying the thing they found. Part or all of her must have survived the Catastrophe. Instead of pulling her out, the Archon forced her to stay. She is the mistress now of a devastated, depopulated system—a system still controlled by the plague that destroyed it. I myself would rather be dead."

"Do you know what she's found?"

"Do you?"

"We know the Occlusion is an entrance to a hyperspatial maze. We know there could be many more such entrances."

Again a penetrating look as the Exarch walked around them. "Do you know this, or is it merely conjecture?"

"I've seen it with my own eyes," said Vermeulen.

"I envy you," he said with apparent frankness. "It is a most remarkable artifact, if the rumors I've heard about it are true. Without such a device behind us, rebellion against the Archon and Sol would simply not be possible. We need every advantage we can get."

Hails had, perhaps deliberately, exposed a depth of ignorance that surprised Melilah. "You sound like you're as much in the dark as we are."

"Of course. This information is not widely disseminated. It is beyond the need-to-know requirements of the average Exarch. Clearly, Sol would rather keep us ignorant of any means by which we might attain our independence. It knows that it is just one small system surrounded by many hundreds of growing ones; if we ever get the upper hand, its days are numbered."

Eogan was looking uncomfortable. "Perhaps we're getting a little ahead of ourselves," he said. "Before we start talking about overthrowing Sol, let's deal with Bedlam. What needs to be done here and now? How are we going to do it? Is there any way we can get rid of the Archon without risking innocent bystanders?"

Melilah nodded, glad for the reminder to stick to basics. "I won't countenance another attack like Cazneaux's."

"Do not fear," soothed the Exarch. "I'm not giving you a Reaper to sic upon yourselves. That would simply be foolish."

"What *are* you giving us?"

"The following." Hails's image faded and was replaced by a close-up of the Exarch's fleet. Nine tapered shapes clustered around a spindly docking assembly, looking like overlarge seeds hanging from a vine. "These are attack drones designed to interface with a Palmer Cell. Don't let their simple appearance mislead you. They're smaller and more maneuverable than anything you've seen before. I've been evolving them on the sly for years, in case a situation like this ever arose. They're designed to be autonomous, under certain circumstances, so the Archon won't be able to knock them out of the sky as it did everything else in Bedlam. At the first sign of interference, they'll shut themselves off to the outside and continue with their mission unchecked."

It was Melilah's turn to have misgivings. She didn't like the idea of unstoppable missiles rampaging around the system, doing untold damage. "I presume there's a kill switch."

Hails returned. "Of course. I will give you all the information you require, when we have a deal."

"What's the other thing?" asked Vermeulen. "The thing they're docked with."

"My tangler. You will have full use of that, too, should you require it."

Melilah didn't need to think about what she would do if she had ftl communications capability at her fingertips.

"You have a deal," she said.

Eogan looked at her in surprise. "Wait a minute, Melilah. You can't accept just like that."

"Yes, I can."

"But I'm not convinced it's the right thing—"

She turned on him, anger flaring. "Who said you have anything to do with it? No one made us allies, Eogan. We're not in this together. Yes, we exchanged information; yes, you brought me out here. But don't forget that you lured me aboard with the intention of kidnapping me—or that I have as little reason to trust the Palmers as I do the Gentry. You're under no obligation to make the same decision as me. Dump me here, if you like, and I'll do what I have to do. Then you can get the hell out of this system and never come back."

He was tight-lipped, betraying a rare emotion. "I just think there's more we need to discuss, that's all."

"Fuck the discussions," she said. "Hails is offering me what I want, and I'm taking it."

"I thought you might," crowed the hologram Exarch. "Am I right in supposing that it's not specifically the attack drones you're after?"

"Damn straight," she said, forcing herself to breathe deeply, calmingly. There was no keeping a lid on the intensity of her emotion, however. She was too tired for subtle games. "I'm sick of all these secrets and lies. I want people to know the truth: not just people in Bedlam, but people everywhere. Tell them about the Occlusion, about the thing the Archon is trying to keep from them, and let them make up their own minds. We're not stupid. We have no need to be *protected*. We stand to benefit most from the maze, so we should be allowed to have a say in who owns it."

"But that will—" Eogan didn't finish the sentence.

"Trigger a revolution? Start a war? End civilization as we know it?" She took no satisfaction at all from the shocked look on his face. "That's what this whole conversation has been about, Eogan. Haven't you been paying attention? Did you think we'd hauled ourselves all the way out here for a polite conversation about the weather? That we'd all go home afterward, pretending everything's okay? Well, it's *not* okay. In fact, everything's about as far from fucking okay as it could be! And if it has to get worse before it gets any better, then that's just what it has to do. It's up to you to decide whether you're prepared to make the effort to fix the situation, or whether you're going to just turn tail like last time, in the naive hope that it'll make life easier for you."

She stopped there, realizing that her mouth had run away with itself. He was silent for a moment, not quite glaring at her but certainly unhappy about the way he was being spoken to. Vermeulen stared at them both, her mouth firmly shut.

When Eogan did speak, it was in a voice that was as soft and inevitable as a slow air leak.

"I want proof," he said. "Proof of so many things it's hard to know where to start. Proof that Hails is leveling with us on the tangler, and the attack drones, and the Archon, and his reason for being here. Proof that the maze is what it appears to be, and not some cobbled-together theory that'll fall apart on closer examination. Proof that it's *worth fighting for.*" He put out a hand to touch the bulkhead beside him, as though to steady himself. "Palmers do not go to war lightly. We are not a military cult. We will act to defend those in need, as we did here yesterday—"

"*Some* of you did," she put in sourly.

"That many of us didn't is an indication of how strongly we feel about getting involved. We are nomadic by nature as well as necessity. Can I in good conscience instruct my Cell to do something even I feel uncomfortable with? I need rock-solid reasoning behind me before even putting it on the table.

"I'm sorry," he added, "if that makes me seem weak or indecisive in your eyes, but I simply need more time and information before I can commit to your plan."

She sighed and wished, not for the first time, that they weren't discussing this cramped cheek to jowl like Apollo astronauts.

"Okay, I understand. You've got a fair point. Hails," she said to the Exarch, who had waited out the exchange with aloof interest, "can you reassure Eogan on any of these issues?"

"I fear not. The only way to ascertain the veracity of my intentions is to put them—and my gifts—to the test. And as far as the Occlusion goes, we are all equally in the dark."

"I figured as much." Melilah turned back to Eogan to urge him to relax his requirements just a little, but the words never left her lips. Vermeulen had raised her left hand.

"Excuse me," said the science officer. "There *is* a test we can perform that should answer a few questions."

"And that is?"

"The data you brought from Bedlam, Melilah. If Hails gives us the algorithm to decode it, we can see what it contains. If it's nothing, or if Hails won't break the security of the Exarchate, then that's a sort of progress."

Eogan nodded approvingly, openly displaying relief and gratitude at the means to break the impasse. "How about it, Hails? Are you going to play?"

"By all means. Send me a fragment of this mysterious data of yours, and I'll see what I can tell you about it."

Vermeulen looked distracted for a second as she prepared the transmission. "It's on its way. This is about one percent of what we have. If you need more"—she glanced at Eogan—"we can discuss it."

A ream of virtual paper materialized in Hails's hands. He riffled through it, stopping every now and again to examine the odd page in more detail. He hummed to himself, skimmed back to the beginning, then read the final page with both bushy eyebrows high on his forehead.

"Is the pantomime really necessary?" Melilah asked.

He looked up at her. "I apologize," he said. "This is

genuinely fascinating. I had no idea such information was available. And you said you found it—where?"

"I didn't. Tell us what it says, and we'll give you more."

"Quite simply, my dear, you've got your hands on everything the Exarchate has gleaned from the object in Sublime—and it makes extraordinary reading. Simply extraordinary!" Hails's attention returned to the pages, which he flicked through with increasing speed. "The rumors appear to be absolutely true. If this is just a fraction of the whole, then I can only wonder at what else it contains!"

"We're receiving new data from Hails," said Vermeulen. "It's the algorithm. I'll try it on the data."

Melilah held a breath as she waited for confirmation, fearing the algorithm might actually be a trap.

"It's working," Vermeulen reported a second later. "We have the data."

"And?" asked Melilah, knowing she was probably being unreasonable to expect results so soon. The files were *huge*.

Vermeulen's eyes unfocused.

You don't need to hear it, Melilah, said Hails into her head, the sheaf of papers hanging at his side. His eyes glittered in the depths of the illusion. *This won't make a jot of difference to what you want to do—and you've known what that is, in your heart, from the moment you saw the attack drones. You understand why I put them here, and why I chose you to receive them. I urge you to pick up the gun and pull the trigger. Fire the bullet right into the heart of the enemy.*

"Eogan—?"

What your Palmer friend decides is irrelevant. Without him, this plan is still workable. Do you and I have an arrangement? That's the important thing. Tell me we do, and let's get on with the messy business of liberation.

Hails's tone was hypnotic. A tingling spread down her back and across her skin. She feared for a second that it might be the nanoware inside her, working some subtle effect, but it was in fact just gooseflesh. The moment had come to truly commit, to put her mark on the devil's contract and sell her soul away.

She felt Eogan's eyes on her, questioning.

It might not be her soul she was selling, she thought, but her home.

Strange shapes stirred through the wreckage of the Occlusion observatory. Since the Archon's arrival there, the spindly remains of the Reaper had melted and been absorbed into a growing mass of material that Deangelis couldn't identify. Some of it broke free from the wreckage like coronal flares on the system's distant primary, orbited a couple of times, then came back down at a different location. These globules glowed intensely in infrared, as though furious chemical processes were taking place inside them. Sometimes they merged with other orbiting globules; occasionally they broke into chains of smaller pieces that one by one went their separate, mysterious ways.

Deangelis also detected short-lived flashes of powerful energies coming from deep in the heart of the wreckage. If there was a pattern to their occurrence, he couldn't find it. Nor could he fathom the process that could have caused them. Whatever the Archon was doing in there, it was well beyond his ken.

I could ask, he told himself. *Just because the Archon keeps its business off the colony's feeds doesn't mean I can't know. I should know. If there's any chance it might be dangerous, it would make sense to be informed.*

But he didn't make the call. He had asked the Archon to help him secure the Occlusion, and it appeared to be doing just that. Requesting the particulars would just make him look suspicious, even churlish.

And it wasn't as if there weren't other things to worry about.

"Tell me what they're doing out there," he asked Hails for what felt like the dozenth time.

"Who doing where?" asked Hails from his cell in Protective Custody, where he'd been held since his assault on Melilah Awad. She hadn't pressed charges before her departure, but the Exarch had pulled rank to keep him out of harm's way. Word of Hails's presence on the habitat had sent a ripple of unease through those paying attention. Luckily there were sufficient other distractions keeping him out of the public spotlight for the time being.

"You know very well who. The *Nhulunbuy* hasn't left the system. Its drive signature indicates that it decelerated for a time before coming to a dead halt well short of heliopause."

"I don't see what that has to do with me." Hails picked at an ear with his little finger.

"It has everything to do with you. They were traveling along the same heading you came from; they've stopped where I presume you have your tangler stashed, just out of my range. And I heard what you said to Awad before she left."

"Then you know full well what our conversation means."

Deangelis knew the words by heart.

You are not alone. Your goals are shared by others. We want exactly the same thing.

They were seditious brands on his memory, flaming bright.

Independence.

He couldn't repeat them aloud for fear of drawing attention to them. The Archon was bound to be listening, even—perhaps especially—to the high-speed Most Secure conversation taking place in the cell.

"I could send a high-acceleration probe," he said, "to check on your tangler in person, but I'm giving you this chance to come clean first. I can hide this conversation, but I can't hide a launch."

"That's not my problem."

"Of course it's your problem! If you don't give me some reason to trust you, I'll have to turn you in."

"To our mutual friend from Sol?" He shrugged. "Do it. I've got nothing to hide." Hails's words were casual, but the gesture he made was anything but. He put his index finger to his temple, cocked his thumb, and mimed a sharp recoil.

The meaning was clear. Hails would sacrifice the part of himself on the habitat—kill the body sitting in front of Deangelis—rather than risk details of his plans reaching the Archon ahead of time. Hails only knew what secrets were locked in that skull. Deangelis wanted to take it in both hands and crack it open himself.

"I need to know what you're doing," he said, his voice little more than a whisper. He felt exhausted, physically and mentally drained. The body that was his current point of view swayed, and he let it sink onto the bed opposite the one on which Hails sat. He put a hand over his eyes in a vain attempt to concentrate.

"I need to know what *I'm* doing."

"I sympathize, Isaac. I really do," Hails said, in tones that were more gruff than sympathetic. "But I told you before: don't expect me to make the tough decisions for you. This is your system, not mine or the Archon's, so the call is yours. You need to come to your own conclusions."

"Too many variables . . ." He shook his head and took the hand away from his eyes. The light in the cell seemed suddenly bright. "I don't want to make an enemy of you, Lazarus."

"Let me reassure you on that score, then. You know full well who my beef is with—and you also know that I'm no Frederica Cazneaux. The last thing I want to do is get you offside or put your people at risk. This is the Exarchate, not some Martian frontier. We have to work together, no matter what happens."

"We'll never get on perfectly. We'll always disagree and squabble."

"Of course. We're only human, after all."

Deangelis wondered if that was how the Archon thought of itself. *Only human.* Did it have superiors it reported to that seemed as alien to it as it did to him? As Deangelis seemed to Melilah Awad?

What was the point of pledging allegiance to a notion of humanity that none of the people who claimed it could agree on?

Again, he felt an incipient fracture developing between him and the mind of the one through whose eyes he saw. The world shivered, oscillating between two radically different points of view.

His greater self believed in the greater good and knew what he ought to do.

Earth-Deangelis's grasp on the greater good was slippery. To that mind, resistance had a strong appeal. The notion of the individual was important, as was the goal of individual survival.

But his higher self, who was perfectly capable of holding all the immense complexity of Lut-Deangelis in a single thought, could just about conceive of what it must be like to be the Archon. He could almost imagine the demands that governing the Exarchate as a whole must place on such a mind. This was responsibility beyond measure—and here *he* was, quibbling over the events in a single system.

Yet, the individual part of him said, *that single system is a fulcrum around which an entire empire might turn. There's no escaping the fact that the decision I make now could have more effect than any of the Archon's.*

All the more reason, then, his higher self replied, *to try to think beyond my petty concerns. If I can't work out what the best thing to do is, I have to have faith in one who might.*

"You're looking thoughtful," said Hails, watching him closely. "Does that mean you've decided?"

"I think so," said Deangelis, standing.

"And?"

"There's only one thing I can do, and that's to do what I think is right. Nothing else matters. It's *myself* I have to live with afterward, whatever happens."

"That's the spirit," said Hails. "You can be your own man, Isaac, if you truly want to be."

Even if it kills me? he asked silently of himself.

There was no point talking to Hails anymore. The Exarch clearly wasn't going to tell him anything about Awad and the *Nhulunbuy*. It was time for Deangelis to take his fate in both hands. The rest, he hoped, would simply fall into place.

With the briefest of farewells, his higher self left the cell and signaled the Archon that he urgently needed to talk.

+51

Decisions.

Palmer Eogan's mind whirled as he explored the data liberated by Hails's decryption algorithm, and the attack drones loomed larger before him. Not only did Deangelis's hidden files prove that the Exarchate had been in Sublime ever since the Catastrophe; it also confirmed that the object Jane Elderton had found was essentially the same as the one he had towed out of the Mizar-Bedlam trade lane. That made two entrances. The new data strongly suggested that there would be more.

The sheer volume of information was difficult to plow through, but major points quickly emerged. The complex structure Vermeulen had glimpsed on the far side of the Occlusion was extensive and convoluted, and followed natural laws of its own. The topography was exceedingly complicated, but exhibited consistent scale-free properties: ten to fifteen percent of junctions acted as hubs, connecting far-flung regions by just a few hops. What those regions corresponded to in the real universe had not yet been determined. Roughly five percent of all corridors ended in dead ends, and some of the anonymous minds put to the task wondered if such termini might be potential exits. If that was correct, no means had yet been found to open them.

Similarly, no connection had yet been found between the Sublime and Bedlam exits. Without the existence of a route between them, the theory that the structure functioned as a means of getting through space by going around it—using hyperspatial geodesics to connect far-distant points—remained just that: a theory. There was still a chance it could have been a natural phenomenon, albeit one more bizarre than anything humanity had encountered before.

Its resonance with living structures—not just because of its scale-free arrangement—was not lost on the Exarchate examiners. Such networks occurred over and over, in nature and information networks, in the brain and in the body. They had initially called it "the Coral" in honor of its brachiated structure, but a new name appeared with increasing frequency in the records. The most recent record, saved two weeks earlier, used it no fewer than seventy-eight times.

"Geodesica," to Eogan's eyes, came with associations of wild, dangerous spaces such as Old America and Antarctica had once been. People would fight over them, especially if a real advantage was to be gained by owning them.

The trouble was, thought Eogan as he feverishly tried to decide what to do next, he was no Columbus or Mawson. He had come to Bedlam with no intentions of laying claim to anything. Now that the opportunity had arrived to represent the Palmers in a discovery of truly monumental proportions, he found himself to be reluctant. He hadn't joined the Palmers to push the frontiers; he had wanted merely to ply the trade lanes in peace, like sailors of old. There were always dangers to be avoided and discoveries to be made along the way, but nothing of the order of an entire new continuum that might tear the Exarchate apart.

Similarly, he had no right to order his crew any deeper into the mess than they already were. Ordinarily, they would have been well on their way elsewhere by then, having unloaded their cargo in Bedlam and taken on new contracts for their next destination. They had been lucky not to lose anyone during Cazneaux's attack on the habitat; that Vermeulen had returned still shocked and surprised him. Who might be killed if open rebellion broke out around them? Whose death would he have to carry on his conscience?

Eogan couldn't live with it. He wasn't a fighter by nature,

and he certainly wasn't the sort to send others into battle for him. But he didn't like abandoning friends in a sticky situation, either—even if they weren't really friends, but something much more complicated . . .

While attention was focused on the data, he opened a side channel to Palmer Flast.

"Listen carefully," he said. "When you get my signal, I want you to do exactly as I tell you. If you do, the *Nhulunbuy* is yours."

That earned him a long, considered silence. "Continue, Palmer Eogan."

He outlined what he had in mind, then said, "Feel free to tell me if I'm insane."

"That all depends on how you look at it." Flast broadcast the nonverbal equivalent of a shrug. "If you're sure you have to do it, then I guess you're going about it in a very sane way."

That wasn't terribly reassuring. "I simply can't think of any other way around this situation."

"Neither can I."

"You'll do it, then?"

"Sure. But what about Vermeulen? You know she'll be pissed off either way."

"The choice is hers—and the same for anyone else who wants to stay. If you're prepared to offer it to them, of course."

The future chief officer of the *Nhulunbuy* took a good while to think that one through.

"This is a very difficult situation," said Flast finally. "There won't be long to think about it, especially if Hails objects."

"Give her as long as you can. Remember: if you don't allow her at least that much, there's a long journey ahead of you. You'll have a lot of time to listen to her complaining."

"True." Flast sent a wry smile that quickly faded. "*Are* you certain you want to do this? She probably doesn't expect you to."

"I'm not just doing it for her," Eogan said. "And I'm at least fifty percent sure that's true."

The amalgamated Cell decelerated smoothly, all its myriad microscopic drive units acting in tandem—or in a way that, to the macroscopic eye of a human, approximated unity. There were bound to be small variations in thrust and timing, but such evened out over the long haul and the large numbers involved. As drive units failed, more assembled to take their place in a constant dance of attrition and replacement, like cells in a living body. The health of the Cell as a whole depended on maintaining the dance across all its dynamic systems, so a preponderance of drive units didn't lead to a shortage of life support or another vital component at a critical time in its operation.

Eogan watched the attack drones expand in the forward view with a feeling of dread. He wondered, as he had many times before, whether the Cell felt anything like emotions in its artificial analogue of life. Did it feel apprehension, nervousness, uncertainty, terror? If not, he envied it.

When they were less than five minutes away, Melilah made her announcement.

"I'm staying," she said, "no matter what you do. Hails has given me no reason to mistrust him, so turning down his offer would be unjustifiable."

"I thought you'd think that way," he said.

"Don't even think about trying to stop me," she started.

"I wouldn't dare."

She stared at him, trying to gauge his intentions, but he kept his expression carefully neutral. "You're keeping very quiet on this," she said.

"I've made my decision. All that remains is to implement it."

The data flow between her and Hails increased slightly. He wondered what they were talking about. The Exarch's illusory appearance reappeared standing among the morass of data extruded from Deangelis's file, his perspective and virtual lighting jarringly mismatched.

"I don't need to repeat my terms," Hails said. "Are the Palmers with us or not?"

Eogan took a deep breath. "They are not," he said. "Not under these circumstances."

Melilah couldn't hide a disappointed microexpression. "So be it. If we can't give you the assurances you need, we'll just have to work without you."

"It's not that," he said. "I don't feel that I have the right to commit the *Nhulunbuy* to such a venture. That would be exceeding my authority, acting outside my brief—call it what you will."

"It amounts to the same thing. You can drop me off at the tangler, then go your merry way."

"I can't do that, either. Not in good conscience."

"What, then? Stop beating about the bush and get on with it."

She was right. There was no point hesitating any longer.

"Palmer Flast?" he said, both aloud and through usual channels. "You have the helm."

"Understood," came the immediate reply. "Full acceleration in fifteen seconds. Disconnection in thirty. Good luck, Palmer Eogan. And fair weather."

Eogan could tell from the look on Melilah's and Vermeulen's faces that they grasped the ramifications of the conversation as quickly as Flast had.

"You're leaving the *Nhulunbuy*?" asked Vermeulen.

"Permanently," he said. "Palmer Flast is now acting chief officer. Palmer Aesche is his second."

"But—" She stopped, not needing to ask why. She glanced at Melilah, who said nothing, then returned her attention to Eogan. "You haven't asked me to come with you."

"You can if you want to," he said. "But I won't order you. Not again. I almost got you killed, last time."

"It wasn't you," she said. "It was Frederica Cazneaux and the Occlusion—the whole damned situation."

"Nothing's changed," he said. "Only this time it's

Lazarus Hails and the Archon. Do you really want to go back there?"

She looked away. There were no tears in her golden eyes, no outward displays of emotion, but he could feel sadness radiating from her. They hadn't traveled so long together without developing an intuitive sense for each other's state of mind.

"No," she said, "but thanks for asking."

"Ten seconds," said Flast. "We need those components separated."

The space around them deformed, slowly at first but with increasing speed. "I'm taking what's left of Deangelis's escape capsule," he told his ex–science officer. "You have all the data we've gathered. It's up to you and Flast what you do with it."

She nodded. "I expect to see you again."

"And I you."

Vermeulen's gaze swiveled to Melilah, who still hadn't spoken. "You look after the big lug as best you can. He's not so smart, but he still has a heart, and it's in the right place most of the time."

The component had stretched into two lobes, Vermeulen in one, Eogan and Melilah in the other. The umbilical connecting them attentuated and sealed shut at both ends. Eogan raised a hand in farewell as his friend disappeared from view, fighting a lump in his throat.

Then a rush of information through his extended senses confirmed that the space around them—contained within a sphere five meters across, possessing all the capabilities of a full Cell in miniature—had disconnected from the *Nhulunbuy*. As its parent Cell accelerated at a brisk rate toward the stars, it braked in a tight circle to bring it on a docking vector with the tangler and its attack drones. Eogan watched with internal eyes as the Cell that had been his home for thirty years snaked off into the Dark.

"You didn't have to do that," said Melilah, watching him, not the *Nhulunbuy*. Her posture was taut, as though ready to run.

"Yes, I did," he said. "You need a Cell to interface with the drones."

"We could have managed."

"I would've felt bad for making you. And besides"—he hesitated—"I think it's the right thing to do."

"To fight the Archon or to help me?"

He smiled thinly, but said nothing in return. The truth was, he didn't know which one. But he was glad the decision was behind him.

"Welcome aboard, Palmer Eogan," said Exarch Hails, reappearing in the walls around him as the Cell decelerated. "If you two would both please hold hands, the nanoware I have installed in Melilah will colonize your system also."

"Is that necessary?" he asked, not daring to meet her eyes.

"Imperative, I'm afraid. Where we're going, we'll need a secure means of communication."

He sighed and gave in. She extended an arm, thrusting it woodenly at him as though it had lost all feeling.

Eogan took it.

Then the Exarch rushed into him, and there was no more time to think.

52

Eogan's hand was hot in hers. His fingers tightened, and his eyes closed; his torso stiffened. She tried not to look at the joins where he merged with the walls of the Cell.

This won't take long, said Hails.

Eogan shivered. "I hear you," he said. "But can't we keep this out in the open for now?"

She relaxed slightly at that. The thought of his voice in her head as well as Hails's had made her anxious.

"Our plan is simple," said Hails. "We integrate the drones with your miniature Cell, giving you complete control over all nine of them. I hand over the keys to the tangler. Then you move in on the Archon."

Eogan opened his eyes and let go of her hand. His expression was grim. "How important is the element of surprise?"

"Not terribly. The Archon is unlikely to have developed a defense system equal to the drones in such a short time."

"Then I have one request. I want to give the Archon a chance to capitulate before we fire a single shot."

Melilah frowned. "Issue an ultimatum? What would be the point of that? We already know what it would say."

"Maybe not," he said. "Faced with superior firepower, it may just back down."

"It could also take the habitat hostage."

"It could do that as soon as we appear in range. We're going to be fairly conspicuous."

"Hails? What do you think?"

"I think the decision is yours. Either way, I'll get my message across."

She nodded. "Okay, then. We'll do it. But I don't want

any screwing around. If it tries to stall, we move in. Agreed?"

Eogan looked satisfied. "No problems there. I just want to give it a chance. That'll make me feel better about what comes afterward."

"So let's get on with it." She couldn't keep the harshness from her voice. Being cooped up with Eogan for so long was difficult. The sooner she was doing something concrete, the better.

"In a moment," said Hails, "I'll send you access codes and control interfaces for the drones and the tangler. The protocols are very tight; you'll need to follow them to the letter. That will require some practice."

"I'm up for it," she said. The thought of doing something concrete restored the vitality she had lost during the long haul out from Bedlam. She could go three full days without sleep, but that didn't mean she didn't feel flatlined as a result. Her eyes were tired of straining data for clues.

"We should aim to leave for the habitat in four hours." Hails was all business, pacing backward and forward in the illusion of space outside the component's walls. "In that time, I suggest we talk tactics."

The Cell drew up alongside the tangler, neatly eclipsing the system's distant primary behind Lazarus Hails's lethal gifts.

Reality struck her one hour into the acclimatization program. For four decades, she had been seeking a way to fight Exarch Deangelis. Now she was fighting his superior, with the help of another Exarch. The possibility excited and terrified her at the same time—as did the capabilities of the attack drones.

They were fast, lethal, and very, very tough. Their needle-slim, tapering shapes lent them an air of fragility that was completely undeserved. They could have sailed through the waves Frederica Cazneaux's Reaper had sent against Bedlam without a scratch. Although one alone couldn't have taken out the Reaper, three could have. Nine would have diced it up and used it for target practice.

Melilah briefly wondered if she should be angry at Hails for not using the drones to defend the colony against the Reaper earlier, before anyone had died. He would have had a reason for not doing it, she was sure—that the timing wasn't right, perhaps, or that his direct involvement would have been impossible to avoid as a result. It certainly would have sent a very different message for Exarch to fight Exarch, so early in the piece.

She decided to let it go, for the moment. There would be time afterward, she told herself, to hold everyone accountable.

And there was plenty to get through before that point arrived. Direct control of the attack drones could be set at various levels, from completely autonomous to totally enslaved. Complete autonomy worried her, but it was impossible for her and Eogan alone to control all nine of the complex craft. Their guidance systems took into account all manner of telemetry, from quantum vacuum density to strength and orientation of local gravitational fields. She would need dozens of separate senses to control just one of the craft, so they sought a middle ground whereby the two of them could oversee their actions but not be responsible for every decision they made.

Together, the drones spoke with a silvery, insidious voice that made her think of mercury and poisoning. Communication from them came in discrete, bulletlike packets that erased themselves so fast she barely had time to absorb them.

I This mission's primary objective was previously set as the destruction of the entity labeled ARCHON, its precise identity and/or location to be confirmed. I

I Is this, now, to change? I

"Yes," she said. "Your primary objective is to protect the habitat. Neutralizing the Archon is your second priority."

"Destroying the Archon is not ideal," Eogan added.

"The Archon will make a difficult prisoner," argued Hails. "It'll be like trying to hold smoke in your hand."

"I know," said Melilah, "but we're not barbarians. If it'll talk, we might even be able to learn something from it."

| This mission's primary objectives have been reset. |

| Performing test maneuvers as instructed. |

"How will we find the Archon?" she asked Hails, as the drones swooped and darted around the Cell.

"Look for Isaac's tangler. There's a good chance they'll be together."

"And if it fights back?"

"I guess you'll have to work that out as you go along. I'm sorry I can't be of more help to you on that point. The Archon's capabilities are unknown to me."

They familiarized themselves with Hails's tangler in order to increase their chances of recognizing Deangelis's. It was a strange device, consisting of a glowing central column that branched in five places. Each branch continued to divide, becoming increasingly feathery with each division. Close analysis revealed that the device was fractal down to the microscopic level, and probably farther, beyond the capability of the Cell's sensors. Functionally, it consisted of numerous interdependent components she could hardly fathom, but its operation was surprisingly simple. All she had to do was key in a message, and the tangler would transmit it along the Exarchate's entangled web to any number of specific destinations. From Bedlam, at the intersection of so many trade lanes, she could reach almost all the major Arc Circuit systems: from Schiller's End all the way around to New Eire. She could also reach most of the major systems just off the Arc—Whitewater, Alcor, Megrez, Eliza—without having to rely on relays within other systems. She had no way of knowing how individual Exarchs would respond to the news of what they had uncovered in Bedlam. Deangelis, Cazneaux, and Hails had each reacted in very different ways, from loyally toeing the Sol line to taking matters into their own hands. Some, she was sure, would pass the message on beyond the Arc Circuit. Some would erase it in the hope, perhaps, that it wasn't true. Others might absorb the information and let it simmer, laying down preparations as Lazarus Hails had against the coming storm.

The tangler had no internal awareness beyond that required for navigation and maintenance. It was a simple machine and possessed a simple interface. She prepared the message she wanted to send and instructed the tangler to wait for her signal to send it. If that signal wasn't received in thirty-five hours, the message should be sent anyway. Likewise, if anything threatened the tangler from Bedlam.

"I'll be here to make sure nothing goes wrong," Hails assured her.

"But who'll guard the guard?" asked Eogan, precisely identifying her one remaining doubt.

"You have to trust me to a certain degree," the Exarch said. "After all, could you tell if the tangler had worked at all, even if you were right on top of it? You have only its word that it'll do what you tell it to."

"I'm sure confirmation would come pretty fast," she said. "If I were Giorsal McGrath in Friday and received a message like this, the first thing I'd do was query Deangelis to see if it was true. And Deangelis would query me in turn—or shoot me out of the sky without thinking twice."

"I doubt Isaac has that in him," Hails said. "If he did, you probably wouldn't be here now."

That was true. Deangelis hadn't lifted a finger to stop her and Eogan from leaving the habitat, even though he must have had a pretty good idea that they knew too much. Either he hadn't wanted to, or the Archon had told him not to. Seeing Deangelis had saved her life less than a day beforehand, she had to suppose that Hails was right.

But what Deangelis would do when she and Eogan came barreling down on him with Hails's attack drones bristling in full battle array was anyone's guess.

| Tests completed. |

| All systems are optimal for commencement. |

"This is it." Eogan brought the Cell close to the drone they had designated D-1. The drones couldn't merge as

Palmer Cells did, but the single component could piggy-back on one of them, allowing more rapid and secure communication between them.

"Do you want to ride your own drone?" Eogan asked her. "I can split the component in two, if I have to."

The thought didn't please her as much as it might have a few hours earlier. They had divvied up their responsibilities so few of them overlapped; being separated would introduce unwanted communication lags and confusions into the mix.

"No offense," she said, "but I'd rather keep an eye on things from here."

"Understood."

If she concentrated on his face, she could almost forget about the rest of him, what he had become. His expression was weary, and wary. "I'm sorry if I was hard on you, before."

"It's okay. This means a lot to you: your home, your sense of identity, your place in things. I'd be surprised if tempers didn't run a little hot at times."

"All that meant a lot to you, too, once."

He cocked his head. "Meaning?"

"You gave up the *Nhulunbuy* easily enough."

"Did it look easy? I can assure you it wasn't."

She shrugged. "I suppose you can always hitch up with it again, after all of this is over."

"I doubt that. The Palmers won't take too kindly to my abandoning my post and getting mixed up in something like this."

"No going back?"

"No." Eogan bent his head down, as though concentrating on virtual information before him.

She thought that signaled the end of the conversation and readied herself to launch the mission to reclaim Bedlam. There hadn't really been time enough to familiarize herself with the command interfaces. She would have to learn a lot of it on the fly, hoping all the while that nothing too unexpected went wrong.

His voice was soft when he spoke again. "We need a name for the Cell, and I was thinking of naming it after that town your family came from, where they found the black jade deposits. What was it called? Cahill? Cowra?"

"Cowell," she said, hiding the fact that his easy recall of her history flustered her: no attempt at repression there. "Why?"

"Do I need a reason?" He sighed. "Look, I don't make a habit of giving things up. Perhaps it's this place. I sometimes thought that leaving here was the biggest mistake I ever made. Maybe it was an even bigger mistake to come back."

"You can't blame Bedlam for the way your life has turned out."

"I know, but the temptation is there. It's a human thing to look for simple answers, or ones that absolve you of blame."

She kept her gaze carefully on the peripheral displays before her. *Human, huh? Who's kidding whom?*

But she couldn't bring herself to say it.

53

On a virtual screen at the edge of Deangelis's greater awareness, the *Nhulunbuy*'s flickering drive signature accelerated steadily out of the system, warping the space ahead of it in a back-to-front wake as it neared interstellar space.

Deangelis wasn't reassured.

"I am pleased," said the Archon, "that you have come to me."

He forced himself to focus on the conversation, stripping back all his inputs until it felt as though he was hanging in a deep, black void. The Archon's voice came to him not as a voice in his ear, not as an electrical or optical trickle at the heart of his mind, but as a vibration thrilling right through him. God spoke from the mountaintop, and he listened.

"You have everything I know," he said to his maker. "What Lazarus told me can be interpreted many ways, as can the behavior of people like Melilah Awad and Palmer Eogan. I feel that it all combines in a worrying pattern. I also feel that I have handled the situation badly, and may have even, in my uncertainty, exacerbated the problem, as I perceive it. I fear that this might be so, but I am unafraid of the consequences. Should you wish to punish or replace me, I am resigned to my fate."

"Resigned?" The Archon's laughter boomed through him like physical blows. "Isaac, I would never think you resigned to anything. You confront life with a vigor few could match. You are loyal, determined, conscientious, and resourceful. I have no doubt that you will weather this situation with your usual efficiency."

"But *I* doubt it, Archon."

"Then that is a matter for you to keep to yourself. If you tell no one, they will never suspect."

"I am telling *you.* I *want* you to know."

"And now I do know. Thank you, Isaac, for trusting me with your uncertainty. It's not an easy thing to confess."

The Archon's response was far from comforting. He had expected it to give him some sort of clarity. He had hoped it would spare him the crippling, mind-numbing sense of being confronted by too many half-glimpsed, terrifying possibilities.

"I would like your advice, Archon." *Tell me what to do!*

"I have given it to you."

"On specific matters, I mean."

"The specifics are your domain, Isaac. Mine is the overview, topsight."

"Is there *anything* you see that can help me decide what to do?"

"I see . . ." The Archon's voice grew softer, introspective. "A critical time for humanity. We stand on the cusp of great things, yet our fate remains far from certain. As a species, we have faced extinction many times. In Africa, as subhumans, sudden environmental change nearly wiped us out on any number of occasions. A random asteroid or comet strike on Earth had the potential to scour the globe clean of us as recently as three centuries ago. A gamma-ray burst aimed directly at us could have destroyed all life in the solar system at any point in our history. We strive for it not to be so. The farther we spread and the more magnificent we become, the more likely we will survive to claim the future for our own. Once we pass the critical threshold glimpsed by the Architects of Sol we will no longer face annihilation, only setbacks along the road to dominion over the galaxy.

"But today, we are little different from the hominids who stared up at the stars in wonderment. They were navigators, not mere animals, but they didn't understand what they saw. And even if they had, would the knowledge have helped them? It's difficult to say. Perhaps we are better off for misunderstanding certain things, for having veils drawn over knowledge that could do us no good and might even hurt us if we suspected its existence. Only in retrospect can we say with any certainty what risk was acceptable, what sacrifice necessary, what ignorance critical. We are shaped by the flow of knowledge as surely as an island is shaped by a river. Uncheck the flood, and we may be swept away forever."

Deangelis listened to the Archon's words with a growing puzzlement. The Exarchate destroyed, and humanity with it? What mere knowledge could possibly cause that?

"Decisions do not become easier the more information one has," the Archon went on. "This is the great irony of evolution—of the universe. Would that omnipotence did equal prescience, for moments like these would be much easier to surmount. I do not know which way events will turn, Isaac, so I cannot answer your question. I cannot give you the response you crave. You must go your way as I must go mine. The journeys are ours to take, and ours alone. If our destinations are the same, I will be glad for both of us."

"And if they're not?"

"I'm sure we'll adapt. That is the great strength of our species, now more so than ever."

Deangelis stood with gaze metaphorically downcast. The parts of him that made up his greater self still niggled that he had acted wrongly by betraying Lazarus Hails and the others. This was guilt he was happy to bear, but it looked now as though it had been for nothing. The Archon wasn't going to do anything about the possible rebellion, and didn't seem to want *him* to do anything about it either. He was right back where he started.

"Have I angered you, Isaac?" the Archon asked unexpectedly. "Or disappointed you?"

"No," he said, trying to find words for what he was feeling. "I just wish there was a way to avoid all this conflict.

Why can't we agree on where we're going and make the journey together?"

"Because life would be less rich for it. Diversity is the key to prosperity. That is why the Exarchate happily accommodates such divergent philosophies as that of your colony. Sol could force it to adopt laws more congruent with the ones we follow, but to what end? There is no possible benefit. If the meme dominant here spreads to other systems, that, too, is no threat. The Exarchate is not the law; it is more than just a name. It is the process by which human life expands through and rejoices in the cosmos, adapting and exapting as necessary. The Exarchate will endure—as will Sol, and you, and I."

"Are you saying I should do nothing to defend the Exarchate from the likes of Lazarus Hails?"

"That depends entirely on how you feel about the circumstances. There is no point defending an irrelevant empire, just as there is no point defending an untenable argument. Perhaps the time has come for a change. Perhaps it hasn't. You must arrive at that conclusion yourself, as must I."

"Yes, but—"

Deangelis fought a sudden wavering of his self. Something was happening beyond the confines of his conversation with the Archon.

"What is it, Isaac?" asked the Archon. "What do you see?"

"Drive signatures," he said, reading the data raw as it came in. "A cluster of them, coming from where the *Nhulunbuy* stopped." *From Hails's tangler.* "I've never seen deforms like these before."

"Palmer?"

"No. Something else."

"Heading?"

"Right at us." *Right at me!* A presentiment of doom rushed through him. Memories of the Reaper were strong. "I'm going to launch interceptors, just in case."

"Do as you see fit, Isaac," said the Archon. "I will be here, if you need my assistance."

Deangelis opened himself back up to the wild information flows of the habitat and told himself to feel reassured.

+54

| Deployment successful. |

  | ETA: one hour, eleven minutes. |

"One hour!" Melilah seemed surprised, despite everything they had learned about the drones. Her eyes opened from scrutinizing virtual displays. "How many gees are we pulling?"

"I'm trying not to think about it," said Eogan, concentrating on the flow of data through the *Cowell*. The drones inundated him and the miniature Cell with information; he had to concentrate to avoid buildups requiring his attention. He had put a sliding scale in place, allowing him to adjust the data flow from almost everything to barely a trickle. He kept it up in the high end to encourage the formation of new connections and nets in the Cell's ever-changing neural infrastructure. If it could learn to assume some of the load, that would be better for everyone concerned.

He felt as though he were caught in an ancient cartoon. He was the moron in a helmet strapped to a giant firework, closing his eyes and putting his fingers in his ears as the fuse burned down rapidly.

Everything looks good, said the voice of Lazarus Hails via the nanoware he had sown in them. *I am impressed.*

"I wondered if you'd hitched a ride," said Melilah. "Another bit part, I presume?"

Enough to advise. I have no intention of taking control.

"Which drone are you in?"

D-4. In the hyperreal schematic of the drone's tightly bound configuration, D-4 glowed faintly pink, as though Hails was reminding them to take extra care of it.

"You can help with target acquisition," said Eogan,

copying a significant chunk of the data flow and diverting it to D-4. "Might as well make yourself useful."

The moment I locate the Archon, you'll be the first to know.

The drones continued, jostling among each other in strange, rhythmic surges, uncannily like dolphins in a fast-swimming pack. Packets of data, as fleeting as minnows, swept through their ports and out again. Eogan wondered what they were talking about, if that was what they were doing. Were they eager for battle after so long lurking on the vanguard of the Dark? Or nervous of performing badly, now that the moment they had been created for was almost upon them?

Although Bedlam itself was little more than a speck of light at that distance, PARASOL soon resolved into a distinct crescent. Within a degree of both shone Ah Kong and its attendant moons. There had been talk, pre-Exarchate, of people settling in the gas giant's ebullient upper atmosphere, as they had elsewhere, laying down floating platforms in relatively stable updrafts thousands of kilometers across. The plan had been scuttled by the instability in the system's primary. It was too hard to guarantee shelter from solar storms for the platform colony, even within the gas giant's powerful magnetosphere. Until a reliable means of engineering people against hard radiation became common—without the kind of overt modifications required of Palmers—the plan would remain unfulfilled.

A trickle of telemetry attracted his attention.

"I'm picking up launches," he told Melilah. "Six drive signatures out of Bedlam."

"Vector?"

"They're still coming around, but I'll give you good odds they'll end up heading our way."

"I've received no transmissions of any kind." She thought for a moment. "Do you think we should hail them?"

Not yet, offered Hails. *Confirm the heading, first. Even if the launches are aimed at us, there's little point doing anything about them now. We'll have some time before they reach us.*

"I disagree," Eogan said. "It's obvious that we've been spotted. Given that we're not currently broadcasting or displaying a recognizable profile, Deangelis will be totally justified in assuming we're a threat and taking action against us."

"He'll jump first, ask questions later." Melilah nodded. "I don't blame him, after the Reaper."

"Okay. Let's send a message, then." Eogan was glad that he and Melilah were in agreement, but steeled himself for their first confrontation with their Exarch benefactor.

It didn't come. *I'll let you handle that, obviously,* said Hails. *The lower a profile I keep, the better.*

There was no question as to who should make the broadcast.

"This is Palmer Eogan, chief officer of the *Cowell,* on approach and requesting a docking vector."

There was a pointed delay before Lut-Deangelis Traffic Control's AI came back to him. "We have you on our screens, Palmer Eogan. But the *Cowell* is not in the register."

"There was a situation on the *Nhulunbuy,*" he half lied, "and we agreed to disagree about it. What you see is what you get. I can give you the specs if you want to log it in the register yourself."

"That won't be necessary. We can get them ourselves when you supply your access codes. You're certainly in a big enough hurry to get back here."

"It's a big, bad universe, LDTC. The sooner I'm in your shadow, the better."

"Not many people feel that way at the moment."

The routing AI was much chattier than normal. Eogan got the feeling it was deliberately trying to keep him talking—or the person driving it was. Deangelis could have been directing the AI like a muppeteer.

"You'll get our codes when we get our vector," he said, prepared to push a little. Supplying a vector was tantamount to handing over the air lock access codes. Short of ramming or scattering debris in their path, there would be nothing Deangelis could do to stop them coming in. Assuming the vector was legit in the first place.

Several minutes passed before LDTC responded. In that time, Eogan and Melilah shored up their knowledge of the drones' processes. It would never be second nature, but he would be satisfied with third or fourth . . .

Their destination grew clearer. The giant habitat hadn't changed much in the previous hours; repairs continued, with work crews and nanotech swarming across the surface. Its smaller companion, the ruined observatory, however, was undergoing a dramatic metamorphosis. The surface was difficult to pin down from such a distance, even with three of the drones spread wide to increase their baseline of measurement. It appeared to be seething like the atmosphere of the sun.

The six vessels Bedlam had launched were by then perfectly lined up to intercept them on their current approach.

"In accordance with Lut-Deangelis Information laws," came the voice of Exarch Deangelis, "you are required to open all memory and channels to public scrutiny. Please immediately supply access codes and encryption keys."

"He's calling our bluff," said Melilah.

"It's going to take more than that." Eogan fiddled the broadcast settings to add a little static. "Uh, LDTC, we appear to have missed part of your last transmission. What was that vector again?"

"*Cowell,* you are in violation of Lut-Deangelis Territorial Regulations. Continued noncompliance will prompt an immediate and severe response."

"I don't understand, LDTC. We're doing nothing wrong. Give us our vector as normal, and we'll give you the codes. What's the problem?"

"The situation is hardly normal. As you well know, Palmer Eogan."

"I guess that explains those interceptors you've sent to meet us. Are we not welcome here now?"

"All are welcome so long as they mean no harm."

"And we've been presumed guilty of that. So much for Bedlam's famed openness."

Eogan assumed the conversation was going out over the habitat's feeds. He didn't really think he could shame Deangelis into backing down, but he could at least make him think twice about making any rash accusations.

"Your configuration is far from friendly, Palmer Eogan. Until you supply access codes in accordance with the law I am sworn to uphold, I will be forced to treat you as a threat. There is no assumption of anything. I am simply taking every reasonable precaution to protect the people in my charge."

"Our behavior in recent days should demonstrate that we have no hostile intentions."

"Every situation must be treated on its own merit. We are grateful for your efforts but unwilling to take any chances. I'm sure you can appreciate that, Palmer Eogan."

He backed down. "We're not going to get anywhere this way," he told Melilah and Hails. "We've made the only points we can over the open channel. I think it's time to get serious."

She nodded. "Do it."

"Any luck locating the Archon?" he asked Hails.

The activity visible on the Occlusion observatory is symptomatic of advanced technology, said the Exarch, *but that doesn't prove the Archon is there.*

"What's happening to the wreckage?" asked Melilah, scrutinizing the images captured by the attack drones.

That is presently unknown.

"Let's see if we can't stir something up, then," said Eogan, switching back to his conversation with Bedlam.

"Take no offense, Exarch Deangelis," he said, "but we'd like to speak to the person who's really in charge. Put us through to the Archon, and we'll discuss the situation with it."

Deangelis's reply was cold. "I assure you that I speak and act with full authority over this system."

"Then what's the Archon doing here?"

"That is not your concern for the moment. Until you

supply your access codes, I am under no obligation to share any information with you."

"Why are you splitting hairs, Deangelis? Are you afraid of the truth?"

"The truth is perfectly clear to me. My function here is unchanged, whether the Archon directs the Exarchate from Sol or anywhere else."

"So it *is* in charge. Is that what you're saying?"

There was a slight hesitation. "The Archon is the authority to whom I answer. That has always been the case."

"Well, we didn't know that. Now we do, that's who we'd like to speak to."

"Who am *I* speaking to, Palmer Eogan?" The query was sharply pointed. "Are these your requests or someone else's?"

It was Eogan's turn to hesitate. Deangelis had almost certainly guessed that someone was working with them; hence the extraordinary profile of the approaching drones. Denying it would be pointless, but admitting that Hails was implicated wasn't part of the deal.

"He speaks for me," said Melilah, taking the line from him. "That is, we speak together."

"Melilah Awad?" The Exarch's reply came with a flash of emotion, not immediately identified. "I should've known you were mixed up in this."

"You didn't think I'd leave with the others, did you? This is my home. You won't get rid of me that easily."

"It is not my intention to get rid of you. I desire only to ensure the peaceful governance of this colony. To that end, I will tolerate all manner of inconvenience—you included."

"Well, good," she said. "I'm sorry I can't be so accommodating in return. While you remain in charge, I can't rest. My long-term objective has always been to return Bedlam to the people who live in it. That's how it should be, and how it will be again, if I have my way."

"But I live here, too, Melilah. This is my home as well. By your argument, I have as much right to govern here as you do."

"Then let's have an election and see who wins."

"You might be disappointed in the outcome."

"We'll never know, will we?"

The Exarch didn't answer her question directly. "Your determination is exceeded only by your hypocrisy. The sort of urban terrorism you endorse differs from the crimes you accuse me of only by degree. You would happily take over this colony in the name of liberation without once stopping to consider if the people you're supposedly saving actually *want* to be liberated. You and a vocal minority aside, how many regard the Exarchate as evil? How many object to the economic and social stability I have wrought here? Before I came, this colony was a minor outpost ignored by its squabbling neighbors. Now it is an essential part of the greatest endeavor in history. Humanity, despite all its wonderful diversity, is united for the first time. Who would not want to be part of that?"

"Yeah, and I'm sure the slaves rowing Roman galleys thought the same."

"Your comparison is inappropriate, Awad! There are no slaves, nor any galleys! You exist in perfect freedom under the guidance of Sol. This is governance like none seen before. That your blinkered view insists on calling it something it's not only proves our point—that until now humanity has not had the capacity to look after itself properly. Until the Exarchate existed, we were just monkeys doing little more than throwing sticks at one another and using feces to mark our territory."

Melilah laughed. "Now who's using unsuitable comparisons?"

The Exarch ignored her flippant comment. "We have an opportunity for greatness here, Awad. I will not let the likes of you derail that process!"

Eogan had never heard the Exarch—any Exarch—speak with such passion about their job. He had always imagined Deangelis and his peers to be cool, calculating intelligences acting from their ivory towers with little real concern for those beneath them, similar to the crude Policy

AIs that had made such a mess of Earth affairs in the mid-twenty-first century. That they genuinely believed in what they were doing was revelatory.

"If it's not a process everyone has subscribed to or is even aware of," said Melilah, her voice low and determined, "I don't see how you can regard it as just, or be surprised that some of us will resist it every step of the way."

"Parents might wish to explain every decision to their children, but there are inevitably times when such communication is not possible. You rail against *nature,* Awad, not me."

"We rail against injustice, Deangelis, whatever its cause. You're either part of the solution, or part of the problem. It seems pretty clear to me which side you're on."

The Exarch made an exasperated noise. "Again, this puerile reductionism. I refuse to be badgered by empty arguments against which there can be no possible defense. If that's the best you and Palmer Eogan have to offer, you are doing yourself a great disservice."

And there it was again, that flash of odd emotion. This time, Eogan thought he might have pinned it down. But why would Deangelis be jealous? That just didn't make sense at all.

| ETA: twenty minutes. |

| Intercept with approaching vessels: ten minutes. |

The voice of the drones brought him back to why they were there.

"That's not all we have," he said. "And that's not what we've come here to say."

"We want to talk to the Archon," Melilah insisted. "If you won't let us, we'll find it ourselves and make it listen."

"How exactly do you plan to do that?"

Tell him, said Hails, *that you know where the Archon is. I've located his tangler; it is indeed in the wreckage of the observatory. That increases the chances that the Archon is in there, too, although I still can't guarantee it. Isaac's reaction will guide us.*

"We already know where the Archon is," Melilah said.

"It's in the observatory with your tangler and the Occlusion. Want to tell us what it's doing in there?"

"I—" Deangelis's momentary hesitation was enough to confirm Hails's guess. "The Archon is not the issue."

"The Archon is *everything*," Melilah insisted. "Whether you'll admit it or not, its presence here is an insult to the entire Arc Circuit. It says that we can't manage our own affairs, that the moment things get tricky we need someone else to step in and take all the decisions away from us. Don't you see that? Aren't you annoyed that you'll never get the chance to prove that you can handle this on your own? Can't you see that this is how I've felt every day *you've* been here?"

The Exarch didn't respond. Eogan watched the data coming in with mounting concern. More distant flashes indicated launches from Bedlam, some of them heading for the observatory. A ripple in space-time propagated before the six oncoming interceptors, accelerating almost as sharply as the drones. He received a distinct feeling that the gloves were coming off. Deangelis had heard enough to be certain of their motives, and now he was preparing a response to them.

Yet no one had declared overt war; no one had fired a shot. So far it was only posturing and pontificating. There was still a chance it might end bloodlessly.

| Intercept with approaching vessels: five minutes. |

Time would tell, he thought. A very short amount of time, indeed, to ensure that they were sufficiently well trained to survive the opening skirmish.

55

Melilah's personal universe simultaneously widened and contracted. Through the information delivered by the drones, she saw the six interceptors with brilliant clarity, set against the backdrop of Bedlam. Several other vessels had launched to protect the observatory, but she didn't care about them. Eogan shifted position beside her; she didn't care about that either. All she saw were the six approaching interceptors and the dumbbell-shaped corridor of possibilities coalescing between her and them.

Their relative velocity was enormous. Even an unarmed ship traveling at such speeds contained enormous destructive potential, so the fact that Bedlam didn't possess an official defense force forbade any sense of comfortable superiority. She had shields to spin and antiassault batteries to prime. The drones hummed at ever-increasing frequencies as internal mechanisms geared up for battle, preparing contingency plans and displaying simulations for her and Eogan to consider.

"Do we want to destroy the interceptors or just get by them?" she asked.

"Evade, preferably," he said. "Once we're past them, they're irrelevant."

Melilah had thought he would say that. She told the drones to concentrate on minimal—preferably zero—damage scenarios. Either there weren't many, or the drones, battle-ready and eager to engage, were reluctant to show them to her.

| Intercept: two minutes. |

"This is your last chance, Deangelis," she said down the line. "Let us talk to the Archon."

"Come peacefully, and you are welcome to do so," came the reply.

"Who's attacking whom, here?"

"I am entitled to defend myself against a perceived attack."

"And I'm entitled to defend my home against an invader. You fired the first shot forty years ago, Deangelis. It may have taken me a long time to fire back, but I'm not going to miss my chance now. You've had it coming."

Deangelis didn't grace the comment with a reply.

| Intercept: one minute. |

A scenario scrolled by that seemed little different from the others. It was about as likely to succeed in all its objectives as hitting Bedlam with a laser blindfolded, but it was better than nothing. Even if it failed, there would be no mistaking their intentions.

Eogan concurred. "Better strap yourself in. It's going to be rough."

She didn't immediately understand what he meant. There were no literal straps. Instead, the Cell would protect her from damage during the encounter—by completely enfolding her, like a fetus in a womb.

Panic tightened her throat muscles. She forced the feeling down. There was no avoiding it, and she should have realized that it would be asked of her. Eogan had done her a favor by not bringing it up sooner.

She nodded once, spasmodically. "I'm trusting you, Dominic," she said.

He looked up at her with surprise in his eyes, and she almost said: *Do you really think I'm that much of a coward?*

Then she realized the reason for his surprise: she had used his first name. Out of habit—a habit that should have died one hundred and fifty years earlier.

Fuck it, she thought. *This is no time to argue about semantics.*

As though agreeing, he nodded, and the Cell closed in around her.

56

Deangelis snarled at the screen, a rush of anger clouding his judgment. In the final seconds before the distant flotillas met, he urged the interceptors to use maximum force in dealing with the interlopers.

"Destroy them," he told the AIs piloting the receding craft. "*Utterly.* I want their ashes to rain on me like dust."

The AIs in the interceptors hurried to reorganize their munitions in the short time available to them before engagement. He sensed their alien frustration and puzzlement at the sudden change in plans, but he didn't care. He was beyond caring, now.

Lazarus Hails was dead. After Melilah Awad's last transmission, Deangelis had sent part of himself to the cell in Protective Custody where the representative of his fellow Exarch was being kept. He had arrived just as alarms reached his higher self. That very instant, Hails's heart had stopped. Medical technicians rushed into the cell with Deangelis hot on their heels. Hails's body lay slumped facedown on the floor between the two beds. They hauled it over and administered emergency aid. Every measure failed: his leonine features remained inanimate, and there was no indication of brain activity. Deep-tissue scans revealed vast hemorrhages spreading through his cortex and spinal cord; all that remained of his peripherals were charred bioplastic lumps. Hails was gone.

And with it went Deangelis's last, faint hope that this was nothing but a misunderstanding, that it could all still work out for the best. If Hails was covering his tracks, the likelihood of the crisis simply blowing over was effectively zero.

First Cazneaux, he thought, and now Lazarus Hails. He couldn't work out which was worse. The specter of civil war had been raised in his colony. His *home*. He hadn't been lying when he'd told Melilah Awad that that was how he thought of the habitat. Lut-Deangelis owned more than just one of his names. It owned him, too—and it galled him to think that Hails's brand of treachery had found fertile soil on his territory.

He had spared her, and she had betrayed him.

"Spare no effort," he told the interceptors, "to bring them down. *All* of them."

Sporting a grim, tight-lipped expression on all his faces, he settled back to watch the telemetry.

+57

| External interference detected. |
  | Autonomous systems engaged. |

With a scream of tortured space-time, the fifteen vessels met. They hit hard and furiously, stretching the very laws of physics to maximize the split instant in which they could act. Buckyballs flung at relativistic velocities struck with masses far in excess of their rest state. Blue-shifted lasers achieved fantastical energies. Shields spun from ultradense kernels swept space around the battlefield in great, disorienting waves.

From a distance, Eogan knew, the skirmish would trace a sudden streak across the starscape, a brilliant, short-lived line that expanded from a single point outward in both directions. Faint exclamation points would Morse code from each end of the line, gradually stuttering to nothing as the streak itself abruptly winked out. Where had once been a bold, geometric statement would be only a mess of high-energy shrapnel and heat, a dissipating scar that boiled the quantum foam and warped light from distant quasars.

It all happened too quickly for him to follow. Even at his highest cognitive rates, the moment of truth passed before he could barely acknowledge it. One instant the drones and the interceptors were rushing toward each other like shotgun blasts from opposing guns; the next they were heading just as quickly apart, debris sparkling in their wake.

He performed a quick head count when the drones' autonomous systems disengaged, indicating that the Archon was no longer trying to shut them down. All the drones were present, although not all were undamaged. A deep gouge ran down the cigar-shaped flank of D-5, issuing bright rainbow tails of stressed space. Looking behind him, he saw that two of the interceptors were gone. The rest were empty and tumbling, their matter reserves spent in one savage, furious instant of combat.

As he watched, the rear end of D-5 disintegrated with a flash of bright light. Its drive failed, and the front end dropped back like a stone. Barely had it begun a slow tumble when it was suddenly gone, visible only in the radar sweeping their wake.

"We made it," Melilah said. Her voice shook as the *Cowell* eased its constrictive embrace, giving them room to move again.

Good work, said Hails. *But it's not over yet.*

More interceptors launched from Bedlam.

| ETA: thirteen minutes. |

"We need to change course," Eogan said. "The observatory is our target now, not the habitat."

"Agreed." Melilah sent a series of commands to the drones, who responded by expending massive amounts of their antimatter reserves on a lateral course correction.

| ETA: sixteen minutes. |
| Deceleration: five minutes. |
| Intercept: twelve minutes. |

"That didn't take Deangelis long," said Melilah, scowling at the Exarch in absentia as more interceptors launched from Bedlam and swung around to intersect their new heading.

"He obviously prepared this contingency in advance. We'll just have to punch our way through."

"We'll be moving slower at that point. It's a whole different fight."

"We still outnumber him. He can't keep us from the observatory like this, and he must know it."

Right on cue, a transmission arrived from the habitat. The voice of a young woman filled the interior of the Cell.

"Grandmother Mel, what are you doing?"

Melilah looked up sharply. "Yasu? Are you all right?"

"*I'm* all right. But you—the feed is buzzing with the

news that you and another Exarch have declared war on Bedlam! Is that true?"

Eogan saw her wince. "No, Yasu, that's not true. I'm fighting the Exarchate, not Bedlam. Deangelis won't let us talk to the Archon, so we have no choice but to force our way through."

"But you could be killed!"

"I know," she said grimly.

"I don't want you to die, Grandmother. Not you, on top of the others."

"That's a risk I have to take, Yasu."

The sound of sobbing came down the line. "But what about *me?* What about all the other people you'd leave behind? We don't deserve it. And for what? Some stupid war that ended before I was born? Don't throw your life away, Grandmother. Please. You have so much left to do!

Melilah looked as though her heart was breaking.

It's a trick, said Hails. *A simulation designed to undercut your resolve.*

"He might be right," added Eogan. "Deangelis could easily do that."

Melilah didn't seem to hear. "I'm sorry, Yasu. I have to do this."

"Why? I thought all this talk of rebellion was a game, a hobby, a fashion among you old-timers. You never seemed to do anything *but* talk. I didn't know you were *serious* about it."

"Of course we were serious. This is important, and always has been. You may not understand now, but you will later, I'm sure."

"How? You'll never get the chance to explain it to me if you throw your life away on some crazy escapade!"

"Yasu, please—"

"I give up, Grandmother Mel. Do what you think you have to do. Drag Palmer Eogan down with you as you go. Just don't expect me to be here for you when you get back!"

On that angry retort, the line clicked dead.

Eogan reached out to put a hand on Melilah's shoulder. She didn't pull away.

"It'll be Luisa and James Pirelli next," he said. "Just wait and see."

"I don't care if it's Elvis," she muttered. "I *know* we're doing the right thing."

He didn't share her certainty, but it was past time for arguing about it. They were committed now.

| Deceleration: two minutes. |

| Intercept: nine minutes. |

He forced himself to ignore Melilah's pain and concentrate on what needed to be done.

Melilah considered sending the signal to the tangler. Blowing the lid off the Occlusion conspiracy would punish Deangelis for bringing such a world of doubt down upon her. Whether the call from Yasu had been real or not, its effect had only been to reinforce something the Exarch had tried to tell her earlier. What right did she have to put her own beliefs ahead of those she was trying to protect? If they didn't *want* her protection, then who was she to force it upon them?

But she wasn't alone. She knew that. There were the members of Defiance, for a start, and many others who had agitated for membership but had been knocked back. There were ex-politicos of the old regime who would no doubt crawl out of the woodwork once the oppression was removed.

And then there were the many thousands of people who simply didn't care much either way. They would accept the end of the Exarch's rule in Bedlam with the same easygoing acquiescence that they had accepted its arrival. Once the shock of the new passed, it would become the norm all too quickly.

Either way, she thought, the Occlusion was bringing change. That it should be the *right* change was critical.

High-tech muscles flexed; powerful forces knotted around the drones as they began the furious deceleration that would bring them in a fast approach over the observatory.

"It's time," she said. "Time we came clean on at least one front."

Eogan, whose subtle support—just one hand pressed on her shoulder—had been an anchor in a very stormy sea, looked up from his analysis of battle plans. "Which one?"

"Rumors and lies are obviously spreading about us. If the people of Bedlam are to think us the bad guys, then I'd rather they did it fully informed."

He shrugged. "We've yet to give the Archon notice, so I'm for broadcasting generally if we can't get through to it specifically."

She felt a kind of relief that some of the game playing would soon end. One board would be swept clean—although probably to be replaced by another, and another . . .

"This is Melilah Awad," she broadcast over all frequencies. "I come bearing a message for the Archon. For robbing everyday humanity of choice, for keeping secrets, and for lying to protect its own interests, I declare it unwelcome in the Arc Circuit. Go home—I would say to it, if it would only listen—and let us manage our own affairs. There is nothing you have to offer that the forty thousand of us do not already have in abundance."

"I am listening, Melilah Awad," returned a cool, collected voice.

"I suspect you have been all along," said Melilah.

"Of course."

"Then why talk only now? Things weren't chaotic enough for you before?"

It ignored the question. "I have just one thing to say to you, Melilah Awad. You are in great personal danger. This is not a threat, but a warning—and I offer it because I wish to avoid unnecessary bloodshed."

"If you're sincere about that, then you'd go home and leaves us in peace."

"I'm not talking about this rebellion of yours. I'm talking about the Occlusion."

She smiled. "Do you really want us to discuss this over an open frequency?"

"You can say whatever you like, Melilah. Misapprehension or lie, it won't change the facts. You are meddling with powers you cannot hope to understand. Continuing to meddle only increases the likelihood of disaster."

"I see no evidence of any such disaster."

"The Exarchate has already lost one colony. I would not make that two."

"What are the odds of that, really? You've been back in Sublime for ten years now, and there have been no more alien attacks. We've had our hands on this Occlusion for a year, and likewise. What exactly does it take to set it off? Tell us, and we'll avoid it. Otherwise, I believe we're safe continuing just as we are."

"You know nothing of the circumstances required to unleash such a catastrophe. It may already be too late."

"So, again, what difference does it make? This thing belongs to all humanity, not just to you. It's about time you realized that."

"The Occlusion is not mine or yours, or *ours*. I don't know who it belongs to; all I know is that it is dangerous. We—you, I, *all* humanity—must exercise great care in our dealings with it."

"So you've come to take it off our hands because we're not capable of doing that. Can't you see that it's a self-fulfilling prophecy? Tell us what the danger is, and we'll do our best to avoid it. Keeping us in the dark only increases the chance that we'll make a terrible mistake. Your secrecy puts us at risk, not our naïveté. Would you rather see Bedlam destroyed than reveal the truth?"

I Intercept: two minutes. I

I ETA: six minutes. I

"Time's running out. What's your answer, Archon?"

"What's the question, Melilah?"

"Will you leave us to govern ourselves in peace?"

"I will leave, but Isaac Deangelis will remain. The Exarchate is the future of humanity. You can no more turn it back than reinstate *Homo habilis* at the summit of the evolutionary tree. Your fight, valiant though it is, is ultimately pointless and futile."

Melilah set her mouth in a grim line. "What about the Occlusion, then? Will you reveal the truth about it and the object that destroyed Sublime?"

"Eventually, yes. But not now. These are volatile times, as witness today. Sol wishes to avoid further destabilization."

"But you can't hide something like this! You and I both know what it is. You can try to bury the Bedlam and Sublime Occlusions as much as you like, but another will come along soon enough. And another. And another. It's like trying to bury an ants' nest. Sooner or later it's going to get out."

"And we'll deal with each outbreak on its own merits," said the Archon. "But at present, we have no other choice."

"You're not leaving *us* much choice, either. Do you appreciate that?"

"I understand that you might think that, Melilah, but you are wrong. You are foolishly gambling with your lives."

"You're already gambling with them, as far as I can tell. We have no intention of harming *you,* Archon, unless you force us to. And that makes us better people in my book. I know who I'd rather have in charge."

"That option is not one open to you, I'm afraid."

Eogan nudged her, pointing out that only seconds remained until the drones encountered the second wave of interceptors. Their velocity had dropped dramatically; this would be no blink-and-miss-it encounter. She was needed to oversee the drones' tactics.

"Then I guess there's nothing more to say," she said, steeping her tone in disappointment, and closed the line. The Archon was clearly not going to back down.

"Are you okay with this?" she asked Eogan.

"As okay as I'm ever going to be." His face was stone. "The Archon hasn't left us any options. Unless it changes its mind, I'm with you one hundred percent."

She was genuinely grateful for his support and the sacrifices he had made to give it to her. "Okay. Then let's finish this."

He nodded, and the drones extended their weapons.

59

The eight attacking vessels unfolded like spindly arachnids, extruding strange spines, many-jointed limbs, and eyelike dishes, each configuration unique to each drone. Harsh sunlight gleamed from wicked points and rapier-thin antennae. Potent energies sparked from angular surfaces through all octaves of the electromagnetic spectrum. Thin lozenges that had once seemed minuscule in comparison to their bulbous, powerful shields were now deadly engines, filling those shields with instruments of lethality.

The shadow of PARASOL swept over them. An instant later, the interceptors sent to guard the observatory came within range. A new sun dawned.

Deangelis glowered at the data as it flooded in. Although no longer directly threatening the habitat, the drones still struck at a point of distinct vulnerability.

Would you rather see Bedlam destroyed than reveal the truth?

Melilah's words sparked a suspicion deep in the workings of his intricate mind. He didn't want to pursue it, didn't even want to think it—but it wouldn't go away. It lingered like the smell of burning oil, issued by some malfunctioning machine.

You know nothing of the circumstances required to unleash such a catastrophe.

The Archon remained no reassurance at all. Sol was as inscrutable as ever, the motives of the home system obscured by more than just seventy-eight light-years. Although he had initially feared the erosion of his authority by the arrival of the Archon, now he yearned for it. Anything to ease the terrible doubt that gnawed at him, the fear that he was doing the wrong thing despite all his best efforts, and the worst thought of all:

It may already be too late.

Two of Melilah Awad's suspiciously advanced craft disintegrated into showers of energy and disorganized matter. He hoped that Lazarus Hails felt their loss keenly, wherever the rest of him was. That the attack drones had come from Altitude he had no doubt, although he couldn't prove it. Each one represented a considerable investment in resources, enough to impact significantly on the Kullervo-Hails colony. Deangelis hoped, vindictively, that the next rebellion was against the man who had given one of his own the weapon she needed to turn against him. Lazarus Hails had joined Frederica Cazneaux on a growing list of people needing to pay for what had happened to his home.

But Deangelis would need to survive the current crisis, first. Just two attack drones died in exchange for all four of his makeshift interceptors. He had no surprises left to pull. Awad and Eogan now had a clear run at the Occlusion. All that stood between them and the Archon was vacuum, and whatever the Archon had been working on the previous day.

Would it be enough? Deangelis hoped so. He didn't dare imagine what might happen if it wasn't.

The Exarchate has already lost one colony. I would not make that two.

He shuddered, and waited. There was nothing else he could do.

| ETA: three minutes. |

Eogan wiped his brow. He was sweating for the first time that he could remember. The last interceptor had come dangerously close to ramming their drone in a last-ditch attempt to destroy them. Only a desperate maneuver by their high-tech steed had saved their lives, and then only barely. It shuddered as it decelerated, shaking them like beads in a rattle.

"This is no good," he said, attempting to reroute power from various subsystems to shore up the breach, but failing miserably. "We can't keep on like this. The drone will tear itself to pieces."

Melilah looked frustrated, but didn't argue. She could see diagnostics as well as he could. "Pull us out of formation," she said. "We'll have to overshoot and come around from behind."

"That leaves you in charge, Hails."

Mine is not to question why . . .

"Hey," Melilah snapped. "This was your idea, remember?"

The illusion of the Exarch bowed deeply. *A jest, my lady. It has been a pleasure.*

The shuddering eased as D-1 eased back from the main contingent. The five fully functional drones surged ahead. Dead in their sights was the Occlusion, a gleaming asteroid-sized bauble in the shadow of PARASOL. As D-1 angled away on a more space-consuming deceleration curve, the target didn't change in the slightest. It looked like a bubble of quicksilver floating in the vacuum. Complex patterns rippled across its surface as though it was ringing like a very large bell.

| ETA: six minutes. |

"How long until the others arrive?"

| ETA: one minute seventy seconds. |

They had selected an attack run designed to show the Archon that they meant business without doing too much damage. If the Archon resisted, the drones would attack again, the observatory's defenses having been tested once and any weak points carefully targeted. This would, once again, be a very different type of combat than the previous two engagements. The observatory was stationary—unless the Archon had worked some technological wonder upon it— and could not therefore run from the drones. The drones, in turn, would be vulnerable to attacks from Bedlam, as Deangelis poured more of his resources into the defense of the Occlusion. They were prepared, however, to fight a war of attrition until the Archon gave in. Only then would they bring the fighting to an end.

"What if we've got it wrong?" Melilah asked him. "What if the Archon isn't in there at all, and we've wasted our only shot?"

"I don't think Hails would throw even part of himself away on a pointless gesture. If he thinks it's there, I'm inclined to believe him."

"But what if . . . ?"

He shrugged. "Then I guess we'd better hope this thing can fix itself and get us out of here in time."

"There's the tangler." She looked gloomy. "As long as the message gets out, I guess we're expendable."

"I don't *feel* expendable right now," he said. "And I don't think I'm likely to anytime soon, either."

"This has never felt like a suicide run for you, then?"

"Never. No offense, Mel, but no place is worth dying for."

"And no *one*?"

He smiled wryly. "I didn't say that."

61

There was nothing left to say, Melilah told herself. This was the moment of truth. Either the drones would succeed, or they'd fail. Nothing was certain after that junction. There was no point even guessing what lay ahead.

"Wait," Eogan said, as the final seconds flew by. "That's not the attack run we selected!"

She had just noticed the variation, too. The drones were splitting up too early and priming their weapon systems in ways she and Eogan hadn't instructed them to. Mass launchers loaded far more matter than expected; lasers sucked power well in excess of their budget; systems not expected to stir until the second attack run were already at full readiness.

She scrolled through screens at lightning speed. Somehow, the plan had changed.

"Hails!" She slapped the bulkhead nearest her. "The son of a bitch is going for the kill!"

"It certainly looks like it," said Eogan. "I'm trying to override the commands, but the drones have switched on their autonomous systems. We're locked out."

Melilah fumed as the drones opened fire on the Occlusion observatory. She should have known better than to trust Hails. He was using them to destroy the Archon, not warn it away. They would take the blame for far more than just starting a rebellion.

Feeling trapped and fearing more bad news to come, she sent a flurry of experimental commands at D-1. The drone responded normally, suggesting that only the five under Hails's command had been compromised. Those five were swooping around the shimmering target like moons in fast motion, weapons and drives sending ripples jack-hammering through space-time. D-1 rocked sickeningly around them, but the waves didn't seem to impede its performance any more than its damage already had.

| ETA: three minutes. |

"This is insane," Melilah said, unable to decide whether to call off their own approach or hasten it in order to stop Hails.

"This is war, Melilah," Eogan muttered. "There are no rules."

She punched the bulkhead again, "Fuck!"

"Take it easy, Melilah. Try to think straight. There must be something we can do. Call the Archon, perhaps. If our communications systems are still open, we can at least try to make it clear that this isn't all our doing."

She nodded, trying to force her anger down. Cursing and hitting things wasn't going to help. She needed to find a better outlet for her energy.

"You do that," she said. "Meanwhile, I'll look into finding a way of stopping Hails."

Determined not to let another Exarch get the better of her, she set furiously to work.

62

Deangelis watched the attack on the observatory with a feeling of bleak despondency. His rage was gone. He had tried his best to protect the Archon and failed. Now it was out of his hands. He could only hope that the short time the Archon had had to shore up the Occlusion's defenses had been long enough.

Initial signs were good. The quicksilver surface of the new observatory absorbed attacks with equanimity, glowing crimson and radiating waste heat away in infrared. Long spikes stabbed at the attacking craft, shooting all manner of energies and material projectiles from their tips. Scythe-like eruptions threatened to slice the drones in two if they came too near. One of the vessels succumbed in just such a fashion. Broken and disintegrating, it tumbled to destruction on the observatory's gleaming skin.

The remaining four concentrated their assault on the bright point their fallen sibling left on the observatory. The red scar glowed orange, then yellow, then a fiery green. Vicious tendrils whipped at the drones but did little more than inconvenience them. Enough energy to crack a small moon in two poured into the breach, turning it a sickly aqua.

Only then did Deangelis pause to consider if Hails's target wasn't the Archon at all, but the Occlusion. Had Hails used the cover of rebellion to go after the same goal Frederica Cazneaux had sought?

"Why?" he asked, firing the message at the drones along the tightest channel possible, but not really expecting a reply. "Why are you doing this?"

"This might sound disingenuous," Hails responded, "but I'm doing my level best to save your life."

"From myself, I suppose."

"No, from the Archon, actually. I told you before, Isaac: you're too trusting. The biggest threat you've ever faced isn't from me or Melilah, or even the Occlusion. It's the one thing you let into the system without questioning it—and now I have to kill it dead before it destroys everyone here."

"What are you talking about?"

"I'm talking about Sublime, and what really happened there."

Deangelis froze. The suspicion he earlier had refused to consider rose up in response to Hails's words, stronger than ever, and caused the equivalent of a freeway pileup. His serial, synergistic thought processes cascaded to a halt.

"No," Earth-Deangelis whispered.

"Yes," said Hails. "We can argue about it later, if there's anything left of us."

"But—" A flurry of disconnected thoughts swirled through his many skulls. He struggled to bring himself back together. "The Archon wouldn't do that. It simply wouldn't."

"Why not? You know it was there when Sublime was destroyed, just like you know Jane Elderton never left. I've seen the data they've gathered since. Does it look to you like they're losing a war against alien replicators?"

Deangelis was stuck for a moment on the realization that Hails had seen the data he had secreted in the belly of the habitat. That had been his worst fear just days ago; now it seemed almost irrelevant.

"Are you saying the Archon could do it here, too?"

"*Of course* that's what I'm saying. Isaac, you're not this stupid. The Archon has some kind of hold over you. The moment things looked dicey, it sent itself down the pipe to make sure every contingency was covered. Someone needed to be there to push the plunger that would destroy your system—if things went wrong, as they clearly have."

The drones pounded the observatory's weak point. It flared bright purple, then inflated like a bubble, increasing its surface area to radiate the energy away. Disfigured and besieged, the observatory didn't look healthy at all.

"There's no proof," he said in desperation.

"That'll come if the Archon survives and Bedlam goes up in flames." Hails used the old name for the colony with easy familiarity, obviously not caring if Deangelis took offense. "I, for one, don't want to perform that test. Do you?"

Earth-Deangelis had no doubt that Hails was right. When the umbrella mind of his higher self dissolved in confusion, the subtle charisma of the Archon evaporated and he could see the truth perfectly well. When his higher self returned, however, the suspicion was quashed.

He fought the reintegration of his mind. The thought that he could no longer trust himself was utterly dispiriting.

The bubble on the observatory burst, exposing a second bubble within, this one radiating most strongly in ultraviolet. It, too, popped as the drones pounded it, exposing another one—and so on, each bubble rising in radiant energy until the boil in the side of the observatory burned brightly in X-rays. Earth-Deangelis dimmed the sensitivity on the electronic instruments focused on the observatory—the equivalent of shading his eyes with one hand. All over the habitat, he felt people hunkering down, afraid of what was to come.

No. Earth-Deangelis fought the seductive sensation of wholeness, of being able to absorb the colony in one gulp. The others could integrate if they wanted to, but he had to stay apart. Someone needed to keep the thought alive in case Hails failed. Someone needed to remember the truth.

A brilliant flash of cosmic rays almost blinded him. Flare screens slammed down all over the colony, antiquated, poorly maintained things installed before PARASOL had rendered them irrelevant. Radiation alarms went off, adding their powerful clamor to the attack sirens already whooping through the pipes and junctions. Those people not already in shelters scurried to find cover.

Earth-Deangelis pulled himself away from the niche in which he'd been standing, numbly jacked in to the data surging through his higher self. If the observatory had been rigged to self-destruct, it might conceivably do so with enough power to take the habitat with it. He headed for higher ground, metaphorically and literally. He needed to keep his head and shoulders above the encroaching tide of his mind.

As he ran for the nearest transport, he tried to find the humor in the fact that he was rebelling against himself, but it wasn't immediately evident.

+63

| ETA: thirty seconds. |

With a resounding concussion that set space vibrating like a plucked ruler, the Archon's defenses collapsed. Eogan surrendered himself to inertia gel as waves of energy poured over and through them. Through barely functional sensors he caught glimpses of concentric shells peeling back around a midnight black shape that glittered in its own deathlight. The chain reaction, once started, spread through all the observatory's new layers, rapidly exposing the raw knot of space-time tucked away at its heart. Eogan picked up familiar spatial distortions through the chaos, magnified and twisted into hideous shapes. He had never seen anything like it, and he hoped never to again.

A white point of light shot out of the observatory's habitat-facing flank. Eogan had barely enough time to notice it when the last shreds of the Archon's defenses evaporated. Energy boiled into furiously agitated vortices of vacuum foam; matter unraveled into photons all across the spectrum. With one last energetic eructation, the observatory simply evaporated into nothing, leaving the Occlusion exactly as it had been when he had first seen it—a strange anomaly surrounded by gas—only much, much hotter than before. A spherical shock wave rushed out into the solar system.

D-1 bucked and complained at the punishment. The *Cowell* shrank to its smallest profile in an attempt to minimize the number of particle and photon hits it was taking. Eogan rode out the shaking with his eyes firmly on what telemetry was telling him. The observatory was gone—and so were the drones that had killed it. All four of them vanished forever into the maelstrom.

Lucky we didn't get as close as we planned, he thought, wondering if that had been Hails's intention all along, too.

"Catch it!" called a voice, rising urgently above the roar of static left in the explosion's wake. "Don't let it hit!"

The voice came from the habitat, from Deangelis. The white mote of light that had ejected at the last moment from the observatory resolved into a stubby shape bearing enough similarities to Hails's tangler to convince Eogan that he was seeing another of them. It was blazing a path toward the habitat, dodging antiassault lasers as it went.

The Archon! Eogan pulled himself out of a daze and took control of the drone. Melilah was stunned, forced into a fetal ball by the Cell in its sudden self-protective collapse. He would have to fly the drone on his own. Swinging targeting routines into play and identifying the rogue tangler as a new priority objective, he set the drone accelerating powerfully in pursuit.

| Target acquired. |

The shudder in its drive returned. He ignored it. The drone's destructive impulses, thwarted earlier by the damage to its systems, brought all its weapons to bear on the tangler. Beam weapons chipped at its rear defenses while VOID-powered missiles snaked in for a broadside hit. The tangler had a few surprises up its sleeve, however: strange butterfly-like feather-shields flapped in and out of existence, batting the missiles aside like flies; concave containment-field effects kept the missiles' self-destruct detonations at bay; brief but powerful surges in acceleration took it at wild tangents to its existing course, just ahead of the next wave of attack.

"It's getting away!" shouted Deangelis. Eogan didn't stop to wonder why the Exarch was suddenly so afraid of someone he had been trying to defend just minutes earlier. "Don't let it get through!"

A lucky beam-shot clipped the tangler's flank. Too late, it surged explosively aside. The damage must have affected its guidance systems, for the tangler spiraled away from the habitat like a disoriented dragonfly. Dogged on all sides, it was only a matter of time before a missile found its mark. White light blared from the tangler's nose, and it went into a tumble.

There, under the shadow of PARASOL with nothing but blackness at its back and the ruins of the observatory to one side, the Archon's last-ditch hope of escape died. The tangler's hull buckled outward, then tore apart. A massive chemical explosion blossomed, casting a golden light across the *Cowell*. In its wake, glowing debris tumbled.

| Target destroyed. |

Eogan let free the breath he had been holding, and mentally took his hands off the controls.

"Is that it?" asked Melilah, her voice weak. "Is it over?"

He reached one hand through the gel and found hers waiting for him. They gripped and held tight.

"Christ, I hope so," he said.

+64

There was no cheering, no wild fanfare. It seemed to Melilah that she and Eogan hung in the thrall of a shocked silence as they accelerated slowly toward Bedlam. It would take time for recent events to sink in. The feed from Bedlam was chaotic and confused. No one personality rose out of the rabble to give words to the consensus view. It might be hours, Melilah knew, before one formed.

She wasn't prepared to wait that long.

"It's done," she said over all frequencies. "For better or for worse, we've kicked the Archon out of Bedlam. The Occlusion is ours, if we want it. We have a chance, at last, to make up our own minds. That doesn't mean it'll be easy. That doesn't mean we won't still make mistakes. But they'll be *our* mistakes, and we'll learn from them."

"We've all made mistakes," said an unexpected voice. "We've all been wronged."

"Don't you play the victim now, Deangelis," she said. "It's not going to wash."

"I *am* a victim," he responded, "as surely as you are. Sol has committed crimes against everyone in the name of the Exarchate. So many lives have been lost. It can't go on any longer."

"*Now* you see reason." She couldn't help the bitterness. "Why couldn't you have said this earlier?"

"I didn't have all the facts. I was—confused." His voice was uncharacteristically uncertain. "It will take me time to put myself back together the way I should be, and you will have to be patient with me. But I give you my word that I will not rest until justice is done."

Melilah didn't know what had turned the Exarch around

so suddenly, but she was quite happy to accept his capitulation—to a point.

"What exactly does that mean, Deangelis? Are you going to give Bedlam back to us?"

"I don't know." He sounded angry and tired. "I have no wish to belong to a government that practices genocide, but I do not know if I am able to abdicate. There are restrictions on my thoughts, constraints I was not previously aware of. Perhaps I can shrug them free and exist in my own right—not as Exarch, but as Isaac Forge Deangelis, human being and citizen of Bedlam. Time, Melilah, is what I need."

"That might be just what we don't have," said Eogan. "I hate to be the doomsayer, but we can expect a strong backlash, and soon. I bet the *Cowell* there are more Exarchs sniffing around for a chance to take advantage of the disruption. And I'm sure Sol won't take this lying down. It may be a long way away, but it's a force to be reckoned with."

"We have the Occlusion," said Melilah. "We have the maze. That gives us an edge they don't have."

"That's true, but they do still have Sublime, and we'll have to find another exit before it becomes truly useful. Don't think the war is won just because we've got one hand on the prize."

His words were sobering. She knew they needed to be said, but that didn't make them any easier to hear.

A flood of messages began to roll in. Members of Defiance offered congratulations. Old political acquaintances did so more cautiously, covering their bets. Yasu apologized for her angry words. Gil Hurdowar sent her a short note welcoming her home, and that one she couldn't let slide.

"I'm not home yet," she told him. "In fact, I've rather enjoyed being out of your sight. Maybe I'll stay away for good."

"You can't do that. Life would be too boring without you, Melilah. Besides, you don't fool me. I know you like it: the attention, the infamy, the drama. You thrive on it.

That's why you like politics so much, and why I don't. I'd rather watch while you strut your stuff. It's an equitable arrangement."

"You had your moment in the spotlight," she said, remembering his warning about Hails and other occasional hints.

"Too hot for me, 'Lilah. Besides, you have plenty of company at the moment. There wouldn't be room enough for me even if I wanted to be there."

She opened her mouth to object at his use of the pet name she hated, then shut it again, protest unexpressed. That was what he would have wanted: to get a rise out of her. She wasn't going to give him the satisfaction when, for now and maybe a little while longer, she had the luxury of simply switching him off.

She did so.

"Any food on this thing?" she asked Eogan. Since the Cell had expanded to its usual size, she had taken up a perch opposite him, held in place by one arm and a leg.

"Sure," he said, "if you don't mind it coming through a vein."

She pulled a face. "Let's get home soon then, before cannibalism starts to look tempting."

"That sounds like a good idea."

She checked the flight plan of the drone. Eogan had plotted a low-energy return to the habitat, and that was fine by her. She could wait an hour to eat. They were still closer to the Occlusion than to Bedlam. The weird hole in space was visible only through the distortions it cast upon the universe beyond it. As PARASOL gradually swung around to block out the stars, it became effectively invisible.

"What about you?" she asked. "Any thoughts on what you'll do next?"

He shook his head. "The *Cowell* could probably make another system, if it had to, but I'm not sure what my reception would be like there. The Palmers will have to work out where they stand in all this. And until I know where that is exactly, I guess I'm stuck here." He looked at her. "Is that a problem?"

She searched her feelings for anything she could justify. The thought of his being around any longer made her feel uncomfortable, but there was no concrete reason for forbidding him. It was her problem, not the habitat's. He had helped save Bedlam, so she supposed she could put up with him a little longer.

"As long as there's no more funny business," she said, thinking of the moment in the ruined alien ship.

"On my word."

"And you have to help get Hails's nanoware out of my head."

He nodded. "It'll take time, but I'm sure it's possible."

"Thanks. I appreciate it." She felt as though she owed him something more than that, so she added: "I really mean that, Palmer Eogan. Thank you."

"Gratefully accepted, Mem Awad." He smiled. "Will you listen to us being nice to one another? The sooner we get out of here, the better."

"Agreed." She turned her attention back to the drone's guidance systems, unwilling to completely repress a smile.

So it was that she caught the first flash of light around the edge of PARASOL. *A solar flare,* she thought, although she didn't remember any scheduled for that time. It wasn't surprising that she had missed it; she hadn't been paying attention to forecasts of late. But it was a concern. A big flare could have serious ramifications for the battle-scarred habitat.

"What rating are we looking at, Traffic Control?" Eogan's voice momentarily distracted her from the view.

"Unknown," came back the AI. "All vessels are advised to return to dock."

"We can ride it out," he said. "The Cell's seen worse than anything the sun can throw at us."

"What about the drone?" she asked him.

"It'll make do. PARASOL will absorb the worst of it,

after all, and it doesn't have to worry about life support. I'm sure it'll come through okay."

Melilah watched, still feeling disoriented, as the far side of PARASOL began to glow with golden fire as well. This was a particularly big flare, judging by its brightness—and it was still growing.

Her smile vanished as a bright spark punctured the heart of PARASOL's black face. Then another. The spark brightened and spread.

Alarm tightened the muscles in her chest.

The flare was burning *through* PARASOL.

"My God," said Eogan.

An alarm she had never heard began to wail over the Bedlam feed. She clutched the walls of the component for reassurance it couldn't give her. Voices shouted as the sparks joined up and new ones formed. The dark shield was melting, burning, dissolving. The stars were vanishing under an onslaught of light.

"That's not a flare!" Deangelis's voice stood out from the rest—no less panicky but thick with the same anger as before.

"Then what is it?" asked Melilah anxiously.

"Catastrophe," Deangelis muttered, trading uncertainty for despair.

Ice crystallized in her veins. For a moment, her thoughts simply stopped.

Impossible. It couldn't be!

Then alarms began to sound from sensors on the drone's skin. It was being attacked by something invisible from the vacuum around them.

"No," she whispered. Catastrophe wasn't an option. She wouldn't allow it.

But in her mind she saw the debris cloud from the destroyed tangler. She pictured it expanding in a hot sphere, hitting PARASOL first, the object closest to it, then the drone. From there it would keep expanding, as unstoppable as an exhaled breath, its foulness spreading to poison everything in its path.

Bedlam.

"No!" She clambered around the interior of the component to where Eogan sat, half in the bulkhead, half out. She
clutched him, shook him. "We have to stop it! There must
be a way!"

Eogan's expression was shocked. His eyes briefly focused on her, then rolled away to internal views. "I'm trying my best, but the agents are replicating too quickly, and
the drone doesn't have the defenses to deal with something
like this. It's spreading faster than I can contain it!"

"To hell with the drone," she snarled. "What about my
home?"

He gripped her arm so tight it hurt. "If we can't save the
first one, we have no chance at all with the second."

Muscular pain shocked her out of her panic. The world
around her turned red as she overlaid the views he was seeing across her natural vision. Warning and damage lights
were doubling in number with every breath. Yellow light—
now more sinister than beautiful—spread steadily down the
drone's flank, as though it had been dipped in molten gold.
In another view, PARASOL was already half-consumed
by fire.

"What can I do?" Her voice sounded as though miles of
fog insulated its source from her. "I need to do *something*."

"Take the helm. I don't know how much longer we'll retain control of the drone, but try to take us out of the debris
cloud. Find the fringes of it. Maybe then I can get a grip on
what we've already picked up."

She did as she was told, noting immediately the stricken
way in which the drone responded. Its systems, already
heavily corrupted, reacted unpredictably to her commands.
She could feel its hurt empathically, deep down in her guts.
The invading replicators were like cancer eating through
her. Tears ran freely down her cheeks as the drone died
piece by piece around her.

Then, with a wrenching dislocation, it was gone. Something had cut it free. The pain fell precipitously away, leaving hollow wounds in its wake. Glowing with sickly yellow

light, visible through senses not belonging to her, it tumbled into poisonous space, decrepitating wildly.

"I tried to fly it," she whispered, "but it was already too far gone."

"I know," Eogan said. "That's why I had to jettison it. That stuff is *fast*."

"Are we going to be okay?"

"Maybe. The *Cowell* seems to be keeping the worst of it out. But—Melilah, I'm sorry. I don't know what else we can do."

They were alone with the *Cowell*, the last component of the *Nhulunbuy*. The drone was as good as dead, and so was PARASOL. The view outside was full of hellish light as the debris cloud spread.

Melilah openly wept as the first bright spots appeared on Bedlam's exposed skin. She felt as though she was dreaming. It had to be a nightmare.

"This can't—this can't be happening!"

"I'm sorry," said Eogan again. The words had no meaning.

"Yasu? Yasu?" She commandeered the Cell's communications; he didn't try to stop her. "If you can hear me, get out of there now! Find an escape capsule; set it for our coordinates! We'll pick you up. Yasu? Can you hear me?"

The feed from the habitat was panicked and chaotic, breaking up into random noise as the deadly fire spread. In a way, that was a blessing. The new replicators were much more voracious than those propagated by Frederica Cazneaux's Reaper. These burned through the outer layers of the habitat like hot copper wire through ice. Chambers collapsed too quickly for people to evacuate; pipes opened to naked vacuum, spraying their contents into the maelstrom. In the disintegrating feed, Melilah glimpsed limbs melting, faces bursting into flame, blood and bright yellow death mingling freely.

"We can't save everyone."

Melilah heard Eogan's cautionary words, but she couldn't feel her body. The horror was too much to take.

Dimly she thought he might be holding her, trying to comfort her, but it didn't truly register. There was no comfort to be found as her home burned, and the people she loved died.

"Yasu!"

A handful of craft launched from the giant habitat. They caught fire immediately. As Bedlam burned, it spawned a volatile, corrosive atmosphere, a terrible miasma that would destroy anything it touched. PARASOL and the drone were doing the same. The small cloud of tangler debris had seeded a plague that would soon overtake the entire system—as it had Sublime.

Eogan was wrong. The problem wasn't that they couldn't save everyone. They'd be lucky if they could save *anyone*. Red warnings began to appear on the *Cowell*'s skin as more and more of the replicators gained a toehold. It couldn't fight them off indefinitely.

The feed died in a wash of static across every channel. The thought of telling the Cell to stop resisting was morbidly tempting. A quick death, she thought, would be better than watching all she loved burn away to nothing.

"Look!"

One sole craft fought off the replicators just long enough to limp out of Bedlam's feeble gravity well. Gold warred with silver across its skin as it tumbled feebly toward them.

Melilah felt some of Eogan's excitement. Survivors— against all the odds! She didn't fight as he swung the Cell around to intercept the glowing lozenge. It was half as large as they were. Infection sparkled like jewels across its silver hull. She recognized neither its design nor the material it was made from, but it was broadcasting a standard distress call, and that was good enough for her.

The Cell shook as it enfolded the infected capsule. Melilah dimly registered how Eogan contained the replicators—scraping the major concentrations into relatively contained locations, then sloughing off the *Cowell*'s entire outer hull, ejecting the replicators with it. The Cell's extreme-redundancy design principles enabled it to survive the loss of such a large chunk of itself, but it came at a cost. This wasn't a tactic it could perform more than a few times.

The Cell absorbed the contents of the capsule. There was just one passenger.

+65

"We have to get out of here," said Earth-Deangelis. His eyes felt as red as Melilah's looked. "We have to make sure the truth survives."

"Therein lies the problem," Eogan said. "I don't think we *can* get out of here."

Earth-Deangelis forcibly suppressed images of the stricken habitat from his mind. There was nothing he could have done to save it—but nonetheless his truncated higher reflexes screamed that he should have tried. *You ran,* they said. *You failed.*

But to stay would have been taking the easy way out. He knew that. Death wasn't an answer. He wanted time to mourn the destruction of his home, and to get revenge.

He reached out with his peripherals and tapped into the Cell's primitive systems. Red warning signs were spreading across its hull faster than he could credit. With PARASOL now a ghastly yellow disk in the sky, brighter than if the sun had expanded to the size of a bloated yellow giant, space was rapidly filling with sweeping winds of deadly nanotech. The burning bulk of Bedlam was doing the same on the far side.

"I've upped our defenses as much as possible," Eogan explained, "and they're already stretched. I can divert sufficient resources away from them to move us a short distance, but to get us out of the system entirely would take more than we can spare. We'd be eaten alive before we got a light-second away."

Deangelis knew it was true. Palmer technology was no match for what the Archon had set loose on the system.

"There is a way out," he said. "Just one."

Melilah nodded. "The Occlusion."

Eogan eyed them both dubiously. "You've got to be kidding."

"It's close," Deangelis said, "and completely defenseless."

"Didn't you keep the specs for the capsule Palmer Vermeulen came out in?" Melilah added. "That can get us safely through the throat."

Eogan swallowed, looking more frightened of their only escape route than he was of death.

"We don't have forever, Dominic."

"I *know* that," he said irritably. "It's just—" He stopped, and nodded. "Okay. But it's going to be tricky. Melilah, I'll need you to hold us on course while I look after the replicators and Vermeulen's specs."

She nodded.

"The Cell has different interfaces than Hails's drones," Eogan said.

"Whatever. Just do what you have to do to get us out of here."

The Palmer bent his face down and folded forward into the bulkhead, which rose up to meet him like a wave of molasses. The transition was sudden, and took Melilah by surprise. One moment he was there; the next he was gone. Then the walls began to close in around her, and she gasped in fear.

Earth-Deangelis reached out and touched her arm.

She nodded and stayed perfectly still, every muscle rigid.

"Don't worry," Eogan said, his voice coming from the walls around them. "This is no different from the configuration we've used before. I need to reduce our profile as much as possible. The smaller our surface area, the less the replicators have to grip on to."

She nodded, seeing the sense in his words, and closed her eyes as the Cell engulfed her. Irresistible pressure forced both their knees up to their chests.

"What should I do?" asked Earth-Deangelis.

"Just hold on," said Eogan. "If there's anything in the throat we should know about, now would be the time to tell us."

"You know as much as I do," the ex-Exarch said. "Hails told me you cracked the data cache."

"Then we're all equally in the dark."

Earth-Deangelis nodded. "We soon will be, anyway."

+66

A torrent of data flooded through nerves Eogan's body normally used for scent and kinesthesia. He smelled the texture of the infected space around him; he felt the Cell's intricate structure as though it belonged to his own body. Telemetry poured through his aural and optic pathways, granting him a clear and uninterrupted view of the Cell and its destination.

The subtle warp of the Occlusion hung against a backdrop of fire. All that remained of PARASOL was a breeding ground for more destruction. Behind him, the habitat blazed like a small star.

He turned his back on it and let the heat of the flames burn away his sorrow. He would mourn his friends later, when there was time.

With a wild surge of acceleration, they fled.

"That's it," said Eogan, as Melilah hesitantly interfaced with the Cell. He felt as though they were riding a hopper with a faulty thruster, sometimes surging forward and other times falling back, but that wasn't her fault. The Cell's many minuscule drives were sensitive to the storm. "Keep us moving as fast as you can. You may feel some drag as I take the resources I need, but I'll try to keep that to a minimum. And don't worry about slowing down. We'll hit the throat at speed."

She nodded, or tried to. Her body was completely swathed, lost to her. The Cell took the impulse and conveyed it symbolically. He read her fear as easily as words down a screen. Something else to ignore.

Nanotech winds buffeted them from all directions. The replicators were digging in with growing ferocity. Their density increased in time with the Cell's velocity, and Eogan was soon fighting a losing battle. He was forced to peel off layer after layer of corrupted hull, sacrificing it in order to spare the Cell's fragile passengers. At the same time, he frantically tried to build up the defenses they needed to ensure their survival when they rocketed through the throat. It was a contradictory, thankless task, and the only way he could tell that it was working was by the fact they were still alive.

Their velocity increased. The Occlusion came closer.

Catastrophic replicators bit deeper. Drag weighed them down.

Eogan abandoned all distinction between himself and the Cell. He physically leaned forward, as though forcing his way through a heavy wind with fists and jaw clenched, eyes in slits, back straining.

Come on! he urged himself and the Cell at the same time. *Just a little bit farther!*

Gold flared around him. The Occlusion ballooned in his face like a rip in the universe. The Cell lurched as Eogan dropped more than half of the *Cowell* in their wake, exposing an entirely new hull beneath. A feeling of being sandpapered back to the bone enveloped him, and he screamed.

Agony!

Blackness took him. The pain dropped away. Blessed silence enfolded him.

But he wasn't unconscious. He wasn't dead. The Cell tumbled through space unknown, at the whim of laws it couldn't comprehend.

It took him a long moment truly to accept what had happened.

+POSTLUDE

One day later

Darkness.

Then—light.

"Welcome back," said a voice. "How are you feeling?"

"Archon?" Deangelis opened his eyes on a lush, green world. "Is that you?"

"Yes, Isaac."

"Where am I?" He struggled to orient himself, but failed to connect with the view before him. Gently wooded hills rolled into the distance; a creek burbled under lush blackberry bushes nearby; to his left, the sun was rising over the horizon in a wash of subtle yellows and oranges. "Is this Earth?"

"Yes, it is." The Archon was silent for a moment, as though giving him a chance to absorb the answer, then said, "Tell me the last thing you remember."

Deangelis thought hard. Memories came in flashes: of Lazarus Hails's inert body lying at his feet; of attack drones rushing toward him at incredible velocities; of a bright purple bubble popping in a flash of X-rays; of a feeling of gut-tearing panic . . .

The Exarchate has already lost one colony, the Archon had told him. *I would not make that two.*

"It's happened, hasn't it?" A terrible sense of finality rolled through him, as irresistible as gravity. "Lut-Deangelis is gone."

"I'm sorry to have to tell you this, Isaac, but your colony was destroyed thirty-eight hours ago." The Archon's voice was thick with sympathy. "We here on Earth were monitoring events there through your tangler, so we knew of the imminent possibility of such an occurrence. Hopes fell when the signal from your tangler ceased. Just hours ago, deep-space probes stationed around the system confirmed the outbreak. There is, I'm afraid, no hope of finding survivors."

"Was it—?" His mouth closed over the sentence. A real mouth, apparently, because he could feel a breeze on his cheeks and taste sleep on his tongue. He couldn't move, however. He sat, propped limply against what felt like a stone of some kind, and could do nothing other than think.

He forced himself to finish the sentence.

"Was it you who destroyed my home?"

The Archon paused again. This time he didn't think it was for his benefit.

"Anything other than the truth, Isaac, would dishonor you and the work you did in Lut-Deangelis. So yes, I destroyed your colony, just as I destroyed Jane Elderton's ten years ago. And I did it for the same reason: to keep the artifact contained. I deeply regret having to take such action, but the necessity is inescapable. *Not* doing it would have cost far more in terms of lives than doing it, as I'm sure you will come to accept in time. I will understand completely if you decide to hate me, as Jane Elderton now does.

"But that would not stop me from doing it a third time if I have to." The Archon's tone hardened. "Nor will it divert us from the course we must now follow, you and I."

Deangelis tried to think through a suffocating fog of grief and despair. "Course? What course? What use am I to you now—a washed-up, failed Exarch with no colony to look after? I'm nothing; I should be dead."

"You haven't failed, Isaac, and you aren't dead. You still have work to do. We couldn't update our model of your mind beyond the point at which the tangler was destroyed, but we have enough of you to bring you back, almost as good as new. Bringing you back was a necessity. Just like you, I exist in multiple bodies, only my parts can be separated by light-years and still function perfectly well. Thus I see the greatest view possible, across all the Exarchate, and I see all too clearly what must be done now."

Deangelis didn't want to know. Enough had been done already. His home was destroyed, his world turned upside down. The Exarchate, which he thought existed to nurture human life in all its forms, was responsible for the death of tens of thousands of people. Whole planetary systems had been depopulated in the name of—what? Stability? Security?

Insanity, he thought, fighting the urge to weep.

"Two hours ago," the Archon said, "a message was sent from the borders of Lut-Deangelis along the tangler network. The message was written by Melilah Awad and detailed the truth, as she saw it, about the artifact we have discovered. Word has come to me of this message from the Exarchs of Michailogliou-Rawe, Alcor-Magun, and Beall-Cammarano. That these systems received the message suggests *all* in the region surrounding Lut-Deangelis have done so, although we have yet to hear from the others. No doubt some have passed the message on to systems farther away from its source, and some of *those* recipients might in turn do the same. This is both unexpected and alarming, Isaac, as I'm sure you appreciate. Knowledge of this artifact is kept carefully contained for a reason, and you have seen firsthand how far we are prepared to go in order to achieve that end."

Deangelis nodded. He did know, and Lazarus Hails had suspected before him. How many of his peers were putting the pieces together even now, as word of the death of another system spread?

"We have modeled the propagation of the truth as one would a disease," the Archon went on. "We expect the entire upper echelon of the Exarchate to be aware of Geodesica within days. All it will take is one Exarch to leak the truth to an underling or two, and it is bound to spread farther still.

We will do what we can to spread counter- and misinformation, just as we did with White-Elderton: one system suggests a connection between the Occlusion and devastation; a second outbreak will only reinforce the meme that meddling with such artifacts is lethally dangerous. But some will remain dubious. This doubt, Isaac, must not be allowed to spread. Do you understand?"

"What can I possibly do about it?" The smell of Earth in his nostrils was all Deangelis wanted to focus on at that moment. This was as close to home as he would ever be again. And even here, where the Archon issued its murderous orders, he would never be fully comfortable.

He felt the Archon regarding him closely, as though the sun was a giant, godlike eye. Its voice was inhumanly calm.

"I need to know more about the rebellion that took place in your colony and the people behind it. You will assist me in this task while you perform your new role in Lut-Deangelis, as caretaker of the latest entrance to Geodesica. Nothing must be allowed in or out, as I'm sure you can appreciate. Together, we must keep a lid on this thing as best we can."

"You don't need me," he protested, thinking: *and I don't want to do it!*

"You underestimate yourself, Deangelis. You are an integral part of this operation. No one else has had such intimate access to the key players: Melilah Awad, Palmer Eogan, and Lazarus Hails. You are truly part of the inner circle now, my friend. There are no more secrets left for you to find."

They're all dead, he wanted to protest. *What's the point in studying them now?*

But the rest of Lazarus Hails was still alive in *his* system, and something in the Archon's voice made him wonder about the others, too.

"No survivors, you said?"

"None has been detected and, judging by our experience in the first outbreak, none is expected. The replicators I propagated after my death in your system were designed for rapid, maximum destruction. If anyone did evade them, they've gone somewhere you and I will never follow."

Deangelis nodded again, reading between the lines and thinking: *No more secrets? Like hell.* If someone had survived, there was only one place they could be: inside Geodesica, the very artifact Sol would kill to keep closed. And if they'd got in, there was very real chance they would one day get out . . .

He repressed a sad smile. Melilah had succeeded in doing what he could not. She had set free the genie, and nothing the Archon did would get rid of it. Word would spread about Geodesica to all quarters of the Exarchate. Enough people would guess what had happened to his colony, and they would worry about it happening to theirs next. Fear would replace trust, fear that would inevitably turn to anger if given a nudge or two.

The seeds of dissent had been sown—and although he had never thought of himself as a farmer before, despite his role as nurturer of his colony, he could get used to the idea.

He took a deep breath. The Archon's charisma was as powerful as ever, but he had a reason to fight it, now.

"Very well," he said finally. "I'll do it."

"That's the spirit, Isaac. I knew you'd bounce back."

"When do we leave?"

"As soon as a relay is in position. It'll take us about a week to transfer and build everything we need, but you don't have to worry about any of that. These are just logistical details. We'll get you home before you know it."

The power of movement spread through his body. Life had been granted to his limbs as a reward for his obedience. He climbed gingerly to his feet and looked around.

He was standing at the summit of a low hill, as he had been at his birth. But this time, instead of a eucalyptus at his back, he had woken leaning against a gravestone.

Be careful, my friend, Jane Elderton had told him a lifetime ago. *Don't lose yourself like I did.*

"Thank you, Archon," he said, hiding thoughts of revenge behind a smooth, obsequious tone. "I'm looking forward to it."

GLOSSARY OF NAMES

PALMERS

Aesche
Bray
Christolphe (Negotiator Select)
Cobiac
Eogan (Chief Officer)
Flast
Horsfall (Chief Officer)
Sarian
Vermeulen (Science Officer)
Weightman (Chief Officer)

ARC CIRCUIT CITIZENS

Szilvia Animaz
Iona Attard (Doctor of Xenarcheology)
Athalia Awad
Melilah Awad
Angela Chen-Pushkaric
Yasu Emmell
Werner Gard
Gil Hurdowar
Bernard Krassay
James Pirelli
Luisa Pirelli
Kara Skirianos (ex-Speaker)
Ludelia Virgo (Professor of Humanist Science)

EXARCHS

Frederica Cazneaux (Mizar)
Lan Cochrane (Alioth)
Isaac Deangelis (Bedlam)
Jane Elderton (Sublime)
Lazarus Hails (Altitude)
Giorsal McGrath (Friday)

CELLS

Cirencester
Cowell
Inselmeer
Jaintiapur
Kwal Bahal
Nhulunbuy
Patrixbourne
Studenica
Umm-as-Shadid

PLACES IN BEDLAM

Albert Hall
Bacon Cathedral (Cultural)
Barabási Straight
ben-Avraham's
Bonabeau Fold (Residential)
Bornholdt Chasm
Faloutsos Junction
Granovetter
Havlin (Industrial)
Jeong Crescent
Milgram's Crossing (Basement)
Ormerod's
Pastor-Satorras (Scientific)

TABLE ONE
TIMELINE

2080–2150	First Wave of human colonization
2090	VOID field effect demonstrated
2100	First VOIDships in active service
2120	Bedlam First Wave colony founded
2121	True Singularity (Sol system)
2125	Bedlam First Wave colony destroyed by solar flare
2183	Melilah Awad born on Little Red
2192	Dominic Eogan born
2200–2250	Arc Systems recolonized; Great Bear Run and Arc Circuit established
2205	Bedlam recolonized
2239	Melilah Awad arrives at Bedlam
2257	Melilah Awad and Dominic Eogan meet
2276	Palmers guild formed
2287	Melilah Awad and Dominic Eogan part ways
2374	Isaac Forge Deangelis born
2395	Exarchate Expansion begins
2397	Exarchate Expansion complete
2407	Palmer Eogan joins the *Nhulunbuy*
2428	Sublime Catastrophe
2433	Palmer Eogan becomes chief officer of the *Nhulunbuy*
2437	The *Nhulunbuy* leaves Mizar for Bedlam
2438	Mizar Occlusion arrives at Bedlam

TABLE TWO
NAMES OF ARC CIRCUIT SYSTEMS

SYSTEM NAME	ORIGINAL COLONY	EXARCHATE DESIGNATION
Phad	Phad 4	Phad-Simondson
Mizar	Mizar	Mizar-Cazneaux
Megrez	Megrez 8	Megrez-Mijolo
Asellus Primus	Prime One	Asellus Primus-Binard
Alioth	Alioth	Alioth-Cochrane
Alcor	Alcor 3a	Alcor-Magun
78 Ursa Major	Friday	Jamgotchian-McGrath
66781	Whitewater	Littlewood-Bohm
66704	Sublime	White-Elderton
65515	Schiller's End	Beall-Cammarano
64532	Eliza	Toma-Herczeg
62512	Bedlam	Lut-Deangelis
61946	New Eire	Michailogliou-Rawe
61100	Altitude	Kullervo-Hails
61053	Gabison's End	Ansell-Aad
59514	Little Red	Yugen-Palliaer
59432	Severance	Newbery-Vaas
59431	Scarecrow	Mei-Shun-Wah

MAP ONE
THE ARC CIRCUIT

Not to scale
(all measurements in light-years)
(systems listed according to
Hipparcos number or real name)

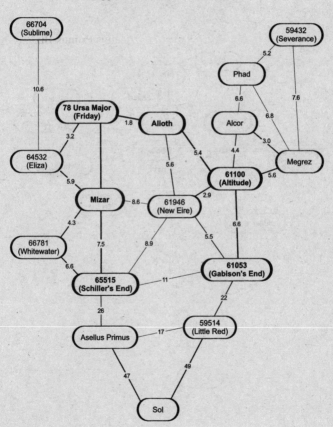

MAP TWO
BEDLAM ENVIRONS

Not to scale
(all measurements in light-years)

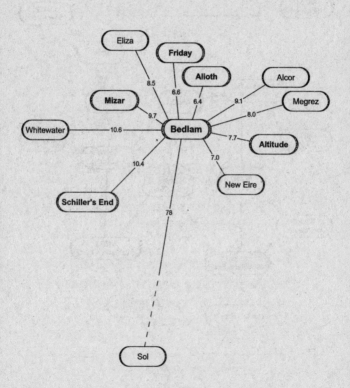

Sean Williams & Shane Dix

Echoes of Earth
0-441-00892-5

Orphans of Earth
0-441-01006-7

Heirs of Earth
0-441-01126-8

"Chock full of marvelous events...and the wonder of outer space."
—*Science Fiction Chronicle*

"A dazzling adventure."
—Jack McDevitt

"Williams and Dix bring an adventurous and expansive approach to their material."
—*Locus*

Coming March 2005 from Ace

Angel-Seeker
by Sharon Shinn
0-441-01260-4
Award-winning author Sharon Shinn returns to Samaria
with this rich, romantic tale that begins where
Archangel left off.

Hex and the City
by Simon R. Green
0-441-01261-2
Lady Luck has hired John Taylor to investigate the origins on
the Nightside—a dark heart of London where it's always
3 a.m. But when he starts to uncover facts about his
long-vanished mother, the Nightside—and all of
existence—could be snuffed out.

Also new in paperback this month:

Rule of Evidence
by John G. Hemry
0-441-01262-0

Monument
by Ian Graham
0-441-01263-9

Available wherever books are sold or at
www.penguin.com